Love and Loss at

Francesca Capaldi has enjoyed writing since she was a child, largely influenced by a Welsh mother who was good at improvised story telling. She is a member of the RNA and the Society of Women Writers and Journalists. Francesca currently lives in Kent with her family and a cat called Lando Calrissian.

Love and Loss
at the
Beach Hotel

Francesca Capaldi

hera

First published in the United Kingdom in 2024 by

Hera Books
Unit 9 (Canelo), 5th Floor
Cargo Works, 1-2 Hatfields
London SE1 9PG
United Kingdom

A CIP catalogue record for this book is available from the British Library.

Print ISBN 978 1 80436 846 6
Ebook ISBN 978 1 80436 848 0

Look for more great books at www.herabooks.com

Printed and bound in Great Britain by Clays Ltd, Elcograf S.p.A.

I

Dedicated to Angela Johnson, Elaine Roberts, Karen Aldous, Sarah Stephenson and Vivien Brown. Thank you for all your support.

Prologue

Littlehampton, Sussex, August 1914

'See you at the station tomorrow, Lorcan!'

'You will so!'

Lorcan Foley walked away from the New Inn a little worse for wear, waving to the pals he'd made just that afternoon. He'd been sharing a few beers with them to celebrate a new chapter in all their lives.

He staggered onto South Terrace, looking ahead to the Beach Hotel in the distance, then stopped. He'd better sober up a bit before his shift, even if it was his last night. Shame he had to work; it was a warm evening with an intensely blue sky, and he fancied having a walk along the promenade with his girl, Hetty, holding her hand, and maybe getting a little closer to her.

Hetty was the head stillroom maid at the hotel, and they hadn't long started walking out. He was going to have to tell her what he'd done, but he wouldn't have time before his shift. She was the one regret about his decision. Surely she'd understand, given the circumstances?

As he approached the hotel, he looked up at the clock of the attached public house. He was already five minutes late for his seven thirty shift. Charlie would be waiting.

He shook himself and took a deep breath before he entered through the staff door. Ignoring scullery maid Annie's greeting, he headed straight into the stillroom, only to be halted by Hetty.

'Lorcan, you're late for your shift.' Her face was creased with concern.

1

'I'll explain later.' He hurried on into the corridor, taking the staff stairs two at a time, to get to his room and change into his porter's uniform. He knew that putting Hetty off was as much cowardice on his part as concern about being late.

Back in the staff corridor, the clock there told him it was nearly twenty to eight. He walked a little faster, not wanting Charlie, who was a good sort, to miss supper. He rushed through the door, only to be halted by the manager, Mr Bygrove. Just his luck; he was the last person Lorcan wanted to see – now or at any time.

'Where on earth have you been?' Bygrove tapped his watch, his face displaying the pompous expression that had become his trademark.

'Sorry, sir. Got carried away celebrating with some new pals.'

Charlie, who'd been a few steps behind, came forward a little, frowning.

Bygrove narrowed his eyes and his lip curled a little. 'Celebrating? You're meant to be working, man.' He looked behind him before coming up close to Lorcan. Too close. His nostrils flared as he took a swift sniff. 'You've been drinking. Disgraceful! You will do a double shift tomorrow and have money taken from your wages.'

Lorcan couldn't help himself. He flung back his head and laughed. 'You can do what the hell you like, so you can.'

Charlie stepped backwards, his eyes wide, as Bygrove scowled, his face taking on a dark pink hue. His clenched fists were held tightly at his sides.

'Gonna hit me, are you?' Lorcan sniggered, though he hadn't intended to. He felt emboldened. 'Well, go on then, for I'm out of here tomorrow, to be part of Kitchener's New Army.'

'You're *what*?' Bygrove shrieked.

'I've enlisted, sir.'

'You bloody idiot,' said Bygrove. 'The war will be over before it's started, then what are you going to do for a job?'

Lorcan shrugged, glad to see a group of people enter the foyer. 'Excuse me, *sir*.' He headed over to greet the newcomers.

He noticed Charlie salute Bygrove, before leaving. Bygrove gave Lorcan another quick glower before following on.

'Good evening, Mr Perryman, Mrs Perryman.' He nodded twice, then wished their companions a good evening, before leading them to the dining room.

—

Hetty Affleck was polishing a silver coffee pot when her fellow stillroom maid, Phoebe Sweeton, returned from her supper.

'Oh Hetty, Lorcan, did you know?'

'That he was late for his shift? Yes, I saw him. I suppose Bygrove gave him an earful.'

'No, well yes, he did, but not just for that.'

The look of anxiety on Phoebe's face panicked Hetty. She placed the coffee pot down. 'What is it?'

'He's enlisted.'

'What? No, of course he hasn't. He's not said anything of the sort to me.' Despite her denial, she felt sick. He had talked a lot about the war, the injustice of it, and how the Kaiser should pay for what he'd started.

'Charlie said that he told Mr Bygrove he'd enlisted. That's why he was late. He'd been celebrating with some pals, he told him.'

Hetty sank into the chair by the dresser that held the silverware, her breathing laboured. He was fond of a joke, was Lorcan, he was probably having them on. But would he do that to the manager?

She closed her eyes. *Oh please, don't let him have enlisted*, went around her head several times, but she suspected it was pointless.

Phoebe knelt next to her. 'Are you all right?'

She opened her eyes. 'No, Phoebe, I'm not. Why would he do such a thing, and not even tell me? Especially when we've only recently started walking out.'

'I don't know, Hetty. You'll have to ask him. His shift ends at eleven thirty, doesn't it?'

3

'Yes. I wonder how long he's got until he goes away.'

'Ah...'

Hetty knew some other bad news was coming.

Phoebe took her hand. 'He said he was leaving tomorrow.'

'Tomorrow?' Did he not really care for her at all? He had seemed very fond of her. 'Why now? And why didn't he tell me before?'

'Spur of the moment, maybe?' Phoebe shrugged. 'Like I said, you'll have to ask him.'

Hetty stood. There was no point fretting until she'd heard the story from him. She still couldn't believe that he'd go this far. 'We'd better get on with polishing these. The dining room is full tonight, and people will be wanting coffee after their meals.'

She picked her cloth and pot up, and started rubbing furiously once more, swallowing back the urge to cry.

–

It was just after half eleven that evening, when Hetty looked up to see Lorcan enter the staff dining room. She was sitting at the table, near the empty fireplace, darning a stocking. Phoebe was the only other person in the room, knitting. Seeing Lorcan come in, she rose, placing the wool and needles in her apron pocket.

'I'll fetch the plate of food Mrs Norris left, and then I'll leave you to it.'

'Plate of food?' Lorcan drawled in his soft, Irish lilt. He looked confused.

'Mrs Norris knew you'd missed dinner, so she saved you some stew. She left it over a pan of simmering water so it would be warm when you finished your shift.'

'That was grand of her. I'm starving, so I am.'

Hetty had so far said nothing. Her lips felt like they were glued together and she didn't have a clue where to start.

'Have a good shift then?' he asked.

Him acting as if everything was normal finally propelled some speech from her.

'Good? No, Lorcan, it wasn't *good*. Do you think I haven't heard what happened?'

'Well, yes, I figured you would.' He hung his head as he sat down.

'And you didn't think it would be a good idea to tell me your plans? Everyone at Charlie's dinner break knew before I did.'

He bit his bottom lip before saying. 'I'm sorry, Hetty. I didn't mean it to work out like that. If Bygrove hadn't been there, Charlie wouldn't have heard, and I'd have told you first.'

She thumped the stocking, needle and darning mushroom on the table. 'I would have liked to have known before you went off and enlisted. That might have been the *courteous* thing to do.'

The anger was a substitute for the tears she'd wanted to shed since Phoebe had told her the news, but she felt more in control of the situation this way. And if he was prepared to treat her like this, an afterthought, he didn't deserve to see her tears.

'Yes, it would have been the right thing to do, you're right. I'm an eejit, Hetty. When I went on my afternoon off, I hadn't even made up my mind to enlist, though I'd been thinking about it. I dunno what came over me. I—'

He was interrupted by Phoebe, returning with the plate. She placed it in front of him, along with some cutlery. 'See you in the morning.'

When she'd gone, he continued. 'I passed the enlistment office and saw a group of men coming out, all cheerful like, congratulating each other and patting each other on the back, and I thought – well, it all became clear to me that it's what I had to do, to help. Especially after the awful things what happened to the people in Belgium, and you know…' His words trailed off and he hung his head once more. 'I didn't mean to make you angry. I wasn't even sure if you'd care. It's not like we've been walking out long.'

5

The fury evaporated, and Hetty was left with the distress and hurt once more. She moved up the bench towards Lorcan and sat next to him, placing her hand on his arm. 'Of course I care. I wouldn't have walked out with you in the first place if I didn't… Come on, you need to eat your dinner before it gets cold.'

He lifted the spoon and half-heartedly scooped up some of the stew, but put it back down. 'I am sorry, Hetty. But, you know, if this war keeps going, I have a feeling all us men will be made to join it. And maybe the sooner we do, the sooner it'll be over.'

'I can't say I agree with you, Lorcan. I don't know why we need to be involved in the first place.'

'Anyways, you know what they're saying: over by Christmas. We won't have even finished training by then.'

She wasn't so sure, but didn't argue. 'I hear you're off tomorrow.'

'That's right. In the morning.'

'I'm not working in the morning, so I'll walk to the station with you. If you'd like me to.'

He turned and took her chin in his hand. 'Of course I'd like you to.'

'Well, good. Then eat your stew now, before Mrs Leggett comes down and tells us off for being up too late. Or at least, me.'

He started eating and she laid her head against his shoulder, as a single tear rolled down her cheek.

–

'Oh Lorcan, I wish you weren't going.'

Hetty turned towards him, examining his face – the light blue eyes and the contrasting black hair – as the pair of them stood on the promenade in Littlehampton, overlooking the beach with its crowd of clamouring day trippers. There was a warm, gentle breeze, the sort Hetty normally loved to feel against her face, but she was too troubled to appreciate it.

'I know. You've said it enough times. But I have got to do my bit, so I have.' Lorcan placed his old, battered suitcase on the ground.

'But why did you have to be so impolite to Mr Bygrove? What will happen when the war's over and you want your job back?' Hetty still couldn't quite believe the account of the argument between Lorcan and the manager that Charlie had related this morning to those who hadn't been at dinner with him the night before. 'I know you can be plain speaking, but turning up late drunk and then cursing your boss when he took you to task... Oh Lorcan!'

'Yes, I suppose, in hindsight, I shouldn't have had quite as much to drink in celebration before I got back to the hotel.'

'War's not an adventure, Lorcan.'

'No, I suppose not.'

She didn't know what else to add to this, so said, 'Let's start walking. We can go via the pier and the river, if you have time to go that way.' She wanted their walk to the railway station to last as long as possible, for once there, his departure would seem real.

He took an old fob watch out of the waistcoat pocket of his Sunday best suit, which he'd chosen to wear for the journey to the training camp. 'Forty minutes until the train for Chichester leaves, so yes, we have time.'

He picked up the suitcase and they walked, speaking of this and that, following the River Arun's course into the town centre. Passing the first of the shops on Surrey Street, Lorcan blurted out, 'Like I said, with the training taking a few months, maybe the war'll be over before we even get to fight anywhere.'

Hetty wondered whether he was regretting his hasty enlistment, but it was too late now, even if he did. 'I hope you're right. Your family won't know about you signing up. You must write and tell them.'

'Aye, I know. Don't suppose they'll be impressed either.'

She placed her hand through his arm, and they walked in silence, towards Terminus Road, where the station was situated. A large brick building came into view, with a horse-drawn carriage and a motorcar waiting in the area at the front. Hetty's heart raced and she felt lightheaded. She could see a few other men gathered, and wondered if they too were on their way to Chichester.

Before they reached the station, Lorcan pulled them into an alleyway. He placed the suitcase down, before taking Hetty's arms and turning her towards him. 'You will write to me, won't ya? *Please?*'

'Of course I will, but you'll have to write first, so I have an address.'

'And, oh, I should have asked before we left. Have you a photograph of yourself you could send me, so I can keep you close to me always?' He took hold of her shoulders lightly to caress them, ran his fingers softly across her cheek. It was so gentle, so tender, that she wanted to cry again.

'I don't have one of me at the hotel anyway, but there are quite a few at my parents' house. I'm sure they won't notice if I take one.'

'Have you told them yet that you're walking out with me?'

She looked down. 'No, as we haven't been walking out for long. And I don't want them interfering so early on.' She looked up at him. 'Have you told your family?'

'No, but as they're so far away, and, as you say, we've hardly got going…'

'Which makes it even more of a shame that you're leaving.' She hoped that sounded disappointed rather than peevish.

'I know. But I'll have leave when I can come and see you.' He looked around, before bending and giving her lips a quick kiss. It was only the third time he'd done that, as they were rarely alone, and it was never more than a peck.

'Would you like me to wait on the platform with you?'

'I think I'd rather we said our farewells here, where we're a bit more on our own, like.'

'I wish we didn't have to say our farewells at all.'

'I haven't enlisted to run away from you, Hetty. And when I come back, we can take up where we left off.'

'If you get your job back.'

'There are other jobs in the area, so there are. Farewell, sweet maiden,' he said, chuckling and acting more like his usual, jovial self. He gave her lips a peck once more but was interrupted by a middle-aged woman as she tried to get past them.

'Not seemly, that ain't,' she complained as she bustled off.

'You'd better get going,' said Lorcan. 'Don't you start a shift at eleven?'

'I've got plenty of time.'

He kissed her one more time before picking up his suitcase. She grabbed his arm as he did so.

'Lorcan, please don't go thinking I'm angry with you for enlisting. I'm upset, yes, very upset, because I'm worried, but I am proud of you too.'

He looked into her eyes for some moments. 'Thank you, Hetty. It means a lot to me to hear you say that.' He walked to the edge of the pavement, lifting his arm in a last farewell, then ran across the road towards the railway station.

She was tempted to linger and watch, but, deciding it wouldn't make the situation any easier, headed back towards the town, and ultimately the Beach Hotel.

Chapter One

Hetty Affleck stood over the large pan in the stillroom of the Beach Hotel, stirring the bubbling gooseberries. She hoped that the meagre bit of sugar she'd added would be enough to make them into a reasonable jam. The sugar shortage was getting worse, and she wondered what would happen if it became entirely unavailable. She'd been using this preoccupation with her latest chore to distract herself from something she didn't want to think about, but the unwanted thoughts kept coming to the forefront.

It was her twenty-fifth birthday. When she'd visited her home in Wick yesterday evening, her parents had given her two birthday presents. They'd wanted her to stay overnight, but she'd told them she had an early shift the next day and didn't want to have to get up earlier than was necessary to get to it. They'd never understood why she wanted to live in at the hotel, with it being only about a mile away from home, but she'd felt she'd needed the independence. And to get away from their interference.

Her parents had informed her that her sister Iris would drop by the hotel with her present later. Her brothers, Hector and Gilbert, would no doubt send birthday greetings in their next letters from the front. But the person she really wanted to hear from hadn't even written in the last three weeks, let alone sent a present, or even a card.

Lorcan. He'd sent a small gift the last two years he'd been away. There'd even been a card in French last year, that Edie

Moore, their undermanageress at the hotel, had translated for her. But it wasn't the lack of a present or card that bothered her so much as the absence of any communication. Was he hurt? Or worse? Or had he simply tired of this distant romance? If that's what you could call it.

The glass door from the scullery was pushed open and the sisters, Annie and Alice Twine entered.

'What on earth's wrong with you?' said Annie, the older of the two. 'Got a face on you, you 'ave. Don't you like the smell of gooseberries?' Annie took a deep breath and sighed. 'I like a nice bit of gooseberry jam, me.'

'Oh, isn't it your birthday today?' said Alice.

'Yes, it is,' Hetty replied.

'Happy birthday to you!'

'You should be a bit more cheerful then,' said Annie, undoing her apron. 'What did you get from Lorcan? He normally sends something nice.'

Did she detect an edge of resentment in Annie's voice? 'The post from him hasn't arrived, so I don't know yet.' That was a better reply than what had been going on in her head.

'All right for some.'

'Don't mind her,' said Alice. 'She's just out of sorts 'cos she got a ticking off from our dad this morning.'

'Here, that's no one else's business.' Annie glared at her sister.

Alice giggled before her face became serious, and Hetty wondered what was coming. 'I was just saying to Annie, I still can't believe that Douglas Bygrove isn't gonna march in at any moment and give us all what for. I'm still thankful, every day, that he's not here bullying us all anymore.'

'Shh,' said Hetty, looking towards the door to the staff corridor. 'You should watch what you say. You don't want Mrs Bygrove overhearing and getting upset. He did die under awful circumstances, after all.'

'Give over,' said Annie. 'Mrs Bygrove was as glad to see the back of him as the rest of us, after the way he bullied and threatened her.'

'Yes, but not the way it happened. He was still her husband and the father of her children.'

'I suppose so. It's not a good way to go, even for someone as evil as Bygrove, being strangled on the beach in a storm. And by a councillor, who we should be able to trust.'

'Well, at least the councillors who were in on it are in gaol,' said Alice. 'And Councillor Bloomfield's soon to get his comeuppance.'

Hetty shook herself to remove the image that came to her mind, of Bloomfield being hanged, as he would be in a few days.

Alice glanced at the door before coming closer and whispering, 'Simon says he spied Mrs Bygrove walking with that Detective Inspector Toshack yesterday evening, down by the river.'

'They'd probably just bumped into each other,' said Hetty, though she was aware that the inspector, who'd overseen the murder investigation into Douglas Bygrove's death, had been for lunch at the hotel a few times recently.

The door from the staff corridor opened and Helen Bygrove entered.

Annie, Alice and Hetty glanced at each other, obviously all hoping that Helen hadn't heard anything of what they'd just said.

'Hello ladies, don't mind me, I'm just passing through on my way out.'

'Isn't it the doll parade today?' said Hetty.

'Yes it is, which is why I'm carrying this around in my basket.' Helen lifted a Mama doll from under a small blanket, tipping it so that it said *Maa ma*.

Hetty had always found the sound of such dolls rather creepy, but she smiled. 'I'm sure Dorothy will enjoy the parade.'

'It's just the first in a week's worth of activities for National Baby Week,' said Helen. 'I believe Fanny has entered Elsie for the baby show tomorrow. Poor Arthur was rather glum when he left for school, saying he wished they had a toy train parade.'

'It does seem a little unfair.'

'By the way, happy birthday, Hetty.' She handed her an envelope.

'Oh, why thank you, Mrs Bygrove.' She opened it to find a card with a picture of blue tits on a tree. 'That's very pretty.'

'And I've asked Mrs Norris to keep a piece of cake back for you to have this evening, with your dinner.'

'That's very kind of you. I thought, with the shortages, you wouldn't do that anymore.'

'I'm still determined to give my loyal staff a treat on their birthdays, while I can.' Helen looked at her wristwatch. 'I'd better get away. I need to visit the solicitor before I take the doll to school for Dorothy. Bye-bye for now.'

When she'd left, Alice sighed. 'Don't suppose any of us will get the chance to get married and have our own children until this war finishes and the men come home.'

'If enough come home,' said Annie. 'Anyway, I'm heading to lunch. See ya later.'

'Aren't you going?' Hetty asked Alice.

'No, I'm on a late lunch today. I only came in to see if you had anything needed washing up.'

'Just these bowls.' She handed a stack of them to Alice.

'Ta. Are you doing anything nice on your afternoon off?'

'I'm meeting Phoebe and we're going to the Harbour Tea Rooms on Pier Road.'

'It's good you keep in touch with her, after Bygrove throwing her out. I like hearing her news from you. I hope she comes back to the hotel after the war. Send her all my best.'

'I will.'

Hetty, pleased to be alone again, was about to dip a spoon into the pan to test the jam when the door from the corridor opened once more. Miss Bolton, the hotel nurse, popped her head around it.

'Just to let you know, I've decided to give you all first aid lessons. I'll have more details tomorrow, when I've worked out how to fit them around the shifts.'

Before Hetty was able to give any kind of reply, Miss Bolton was gone.

'Well,' she said to herself. 'Whenever am I going to have use of *those*?'

She shook her head and grinned, but soon thoughts of Lorcan crept back in. She shouldn't worry too much about a lack of letter, as they were all very busy on the front, according to the newspapers.

She couldn't help wondering whether he'd still want to walk out with her when he returned. It's not like she'd seen him since he'd enlisted, as he'd spent any leave he'd had in Ireland with his family, though that had been partly because Mr Bygrove wouldn't allow him back in the hotel. Perhaps he would come to see her now the manager was gone.

Would they get married, or would she end up being a stillroom maid forever? A head one, in charge of others, but a stillroom maid nonetheless. Where would they live if they did get married? Lorcan had lived in at the hotel when he'd worked here too. Would they be able to afford a place of their own? Or would he expect her to move to Ireland? She wasn't sure what she felt about that, being away from her family, however annoying they could be. And her friends. Not seeing Lorcan for so long made it all rather confusing for her.

The door opened once more, and Hetty was about to groan inwardly when she saw that it was Tilly and Milly, her two underlings, who were cousins and quite lively young girls.

'You took your time,' said Hetty.

'Sorry,' said Tilly. 'We split up and went to different grocery stores looking for sugar, but we couldn't get as much as you wanted.'

'It was worth a try. We'll just have to do our best until the next delivery.'

She looked up at the clock on the wall. Only an hour and twenty-five minutes until she got off for the afternoon. She couldn't wait.

Hetty spotted Phoebe as she reached the pond at the end of South Terrace. She was standing by the river, her hand shading her eyes, as she looked over at something. When Hetty reached her, it became evident what had caught her attention.

'It's one of the flying boats!'

Phoebe twisted around. 'Oh Hetty, hello!' The friends embraced briefly. 'Yes, it's fascinating.'

'They've been building the hulls for them down on the quay for a while now. They test the finished items out on the water here quite often.'

They both rotated to watch as the flying boat cruised along towards the mouth of the river. The sun, in a completely blue sky, shone down on the water, making it sparkle, and a warm breeze caressed Hetty's face. It was at times like this that she could experience a brief respite from work and the reality of the war, and enjoy contentment, if only for a few seconds.

When the flying boat was out of sight, Phoebe unclipped her leather handbag and retrieved a present wrapped in newspaper. 'Happy birthday, Hetty.'

'That's so kind. Thank you.' Hetty took the present and unwrapped it to reveal a hair comb with faux tortoiseshell teeth and a metal floral top with rhinestones. 'That is lovely, Phoebe. I'll look forward to wearing it when I go somewhere special next.'

'You heard from Lorcan?'

'No, but it's meant to be frantic out at the front at the moment.'

'I'm sure he'll write and send you something when he has time.'

'I'm sure he will.' She had to keep convincing herself of that.

'Ready for afternoon tea?'

'Oh my, yes.'

They linked arms and crossed over Pier Road to the fishermen's cottages, among which was the Harbour Tea Rooms.

Inside, she spotted Mr Crolla, the Italian owner of the business, next to the counter at the back of the room. He smiled and raised a hand in welcome. The tall glass display next to him didn't seem as full as it had been in the past.

'There ees a nice table by the window, ladies,' Mr Crolla said as he approached them.

They sat where he suggested, at a square table already laid up, overlooking the boats, lobster pots and a fisherman mending a net. He placed two menus down on the lace tablecloth.

When he left, Phoebe said, 'Oh dear, there's very little choice now; only two types of sandwiches and one cake.'

'They'll be having the same problems as us, getting supplies.'

'I think I'll have an egg and watercress sandwich, a scone and jam and a piece of fruit cake.'

Hetty placed the menu down. 'Me too. I dare say if the jam's anything like what I've made recently, it won't be very sweet.' She took the opportunity to look around at the walls with their wooden boards on the bottom half and flowers painted on a cream wall above.

'It's very stylish in here,' said Phoebe, who must have seen her looking around. 'It could rival the Beach Hotel.'

'Don't let Mr— I mean, oh goodness.'

'Were you about to say "don't let Mr Bygrove hear you say that"?' Phoebe widened her eyes.

'Yes, I was. How could I forget, even for a second? It happened going on three months ago now, so it's not like it's new.'

'And especially as everyone at the hotel must have been delighted about his demise.'

'Phoebe!'

'Come on now, tell me it's not true.'

Hetty looked down. 'Well, yes, we were all glad to see the back of him, I can't lie, but maybe not in the way it happened.'

'No, I suppose not.' They were quiet for a moment, before Phoebe continued with, 'How is everyone getting on?'

'They've got over the shock of it all, I think. Life seems to have got back to normal, if that's what you can call it. As normal as it gets during this war. Rumour has it that Mrs Bygrove is walking out with Detective Inspector Toshack. But don't tell anyone.'

'Good luck to her. And who could blame her? I got a glimpse of him a while back. He's so handsome.'

'Phoebe!'

Her friend giggled. 'Are you going to keep admonishing me?'

'No. You're right, he is handsome. Lucky Mrs Bygrove, eh?'

Phoebe took her hand. 'Lorcan'll be back, you'll see. I don't think this war can go on for much longer.'

'That's what people have been saying since the thing started. "Over by Christmas," they said then. And nearly three years later…' She recalled Lorcan saying much the same thing, the day she walked with him to the railway station.

Mr Crolla's daughter arrived and took their order. As soon as she'd gone, Hetty said, 'Well, that's enough of me; have you heard from Günther?'

'I had a letter last week. He's still in the internment camp on the Isle of Man. It seems so much further away than Newbury. Not that I could have visited him there.'

It was Hetty's turn to take Phoebe's hand as she continued.

'He seems all right… I wonder, you know, whether we'll be able to take up where we left off, when he returns. *If* he returns, and doesn't decide to go back to Germany. Our relationship had hardly started when he was hauled off.'

'It was much the same for me and Lorcan, and I've been wondering the same. Especially with all the trouble there's been in Ireland. He does worry about his family.'

'My mum keeps asking when I'm going to meet a nice boy and get married, being a sad old spinster of twenty-seven.' Phoebe raised her eyes heavenward.

'Doesn't she know about Günther?'

'Yes, but she doesn't approve, of course, and thinks I'll get over him. I do have to remind her that the chances of meeting a young man currently, nice or otherwise, are slim.'

'My mother's much the same. Only yesterday evening, she said, "Twenty-five already, and no husband and family," before clucking her tongue in that way she does.'

'They still don't know about you and Lorcan?'

'They know I write to him, but I made it sound casual, like I was doing it to keep his spirits up. That was near the beginning of the war, and I've never got around to telling them otherwise. I suppose, in a way, I'm protecting myself.'

'From what?' Phoebe looked confused. 'Oh, you mean, if he doesn't come back?'

'That, and also, if he comes back and doesn't want to continue the relationship. Or, oh, I don't know, maybe it will be me who has a change of heart.'

She wished she hadn't expressed that last thought, though it was something she'd thought about for a while. She hadn't seen him in nearly three years. What if he'd changed in some way that she didn't like. That part sounded too heartless to voice.

'I suppose you might have grown apart,' said Phoebe. 'And maybe Günther and I have too. We won't know until we see them again.'

'You're right. I think too much sometimes. That's the problem with having so many monotonous jobs to do in the stillroom. It gives you too much time to ponder.'

'Oh yes, I remember those days. I suppose it's not much different working the land. My jobs there can be repetitive too.'

'Come on then, tell me what you've been getting up to as part of the Land Army.'

Phoebe leant forward to tell her the first of many stories, and Hetty was glad of the distraction.

Chapter Two

Despite being the undermanageress now, Edie Moore enjoyed her occasional stints in the conservatory, serving afternoon tea. Mixing with people was more satisfying than drawing up rotas, telephoning tradesmen or helping with accounts. And it was such a lovely room, with its large plants and glass panes, overlooking the south-facing garden, bright in the sunshine today. The outer doors had all been opened and the tied-back net curtains fluttered gently in the breeze.

She smoothed down the grey dress and white apron that was the waitresses' uniform, and made sure her cap was straight, before strolling over to a table by the window.

'We don't see you so often in here these days, m'dear,' said old Major Thomas, a permanent guest at the hotel, as he looked up.

'Sadly not, Major,' said Edie. 'Though I do prefer it to sitting in the office.'

'Don't blame you, m'dear. I always preferred being a man of action. Now, let me see...'

He perused the menu once more. Goodness knows why, he must know it off by heart by now, especially as it had become more restricted and predictable in the last year or so.

'I'll have the smoked salmon and chive sandwich, and a palmier.'

'No scone for you today, sir?'

'Not today, no. I'm meeting an old army pal for a walk, so haven't got much time. It's not very busy in here today; looks like everyone wants to be out in the sun.'

'And who can blame them, Major? And a pot of your usual coffee?'

'Of course, goes without saying.'

Edie took the order to the stillroom and kitchen. As she re-entered the conservatory, she noticed James Perryman, the owner of local shipyards, being shown to a table by young Simon, along with his wife, daughter and son. Edie stopped beside the dresser, where head waitress, Liliwen Probert, was standing.

'We don't often see Victor in here,' Lili said, in her lilting Welsh accent. 'And Sophia doesn't come that often.'

'You mean young Mr and Miss Perryman,' Edie corrected, though she said it with a grin.

'Them too,' Lili joked back. 'Always saying how hard her Sophia works, is Mrs Perryman, what with the various charities, even though we already know that 'cos she's helped out with it at the hotel.'

'Yes, Mrs Perryman is inordinately proud of Sophia and all she does, and rightly so.'

'I wonder why young Mr Perryman is gracing us with his presence today. Rather handsome he is, don't you think, with his auburn hair, large brown eyes and sculptured cheekbones?'

'I'm sure, Miss Probert, that we are not paid to think such things.' She turned and regarded Lili with a smile. 'But I do concur, and he's an agreeable young man, too.'

'Would you be interested if you weren't already walking out with Charlie?'

Edie shook her head. 'No. I've left the life of a baron's daughter behind, you know that. Besides, wouldn't it be strange, if I married the man whose father now owned the shipping business that once belonged to my mother's second husband and was left to her?'

'Haydon's Shipyard you mean? Might be rather appropriate. If your mother hadn't sold it when she married your father, it would have belonged to your family now.'

'I suppose… Would you be interested in Victor if you didn't have Rhodri?'

'Heavens no! Besides which, he's a different class to me.'

'As is Charlie to me.'

'True, but you two are the other way round, with you being from a higher class than Charlie. I have wondered why he hasn't been conscripted. Victor Perryman, I mean.'

'Because of the business I should think. They do make vital parts for the ships and the flying boats.'

'I suppose,' said Lili. 'By the way, Simon told me that he saw Mrs Bygrove walking out with DI Toshack yesterday evening.'

'He shouldn't be spreading idle gossip. I'll have a word with him later. She was simply taking a walk with him because he was concerned about how she was coping with the hotel, being a widow now.'

'She coped well enough when Bygrove were conscripted. Better even.'

That was certainly true, and Edie knew that there was more to Helen's relationship with the inspector than simple friendship, but it was nobody else's business at the current time.

Edie spotted a young woman enter the room. She was wearing a sand-coloured silk dress with large decorative green buttons on the bodice. The top skirt reached her knees and had box pleats, while the purple underskirt reached just above her ankles. Over it she wore a short, teal jacket. Her shoes, which matched the dress, had a pointed toe and a Louis heel. Her black hair was short, with a slight curl at the ends.

'There's Ebony Girard, looking as glorious as ever,' said Edie, pronouncing the surname in a French accent, the way Ebony herself did.

'I wonder if she has French ancestry? I was going to ask her once, but it didn't seem my place.'

'She told me a while back that her father is half French, and her mother half Italian, and that she speaks both languages fluently.'

'There's impressive. It looks like she's had her hair cut into one of them bobs I've seen in the magazines. I wonder where the other two artists are. She's never stayed without them before.'

'I've no idea. I'll direct her to a table.'

'And that were the bell for my order.'

They walked in opposite directions, Edie meeting Ebony halfway across the room.

'Good afternoon, Miss Girard.'

'Good afternoon, Edie. Now I've told you before to call me Ebony. Miss Girard sounds so stuffy and old fashioned. I was heading to one of the window tables, if they're not reserved.'

'No, we're very quiet today, so take your pick.'

Edie fetched a menu and placed it on the table as Ebony sat down.

'I suppose everyone's wondering why Hazel and Marigold aren't with me on this visit,' she said.

Edie didn't like to say that it had been mentioned a few times by the staff since she'd checked in. 'I suppose they're otherwise engaged.'

'You could say that. Marigold joined the Women's Army Auxiliary Corps in February and is a signaller in France now. Hazel became a Voluntary Aid Detachment nurse in April. She's at Netley Hospital, in Southampton.'

'Oh, I see.' Edie had thought she would say that they were on some painting expedition somewhere, and this was the last thing she expected.

'I can see that you're as surprised as everyone else. I keep wondering if I should go and do "something useful", as Hazel put it. I do feel so terribly lonely without them, as we shared a house, as well as coming away together. I've brought my art materials with me and am hoping for some inspiration from the coast to distract me.'

'It's certainly a lovely day for painting,' said Edie.

'Yes, I may go and do some sketches later, on the pier maybe.'

'What can I get you, Miss— Ebony?'

'A pot of Earl Grey tea, and I think just a scone with the usual accompaniments this afternoon. Thank you.'

Edie felt sorry for her as she walked away. But really, why should she? Hers was a tiny problem compared to those of so many others in this war. She looked back briefly. Still, she looked quite forlorn, as if she'd lost two triplets, though they were all only cousins. They had visited the hotel together several times a year since before Edie had started working here in 1914. She could understand why she might feel lonely now.

Hopefully, she would find something to do while she was here, to cheer herself up.

–

Ebony had just finished the last piece of her scone when she heard a loud male laugh from a few tables away. It brought her out of a self-pitying reverie about the last time she was here with her cousins, and at first, she was cross. She looked up to find out who the offending gentleman was when she spied a young man, grinning widely. He was sitting at the table with a young woman she knew to be Sophia Perryman, who had organised many charity events in the area. She vaguely recalled the middle-aged couple, with their backs to her, having dined in the hotel before, when she was here last Christmas. She looked around the room now, to see who else was here, but there were only two other tables occupied. At one of them sat Major Thomas, his head in a newspaper. She had been so wrapped up in her own misery, that she hadn't even noticed who was in the room.

As she was looking around, Edie stopped by her table.

'Is there anything else I can get you, Ebony?'

'No, thank you, that will be sufficient. I was just wondering, though, who the people with Sophia Perryman are.'

'The young man is her brother, Victor. He is considered to be rather attractive,' she mouthed.

Ebony was confused at first as to why Edie would say that, then realised that her enquiry must have sounded like she was interested in this Victor. 'I'm an artist, Edie. I'm interested in people in general, not young men in particular. I've seen the older couple before, I think. Last Christmas?'

'Yes, you will have done. They are James and Barbara Perryman, Sophia and Victor's parents. Mr Perryman owns several shipyards along the coast, including Haydon's and Humphrey Wilmot's, here in Littlehampton.'

'I see. Well, I will just finish my tea, and I'll be off to the promenade with my sketch pad.'

'We will see you at dinner, no doubt?'

'Of course.'

As Edie walked away, Ebony considered her assumption about Victor Perryman. He *was* good looking, but he didn't raise any interest in her in *that* way.

She rose gracefully from her seat and made her way towards the door.

'Good afternoon, m'dear,' came a voice as she started to walk away. It was Major Thomas, looking up from whatever he'd been reading.

'Good afternoon, Major. How lovely to see you here again.'

'Oh, I'm always here. But it's certainly good to be treated to your colourful presence again. Where, may I ask, are your fellow artists?'

'They were unable to accompany me this time.' She didn't feel like explaining again. It could wait for another time, when she wasn't keen to get out and enjoy the sunshine.

'What a shame. Enjoy the rest of your afternoon, m'dear.'

'Thank you, Major. I hope you do, too.'

She did tire of these polite encounters with people some-times, but they were the way of life. A courteous if brief, 'Good afternoon,' would have sufficed.

She was pondering this when something knocked her arm, and she was pushed sideways a little.

24

'Good heavens, I am so sorry, madam.'

Ebony took a few moments to compose herself, before she realised who her accidental assailant had been. Now she could see him up close, she noted that James Perryman was tall, with broad shoulders. His hair was partly grey, though there were more than enough dark streaks to show that his hair had been brown in his younger days.

'I–I'm fine, thank you.'

'I was so involved in conversation with my son, that I wasn't looking where I was going. He doesn't often come here with us, but it is my wife's birthday today, so it was good...' His voice trailed off and he looked a little embarrassed. 'But you're probably not at all interested in that.'

Ebony looked towards the door, where the rest of his family had carried on, though his wife was now peering over.

She looked up at him once more. 'I hope she's enjoying her birthday. And it – it's all right. These things happen. I was in a world of my own, so was not looking where I was going either.'

After a few awkward seconds, she glimpsed the door briefly. His family had left.

'You're one of the three artists, aren't you? You were here at Christmas, I remember because that woman came in accusing Mrs Bygrove of writing those very unsavoury libellous letters, that almost ruined this hotel.'

'That's right, I'm Ebony Girard. Of course, I thought I recognised you and your wife. That dreadful woman! I remember now that you both defended Mrs Bygrove. Good for you.'

'As did you, as I recall.'

'Well, the woman was appalling. Now, do not worry unduly about me,' she said. 'I am not in the least bit injured. Good afternoon to you, sir.'

'Good afternoon, Miss Girard.' He bowed his head, taking a last glance at her, before carrying on to the door.

She carried on with her mission to collect her sketch pad and pencils from her room. Dressed as she was – colourful, Major

25

Thomas had called it – Mr James Perryman probably thought of her as one of those silly avant-garde artists. He wouldn't be the first and, no doubt, wouldn't be the last either.

Chapter Three

A week had gone by since Hetty's birthday. She was currently in her room, feeling a mixture of nerves and excitement, as she changed into the grey dress, white apron and cap of a Beach Hotel waitress.

Simon had been coughing far too much during luncheon and had been sent home towards the end of the shift, so they were now a person short to serve afternoon tea. Hetty had served trays of food at parties and charity functions since the war, but had never served during any of the meals. Phoebe had gone from being a stillroom maid to a waitress after most of the waiters had enlisted, and she'd managed it fine, so why shouldn't she? Then Hetty worried about everything being done properly in the stillroom while she was absent. She didn't want to find it in chaos later.

She shook her head at her foolishness. Tilly and Milly, though young, were perfectly capable of pickling onions and gherkins on their own, as they would be today, and of producing any beverages needed. And Annie would be popping in to keep an eye on them.

There was a tap at the door, before Lili's voice called, 'Are you all right? We need to get to the conservatory as people will be arriving soon.'

'Yes, just coming.' She left the room to find Lili at the top of the stairs. These led up from the staff corridor, past Mrs Bygrove's rooms on the first floor, and up to the staff quarters on the second floor. 'I was just struggling with the buttons a little.'

'Come on then, for your first go at being waitress. Ooh, don't look like that; you'll do all right. Managed it fine, Phoebe did.'

'I was just thinking that, funnily enough.'

Reaching the conservatory, Hetty was a little disappointed. Today it was dull, and there was even a little drizzle spraying against the windows. Still, the large pot plants in here at least gave it the feel of a garden. Edie was walking around the room, inspecting the tables.

'Good afternoon, ladies. It might be a little busier than we expected for tea, as we've just had half a dozen people book in, who we expected later in the day.'

'Were they the ones from London, wanting to flee the air raids?' Lili asked.

'That's right. Except one couple is from Margate, but here for the same reason.'

'I read about the air raids a couple of days ago in the newspaper,' Hetty said. 'They sounded awful.'

'Indeed,' said Edie. 'There were a lot of civilian casualties. We always seem to get a surge in bookings when these raids happen. Right, I will leave you to it as I'm relieving Grace on reception. And Hetty, there's no need to be worried. You're well turned out, efficient and very polite, you'll be fine.'

'Oh dear, do I look worried?'

'No, but I know how I felt when I first started waiting, and I was used to mixing with such people. I'll see you both later.'

When she'd left, Hetty said, 'Goodness, it looks like we'll be busier than we thought.'

'Stop worrying. And if anybody asks you anything what you don't know, just come and ask me.'

The door was opened by the head portress, Gertie Green, to admit the first of the guests. How glad Hetty was that her mother had regularly taken her to tea rooms and had always been a stickler for etiquette.

'Ready?' said Lili.

'Ready as I'll ever be.'

–

Hetty had served two tables so far, and everything had gone off without a hitch, much to her relief. Tilly and Milly had seemed to be doing well when she'd gone to the stillroom to order the tea. Around half an hour had gone by when a middle-aged woman entered with a young man.

Hetty was taken immediately by his tall and confident stature. He had thick, light auburn hair, wavy, with a side parting. He was smiling at something the older woman was saying.

'Who are they?' Hetty asked, standing next to Lili by the dresser.

'That's Mrs Perryman, whose husband owns several local shipyards, with Victor, their son.'

'He must be on leave.'

'No, I believe he runs one of the shipbuilding businesses in Littlehampton, so has a reserved occupation. He doesn't often come here, but twice in a week that's been now.'

'Should we show them to a table?'

'No, they'll sit where they want. They always do. There, they've sat at one of your tables by the window.' Lili picked up two menus and handed them to her. 'Off you go.'

Hetty put her smile in place and walked over to the table, noting that the rain seemed to have finally stopped. Nevertheless, the young man's hair was slightly damp, as was the woman's turban hat with its ostrich feather tips and velvet pansies.

'Good afternoon, madam, sir.' She gave them a menu each.

'Hello. I don't think I've seen you here before,' said Mrs Perryman.

'No madam, I've been brought in as we're a little short-staffed today.'

'And what's your name?'

'Henrietta, madam.'

29

Only her mother referred to her by her full name, and then only in public, but she knew management preferred the use of 'proper' names when dealing with customers, as Douglas Bygrove had always put it. She wondered whether Helen was as bothered about it as he had been.

'Do you usually work somewhere else in the hotel?'

'Mother!' said Victor. 'Don't give the poor girl the third degree.'

'I'm the head stillroom maid, madam.'

'Ah, the person who normally makes our delicious beverages. I hope they have someone in there today equally skilled.' Mrs Perryman said this in a light-hearted manner and with a smile, which put Hetty at her ease.

'Yes, they're very skilled, madam.'

'Now let me see. A pot of Darjeeling for two, of course, but what sandwich do I fancy. I don't suppose you have any ordinary bread yet.'

'No, we're still having to use the war flour, madam.'

'That is one thing I will *not* miss when this war is over.'

'There are worse things, Mother.'

'Yes, I suppose,' she said on a sigh.

Hetty found that, now she'd got used to the rougher bread, with its barley, oats and rye flour, she rather liked it. Mrs Norris, the head cook, hadn't appreciated her saying so at lunch a few days ago, though.

'I think I rather fancy the roast beef and chive sandwich today,' said Mrs Perryman. 'Though the devilled egg and cress is tempting too, oh gosh, and the smoked salmon and dill.'

'Why don't we order a selection for us both, Mother?'

'What a good idea, Victor. Along with scones for both of us, with cream, and the delicious strawberry jam, of course.' She looked up at Hetty. 'Do you make that in your stillroom?'

'I do, madam.' She resisted looking proud and smiled only slightly.

'Now, what cake shall I follow that with? Hmm, only three to choose from again. I'll have the hazelnut dacquoise. What about you, Victor?'

Hetty now turned her attention to the young man, only to feel a jolt – yes, that was the only way she could describe it – when she considered him close to. He looked up at her, and she found it hard to breathe. My, he was striking, with his dark brown eyes contrasting with the light auburn hair. His skin wasn't as pale as she normally encountered with redheads either but was a light olive. He grinned broadly before saying, 'I'll have the walnut torte, please.'

'Very well, sir, madam.'

'I wonder how long these treats will be on the menu,' said Mrs Perryman, 'what with the increasing shortages.'

Hetty had wondered this herself, but knew that Mrs Norris had ways to get around things they were short of to produce such treats. She could hardly tell a guest that though.

'I wouldn't like to say, madam.'

She was disappointed and glad all at once, to be leaving the table. Whatever that was, what she was feeling, it was rather disturbing. She needed to pull herself together before she returned to them.

As she walked back to the table with the tray containing the teapot and accompaniments, she became anxious once more. What if she were asked to pour the tea? She'd done it a thousand times at home and in the staff dining room, but here, she was afraid of spilling it. She reached the table and started to unload the items.

'So, I think we really should make a supreme effort for Sophia's thirtieth birthday, Victor,' Mrs Perryman was saying. 'She certainly deserves it, after all the hard work she's put into her charity endeavours during the war.'

'I agree, Mother. What about having a party for her here, at the hotel?'

'That's not a bad idea.' She looked up at Hetty, who had just unloaded the last item, a pot of hot water. 'What do you think, Henrietta? Can the hotel throw a good party?'

Hetty was taken aback to be asked her opinion. 'Why yes, madam. The ones at which I've had the privilege to serve food have certainly gone very well. However, either Mrs Bygrove or Miss Moore would be able to advise you further. Miss Moore is on reception currently, so you might be able to speak with her before you leave.'

'Excellent. Thank you, Henrietta.'

'You're welcome, madam.' Hetty gave a slight bow and walked away.

Lili made a signal to her that indicated she'd been summoned by the bell – two tings for her, one for Lili – and hurried to the kitchen, the image of Victor Perryman's face still lingering in her mind.

–

Victor had been wary of an afternoon tea out with just his mother, especially when she'd mouthed that she had something she wanted to discuss with him. He'd feared it would be an attempt to inveigle him into going to yet another party to meet 'young ladies'. She'd said last time that it was the perfect opportunity, while most of the young men were away. That seemed rather cold reasoning to Victor. When attending such functions in the past, he had not enjoyed being ogled by the young women in question while being discussed behind cupped hands.

He was relieved when it became evident that it was Sophia's birthday she'd wanted to discuss, and that the secrecy had been because his sister had been in the room at the time.

He was sitting now in the drawing room at home with his mother, after both had changed for dinner. They were awaiting the call to the dining room, along with his father's homecoming, though the latter was not certain at this hour.

Sophia, who had a meeting with her charity committee this evening, had eaten earlier.

The front door could be heard opening and shutting, and his mother, Barbara, said, 'Here he is, on time for a change… I meant to say, I wonder if Henrietta, the girl who served us today, is a little like Edie. Not as high class, but she did have rather nice diction, quite middle class, not like most of the staff, although they try.'

'Really, Mother, I don't notice such things. I believe Liliwen, the head waitress, is Welsh, so maybe that is the middle-class diction, as you put it, in Wales. Who knows?'

'You're being flippant, Victor.'

'I'm being non-judgemental, Mother.'

'I wasn't being judgemental, I was making an observation. It matters not a jot to me where the staff serving us come from, only that they are good at their jobs. And at the Beach Hotel, they are all exemplary. Well, they are now that Douglas Bygrove has met his maker.'

'Mother! Though I suppose I can't disagree. What we've heard since Bygrove's death about his behaviour makes it unsurprising that he met his end the way he did.'

Not long after, James entered the room. He greeted them both and bent to give Barbara's cheek a cursory kiss.

'How were things your end today, Victor?' James sat in an armchair.

'Running smoothly, Father. The orders we have are all due to go out on time.'

'That's what I like to hear.'

'The pair of us have also been busy organising a thirtieth birthday party for Sophia,' Barbara added. 'We went to the Beach Hotel for afternoon tea to talk about it, and Victor came up with the splendid idea of actually holding it there. I don't know why I didn't think of it before. We spoke to Edith Moreland about it.'

'Edie Moore,' James corrected.

33

'Yes, of course,' said Barbara.

'Edith Moreland?' Victor was confused.

'Of course, you don't know,' said his mother. 'Edie is actually the Honourable Edith Moreland, daughter of Baron and Baroness Moreland.'

'As in the Agnes Moreland you bought Haydon's shipyard from?'

'That's correct,' said James. 'I thought you knew. I'm surprised Sophia didn't mention it. Edie decided that the life of a baron's daughter wasn't for her anymore.'

'My goodness,' said Victor, while harbouring some understanding of why Edie Moore might want to escape the pressure of such a life. He wouldn't say this to his parents though. He'd often wondered what it would be like to simply be a worker in the business, a clerk in the office or one of the skilled workmen who built the ships and flying boat hulls. Or what it would have been like to have been given some choice about his future. His father had been keen when he'd gone off to university, but what had been the point when he was only ever destined to help run the shipbuilding businesses?

'Anyway, Barbara, you can't keep taking Victor off for afternoon teas when you feel like it. He has a business to run.'

'I don't *keep* taking him off. He came with us on my birthday last week, yes, but when was the last time he came with me, or us?'

'I hadn't been there for some years,' said Victor. 'And it was my afternoon off, Father, to be fair, and there have been many weeks recently when I have not taken my afternoon off. And you and Mother dine regularly at the hotel.'

'But I work late to make up for any shortfall in hours.'

'Yes, you do,' said Barbara, a little peeved. 'Anyway, we booked the ballroom for Saturday eighteenth of August for Sophia's birthday.'

'You'd better tell her then, so she doesn't organise something else that day.'

'She already knows we're doing something. She just doesn't know what.'

Barbara started to outline the arrangements to James, and Victor's mind wandered. He hoped that their waitress today, Henrietta, would be helping to serve at Sophia's party. She seemed like a thoroughly pleasant young woman, and very pretty, with her thick fair hair arranged into coils at the back of her head, her sparkling blue eyes and constant smile. She looked... sweet.

'Could you do that, Victor?'

He looked around in surprise. 'Sorry, Mother? Do what?'

'That's not the first time today that you've been miles away. Is some pretty young woman taking up your thoughts?'

'What? No, of course not. I was just thinking about Sophia's party.'

'Which is what I was asking about. You must have some young male friends you can invite along.'

'First of all, Mother, most of my friends are at war.'

She looked down. 'Yes, of course they are. I should have thought of that.'

'Secondly, Sophia appreciates, as little as I, having her prospective love life organised.'

'I know. But she'll be thirty years old soon! She should be married by now with at least two children. I fear she'll be left on the shelf. Oh, this wretched war. Hopefully, when the men come home...'

'She has always been rather scathing of men,' Victor pointed out. 'In her suffragist days before the war, she told me that she wouldn't even consider marrying until women were granted the vote and she felt she was more equal.'

There was more to it than that, but it wasn't Victor's story to tell.

'Oh dear,' said Barbara. 'And I dare say she'll go back to campaigning after the war has ended.'

'I would lay good money on it,' said James.

The door opened, and their butler, Harries, entered.

'Dinner is served, sirs, madam.'

'Wonderful. I could eat a horse,' said James, as they all rose and followed Harries to the dining room.

'Let's hope, with the shortages, that it doesn't come to that,' said Barbara.

Chapter Four

A couple of days after serving Victor Perryman and his mother in the conservatory, Hetty was out on an afternoon off. Her mother had been keen for her to spend the time off at home, but she'd managed to persuade her that she needed a trip into town to look for some new shoes for best.

It had been a busy morning, shut up in the stillroom, and as she left the hotel and saw the wide blue sky and felt the warmth of the sun, she decided to walk the length of the long common, past the pond, and make her way into town that way, rather than take the short route.

She took her time as she walked along the River Arun on Pier Road, greeting a couple of fishermen along the way, enjoying the freedom of the open space and fresh air. The stillroom didn't have an outside window, only an inside one, and a glass door, both of which looked onto the scullery, so they didn't even get as much light as the scullery maids. As her mind wandered, she pictured Victor Perryman's appealing face. She'd done that a lot the last two days. Silly really, but it didn't do anyone any harm just to dream, like she might do about a matinee idol.

She passed the drill hall, houses and warehouses, until she reached the entrance to Fisherman's Quay. She strolled down past the Britannia public house, pebbles crunching underfoot, until she reached lobster pots and the river's edge. She didn't often come down here as her mother reckoned that drunks and women of ill repute hung around the public house, but she doubted she'd see much of that in broad daylight. There were some boat building workshops on one side. She looked out across the water, to the riverbank opposite, where there was a small beach and a wharf.

'Good afternoon, are you looking for something?'

She turned, surprised. It was Victor Perryman standing there, looking dapper in a blue pinstriped suit. It was as if her thoughts had conjured him up.

'Oh, hello, it's you,' said Victor, as he smiled warmly and stepped a little closer. 'Don't look so shocked.'

'Good afternoon, Mr Perryman.' After a brief delight at seeing him, she felt immediately silly in his presence, outside of her proper place.

'It certainly is a good afternoon for a walk, not like when my mother and I visited the hotel a couple of days ago.' He turned to look over the river, like she had been.

'Are you out for a walk too, sir?'

'Goodness, no.' He pointed to the buildings of the Britannia Works to the side of them. 'I run the Humphrey Wilmot factory here for my father. We make the hulls for the flying boats, which then go to Middleton to be put together.'

'I've seen the flying boats being tried out on the river here a couple of times.'

'That's right. They take them down the river and out to sea for a test run.'

'I do enjoy watching them, sir.'

'Please, we're not in the hotel now. You can drop the "sir".'

'Oh, all right then – um… all right.'

'You were about to say "sir" again, weren't you?' He chuckled.

'Yes, I'm afraid I was.' She started to feel more at ease in his company, but wary of overstaying her welcome.

'I'm Victor, which you may already have gathered.' He put his hand out towards her.

As she took it, she said, 'And I'm normally called Hetty. Henrietta is only for formal occasions.'

'Nice to meet you again, Hetty. What's brought you down to the quay?'

'Nothing in particular. It's my afternoon off and I fancied a walk. As I passed here, I thought I'd take a look. I love walking by the river but I only normally come down this bit when the fair's in town, if I have the time off.'

'Yes, I love a walk by the river, too. I have been known to walk all the way to Arundel.'

'Oh, yes, me too!'

'Fancy that! It is interesting working here when the fair's around. My father thinks it's a nuisance as it's a distraction to our workers, but it's only one day a year, and people do enjoy it. So, do you live-in at the hotel, Hetty?'

'That's right, um, Victor. Though I used to live in Wick, with my parents. My father is the headmaster of the Lyminster Council School, and they live in the schoolhouse.'

'A headmaster's daughter, eh? That would account for your "rather nice diction", as Mother put it.'

'My what?'

'My mother pointed out, when we got home, that your diction was rather more middle class than many of your work colleagues.'

Hetty, not knowing what to say to that, frowned a little.

'I'm sorry, I didn't mean to offend you. My mother said it wasn't a criticism of your colleagues, just an observation that you might be middle class, whereas most who work there aren't.'

'I don't know about that. Mother was always keen on our elocution, though.'

Her mother had been sure it would allow her brothers to get better jobs, and that she and her sister, Iris, would marry into a better class. She'd always been a bit of a snob. That's why Hetty had never confessed to her true relationship with Lorcan.

There was an awkward silence which made Hetty squirm inside. Even though he'd meant it as a compliment, somehow

39

it felt like the opposite, like he'd only talked to her because she might not be considered working class, like most of her colleagues. How she hated this whole 'class' thing!

'I had better get going,' Hetty said. 'I'm supposed to be shopping for new shoes. Good afternoon, sir.' She bowed her head a little.

'Good afternoon, Hetty.'

She crunched her way up the pebbles with purpose, feeling a mixture of loss at leaving him there and annoyance at his assumptions. As she passed the Britannia, she looked back to see him, hands in pocket and head down, walking back towards the workshops. Regret filled her, but she soon shook it off. Regret at what? They were worlds apart, and it wasn't like she could ever be anything but a maid to him. And she had a sweetheart, didn't she? Sort of. Though she still hadn't heard from him.

The crushing worry of what might have happened to Lorcan overwhelmed her, along with the guilt at looking favourably on another man, and she felt the tears in her eyes. She raised them skyward to stall them, a trick her mother had taught her, then took a handkerchief from her bag to wipe the drop that had already fallen.

–

What a clumsy clod he was, thought Victor, as he padded wearily back to the workshops. He had thought when he'd first started on his mother's comment about her diction that she would see it as a compliment, but she clearly hadn't. He probably looked like another upper-class snob, the sort she likely encountered all the time at the hotel. Then he remembered that she was usually in the stillroom so wouldn't have often met the guests. That didn't make it any better.

What did it matter? It wasn't like they were ever going to mix in the same social circles. A regret washed over him. She seemed so much more straightforward, more… *natural*, than most of the women he'd met recently. Especially those at the silly parties he was taken to. Yes, she was the first girl in a long time to take his interest, and she would no doubt be considered unsuitable by his parents. Just his luck. And for all he knew, she had a sweetheart.

As he reached the door, his secretary opened it. 'There you are, sir. Your father is on the telephone, wanting to speak to you.'

'Very well.' No doubt he'd get a ticking off for not being at his desk, but he could make the excuse that he was inspecting the wares or talking to the men. His father didn't need to know he'd gone for an indulgent stroll, as he would no doubt have referred to it.

He looked towards the public house, to see Hetty disappearing down the lane beside it, before he followed his secretary in.

–

Hetty returned to the hotel in time for early staff dinner at half past five. She'd finally managed to purchase a pair of brown leather shoes with a strap and Cuban heel from Freeman, Hardy and Willis. Her mother would complain that they were a little expensive when she saw them, and probably too fancy for her, but it was her own wages she was spending.

In the staff dining room, people were already gathered around the long, rectangular table, wishing Simon a happy seventeenth birthday. There was a stew in the middle, waiting to be served. Mrs Leggett the housekeeper, as usual, was at the head of the table in a proper chair, not sharing benches, as the rest of them did.

'I can't believe you're already seventeen,' said Mrs Norris, shaking her head at Simon. 'Don't seem five minutes since you came here as a skinny fifteen-year-old, with young Dennis, and now look at you.'

'What did you do with your afternoon off then, lad?' said Will Fletcher, one of the older chefs who'd come out of retirement after the war started, looking up from his newspaper.

'Went to see *The Love Liar*, with a couple of other films at the Empire in Church Street, with me mum and sister.'

'Only a year til you're eighteen. Let's hope the war's over by then.'

Mrs Norris flicked Will's arm. 'Let's not be talking like that, eh?'

'To be honest, I'd like to do something useful in the war,' said Simon, 'so I wouldn't mind if it was still going on.'

'Other people might, though.' Hetty was thinking of Lorcan once more.

'I 'spose.'

'Come on, let's get this served while it's still 'ot,' said Mrs Norris.

They all helped themselves and started to eat.

Bridget Turnbull, the storekeeper, turned to Hetty. 'And what did you do with your afternoon off, pet?' she intoned in her Geordie accent.

'I went for a walk to begin with, down to Fisherman's Quay. Funnily enough, Victor Perryman was there, and remembered me from when I served him and his mother a couple of days back. He was telling me about them making the flying boats in the workshops there.'

'You should not be associating with the guests, even if they are only day guests,' said Mrs Leggett.

Hetty thought she'd better explain so she didn't get into trouble. 'He came and talked to me, and I could hardly be rude.'

'I hope you didn't encourage a long conversation,' said the housekeeper.

'No, not at all.'

Though it might have been longer if he hadn't said that thing about the way people spoke. How she wished she hadn't taken offence and had lingered longer, despite what Mrs Leggett had just said. When she'd thought about it later, it wasn't as if he was trying to insult her.

Gertie ran in from the corridor, letting out a huge sigh. ''Ope you've left some for me. I had to go on an errand for Miss Girard, and then I met Clarice the postwoman on the way in, and she gave me this.'

Gertie stopped by Hetty and handed her a letter. She recognised the writing immediately. Relief washed over her, and she was now glad she'd felt guilty for enjoying Victor Perryman's company.

'Lorcan, by any chance?' said Lili, on her other side.

'I think it might be.' She put down her fork and opened the slightly bulky letter, to find a birthday card embroidered with violets.

Lili peeped over, saying, 'Ooh, there's pretty.'

'Don't be so nosy, lass,' said Mrs Turnbull.

Inside, Lorcan had written an apology for being late, and a few lines. There was also a little package wrapped in tissue paper. She opened it to find a coil of French lace, with a note from Lorcan saying that he hoped she could find something to sew it onto. She wrapped it back up and replaced it in the envelope. She'd have a better look at it later.

'I trust everything is all right with Mr Foley,' Mrs Leggett asked.

'Yes. He says it's very busy out in France at the moment.'

'Which is what the newspapers are saying too,' said Will. 'Whatever that means, exactly.'

'I meant to ask,' said Mrs Turnbull, 'whether Lady Blackmore's been back to the hotel recently.'

It was a complete change of subject, but something that the storekeeper often did when people dwelt too long on the war. The rather bossy Lady Blackmore had been a regular customer at morning coffee and afternoon tea for several years. She'd always come with her plain but pleasant companion, Cecelia, who was invariably being belittled and harassed. That was, until Miss Harvey, the perpetrator of the libellous letters that had nearly put Mrs Bygrove in gaol, had sent notes to people claiming they were actually sisters.

Lili shook her head. 'No, not seen hide nor hair of her in the hotel, we 'aven't. She doesn't seem to have forgiven us for the revelation, even though nobody here were responsible. Edie saw her in town a coupla days ago on her day off, and Lady Blackmore ignored her. Cecelia wasn't with her.'

'I wonder if the rumour about Cecelia being 'er sister is true,' said Gertie.

'Nobody seems to have got to the bottom of the rumour yet,' said Lili.

'If it is true, it's a shoddy way to treat your sister,' said Hetty.

At this point, Miss Bolton came into the room, but didn't take a seat.

'Just to let you know, I'll be running the first of my first aid lessons this evening, at ten o'clock, for half an hour. Anyone who can't make it, I'll be repeating it tomorrow morning at seven o'clock. I advise anyone who can come to do so. You just never know when you might need them. Especially if we start to get air raids here.'

'Do we all 'ave to do them, Miss Bolton?' said Gertie.

'If you're free, yes. I'm doing them at different times so as many people as possible get to participate. And I've decided you are all to call me Nurse Bolton from now on. It was nice to be out of the hospital and not be called that for a while, but now I think it's only proper.'

'It might take us a while to get used to that, Miss— I mean, Nurse Bolton,' said Mrs Turnbull. 'See, I'm gettin' it wrong already.'

'I'm sure you'll all get the hang of it eventually, Bridget.'

She exited the room swiftly.

'She wants to give us first aid lessons because she thinks we might get air raids?' said Lili. 'There's cheerful.'

'I was looking forward to reading the book I got out of the library,' said Hetty with a huff.

44

'Go on,' said Lili. 'It might be 'andy, you never know. Doesn't hurt to know how to deal with accidents and the like.'

'I suppose ·so.' Hetty could always take the book out for another few days, and if she didn't attend, *Nurse* Bolton would probably never let her hear the end of it.

—

The following day, just as afternoon tea was beginning, Hetty took a large tray of cups and saucers to the conservatory and started placing them on the dresser, ready for when the waiting staff needed to relay tables.

The room was already quite busy, but there was no sign of the Perrymans. She didn't really expect there to be, especially not Victor, but had harboured a vague, guilty hope. She was, however, surprised to see Miss Cecelia enter, without Lady Blackmore. Lili, who'd also spotted her, glanced at Hetty. Simon approached her and showed her to a nearby table.

Once seated, they heard her say, 'I know that people have been speculating on the true nature of the relationship between Lady Blackmore and me, but the only thing I will confirm is that she is my sister. That is all people need to know, so if anyone asks you, you can tell them that, Simon.'

'Very well, Miss Cecelia. Will Lady Blackmore be joining you today?'

'No, Simon, she will not.'

Lili approached Hetty as she placed the last cup on the dresser. 'Well, now we know,' she whispered.

Hetty simply nodded and returned to the scullery, eager to tell Annie and Alice the latest news.

Chapter Five

Ebony was enjoying her evening walk on the promenade, though she wished she'd brought her sketchpad and pastels to capture the mixture of blue and orange sky with the pink clouds. She'd been painting in her room during the afternoon, basing the work on sketches she'd made of the sunny beach and green sea a couple of days previously.

She reached the pier and strolled onto it to look eastwards, along the stretch of shore and promenade. Her thoughts wandered to what she might do tomorrow. Some sketching by the river maybe, or perhaps take a trip out, to Arundel or Chichester? It might depend on the weather.

As she stared at the scene, she was aware of someone approaching her. She turned to see James Perryman.

'Miss Girard, I thought it was you. I'm sorry, I realised when you told me your name the other day that I did not tell you who I was.'

'It's all right, Mr Perryman. I already knew who your daughter was, as I've encountered her at charity events.'

'I'm so glad I've bumped into you, as I was thinking of seeking you out at the hotel.'

This was a little forward. 'And why was that?'

'Because I seem to recall that you're an artist, and I'm looking for someone to paint Sophia, for her thirtieth birthday. Of course, I realise you might be an impressionist, or an abstract artist, or whatever the current trends are. Do you do portraits?'

She chuckled. 'I have tried my hand at several different styles, but I am more than capable at what I'll call "normal" art, for want of a better word. And yes, I have done portraits. But you have no idea whether I'm any good or not.'

'Do you have any examples?'

'I do have a catalogue of my paintings from an exhibition I did with Hazel and Marigold.'

'The two ladies you were with at Christmas?'

'That is correct. It's in my room at the hotel, though it is in monochrome, of course.'

'It wouldn't be right, to visit your room, Miss Girard.'

She tried not to grin but failed. 'Mr Perryman, I wasn't suggesting you should, but was merely illustrating that I had examples of my paintings nearby.'

'Oh, I see.' His face went red, which she found rather charming.

'If you like, and if you're available, I could bring it on my walk tomorrow evening, then you could see for yourself.'

'Um, tomorrow?' He thought for a few seconds. 'Yes, yes, that would be agreeable. Would around eight o'clock be all right for you, here on the pier?'

'Yes, that would be fine. I always dine early, so will have finished by then.'

'Good. Very well.' He looked awkward for a while. 'Yes, until tomorrow then. Good evening, Miss Girard.'

'*Bonne soirée*, Mr Perryman.'

As soon as he started walking away, Ebony regretted his departure and the prospect of being alone once more. At least she had tomorrow evening to look forward to.

–

James walked away from Miss Girard, down along the River Arun. *Ebony*. What a fitting name, with her raven hair. If it was natural, of course. You couldn't always tell these days. After all, Barbara's hair wasn't really blonde, not anymore. He glanced back at Ebony, but she was now leaning against the pier wall, looking back towards the beach. He was gripped by a feeling of déjà vu. Looking away, he tried to work out why.

Irene Belfiore. That was it. How many years had it been since he'd seen her? He counted in his head. Thirty-four. She'd been elegant too, an artist like Ebony, and a most interesting young woman. Her surname had been fitting. *Bel fiore*. Beautiful flower. He'd walked out with her a few times as a young man, on days that she'd managed to escape her house without a chaperone. She'd given him up in the end, saying she was moving to London and wanted to see more of the world, to meet different people. They'd been on the pier when she'd announced to him that she was leaving. How strange life was.

He'd been heartbroken for a while after Irene's departure, but being introduced to Barbara at a soirée, held by her parents, had changed all that. He'd only been vaguely aware of her as part of society until then. He hadn't even wanted to go to the soirée, but his parents had insisted. They'd married within the year.

He passed the Nelson public house and waved to the old fisherman he'd spoken with a few times, as the man mended his net. Now, he'd better fetch his motorcar from the shipyard and hurry home, before Barbara once again made a fuss about his absence.

–

The following evening, on the pier once more, Ebony lifted the sleeve of her teal velvet jacket to examine her watch: seven minutes past eight. James Perryman was late. Or he wasn't coming at all. That would be a shame. She'd been thinking about this possible commission since yesterday evening, and was excited at the prospect of a new project, a new *purpose*, to take her mind off missing Marigold and Hazel.

She sighed deeply and rose from the bench, where the leather bag holding the catalogue and other credentials for this assignment was laid. She regarded the beach, still fairly busy on this warm evening. From the corner of her eye, she caught a glimpse of someone she recognised. Yes, there was Lady Blackmore striding down the pier in a brown raincoat that reached her boots. What a thing to be wearing on such an evening. On her head was a broad, mushroom brimmed hat. Ebony hadn't seen her since her return to the hotel, and nor had she missed the judgemental glares and talking behind her hand to Cecelia, who had been a lot friendlier towards her and her cousins.

Still, she could hardly ignore the woman.

'Good evening, Lady Blackmore. And how are you this fine evening?' She smiled, even though she was sure it would not be reciprocated.

Predictably, Ebony was treated to the woman's condescending gaze, and a clipped, 'Good evening,' as she came to a halt.

'I haven't seen you at the hotel since I arrived, and only seen Miss Cecelia once.'

'Cecelia?' There was a pause, before she added, 'We've found somewhere more salubrious to frequent. Excuse me.'

Lady Blackmore did an about turn, then marched swiftly in the opposite direction.

'Excuse me for existing,' Ebony mouthed, as she watched her leave the pier.

She was wondering whether her ladyship hadn't known about Cecelia's trip to the hotel, and was hoping she hadn't got her into trouble, when she spotted James walking onto the pier. He was wearing a pale blue linen suit today, with a narrow navy tie. On his head was a straw boater. He looked very dashing.

'I'm so sorry for being tardy, Miss Girard. Dinner was a little later than we normally have it, and I couldn't very well leave until it was finished.'

'Don't worry, Mr Perryman. It's such a lovely evening that it's been a pleasure just to stand here and take it all in. Now, I have what you came for, and a little more.'

She picked up the leather bag from which she removed the catalogue she'd told him about. 'This was from an exhibition we gave in London last year.'

He flicked through the book, smiling and nodding. 'You and the other two artists are talented.'

'Thank you, Mr Perryman.'

'A shame they're not in colour; I would so have liked to have seen them in a little more detail.'

'Then you must attend one of our future exhibitions.' *If we ever have another*, she thought, wondering if this was the end of their little artistic trio, now Marigold and Hazel had abandoned her.

When James had got to the end of the catalogue, she said, 'As it happens, your wish can be granted in a small way.' She put the book back in the bag, and removed two small canvasses wrapped in tissue paper, portraits she had made of Marigold and Hazel, not long before their departures. She hadn't known whether to bring them or not, afraid she might drop them, or get sand on them, but had persuaded herself that she was being ridiculous.

She unwrapped them and passed them to him. He held one in each hand, looking from one to the other. 'My word, such good likenesses. I can tell, of course, that they are your companions. I say companions, are they, perhaps, your sisters? There is some small resemblance.'

'They are my cousins, Mr Perryman. It's our mothers who are the sisters.' She took the paintings one by one from James, wrapping each before placing it back in the bag. 'And despite what people think, we really are called Ebony, Hazel and Marigold.'

James sat down, reclining in a relaxed manner, crossing one leg over the other. 'How extraordinary. Yet your names match your hair colour, which surely wouldn't have been quite the same when you were born.'

'Au contraire, Mr Perryman. I had a full head of black hair when I was born.' She sat next to him. 'And it's never changed.

Hazel had light brown hair, which went a little darker as she got older, and Marigold was white-blonde, which her mother said she knew would end up a yellow-blonde, as did her own.'

'They've not come with you this time, your cousins?'

She huffed out a breath and looked towards the west bank of the river. 'No. Hazel has enlisted in the WAAC and Marigold has become a VAD nurse.'

'Did you not think of joining something, with them gone? Sorry, I'm being nosy now. Do tell me to mind my own business.'

'I didn't, no. They still needed people to organise charity events in Richmond – in Surrey, where we live – so I did that for a while, much like your daughter does. But then… I needed to get away for a rest, to experience the sea air.' As she said it, she hoped it didn't make her sound selfish or indulgent.

'If you're planning on staying any length of time, Sophia is always glad of help, especially from those who have experience.'

'I will give it some thought, Mr Perryman. Now, talking of Sophia, about this portrait…'

He sat forward, straight backed, as if to do business. 'I presume you're willing to take on the commission?'

'Indeed. It would come with a fee, of course.'

He pulled a piece of paper from his jacket pocket and unfolded it before handing it to her. 'I've done a little research and come up with this figure, if you're agreeable?'

She was quite surprised at the fee suggested on the paper, which was half again what she would have charged. 'Why yes, that would be fine, Mr Perryman. We will need to organise some sittings. And when would you like the painting finished by?'

'Well, that's the thing. It might be rather short notice. Her birthday is on the eighteenth of August, so a little over a month. Is that enough time?'

With the extra money he'd offered, she could make it enough time. 'Of course.'

'Then if you could come to the house for the first sitting on Monday, we'll take it from there. We have a room with good light that you can use. I will pick you up from the hotel, so that we can transport your equipment. I will send a note to the hotel, or telephone them, to confirm a time.'

'Very good.'

'How fortunate I was to have happened upon such a good artist just when I needed one. Tell me, Miss Girard, why is it you and your cousins often come to Littlehampton for painting holidays? There are many other places on the coast worth painting, especially in the west of the country.'

'And we've been to some of them too. But our trips here are to do with nostalgia as much as anything. We were brought here as children, you know, for seaside holidays.'

'I see.' He checked his wristwatch. 'I suppose I'd better get back,' he said, with some regret in his voice. 'It is a nice evening, but I did promise Barbara that I'd play some games of bridge with her and the children, since they'll both be home.'

'I'm going to stay out a little longer. The sky over there looks like it's developing into a gorgeous sunset, and I've brought a sketch pad and pastels with me.'

'I'll see you in a couple of days then, Miss Girard.'

'Indeed, Mr Perryman.'

–

It hadn't occurred to Ebony that she had no idea where the Perrymans lived until after he'd left the pier a couple of evenings before. She was standing at the window of her room, all the items she needed packed or folded, awaiting James Perryman's arrival at two o'clock, as outlined in the letter he'd had delivered at the front desk for her.

There was a knock at her door and she went immediately to answer it. The head portress, Gertrude, stood there, smiling.

'I understand you might need some help downstairs with your art equipment, Miss Girard.'

'Mr Perryman has arrived then?'

'That's right, madam.'

'If you could manage the easel, I can carry the two bags.'

'Very well, madam. I'll take it down the stairs and you can take the lift.'

'No, you take the lift, Gertrude, as the easel is far more cumbersome.'

'But—'

'I insist.'

'Very well, madam.'

'Miss Girard.' James came towards her as she reached the foyer. His brow was furrowed. 'The portress was supposed to carry those for you.'

'She is carrying the easel, and that was enough. I'm not incapable, you know.'

'Of course not. I'm sorry. Ah, here she is,' he said looking towards the lift. He went forward, relieving the portress of the easel and handing her a couple of coins, for which she thanked him.

'It's only up the road,' he said, leading her out of the hotel, 'but I have of course brought the motorcar.'

'I completely forgot to ask you where you live. Is your house on South Terrace?'

'It is, though right at the eastern end. Surrey Cottage.'

'Next to Surrey House?'

'That's right.'

'Cottage' it might be called, but she'd passed it enough times on walks out to know that it was a fair size.

When they arrived, she stepped out of the motorcar and gazed up at the building.

'It's not Surrey House,' he said, pointing to his neighbour, 'but it's home. I have offered a good price for next door, but Lady Violet St Maur is not ready to move out.'

'I think you'd do well to remain where you are,' said Ebony. 'Surrey Cottage is infinitely more charming than its neighbour.'

James chuckled. 'It's very nice of you to say so.'

They entered the hallway and Ebony looked around. It was elegant, with its light wooden flooring and cream walls. She detected a deliciously sweet scent, before she noticed the vase of mock orange and roses on the occasional table against one wall. At the windows were William Morris curtains. It all looked new, and she wondered whether they'd recently redecorated.

'James, now what is all this— oh.' Barbara Perryman, walking out of a door, came to a halt on seeing Ebony. She looked around at the painting equipment they'd brought in. 'Miss Girard, isn't it?'

'That's right.' Ebony stepped forward to take Barbara's hand to shake.

'What's going on?' said a new voice, just before Sophia appeared at the door.

'That's what I was about to ask.' Barbara tipped her head slightly to one side, regarding James.

'Surprise!' he announced, smiling. 'I've hired Miss Girard here to paint Sophia as a thirtieth birthday present.'

The look of confusion on Barbara's face made Ebony even more nervous, but this was tempered a little by Sophia's enthusiasm.

'Oh my goodness, Father, how splendid. That's a bit more imaginative than your usual presents.' She turned to Ebony. 'I have heard from someone who has attended them, that the exhibitions put on by you and your cousins in London are quite something, Miss Girard.'

Sophia clearly knew a little more about her than her father had. 'They have certainly had a modicum of success.'

'How modest of you. Now, where are we going to do this?'

'I thought in the old playroom,' said James.

'I've just had it decorated with a view to making it into a study for Sophia,' said Barbara rather sternly. 'We wouldn't want to get artist's paint all over it.'

'Nonsense, I'm sure Miss Girard will have brought adequate protection with her,' said Sophia.

'I do have some heavy canvas cloth which I use to protect the floor at the hotel when I'm painting.'

'Oh Mother, I can't think of anything better than being painted in a room I spent such a lovely time in as a child. Come on, Miss Girard, I'll show you the way.'

Buoyed up by Sophia's excitement, Ebony followed her up to a decent-sized first-floor room, which indeed looked – and smelled – like it had recently been decorated. It was a light yellow. There were currently no curtains, but this would allow more light into the room. She followed Sophia to the window. It faced south, and they could just spy the promenade and beach through the trees.

'Would this room suit your requirements, Miss Girard?'

'It would indeed, Miss Perryman.'

'Wonderful. I do love your outfit, by the way,' she said, indicating the layered dark green and purple crepe de chine dress with a long, tasselled sash. 'I wish I had the courage to wear such bold colours. Ah, here's Harries and Fairfax.'

A butler and maid entered, carrying Ebony's equipment. They placed it in the middle of the room and left.

'While you set up, I will go and choose an outfit to wear for the sitting. Is there anything in particular you'd like to suggest?'

'Your favourite day dress perhaps, Miss Perryman?'

'Very well. And please, it's Sophia.'

'Then you must call me Ebony.'

'Splendid. See you in a while.'

On her own now, Ebony put on her overalls, doing up the buttons as she went to the window once more to peep out. What a welcome she'd had from Sophia and James. But Mrs Perryman did not seem so enthusiastic. She only hoped this wouldn't cause trouble between husband and wife.

'Time to set up,' she told herself, and started with the easel.

Downstairs, James was now in the drawing room with Barbara, having been beckoned there by her.

'I really must get back to work now, my dear. I have an order arriving in a couple of hours at the Shoreham site and want to be there.'

'I won't keep you long. I'd just like to know when you organised this portrait.'

'Having heard that Miss Girard was an artist, I went to see her.'

'How do you know she's any good?'

'Because she showed me a catalogue of one of her exhibitions, and she also had a couple of portraits she'd done of her cousins.'

'Why couldn't you have told me? I would like to have come and seen the catalogue and portraits and discussed the matter with her.'

'Because I wanted it to be a surprise for you too, my dear.' He took her hand and gave it an affectionate squeeze.

'It is certainly a very nice gesture, and a lovely present for Sophia.'

'I'm glad you agree. Now, I really must get away. I'm sure Miss Girard would appreciate afternoon tea with you here, when you have it.'

'Of course. She's a guest, so that goes without saying.'

'See you later, my dear.'

She was calling, 'Don't be late for dinner,' as he exited back into the hallway.

—

Ebony's first day at Surrey Cottage had gone so well that she looked forward to her next session there on the Wednesday, two days later. At least, the part where she'd be painting Sophia. Mrs Perryman had been pleasant to her, after the shaky start, but Ebony still felt a little uneasy in her presence.

The young women were having a brief rest now, looking out of the window at the late morning overcast sky and the wetness on the road from the light drizzle.

'Such a shame after the lovely sun we've had,' said Sophia. 'And there's meant to be a couple of performances from Mr Janus's players this afternoon on the common. I do enjoy them, and they seem to be put on less often these days.'

'He was having tea at the hotel the other day and told me that with most of the male entertainers conscripted, the performers left have to be shared out between the outdoor events and his other shows, like the ones at the Casino Theatre. He is a dear soul.'

'He is. I've worked with him on charity events where he's been kind enough to donate performances from his troupe, including at the hotel. Talking of which, my father mentioned that you organised events in Richmond, and might be looking for a similar project here?'

It wasn't exactly what she'd said to James, but maybe it was what she needed. It would be an opportunity to get to know a few new people, at least.

'I do like to be useful, especially now that Hazel and Marigold have gone off to do war work.'

'Then you must come to our meeting tomorrow, it's at the hall behind the Congregational Church.'

'I know just where you mean,' said Ebony. 'Yes, I will. It's funny to think that in recent years I've frequented church halls with groups of women to arrange charity events, when once upon a time I used to meet up with them to arrange marches and demonstrations as a suffragist.'

'You too?' Sophia seemed surprised. 'Oh yes, those were the days. And I'll be doing it again when the war's finished, if something isn't done about giving women the vote.'

'Me too,' Ebony said with gusto, swinging her arm in front of her.

The two women laughed heartily.

'Did you read in the paper about the royal family changing their surname to Windsor?' said Sophia.

'Major Thomas read it out at breakfast this morning. I can't say I blame them. Having a German surname probably doesn't make them very popular.'

'And Saxe-Coburg-Gotha is such a mouthful. By the way, you are invited to eat with us.'

'Why, thank you. That is most kind.'

Chapter Six

It was August bank holiday Monday, and the crowds were seated in deckchairs in front of a temporary stage between the hotel and the promenade. Hetty had an hour off between shifts and had wanted to experience some of the entertainment taking place. On stage was a twelve-piece women's string orchestra, playing a tune she didn't recognise. It was pleasant enough, but she wanted to take a walk and see what else there was.

Although a warm day, the clouds skittered occasionally across the sun, creating patches of shade as she headed towards the beach. The sound of violins and cellos faded as she reached the promenade. There were shouts of delight from a group of children, who she saw were playing catch on the sand. The edge of the beach, nearest the promenade, was filled with no end of striped fabric huts and various entertainers, making the most of the bank holiday crowds.

She stopped to watch a man in a clown costume with a guitar, whose signboard announced that he was Bertie Fisher. With him he had a talking cockatoo, and a dog called Toby who did tricks. Hetty found him entertaining, laughing at the antics of the group, the funny songs and jokes. Quite a crowd gathered around and were soon applauding Bertie's exploits. This was the kind of 'nonsense', as her mother would call it, that she needed to escape the frantic busyness at the hotel. At the end of their routine, the audience clapped enthusiastically, and were more than happy to give up a few pennies for the man's box, as was she.

Further along the promenade, she passed a Punch and Judy performance, a hurdy-gurdy man with a monkey, a magician and several refreshments stands. She was approaching the donkeys, watching as two children were enjoying a ride, when she came to a sudden standstill.

Victor Perryman was standing on the beach, watching the donkeys. His golden hair shone in the sunshine and he looked very smart in his cream linen suit. Next to him was a young woman with auburn hair, a little darker than Victor's. She was petite, in a mid-blue glossy dress with embroidered panels. Very fashionable it was, the sort of thing that young ladies visiting the hotel would have worn. On her head was a matching silk hat with a small brim and a buckle and bow at the front. She put her arm through Victor's, saying something to him in an animated way before placing her head on his shoulder.

Her heart sank. She hadn't seen Victor in over three weeks, and some small, irrational part of her had been hoping she would. Served her right for being so silly. Of course he had a sweetheart, maybe even a fiancée. He was an incredibly eligible bachelor, and with the war, there weren't many of those.

She did an about turn and headed back the way she'd come. She didn't want him spotting her. Not that it would have made any difference, as it was highly unlikely he'd have spoken to her under the circumstances. Noticing a woman selling ginger beer, she stopped to purchase a bottle.

Her mood had dipped now, and the walk in the fresh air didn't seem so inviting. She'd be glad to get back to the clatter of the stillroom. She had a letter there, in her apron, that had arrived from Lorcan the morning before. That would remind her where her loyalty lay.

–

What a day it had been, considered Hetty, as she polished yet another crystal champagne glass, ready for the evening's big do. She tried to forget that it was Sophia Perryman's thirtieth birthday party, and that Victor would almost certainly be there. And maybe also the young woman she saw him with on the beach. Thank goodness she'd be tucked away in the stillroom.

She took a short break from polishing. It had been a hectic day in the hotel generally, but she didn't mind that. She preferred being busy to standing around, and business would drop a little during autumn, before building up for Christmas again. She looked at the clock. Tilly and Milly should be back from their afternoon tea break soon, to help with the polishing.

She put the glass down and picked up another, just as Helen Bygrove entered the stillroom. Her brow was creased, and Hetty had known her long enough to gather that something was up.

'Oh Hetty, what a marvellous job you and the girls have been doing. But I'm afraid we've had a bit of bad news.'

Hetty feared the worst. Had yet another of their male staff been injured – or worse – in the war? 'What's happened?' she said, breathless.

'We thought Simon had gone home for his afternoon off, but we've just had word from his parents that he's left them a note saying he needs to do his bit in the war.'

'He enlisted? He's not old enough. And won't the authorities know that, since he hasn't been conscripted?'

'They might think it's an oversight. He wouldn't be the first underaged boy to be accepted.'

She knew Mrs Bygrove was right; they'd read of such cases in the newspapers, and even of some boys being killed. She shuddered. It didn't bear thinking about.

'Did he say where he was going?' Hetty asked.

'No, but my guess would be Shoreham-by-Sea, as that's the closest camp. His family are making various enquiries.'

'Oh dear, I hope they find him in time and bring him back.'

'So do I. But in the meantime, we will be a waiter down at the party later. I wonder if you would mind taking Simon's place serving this evening. Tilly has said she can do an extra shift here with her cousin. You've done very well when you've filled in for absent staff recently.'

Hetty's immediate reaction was to say yes, but before the word reached her lips, she remembered that Victor would be there. What difference did it make? She was a humble hotel worker, and that's what she'd always be, and he knew that. He probably wouldn't give her a second glance this evening.

Although all this flashed through her head in an instant, Helen said, 'You're hesitating. Do you not feel confident in the role?'

'Sorry, it was just the shock of the news about Simon. Yes, of course I will.'

How different Helen was to Mr Bygrove, who would have told her, in no uncertain terms, that she *was* replacing Simon, not asked her if she minded doing so. But then, that's why Helen had such a loyal staff.

'Thank you, Hetty. I'll get Lili to organise a uniform for you.'

Helen departed, the worry creases on her face smoothed out. Tilly and Milly came into the room a few seconds later.

'Good, you're back,' said Hetty. 'One of you can finish polishing the glasses, and the other can start on the cutlery. You choose. I'm off for a very quick tea break.'

'You look like you need it,' Milly quipped, as Hetty walked to the door. 'Have you heard about Simon?'

'Yes, I've heard.'

–

Hetty admired the gleaming glasses on the tray as she did the rounds with the champagne in the ballroom. She and Tilly had done a good job, even if she did think so herself. So far, she'd managed to avoid going anywhere near Victor Perryman, as Lili had been serving on his side of the room. Not far away, Dennis was also carrying a tray. Despite giving herself a good talking to, her heart was still thumping.

Ebony approached her and lifted a glass from the tray. 'Are you having an evening off from the stillroom again?' she asked, smiling.

'That's right, Miss Girard.'

'All hands on deck, as they say. It must be nice to have a change.'

'It is, madam.'

While she appreciated a guest taking the time to talk to her, she was also embarrassed, knowing she couldn't carry on a conversation, but feeling awkward about her brief replies.

'Oh look, the orchestra is about to strike up. I do usually prefer something a little more modern, but these ladies were rather splendid when I heard them at the bandstand a couple of weeks back.'

Ebony walked away as the twelve young and middle-aged ladies took their seats by the instruments.

There were about a hundred guests in a room that could have taken a lot more, and the lack of young men present stood out. The chatter dimmed only a little as the orchestra struck up with the 'Blue Danube Waltz'. Hetty recognised it as her parents had it on a gramophone record. A few older couples started dancing, and the rest of the guests moved to the edges of the room to continue their conversations.

Hetty carried on down one side of the elegant room, with its arched mirrors, pillars and crystal chandeliers. By the time she'd reached the door to the corridor, her tray was clear of glasses, so she slipped out to return to the staff area for more.

In the corridor, she was detained by Helen. 'When your next tray has been emptied, would you come back and help carry the buffet food to the lounge please, Hetty?'

'Of course, Mrs Bygrove.'

Back in the ballroom, a few more couples had taken to the floor, doing the polka. There were a few younger women dancing together, presumably because of the lack of young men. Sophia was dancing, but with an older man, the sort that looked like a jolly old uncle.

As Hetty started off on her rounds of the room, she spotted Victor a few feet away, looking at her. Many of the older men were sporting tailcoats, but he looked very handsome in his modern black dinner jacket and bow tie. He smiled briefly, but her attention was soon taken by a couple wanting to swap their empty champagne glasses for full ones. By the time they'd done that, Victor had his back to her, speaking with a man in uniform, a captain by the looks of the three stars on his epaulettes.

She gazed around at the guests. Never having had a hankering to be part of the upper classes, she did wish now that she could join the party, be one of the bright young women who were either dancing or chatting and laughing. She imagined herself taking to the floor with Victor for a few moments, before berating herself because of Lorcan. But, as she kept telling herself, she and Lorcan were not really a couple, not at the moment. And if he'd been that interested in her, wouldn't he have at least spent *one* leave in Littlehampton? Now Bygrove was gone, she wondered if he would indeed show up here. Probably not. Despite this pessimistic thought, she tried to imagine her and Lorcan dancing in here. Perhaps, if he did come home, they could sneak in here late one evening for a dance to an imaginary band. He could hum the tune, having a good singing voice.

She was enjoying this reverie, when a young, red-headed woman approached her. Hetty stopped herself from gasping, and instead smiled. It was the woman she'd seen Victor with on the beach, his sweetheart, fiancée, whatever she was.

'I'll have a glass of what I'm told is most excellent champagne,' said the woman, picking one up. 'Oh, and one for my husband,' she said, picking another.

Husband? Hetty was confused. Hadn't someone mentioned that Victor Perryman was single?

A young man in a lieutenant's uniform approached them. 'There you are my darling Maria.'

'And here's a glass of champagne for you, my darling Ben.'

He took it and they clinked glasses before turning away.

Was Victor… *carrying on* with this woman while her husband was at war? On the beach, in front of everyone? That being the case, it was as good a reason to put Victor Perryman out of her mind as any she could think of. Men! Was Lorcan perhaps not visiting her because he'd found love in France? After all, Lili's previous sweetheart, Norman, had done just that.

Forget it, she told herself, as the last glass was removed from her tray. She could now leave and help with the food.

—

'How are you, old chap?'

Victor swung around to find a childhood friend standing beside him, in uniform. 'Gerald! How are you? Been an age since I've seen you.'

'That's the trouble with this bally war. First time in a year that I've got any leave. You're looking hale and hearty.'

Victor examined Gerald's face. It looked careworn, but he'd managed a smile. He had a scar across his right eyebrow. 'How are things on the front?'

'Can't give away a great deal, but let's just say bally awful, shall we? It's jolly nice to have a party to come to while I'm on leave, I can tell you. Still making ships to fight the Huns with, I presume?'

'We are. My part at the moment is making the hulls for the flying boats.' Although it was war work, it made him feel inadequate next to Gerald's efforts.

'Good, good. They do a good job of keeping an eye on the coast and enemy movements.'

'Gerald Carruthers!' said Sophia, as she approached the pair of them. 'Or should I say, *Captain* Carruthers now!'

'Oh please, being called Gerald makes me feel normal for a change.'

'Then come and dance with me and feel even more normal!'

'How can I refuse?'

Sophia whisked him away, giving Victor a chance to look back at Hetty. But she had moved further around the room and was serving champagne to Maria and Ben. Shortly after, she left the room.

'Victor, stop standing around daydreaming,' said his mother, who'd come up behind him.

'I was just talking to Gerald, before Sophia took him to dance.'

'Good for him. You know, Gerald is a very eligible bachelor, even if he is a couple of years younger than her.'

'Mother, they're just friends.'

'What a shame. It's way past the time that she should have settled down. Soon nobody will want her as she'll be considered too old for childbearing.'

'Some women have children in their forties.'

'Anyway, we have far more young women here than men, and I think maybe you could oblige by dancing with a few. You may not be interested in any of them, but at least give them some fun. It *is* a birthday party.'

'Yes, Mother. Of course.' As he followed her, he pictured himself leading Hetty onto the dance floor. That was never likely to happen, so he'd better content himself with some 'fun', as his mother put it.

Before he'd managed to ask the first young lady to dance, his mother had whisked his father off to the dance floor.

—

Ebony had been relieved when she'd spotted someone she recognised from one of Sophia's charity meetings, standing on their own, listening to the orchestra. She was a young woman, about her own age, and they had got on well the two occasions they'd met.

What on earth was wrong with her? She normally thrived at parties, able to talk to anybody. But then, she'd always had Marigold and Hazel somewhere around. They'd been like backups in case she had no one to talk to, even though that had never happened. And maybe there was a little feeling of being an... intruder? After all, how long had she known the Perrymans?

She reached the woman as the orchestra stopped playing and the audience was clapping. 'Emma, how splendid to see you.'

'Ebony, what a surprise. I didn't know you'd be here.'

'I think the reason I'm here will be revealed shortly,' she whispered.

'That sounds intriguing.' Emma leaned towards her and giggled.

James Perryman stood in front of where the twelve women had left their instruments and coughed to get people's attention.

'Ladies and gentlemen. More musicians will be joining us later for your entertainment, and soon we will be repairing to the lounge room for our buffet. But before we do that... Sophia, join me please.'

As he was saying this, Bert, one of the young porters, carried in a medium-sized canvas covered with a sheet. Behind him, Wilfred, the other young porter, carried an easel.

Ebony knew what was coming, and, rather than being excited like she would normally be, she was as nervous as she had been at her first exhibition. Sophia hadn't seen the finished portrait yet, only James had, saying that he wanted it to be a surprise on the night. She just hoped Sophia, and her mother, considered it a *nice* surprise.

'Barbara and Victor, please join us too, as you haven't seen what is about to be unveiled either.'

When the painting and easel were put in place, and everyone was quiet, James lifted the sheet to reveal the completed portrait.

'Oh, it's lovely,' said Sophia, placing her hand on her chest.

The relief that ran through Ebony almost had her weak at the knees. She looked to Barbara and Victor, for their reaction, to see delight on their faces also.

'And now I must introduce you to the artist who made this surprise possible,' said James. 'Miss Ebony Girard!'

He beckoned her forward as people clapped heartily, and she went hesitantly towards the family. She really could have done without the fuss.

Sophia went to her and hugged her arm. 'Thank you, Ebony. I must admit I was nervous, never having seen any of your work. But, well, I'm *so* pleased.'

'Yes, well done,' said Victor, shaking her hand.

As the clapping died down, Edie Moore came into the room, and towards the family.

'Sir, madam, the food is ready when you are.'

James turned back to his guests. 'If you'd like to make your way to the lounge room, the buffet is ready.'

Still holding Ebony's arm, Sophia led her out of the room. 'Come, let's eat. I've been saving myself all day for this, and I'm starving.'

James looked around at the guests, helping themselves to food in what was normally a guest lounge, but had been turned into a dining room for the evening. So far, the party had gone very well.

Edie Moore came to a halt next to him. 'Is everything to your liking, Mr Perryman?'

'It's all magnificent, thank you, Miss Moore. I haven't found a thing so far to complain about, and probably never will.'

'I'm afraid the food isn't as varied as it once was.'

'That's not your fault. I'm amazed it looks as wonderful as it does. Compliments to your cooks and chefs. They do an exemplary job, given the circumstances.'

'Thank you, sir. I will pass that on to the kitchen staff.' She bowed her head briefly and made her way to the door.

Eventually, people finished eating and made their way back to the ballroom to find a new group of musicians had set themselves up. James wasn't sure what was coming next, as Barbara had said it was a surprise. It was an older male quintet, with a piano, drums, trombone, trumpet and clarinet.

'It's the Jack Peters Dance Band!' said Sophia, with great enthusiasm.

'Who?' said James.

'Oh Father, you're so old fashioned! They've appeared at a lot of parties and venues, and they tend to play ragtime.'

James felt suddenly out of date, an irrelevance from the past, with so many young women in attendance at Sophia's party. 'Ragtime? That's a type of music, isn't it?'

'Yes, of course. We have gramophone records by Scott Joplin and Gene Greene at home, you should recognise it. Victor and I went to a few parties where this band performed, before the war.'

The band leader introduced himself and announced that they'd be playing something called, 'Maple Leaf Rag'. The younger members of the audience cheered as well as clapped.

James vaguely recognised the tune and had to admit that it was catchy. Part way through, he noticed that Sophia had started dancing with Gerald Carruthers, and Maria was now on the dance floor with Ben. It was a lively dance, not unlike the galop or polka of his day, but less elegant, less – *proper*, with legs and arms thrown out at odd times. It looked particularly strange with Gerald being in uniform. Not long after, his son was doing the same dance with Ebony. Were they a likely pairing?

His attention was taken by a hand on his arm. 'Makes you wish you were younger, doesn't it?' It was Barbara beside him.

'I don't know. There are certain things about being young that I'm glad I don't have to put up with now,' he said, but he knew he'd been thinking the same thing.

'Maybe,' she laughed. 'But on balance, I think I'd rather be in my twenties again.'

For a while she looked thoughtful, and he wondered where this had come from. She always seemed so comfortable, so at home, with their current stage of life.

'Was it your idea to hire a ragtime band?'

'I asked Edie for something modern, as I knew Sophia would appreciate it, and she suggested them.' Barbara smiled. 'Come on, this is an opportunity to talk with the older contingent while the young enjoy the dancing. Oh and look, the waitresses are back with more trays of champagne. Wonderful!'

—

Most of the guests had departed, declaring what a 'splendid' evening it had been. Only James's immediate family was left in the ballroom, along with Ebony. She was standing by the painting with Sophia, who was clutching her hands and saying something enthusiastically that he couldn't hear.

'I suppose we'd better head home,' said Barbara, as Ebony and Sophia caught them up by the door.

'But what about the painting?' said Victor.

'You all go ahead and take the motorcar,' said James. 'I'll make sure the painting is stored somewhere safe until we can pick it up tomorrow. I'll walk back, as I could do with the fresh air.'

'Very well, if you're sure,' said Barbara.

'Goodnight to you all,' said Ebony.

'And a very good night to you, Miss Girard,' said Barbara. 'Your wonderful portrait was certainly a talking point this evening.'

'I'll see you next week, at the meeting,' said Sophia.

Ebony nodded and smiled. Barbara, Sophia and Victor left the room.

'I'll wish you a goodnight too, Mr Perryman.'

Something about Ebony in that moment, the way she smiled, gave him a feeling of being back in his youth again with Irene Belfiore. He caught hold of her arm gently. 'Wait a moment.'

'What is it?'

'I just want to say thank you again for the painting.'

70

'You've already thanked me several times, Mr Perryman, and paid me handsomely for it.'

'It's more than worth it. And I just wondered if, to show our gratitude, and as you don't seem to get out of the area much…'

She looked confused. 'And?'

'I wondered if I could take you on a trip somewhere, maybe out on the South Downs. As one last thank you.'

'I presume your wife would be coming too?'

'Of course. It would be nice to do something while it's still August, and we have good weather. September may not be as good.'

'I am helping with a couple of upcoming events with Sophia, as you know, but I won't be needed every day, so yes, why not? Saturdays and Mondays are the best days. I have my own car, of course, but I have missed having Hazel and Marigold around to go on trips with.'

'I will pick you up next Saturday then. I will be in town at the council offices for a meeting until around nine thirty, so perhaps I could meet you, and Barbara, on Fitzalan Road, by the library, at eleven o'clock? Just in case the meeting runs over.'

She went quiet for a while, and he thought she might change her mind.

'Very well. Eleven o'clock it is. I'll look forward to it. Farewell, for now, Mr Perryman.'

'Goodnight, Miss Girard.'

When she'd left and closed the door, he carried on looking at it, wishing she'd stayed a little longer to talk. She was an interesting young woman.

The door opened and Edie Moore stepped in.

'Still here, Mr Perryman? The staff will be in soon, to clear up.'

'I was just about to find someone to speak to about the painting.' He pointed towards the other side of the room. 'Could it be stored until tomorrow, when I'll bring the motorcar to pick it up?'

'Of course. I'll arrange that myself.'

Chapter Seven

Lili was still talking about Sophia Perryman's party four days later, and how she'd enjoyed watching the young people dancing to the ragtime music as they'd served the second round of champagne in the ballroom. As much as she'd enjoyed the music and dancing herself, Hetty was fed up with hearing of it. Apart from which, she wanted to forget about Victor.

'Is it possible to talk about something else, Miss Probert?' said Mrs Leggett, sitting at the end of the table in the staff dining room. 'I'm sure the band was as *wonderful* as you keep telling us it was, but we've heard it enough times now.'

The housekeeper could be rather sharp with her criticisms, but Hetty was glad of it on this occasion.

'Sorry, Mrs Leggett,' said Lili, not sounding as if she meant it. 'I thought it would make a change to the depressing reports in the newspapers.'

'A German airship was apparently destroyed over the North Sea yesterday. That's good news,' said Will Fletcher, holding up his copy of the *Daily Mirror*. 'And agricultural workers are set to get a minimum wage.'

'News of the end of the war would be better,' said Lili.

'I can't argue with that,' said Hetty.

Edie entered and stood in the doorway. 'Ladies and gentlemen, and Hetty in particular, we have a surprise for you.'

Hetty was feeling more anxious than intrigued at this news, wondering what on earth it could be about.

Edie stepped properly into the room, and behind her, came Lorcan Foley.

Several people gasped or called, 'Welcome back!' before Hetty stood and stepped over the bench seat. Having done that, she didn't know what to do next. Would it be considered improper to run to him and fling her arms around him? Did she even want to?

He looked over at her and beamed, so she trotted quickly to his side, putting her arm through his uniform-clad one. 'Lorcan, why didn't you write to say you were coming?'

'It was a last-minute decision, so it was, to give some of us leave while things were a little quieter.'

'You didn't go to Ireland this time.'

'No. With Bygrove no longer here, I thought it would be safe to turn up.'

He looked at her with a little concern, and she wondered if she hadn't shown enough enthusiasm.

She grinned widely at him, squeezing his arm. 'Well, I'm so glad you did.'

This put the smile back on his face and she was relieved.

'Where are you staying, lad?' said Will.

'Mrs Bygrove has kindly allowed me to stay here, as there are staff rooms spare.'

'That's great to hear,' said Hetty, making her grin even wider. But it was strange him being here after so long, strange to be so close to him like this. 'Come and sit down for a cup of tea. And there's even a biscuit left.'

'And you can have mine too,' said Annie, who'd been quiet up til now. She gave Lorcan a big smile, and Hetty was grateful to people for making him feel so welcome.

'I've missed the hotel's biscuits,' he said, heading to the table, holding Hetty's hand. 'The ones we get are like eating cardboard.'

'You tuck in, me boy,' said Mrs Norris, standing. 'Despite the shortages, I've got a couple more where they came from. You deserve an extra treat after what you've been through.' She stood and patted him on the shoulder, before heading off to the kitchen.

Edie came over to the table. 'Mrs Bygrove is aware that you had yesterday afternoon off, Hetty, but since Lorcan is only here for two days, she wonders if you'd like tomorrow afternoon off. Providing you can cover an evening shift on Sunday, for one of the stillroom maids.'

This Sunday evening she'd been due to visit her parents, join in evensong at the local church, and have supper with them. But this was more important.

'Yes, tomorrow off with Lorcan would be perfect, and that's very kind of Mrs Bygrove.'

'I'll rearrange it on the rota then,' said Mrs Leggett, who didn't seem at all put out, as she often would have been.

Lorcan was dipping his first biscuit in the tea Hetty had poured him, when Gertie came careering through the door.

Mrs Leggett stood abruptly. 'Whatever is going on, Miss Green!'

'It's Simon! His parents found him at Shoreham camp. They proved to the authorities that he's only seventeen. They've brought him to the hotel to apologise to Mrs Bygrove.'

'Thank the Lord!' said Mrs Norris, returning with a small plate of biscuits.

'What's all this then?' said Lorcan, his mouth half full.

Hetty told him the story.

Simon entered with Mrs Bygrove as she was finishing, looking down at his feet, his lips pushed to one side as if he were biting the inside of his mouth.

'Ah, is this the lad himself?' said Lorcan.

Simon looked up, narrowing his eyes.

'This is Lorcan Foley,' Helen explained. 'One of our porters who enlisted early in the war.'

'More fool me. If I'd known then what I know now, I'd have left it til I was conscripted, so I would. The front's no place for no living soul, let alone a boy, let me tell you. So don't you be so keen to be heading off to no war.'

'And that's told you,' said Mrs Norris, folding her hands over her stomach. 'Now young Simon, I presume there's time for you to have a cuppa tea and a biscuit before you start on dinner preparations in the dining room.'

'Yes, there is,' Helen confirmed.

Simon sat at the table, his hangdog expression back in place.

'Ah, don't look so downhearted,' said Lorcan. 'Come on, tell us ya tale.'

Simon brightened a little and they all leaned in as he told them his story. Hetty sat close to Lorcan, half listening, but also wondering what she and Lorcan might do tomorrow.

–

Hetty had suggested a trip to Arundel, as she'd fancied getting out of Littlehampton for a while. Lorcan, however, had been looking forward to his stay by the seaside, and had been content to stay in the town.

They were walking on the promenade now, side by side, the weather sunny and warm. The area wasn't as busy as it had been a couple of weeks before, but it was still noisy with the constant chatter. There were several fabric-covered bathing huts on the sand, with only a few brave souls, mainly women and children, in the water. A couple of long rowing boats were at the edge of the sea on an almost high tide, being pushed out by two men and a few boys.

'D'ya fancy a hokey pokey?' he said, pointing to the ice cream hut nearby.

'I haven't heard it called that for a few years.'

'Especially not in the hotel,' he chuckled. 'Are you still making the ice cream in the stillroom?'

'Of course. And yes, I'd love a *hokey pokey*.' She laughed.

He bought them an ice cream each, and they sat on one of the bench seats to eat it. Its creamy coolness was welcome.

'What have you been doing on the front lately?' she asked. 'You haven't said anything about it so far.'

His smile disappeared and a frown replaced it. 'Sitting in mud, waiting, mostly. Cold, sticky mud. Wonderin' who'll be next to get trench foot, and whether it'll be me.'

'Even in the summer?'

'Well, not so much in the summer, admittedly. But it's still muddy and wet. And boring. I've never been so bored in all my life, so I haven't. And when there is some action, it's terrifying. And when someone nearby is shot...'

He was looking ahead, towards the sea, but Hetty had a feeling he wasn't seeing it, but rather was picturing the trenches.

'I'm— I'm so sorry, Lorcan. You're always quite cheerful in your letters. I hadn't realised it was quite so awful for you.'

'I didn't want to worry you... And to be honest, Hetty, I'd rather forget it for a while, so I would, and enjoy this lovely day by the seaside. Who knows if I'll see it again after I go back.'

'Don't say that, Lorcan.' A sadness enveloped her, to think that he felt like that. Then she wondered whether he meant he wouldn't see it because he'd be going back to Ireland for good after the war.

'Not that I can completely forget it with the sound of the guns here now. Is it always like this?'

'Yes. Often it's louder.'

'Saints preserve us. Is there no escaping the damned war? Talking of noise, I was woken in the night by Fanny's wean. Elsie isn't it?'

'That's right.'

'Why's Fanny in the men's area now?' he asked.

'It's only temporary, while the men are away, to give Gertie some peace from Elsie's fussing at night, since she was sharing with Fanny.'

'You didn't tell me much in the letter about it all, only that none of you knew she was expecting until she'd had the baby. Has she ever mentioned who the father is?'

'Not a word. All we gather is that he enlisted when he found out she was pregnant.'

'Rotten little eejit. He wants to hope none of us find out who he is when we return from the war.'

'I'm not sure that beating him up will help matters, if that's what you're implying.'

'No, maybe not. Fighting hasn't got anyone anywhere the last few years… There's been an awful lot of change since I left. I wonder how the women who've taken on the men's jobs will feel when the men return and they have to go back to their places.'

'Their places? Meaning what, exactly?' She was surprised to hear this from Lorcan, who'd never struck her as a particularly chauvinistic man.

'You know what I mean, Hetty. I'm not saying it's right that the jobs are divided up the way they are, but what else can the men do? They'll need their jobs back, so.'

'Apart from Alex, James and Anton,' Hetty said sadly.

His frown returned. 'I still can't believe it. And who knows, maybe none of us will come back, and the women will be able to keep the jobs.'

'Oh Lorcan, *don't*. I thought you wanted to escape talking about the war. When we've finished our ice creams, let's carry on walking.'

'Aye, you're right.'

When they started off towards the pier again, he took her hand. The smile was back, but she wondered how much of a mask it was. He'd been jolly last night and this morning with the staff in their breaks, but had that all been an act too?

Being here with him, she felt a kind of contentment, but was that enough? They needed time for their feelings to grow properly, and that chance wouldn't happen until he came back for good.

'After the war, you will be coming back to the hotel, won't you?'

'Of course. Mrs Bygrove's already told me my job will be waiting for me. Where else would I go?'

'Back home, to Ireland?'

'I know I've spent my leaves there, but it doesn't feel like home anymore. And all the troubles...' He shook his head. 'Besides, I want to be where you are. If only I could persuade my family to come here, but they're not keen, like.'

'Come on, I'll treat you to afternoon tea at the Harbour Tea Rooms, try and cheer you up.'

'No you won't,' he said, bucking up. 'I'll treat *you*.'

'We'll go halves, how does that sound?'

'We'll see when we get there,' he said, half frowning and half grinning, as their pace became a little quicker.

He wanted to be where she was. That was encouraging. Perhaps everything would be all right between them when he came home after all.

–

'Well, Hetty, I'll see you when I see you,' Lorcan said, standing with her in the yard outside the scullery two mornings later. 'I suppose if I have another leave before the end of the war, that I might feel obliged to visit my family. It'll depend on what's going on with them, so it will.'

Hetty saw Annie looking out of the window, who seemed to be scowling at the pair of them. Goodness knows why. Lorcan turned to see what she was looking at, and Annie's frown turned to a smile and a wave. How curious.

'I can understand why you'd want to make sure your family's all right,' Hetty said finally. 'It would be the right thing to do, so don't worry about me. And it's not like we're betrothed or anything.'

'I suppose it's still hardly more than a friendship at the moment,' he conceded with a sigh. 'But when I come back...'

'We can start again,' she said. 'If we both want to. Then see how it goes if we do.'

He nodded. 'That would be grand. And keep those letters coming. I know I can't always reply straight away, but I do look forward to them, so I do.'

'I wish I could walk with you to the railway station, but I can't swap another shift, especially as I'm involved in the children's tea party this afternoon.'

'What's it for again?'

'To raise money for the Arun Children's Aid Project.'

'That's good. And it's fine, you not walking to the station with me. Better to say our goodbyes here, alone.'

'Except for Annie peering out at us.'

'Let her.' He leant down and planted a peck on her lips, as he had done the day he'd left for the training camp. There was that slight tingle, but nothing earth shattering. Perhaps she was expecting too much. Even standing near Victor Perryman, she'd felt more... excitement. But that was a fantasy, and she needed to build something real.

They hugged, then he picked up his rucksack and walked away, looking at her one more time before he went through the gate. Hetty looked at the empty space where he'd been for a few seconds, before going back through the scullery.

'So, he's gone then,' Annie said.

She felt annoyed at Annie for spying on them when they should have been allowed some privacy, so her, 'Obviously,' was a little curter than it should have been.

'You're lucky to have such a nice man as a sweetheart.'

Hetty's irritation with her faded. 'I'm not sure "sweetheart" is quite the right word. Not yet, anyway.'

It was hard for young women to find sweethearts now and had been for three years. She couldn't blame Annie for feeling frustrated.

'The war can't last much longer. Then the men will be back, and you'll find a sweetheart, you wait and see.'

Annie hmphed, then continued with the washing up. Hetty left her to it.

Hetty's patience had worn thin by the end of her morning break. Everyone was tiptoeing around her, trying to be sympathetic about Lorcan's departure, and she'd had enough of being treated like a poor little wilting flower. She said as much to Lili as they left the staff dining room.

'They're only trying to be kind, Hetty. But I do remember feeling the same when Norman disappeared. Treated like a child I was.' They stopped in the corridor.

'Exactly. But Lorcan hasn't disappeared. And, talking of children, I'd better go and start making that ice cream we're serving at the children's party this afternoon.'

'I'm looking forward to it. They're always such happy little souls, with their giggles and smiles. And I love the idea of us being dressed as characters from *Alice's Adventures in Wonderland*. I'm sure the kiddies will love it.'

'I think *I* will too,' said Hetty, grinning.

They went their separate ways. It was busy in the stillroom for the rest of the morning, and early afternoon, with there being so much to prepare for. Hetty was glad to get out of the staff area after the lunch period to prepare for the party, leaving Tilly and Milly to make the beverages for the normal afternoon tea in the conservatory.

Lili was coming out of her bedroom, already dressed in her blue Alice costume when Hetty reached upstairs.

'Mrs Leggett and Mrs Turnbull have done a wonderful job of the costumes,' said Lili.

Hetty smiled. 'My Queen of Hearts outfit is very like the illustration in the book. I've even got a triangular headdress that Mrs Turnbull managed to fix onto a hairband!'

'They 'ave been inventive. I'll see you downstairs.'

Dressed and in the ballroom now, ready to set up the tables, Hetty was delighted to see Dennis in his King of Hearts costume. He was playing up to the part as they prepared the room, quoting lines from the book.

'Have you been practising?' asked Lili.

'Had a read of me little sister's book. Thought I'd get into character.'

'I 'ope Hetty isn't going to say "Off with your head," to me, as the Queen of Hearts!'

'Depends how naughty you are,' she joked.

Edie came through the door at that moment, with a yellow waistcoat and red jacket over her skirt, and a check scarf around her neck. In her hand she held a pocket watch that she tucked into her waistcoat pocket.

'Oh my, you do look the part of the White Rabbit,' said Lili.

Then Gertie entered, with a long green jacket, a huge spotted bow tie around her neck and a top hat with a piece of paper sticking out announcing, 'In this style, 10/6'.

'That's got to be the best one yet,' said Edie.

'I'm looking forward to doing something a bit different,' said Gertie. 'The top hat belonged to Mrs Bygrove's father, but she said it was time it was put to some use.'

'What with this and the games, everyone should have a lovely time,' said Edie.

She looked at her pocket watch. 'It's just coming up to three o'clock, so we'll open the doors in a moment.'

Hetty looked around the room. At one end, the tables were in two lines, all laid up with cloths, crockery, cutlery and flowers. There was another table by the wall with cups and saucers, ready for the teapots for the adults. The doors to the outside were open onto a lovely sunny day. At the end of the room, where they were standing, stood a table with the items for the games, plus an easel that Ebony had leant them with a picture of several items she'd drawn for Kim's Game.

When Edie opened the doors, there was already a queue of adults and children waiting in the foyer. Edie invited them in. The children, thirty of them, sat cross-legged on the parquet flooring, some of them pointing out the staff's costumes with glee. The adults took the seats placed around the walls, a few of them clearly nannies.

Hetty smiled, her spirits rising: the presence of children always made her happy. She wondered what it would be like to settle down and have her own, either with Lorcan or... someone else.

As she was considering this, a young red-headed woman with two children entered. It was Maria, as she'd discovered she was called, the one she'd seen with Victor on the beach on August bank holiday and at the party with her husband. They had children too?

It was none of her concern. They were guests, nothing more.

'It's rather lovely to be in this beautiful ballroom again,' she said to the woman she'd walked in with. 'I was here for Sophia's party, only a week ago you know.'

'Such a splendid place,' said her friend. 'I often come for dinner.'

Hetty didn't recognise the friend, but then she'd never served dinner.

'Oh, and look,' said Maria. 'The staff are dressed as characters from *Alice's Adventures in Wonderland*. How splendid!'

Edie settled everyone down, explained the order of events for the afternoon, and then invited the children to play the first game, Pass the Slipper.

They'd played Pin the Tail on the Donkey and a couple of other games when the door opened and a man entered, the only one so far.

It was Victor.

Spotting Maria, he went over and joined her where she stood watching her son and daughter. She took his arm and they kissed on each cheek. They spoke animatedly to each other, as excited as the children. At one point he tapped her nose playfully.

Really? Here, where everyone could see them? Just like on the beach. What on earth were they thinking? He went down a little further in her estimation.

Hetty was starting to get nervous. She knew that soon she'd be in the limelight. She'd already had the collywobbles, but now

Victor was here, whatever her opinion of him, she didn't want to be the centre of attention.

'Right children,' said Edie, once the game was over. 'Miss Affleck here is going to play Kim's Game with you, while the rest of us bring your tea in.'

Some of the children cheered, encouraging the others to do likewise.

Hetty stepped forward. 'If you'd all like to come and collect a piece of paper and a pencil each, we'll begin.'

–

Hetty was leaning over, serving lime cordial to some of the children, when Victor approached her. He waited until she'd finished before speaking.

'Hello, Hetty, or I suppose I should say Henrietta here. I have to say, you and the others have put on a jolly good party for the children. I just love your costumes. You're all jolly good sports for getting dressed up.'

'It's nice to give them something to smile about, especially as some of their daddies will be away in the war, no doubt.'

'I know Lionel and Sylvia's is, poor little mites.' He looked towards the other end of the table, where Maria's two children were sitting. 'You might have spotted him at Sophia's party last week, with my cousin. He just happened to have leave that week.'

'Your cousin?'

'Yes, sorry, I'm not explaining it very well. The lady over there with the auburn hair, Lionel and Sylvia's mother, is my cousin. And I'm her children's godfather. With their father away, I try to spend a bit of my spare time with them, take them on little trips out. It just so happened I had an afternoon off.'

'I see.'

What an idiot she'd been! Of course there was some perfectly simple explanation, but she'd had to jump to the worst of conclusions.

'That's good of you, to keep an eye on them.'

'It's the least I could do. Maria was like a second sister to me, growing up. We've always been close.'

He had suddenly gone from a cad back to a thoroughly decent man in her estimation. He'd regained the appeal he'd had when she'd first spoken to him. In a way, she wished she hadn't found out that it was all innocent. She could cope better with thinking he was a rotter.

'I'd, um, better go and see how Maria and the children are doing.'

'Of course.'

With the children occupied eating the savoury course now, the staff hung around until they were needed. Edie stood next to Hetty.

'I didn't get to tell you earlier. I had a letter from Charlie.'

'Is he coming home on leave?'

'No, sadly, but he has been made a lance corporal. I'm very proud of him.'

'And so you should be. Tell him congratulations from me when you write back.'

'I will. That carrot cake that Mrs Norris baked for the children looked jolly moist and tasty, despite the war flour. I hope there's some left over from the party that we can celebrate with later.'

Hetty chuckled. 'Unlikely, the way this lot are going at the food. I doubt she made more than was needed, like she used to.'

–

Hetty had been right: the carrot cake was all gone by the time the children finished eating. Lili and Dennis cleared away while she, Gertie and Edie took the children back to the other end of the ballroom for another couple of games. Despite her best efforts to ignore him, Hetty was aware the whole time of where Victor was standing.

The final game of the day was a treasure hunt, taking place in the garden as well as the ballroom. Dennis and Lili were back to help by this time, guiding the children and dropping hints as they scouted the area for clues, to make sure that they were all successful.

At the end, Edie gathered the children in the ballroom once more.

'It's been lovely having you all for tea, and I hope you enjoyed it.'

The children all cheered, some dancing or jumping around with enthusiasm.

Edie addressed the adults next. 'I'm sure the children who benefit from the Arun Children's Aid Project will appreciate the money raised too. Cheerio, children, and hopefully we'll see you at another tea again one day.'

As people started to leave, Hetty said to Edie, 'A couple of years ago we had a tea for some of the less privileged children from town. I wonder if we'll ever do one of those again.'

'I believe Helen is planning something along those lines.'

'Good.' She was about to say more, when she noticed Victor approaching. She had hoped he'd leave without saying goodbye. Edie went to talk to one of the mothers who'd caught her eye.

Hetty expected a thank you from Victor, but instead he said, 'Have you a day off soon?'

'Monday, so only a couple of days away,' she said, thinking it was a comment on how hard they'd worked.

'Would you allow me to treat you to afternoon tea somewhere, as a thank you for helping make the party so special for my godchildren. They really did enjoy it tremendously.'

This was so out of the blue that she was stuck for words for a couple of seconds. 'It wasn't only me doing it. And besides, you're a guest, so I'm not allowed to.'

'Only a day guest, not a resident. Please?'

She thought about how she should go and see her parents, but remembered they were away in Brighton, visiting an aunt. And what about Lorcan? But Victor was only being friendly; that's all it could be in their positions.

'I'm sorry, I've put you on the spot,' he said.

'Th–that's all right. And yes, I will allow you to treat me to afternoon tea. Thank you.'

His smile lit up his face and his brown eyes widened. 'Shall I meet you somewhere, at say, two o'clock?'

'By the windmill,' she said, picking somewhere away from the hotel, and already wondering if she'd made the right decision.

'The windmill it is. I'll look forward to it.' He bowed slightly and took his leave.

Edie came back over, grinning. 'What was all that about then?'

'He was saying thank you for us making it a wonderful party for his godchildren.'

'Our efforts do seem to have been appreciated. Come on, let's get out of these costumes and get a cup of tea.'

'Ooh, yes please.' Hetty looked forward to that, and, despite her misgivings, now had a reason to look forward to her day off.

Chapter Eight

'What an absolutely splendid day for a jaunt,' said Ebony, as James's car negotiated a long tree-lined bend on the road going downhill. 'I haven't been out on the South Downs for a while now.' She leant her arm on the door of the Ford Model T Tourer.

'Yes, couldn't have picked a better day if I'd tried.'

'It's a shame that Mrs Perryman couldn't make it.'

He nodded and half smiled, making her wonder whether they'd had some kind of argument. Not over this trip out, she hoped.

As they came out of the bend, she saw the wide spread of countryside ahead, the gentle slopes and vibrant green grass contrasting with the brilliant blue sky. The air was warm against her skin. In the distance she could see the exposed chalk of one of the hills.

Ebony sighed with contentment. She was so glad she'd agreed to come. They continued to go downhill, passing a sign saying Houghton, before dipping back into the shade of the trees once more.

'Was it Amberley you said we were heading for, Mr Perryman?'

'That's right. And please, you must call me James.'

She wasn't sure about the familiarity, but it did seem a little daft to remain on such formal terms. 'Then I'm Ebony.'

'Have you been there before Ebony?'

'A very long time ago, with my mother.'

'I thought we'd have lunch at the Houghton Bridge Hotel, then have a look around Amberley village. It is rather pretty. If that's all right.'

'I'm happy to be out as long as possible, on a day like this.'

They finally came to the beginning of a village, crossing a low, long-walled bridge over the River Arun. They turned right and immediately left, stopping in front of the Houghton Bridge Hotel.

'People are eating outside on the lawn. How lovely,' said Ebony.

'I telephoned this morning and booked a table.'

'How organised.'

Having ordered their meals, they sat at a table for two, underneath a small canopy, each holding a glass of white wine. There were a few larger tables with families, and two others with what she assumed were couples.

'You said your wife is involved with some charity event today?'

'She's helping Sophia distribute the leaflets about a white elephant sale, to raise money for a local War Supply Sub-Depot, which is making medical supplies.'

'I'm not involved in that one. I'm helping with the garden fete next week, to raise money for a tobacco fund for the soldiers. Does Victor help too, on his days off?'

'Good heavens, no. We leave that to the women.'

Ebony, about to raise the glass to her lips, raised her eyebrows instead. 'Is that so?'

His widening eyes told her that he clearly realised he'd made some kind of faux pas. 'It's very important, the charity work, but we chaps don't really have a clue what we're doing. And we're not free to help, most of the time. Besides, Victor is attending a children's tea party with his godchildren, Sylvia and Lionel, and their mother, Maria, who's Barbara's niece. He likes to keep an eye on them since her husband, Ben, joined the war. You might have seen Maria and Ben at Sophia's party.'

'Yes, I was introduced to them briefly. Is that the tea party that they're holding at the hotel?'

'That's the one. I hope this isn't too staid for you, going for a drive and having lunch in the country.'

'Why would you say that?'

'Being a Bohemian and all that.'

She put her head back and laughed, eliciting looks from some of the other diners. 'I am very definitely not a "*Bohemian*", James, as you put it. Avant-garde, yes. To be a Bohemian, I would have to deny all worldly goods for the sake of my art and sacrifice myself to poverty. And believe me, there is no way I am doing that. I don't believe my art is only worth something if I do it for nothing.'

'Is that what Bohemians believe?'

'Indeed. Hazel, Marigold and I visited a few in Paris once, artists, writers, poets, thinking how romantic it would be, and wondering whether it was maybe a way of life for us. I can tell you, there is nothing romantic about it, and we soon changed our minds. Many of them live in total destitution and have even died from lack of food.'

'I never realised that.'

'I'm just somebody who likes to be a little different.' She ran her hand down her loose summer coat with its green and teal swirls.

Their food arrived and their conversation turned towards her favourite artists.

–

After lunch, they drove into Amberley village, parking the car to take a walk. It had been a while since James had come here. Passing old flint houses and thatched stone cottages, they headed towards the castle.

'This is thoroughly charming,' Ebony said, as the lane narrowed.

'Would you like to live somewhere like this?'

'It seems very peaceful after living in Richmond and visiting London for business so often, but no. It's pleasant to visit, but I'm sure I'd be utterly bored within a week.'

'So would I.' He chuckled, but at the same time felt guilty that he was enjoying this trip out so much, especially as his wife had been unable to come. Anyone looking on, who knew him, might surmise that he was carrying on with Ebony. What made it worse was that Barbara had assumed he was going to cancel the trip, but he'd explained that he didn't want to disappoint Miss Girard. Barbara had been rather annoyed.

'Look, there's the castle.' Ebony walked a little faster. Taking the path around it, she said, 'It is rather run down and over-grown, but it makes it all the more charming.'

After some moments staring at it, James said, 'Shall we walk back? We can take a trip further into the downs, through Bury, then do a loop around Pulborough, before we head back to Littlehampton.'

'Very well. I'd like to see a bit more of the Downs.'

And then he'd be satisfied that he'd thanked her enough for the painting. It would be too easy to get drawn in by such an attractive young woman, so after this trip out, his gratitude to her for producing such an accomplished portrait, in so little time, would have been fully expressed.

–

Hetty had changed her blouse twice before heading out on her afternoon off with Victor on the Monday, looking at herself this way and that in the mirror. She'd opted in the end for her new crepe de chine blouse with its square neck and large, square collar, with tiny buttons down the front. She'd saved up for a few weeks to be able to afford it, and she wanted to look her best for such a distinguished gentleman.

How excited her mother would have been to hear that Hetty was to have afternoon tea with the son of a local shipbuilder.

She turned away from the mirror to put her jacket on. Not that her mother would ever hear about it, Hetty would make sure of that, for she'd be sure to tell her friends and make it look something it wasn't. She picked up her handbag and left the room, marching purposefully towards the staff entrance.

On her way to the windmill, a thought struck her. What if he'd thought better of meeting her and decided not to turn up? She felt a good deal of disappointment at the thought, but decided that if he didn't turn up, she'd go and have tea somewhere by herself. She was her own woman, and she could do what she liked.

When she turned right at the pier, to walk past the old gun battery mound, she was relieved to see that her concern had been unfounded. She looked at her wristwatch: it was only five to two, so he was early. As she got closer, she saw him look towards the oyster pond and check his watch. He stayed looking in that direction until she caught him up.

'Good afternoon, Victor.'

He turned abruptly, starting a little. 'Oh, good afternoon, Hetty.'

'Sorry to make you jump.' She couldn't help but laugh a little, regretting it immediately. But then he laughed too.

'I assumed you'd come along South Terrace.'

'I like an opportunity to walk on the prom.'

'I was wondering whether we should go to Read's Dining Rooms for tea. I've heard it's quite good.'

Read's was somewhere her mother often went, as did other people she knew. Not wanting to risk being spotted there, she came up quickly with an alternative.

'Or we could walk just down the road here and go to the Harbour Tea Rooms. I've been a few times with my friend Phoebe, and it's rather nice.' And she'd never seen anybody she knew in there who might report her to the hotel or tell her mother.

'I've often passed it, but assumed it was an eating establishment for the fishermen.'

'Goodness, no. You never see any fishermen in there. It's quite sophisticated and has nice food. The war notwithstanding.'

He didn't look convinced, but said, 'All right then, if you recommend it.'

As soon as they stepped into the tea room, he said, 'Oh. Yes, it is rather attractive in here.'

They were greeted by Giovanni Crolla, who added, 'Ees nice to see you again, *signorina*. You are lucky we have one free table.' He showed them to one in the middle of the room.

'Thank you, Mr Crolla.'

After they ordered, Victor said, 'This is a bit of a surprise,' indicating the room.

'I did tell you. And it has a nice view of the river. Lili reckons it's better here than at Read's.'

'Lili?'

'Liliwen, the waitress at the hotel.'

'Ah, the Welsh waitress.'

'I assume you have the day off too, or can you just take any time off you like, being the owner's son?' That hadn't come out the way she'd meant it, but he didn't seem offended.

'No, I only have a certain amount of free time, like anyone else. My father is quite strict about that, even with himself. *Especially* with himself. If he has afternoon tea with my mother at the hotel, he always works later in his office.'

'I suppose there's a lot more work for a shipbuilding company, what with the war.'

'There certainly is, but Father was always like that. I think sometimes that my poor mother... well, never mind, you don't want to hear that. You said your father is a headmaster. That probably has its advantages and disadvantages.'

'You could say that. He made sure I was quite well educated, but my mother said there wasn't any point in trying to get qualifications, or a good job, as I'd have to give it up when I got married.'

She recalled the numerous arguments they'd had about it when she was younger.

'Would you have liked to have done something else then?' He sat forward, seemingly genuinely interested.

'Oh yes. I did think about going to college and training as a teacher. I think my father would have been happy with that, being a headmaster. But he was overruled.'

'I'm sorry to hear that, Hetty. It is about time women were able to get on in life, do what they want, the same as men.'

'Not all men can do what they want, especially the poorer ones.'

'But they do have more options than women.'

'Yes, they do.' She couldn't quite believe that someone of his class was as enlightened as this. 'What about your sister, Sophia? I know she does tremendous work with the various charities, but did she ever want to do anything else?'

'You might be surprised to hear that she went to Oxford University.'

'Really? So women are allowed to go there?'

'A few. She got a first-class degree, that's the top pass, except she didn't, because women's degrees aren't recognised. Not at Oxford or Cambridge anyway. Other universities do now allow it.'

'What?' She was leaning forward now. 'Why not Oxford and Cambridge then?'

He shrugged. 'It's outdated and an abomination, if you ask me. I think Sophia would have liked to have been a university tutor at Oxford eventually, but there weren't the same opportunities as for men. While she was there, she met a lot of suffragettes, and when she came home, she made women's suffrage her mission. She joined the local branch of the National Union of Women's Suffrage Societies and was soon very active in it.'

'I remember the march they had in Littlehampton, about a year before the war. I so wanted to join them but didn't have any time off.'

'That's right, the Pilgrim's March, as they called it, led by Lady Maud Parry, the leader of the Littlehampton branch. Sophia was on that.'

It made her own life feel very dull, and unproductive. 'It sounds very romantic, to have something to fight for.'

'But hard work, too. And of course, many of those women are doing war work of some sort now.'

The tea arrived, shortly followed by the smaller than usual scones and a piece of the fruit cake each, one of only two choices.

'I wonder how long until there are no scones or cakes on offer,' said Victor. 'You still seem to have a little more choice than this at the hotel.'

'For now. But Mrs Norris, the head cook, is forever bemoaning the decreasing supply of ingredients. She is very good at being what she calls "resourceful". And growing more of our own vegetables, and so on, has helped.'

The conversation halted for a while, as they started to butter their scones, but, having heard about Sophia's education, she wondered about his.

'Did you go to university, Victor?'

'Yes, yes I did. I went to Oxford too.'

She should have guessed that. 'What did you do there?'

'Engineering Science.'

'That must be useful for what you do in your business.'

'Hmm. To be honest, I feel my skills are rather underused in the business, as my father employs other engineers too. I know there was an understanding that I would eventually take over the business, but I would like to have gone to work for other firms for a while, to build up my experience. But as soon as I graduated, my father expected me to come and work for him.'

'I suppose it's, in a way, a bit like me not being able to train as a teacher. Sort of.'

'No, it's very like it, because both our situations are about a parent making a decision that will affect our future lives.'

'In that way, yes.'

'And I do wonder whether I should have enlisted and used my engineering skills in the army. Or the navy. But my father said I would be doing a better job for the war in the company. Then, when conscription came in, he applied straight away for my exemption, which was granted without any fuss.'

'Well, he's not wrong. What you do is a huge help towards the war effort. Do you ever get any...' Now she'd started, she wasn't sure how to word it. 'Um, trouble, about being a young man who's not in uniform? I remember some of the men at the hotel, those who hadn't enlisted before conscription, getting a lot of grief from those white feather women who used to gang up on men in the town.'

'Oh yes, I remember them. I did get a bit of harassment, so I'd always have to show them this.' He took hold of the lapel on his jacket and pulled it forward to show her. He looked down. 'Oh, I haven't put it back on.'

He reached in his pocket and pulled out a blue-and-gold badge, pinning it on to his lapel.

'Ah, an "On War Service" badge.'

'That's right. The admiralty gave them to all of those at the shipyards, as we're working on vital components for the Royal Navy.'

'So, in a way, you are working for the navy.'

'I suppose.' He shrugged. They ate their scones and cakes, commenting every now and again on the view, or about someone passing by.

'Do you have any family on the front?' Victor asked when he'd finished his cake.

'My brothers, Hector and Gilbert, my sister's husband and a couple of cousins. What about you?'

'A few cousins. And quite a lot of friends,' he said, sighing heavily. 'A few who've been lost.'

'Most of the younger men from the hotel are in the war too, as you've probably noticed on your visits. Three of those who enlisted early on were killed at the Battle of the Boar's Head, last summer.'

'I heard about that. How terrible for you all. Do you have a sweetheart in the war?'

She didn't answer for a couple of seconds, not quite knowing how to describe her relationship with Lorcan. 'Not exactly. That is, we'd just started walking out when he enlisted, right at the beginning of the war. We didn't get to know each other well enough before he left, so I'm not sure what will happen when he returns.'

'Do you write to him?' He seemed very solemn as he asked this.

'Yes, I write to him, but he's only been back here once, as he's taken leave in Ireland with his family the other couple of times. When he came back here, very recently, we agreed to see how we felt when he returned. Do you have a sweetheart?'

'Me? No, despite my mother's *best* efforts to get me married off.'

They both laughed.

'My mother's the same. She seems to think that at twenty-five I'm in danger of being an old maid. I told her once that if she'd let me train as a teacher, I might have met a fellow teacher and settled down. She was not amused.'

'I can imagine. My mother thinks that twenty-seven is a reasonable age for a man to settle down. She also keeps on about it being the perfect opportunity to find someone now that there's a shortage of men in the country, which I do rather feel is in poor taste.' He pushed his fingers sideways through his neat auburn hair.

'Oh dear, yes.'

'When we've finished our tea, would you like a trip on the ferry over to West Beach? Despite the workshop being not far from the bridge, I haven't walked over there for a while.'

She didn't hesitate in her reply. 'Neither have I, and I do like it over there, so yes, that would be nice.'

'I'll get the bill then.'

As Victor lifted his hand to attract the waitress's attention, Hetty went briefly over their conversation in her head. What a lot they had in common, despite their class difference. She wondered what would be revealed on the next part of their afternoon.

Hetty had an evening off on Friday, and, with her parents still away, she decided to take a walk to the promenade to enjoy the still warm weather and late sun of the day.

The nearest benches were occupied, so she sat on the wall bordering the beach, her feet dangling. There were still a fair amount people on the sand, sitting with a picnic or like herself, enjoying the evening. The tide was out, so a few children were digging the wet sand.

She thought back to Monday, to her afternoon with Victor. After their visit to the tea room, the walk to the beach on the other side of the river had been very pleasant, chatting about this and that. She'd been surprised how relaxed she'd felt with him, after her initial nerves. He'd offered to walk her back to the hotel afterwards, but she'd wanted a quick trip into town, and wasn't sure how she'd explain his presence to the other staff, so he'd gone back to the workshop on Fisherman's Quay. Before he'd left, he'd asked whether they could meet again, two weeks hence. She smiled as she recalled her effort not to sound too excited as she agreed to the meeting.

'Hello there Henrietta, mind if I join you?'

Hetty looked up and was surprised to see Ebony Girard standing there, in a loose, green cotton dress, sleeveless and barely below her knees. On her feet were a pair of open sandals, the sort children normally wore, and she had no stockings on. She was hatless, without even a hairband or a clip. Fashion had become more daring recently, but Ebony's outfit went one step further.

'N–no, of course not.'

'Don't worry about all that staff shouldn't mix with guests lark,' she said as she sat down. 'It's a lovely evening, isn't it? Or would be if we couldn't hear the guns going off in France.'

'It's quite loud this evening.'

'I hope that's to do with the weather, rather than anything – more. They can even be heard on the Downs sometimes.'

'We can hear it here most of the time now,' said Hetty, 'especially in the evening when there are fewer people around.'

'I've noticed that. It is a constant reminder of what's going on. Maybe that is as it should be; it can be easy to forget sometimes, when things here don't seem much different. Apart from the lack of men, of course. Do you have a sweetheart in the war, Henrietta?'

That question again. She wanted to keep it brief this time. 'I'm writing to someone on the front, but we're just friends. If it's not cheeky to ask, do you have a sweetheart in the war?'

'Of course it's not cheeky to ask. I asked you. And no, I don't. I have, well, I suppose I have too high standards, and have turned down all the young men who were interested in me.'

'I wonder if I may ask how Miss Hazel and Miss Marigold are. I heard about one becoming a VAD and the other joining the WAAC.'

'It's very good of you to ask, Henrietta. I've received letters from both recently, and they seem to be enjoying their new roles. I do worry about Hazel being in France, naturally.'

'Yes. I have brothers in the war who I worry about.'

'I don't have any brothers myself, in fact, no siblings at all. Neither do Hazel or Marigold. It's why we've always been like sisters.' Ebony stood up, putting her hand to her forehead as she looked out at sea. 'There's one of those flying boats.'

'So it is,' said Hetty, reminded once again, of Victor.

After a few seconds, Ebony looked down towards her. 'I'm off for my evening constitutional now, so I'll wish you good evening.'

'Good evening, Miss Girard.'

Ebony turned and was soon striding away, her eccentric style drawing looks from passers-by. She'd never seen her look quite that informal before.

Hetty looked back at the beach, wondering if she should take a walk too. Maybe in a while she'd get herself a ginger beer from the seller a few yards away, but she'd been on her feet all day and for now she was enjoying just sitting here, thinking about Victor and the proposed afternoon out. She felt a rush of excitement, yet a voice at the back of her head advised caution. His friends were in the war, he had no sweetheart. He was lonely. She was a friend, that was all.

Well of course, because what else could it possibly be? And Lorcan, oh Lorcan.

She stood up, not managing to do it as elegantly as Ebony had. She'd get that ginger beer and take a walk, and maybe she'd stop thinking up such nonsense.

Chapter Nine

Hetty and Victor had agreed to meet at noon, meaning that Hetty had to miss the early staff lunch, but she didn't mind. It was a lovely September day, with a golden light and no breeze at all, and she was glad to be out of the hotel. They'd agreed to meet in town, outside the bank on Beach Road.

As before, despite her being slightly early herself, he was already there, smiling and waving at her as she approached.

They greeted each other awkwardly and both seemed lost for words for a few seconds, which was odd considering how well they'd got on before.

'I suppose we should start by having lunch,' he said. 'Unless you had yours before you came out.'

'No, I didn't. Have you somewhere in mind?'

'I do, but it would require a train journey to Worthing.'

'Worthing? I like Worthing. It's where my brother Gilbert lived, but I've not been there since he enlisted. Yes, I like that idea. But I insist on paying my fare there.'

'But—'

'No buts.'

His body slumped as if in submission. 'Very well. Let's head to the railway station.'

—

In Worthing, Victor stopped part way down Montague Street, outside Roberts Dining Rooms, housed in a large, white, Georgian building.

'This looks nice,' she said, admiring the large windows and classical style of the structure.

'I used to meet up with my old chum Timothy here on occasion. We were at school together, but he lived in Brighton, so it was a sort of halfway spot. It has a much simpler menu than the Beach Hotel, but it serves good food. Shall we?' He opened the door for her and indicated that she should go in first.

Inside were about a dozen round tables with no cloths, showing fancy woodworking on the surface. Those not occupied were laid up with cruets and a menu in the centre. One side of the room had dark wood panelling, and from the ceiling hung several chandelier-type lamps, with five glass lampshades each. The room was only half full, with mostly women.

They were seated by a mirror, and Hetty was glad to be sitting with her back to it, not wanting to forever feel self-conscious about how she looked.

'The menu is, of course, limited compared to the last time I was here,' Victor said, looking at the single sheet of card.

'I think I will have the ham with boiled potatoes and green vegetables,' she said, suspecting he'd insist on paying and not wanting to pick anything too expensive. 'And the iced lemonade.'

'A good choice. I'll have that too.'

When their order had been taken, Hetty asked, 'Does your friend Timothy still live in Brighton?' hoping that he hadn't been killed in the war.

'When he's home, yes. Tim's in the army now, and recently been made a captain. Unfortunately, it was because his captain was killed.'

'Charlie Cobbett was recently made a lance corporal, and I did wonder if it was for the same reason.'

'Is that Charlie the porter at the hotel? The chirpy, happy chap?'

'That's right. At least, the side he shows to guests. He can be quite serious too, especially since the war. He's in one of the Royal Sussex battalions.'

'Let's hope now the Americans are involved, that the war will be over a bit sooner than it might have been. Did you know there are plans to build five aerodromes in Sussex for the Air Service of the American Expeditionary Force?'

'For the what?'

'That's the American equivalent of our Royal Flying Corps. I believe Rustington has been suggested for one of the aerodromes.'

'That would be very close to us.'

'Yes, it would. And it might give the hotel more custom, from the officers. But nothing's decided yet, so don't mention it to anyone. My father gets to hear these things and I probably shouldn't be telling you.'

'Don't worry, I'm not a tell-tale.'

'I'm glad to hear it,' he said, smiling.

–

After the meal, the pair of them went for a walk along the wide promenade. Here, it was next to the road, not separated by a large common like in Littlehampton. The tide was fairly low, exposing stony sand beyond the pebbles.

'September's a good time to come for a day out here. Or anywhere by the beach,' she said.

'Why is that?' he asked.

'You get some nice sunny days, without it being too hot, and there are far fewer people on holiday, or taking a day trip.'

'I bet you prefer the autumn and winter months in the hotel.'

'It is quieter than summer, but still busy. It seems the rich are happy to up sticks for a holiday at any time of year.' She hoped that didn't sound too critical, so tempered it with, 'Some have told us that they prefer it in the quieter months.'

'I think some of your guests clearly don't have anything better to do. I wish I could up sticks for a holiday whenever I wanted. I have a business to run.'

'I'm sorry, it wasn't a criticism of you.'

'And I didn't take it that way, Hetty.' He stopped, turning to face her. 'I know some of your guests think a great deal of themselves, and think they are better than the people who serve them, but I'm not like that. My great grandfather built up the business and worked hard doing it, as does my father, and as do I. Yes, we've made money, but we have earned it, and we make sure our employees are fairly recompensed, because that's how my great grandfather started out, so he knew what it was to work for someone else.'

This was said with some passion, and Hetty found herself liking him all the more for it.

'I'm glad to hear that, Victor. And yes, some of the guests do think highly of themselves, and they're often the ones who've never had to work a day in their lives. But there are others who are more appreciative of our efforts. Take Major Thomas for instance.'

They started walking once more.

'He's been there a few years, hasn't he?' said Victor. 'I've always liked him. Says it as it is and is invariably right.'

'Did you know he helped save Edie from being murdered a couple of years back? Him and Charlie.'

'I knew Edie had been attacked but didn't know Charlie and Major Thomas had been involved in defending her. What heroes.'

'And guests like Ebony Girard, who painted your sister's portrait, are always very friendly.'

'She does seem immensely pleasant.'

'Do you know, she actually came to sit next to me on the promenade wall a few evenings ago and chatted to me like I was an old friend.'

'She is rather a free spirit, and hopefully a sign of things to come,' said Victor.

They stopped once more to regard the sea and the long pier in the distance for some moments before Victor pointed in the other direction, towards the bandstand.

'I didn't expect anything today, but it looks like a small group of musicians is setting up there. Would you like to watch them?'

There were five women with wind instruments, and a small audience was starting to gather on the deck chairs provided.

'That would be most agreeable.'

To her surprise, he took her arm, and they headed to the bandstand.

–

Hetty arrived back at the hotel on a wave of euphoria that she was sure would last her the whole evening. But as soon as she entered the scullery, Annie's rushed, 'Your mother's waiting for you in Mrs Bygrove's office,' brought her back to reality.

She sped along to the office, knocking rapidly on the door.

Helen called her in at once. Her mother, Miriam, was sitting opposite the manageress with a handkerchief in her hand, dabbing at her eyes. This was greatly out of character for her mother.

'There you are, Henrietta! Where on *earth* have you been?'

'I… took a trip to Worthing, just for a change.' There was no need to mention Victor. 'What's happened?'

'If you had a day off, why didn't you come home? It's only half an hour's walk away. You haven't been to see us much recently.'

'Is that why you're upset?' It seemed an odd reason to turn up and start crying.

'No, of course not. It's Hector.'

'What's happened?'

'Take a seat, Hetty,' Helen said kindly, indicating the chair next to her mother.

Hetty sat down. This didn't sound good. She felt sick, anticipating what might be said.

'Hector has been shot in the shoulder,' said Miriam. 'He's currently in a casualty unit in France but will be sent home in the next few days, hopefully to the Belgrave Hospital, here in Littlehampton.'

Not as bad as she'd feared, but then, she didn't know the details. She took a few slow breaths to still her heart. 'Is Victor all right? How badly is he injured? I mean, is there any chance he could…?'

'Victor? Who's Victor?'

'S—sorry, I meant Hector. I'm so upset I just got confused.' She lowered her head and closed her eyes.

'He's through the worst now and recovering well, according to the letter, thank the Lord, but it was apparently touch and go initially and it's still a pretty bad wound.' She dabbed at her eyes once more. 'We won't know for sure how debilitating it will be until, until, h—he arrives.'

She started crying and Hetty took her hand. 'I'm sure it will be all right, Mum. Lili's Rhodri was shot in the leg, and Detective Inspector Toshack even lost a leg, but they're both fine now.'

Miriam snatched her hand away and sniffed. 'We're in company, so it's "Mother". And you can hardly compare them when we have no idea how much of his shoulder is damaged.' She turned to regard Helen. 'Hector was already in the army and a lieutenant when the war started. Who knows if he'll be able to continue his career.'

Is that all she cared about?

'We'll cross that bridge when we come to it, Mother.'

'You would say that. Now when is your next long afternoon off?'

'Next Monday.'

'Then you are to come home instead of gadding about. With any luck Hector will have arrived and we can visit him at the hospital. And you can help me get his room ready, for he will want to recuperate with us once the hospital discharges him.'

Hetty thought of the meeting she'd arranged with Victor and her heart sank. Still, this was her brother who was injured.

Somehow, she'd have to get a message to Victor. Perhaps Edie could help?

'Very well, Mother.'

–

Hetty didn't get a chance to talk to Edie alone until the following day. Tilly and Milly had gone for their morning tea break when Edie came into the stillroom for a glass of lime cordial.

'How are you today, Hetty?' She rubbed her arm and looked sympathetic.

'I'm all right, thank you. Knowing that Hector is out of mortal danger… Edie, do you have a moment to spare?' she half whispered, closing the door to the scullery so nobody in there would hear.

'Of course, Hetty.'

'I wonder if I could ask your advice. I think you might have some understanding of my situation, even though Charlie and you are the other way around.'

'The other way around?' Edie narrowed her eyes curiously. 'Perhaps you should start at the beginning.'

Hetty told her about the two meetings with Victor, and how she'd arranged to see him the following week. 'But now, of course, I won't be able to meet him, and I need to get a message to him but what if a letter doesn't get to him on time and I don't feel I can go to his office on the quay to tell him and definitely not his home.' It all came out in a rush.

'Calm down, Hetty, it's all right. First of all, I have to ask, what about Lorcan? I thought he was your sweetheart.'

'Not really, no. We agreed to decide about our relationship when he comes home. And as I said, Victor and I are only friends. But it is awkward.'

'Be careful, Hetty. I know Charlie and I are in a similar situation, but you don't know what Victor's intentions are, do you?'

'No. I don't think he does either though.'

'Listen, if you choose Victor, and the relationship develops between you, you must tell Lorcan.'

'I don't see how our relationship will develop, and I'm sure his mother is keen for him to find someone, well, higher up than me. I wouldn't want to say anything to Lorcan that might upset him while he's on the front, as it might, I don't know, make him lose concentration or something.'

'I can understand your concern. So, the problem is letting Victor know you can't come next week.'

'I daren't use the hotel telephone, as I don't know who will answer. And I don't even know his home or his work telephone number.'

'You won't have to. If you write a note explaining your predicament, I will take it to Humphrey Wilmot's and hand it to him personally. It's my afternoon off tomorrow, so I'll do that first. The family are associated with mine, so nobody will think twice about me being there.'

Hetty was so relieved that she gave her a hug and was hugged in return.

'You're a good friend, Edie. Thank you.'

—

Victor was talking to two of his staff just outside the workshop area, where one of the finished hulls sat on the ground, when he recognised Edie Moore traipsing across the pebbles towards his office.

'Excuse me, gentlemen, I'll speak to you later.' He went to meet her.

Oh dear, had they found out that Hetty had been meeting a guest and wanted a word with him about it? He hoped he hadn't got her into trouble over this.

'Good afternoon, Miss Moore. Can I help you?'

'I must say, the work you do here looks impressive. I've seen the flying boats a couple of times on the water here.'

'That's right.'

'Um, I'm glad I caught you out here,' she said.

Oh dear, here it comes.

She undid the clutch of her handbag and pulled a letter out from within. He felt a mixture of curiosity and dread as she handed it to him.

'You can probably guess who this is from.'

He took it and regarded it forlornly.

'Don't look so downhearted. But I would say, Mr Perryman, that if your intentions towards her are dishonourable, I would rather you gave her up now and saved her any pain.'

He looked up, shocked and not a little hurt. 'I can assure you, Miss Moore, that I have nothing but the utmost respect for Hetty – Miss Affleck. At this moment in time, we are simply friends, and I would never do anything discourteous towards her.'

'I'm glad to hear it, Mr Perryman. Anyway, I will leave you to read the letter.'

She walked back towards the Britannia public house, the pebbles crunching beneath her shoes as she went. He placed the letter in his pocket a moment before noticing his father emerge from the passageway leading to Surrey Street.

'Victor, my boy, was that Edie Moore I saw just leaving?'

'Yes, it was.'

'What did she want?'

'She was just taking a walk and noticed me, so came over to say hello and have a look at what we do here.' He stopped there, afraid of over explaining.

'I see. I've just popped over to have a look around, see how the new order is progressing.'

'Of course.' Victor extended his hand towards the workshop.

James spotted the two men that Victor had been speaking with a short while before and started asking them about progress. Victor stood close by patiently, smiling, but he was greatly irritated by his father's interference. He was perfectly capable of managing the men and achieving what was required of him.

'I'm just going back to the office, Father, to do some work.'

'Very well, my boy.'

My boy! The least he could do was refrain from treating him like a child in front of the men. What did that make him look like? It was almost as if his father was reminding him – and them – who was ultimately in charge.

Back upstairs in his office, out of the way of prying eyes, he quickly opened the letter. He was disappointed by its news, but not devastated, as he'd expected. And poor Hetty, having her brother so injured in the war. He wished he could meet her, if only to console her.

But there was no mention of meeting in the future, and he wondered whether Hetty was using this to break it off for good. Break what off, though? Maybe she'd decided that this Lorcan chap was who she really wanted to be with.

He heard his father's voice downstairs, talking to his secretary, and he placed the letter in a drawer. His father ran up the stairs, remaining at the top as he spoke to him.

'I'll be off now, as I have a meeting up the road with the Butt family about renting some warehouse space for the hulls.'

'Would you like me to come?'

'No, no. It doesn't need two of us.'

'I could have attended the meeting myself, as it's nearby, and I am running this side of the business.'

'But I am the overall owner, so I should go. I'll see you at dinner.'

'Very well, Father.'

This, along with Hetty's bad news, left him in a gloomy mood for the rest of the afternoon.

–

When Victor arrived home that evening, his mother was in a buoyant mood, greeting him with a smile.

'Up you go to change and then join us in the drawing room. Dinner will be ready in about twenty minutes. Your father's already here, getting changed.'

Was that why she was so happy? His father was invariably either late or turned up last minute.

When he entered the drawing room ten minutes later, his mother was alone. She greeted him with another broad smile, inviting him to sit next to her on the settee.

'So, Victor, you're walking out with Edie Moore, are you?'

'What? No! Why would you think that?'

'Your father said he saw her at the workshop, and that she gave you a letter. Was it a missive expressing her undying love?' she quipped.

'No, Mother, it most certainly was not any kind of romantic missive. I don't know where you get these ideas from.' All the while he tried to think of a reason why Edie would have been giving him a letter. He hated lying, but it would benefit nobody to reveal anything of the true nature of the letter at this point.

Yes, that was it. 'I thought about organising a Christmas dinner for the men at the Beach Hotel, to thank them for all their hard work, and Miss Moore was simply giving me a rundown of costs, should I decide to. That's all.'

His father entered with Sophia as he was explaining, and looked askance.

'What's all this?' said James. 'If you want to treat the men, you'd be better off taking them somewhere like Read's Dining Rooms in Surrey Street, not taking them to a luxury hotel. That is way above their expectations.'

'It was only one of several ideas to look at, Father.'

'Then you can take it off the list now.'

'So, there is nothing between you and Edie?' said his mother, looking disappointed.

'Nothing whatever.'

'What a shame.'

The butler entered. 'Dinner is served, sir, madam.'

'Thank you, Harries,' said James, leading the way to the dining room.

Victor sat with his sister, opposite their mother, with James at the head of the table. He had even less of an appetite than he'd had when he'd entered the house. That was twice today that his father had made him feel a dolt.

Perhaps, after dinner, he could go for a walk on the promenade. He knew that Hetty liked to take a walk at that time if she wasn't on duty. He might bump into her. He'd forego dessert and make his excuses – but no. The evenings were drawing in now, and it was already sunset so it would be too dark for her walk. He'd go to his room and read his book after dinner. He was in no mood for his parents' company tonight.

'I thought, since we're all here for a change, that we could have a game of Whist,' said Barbara.

With Sophia and his father readily agreeing, he didn't think they'd appreciate him making excuses.

'Yes, why not?' he said, and took a spoonful of soup.

Chapter Ten

Three days had gone by in which Victor had hoped to take a walk on the promenade in the evening before sunset, on the off chance of seeing Hetty. It wasn't until the following Saturday that he managed to organise leaving work early enough to do so.

Locking the office door at five thirty, and having no intention of going home first, he headed down Pier Road, with the aim of carrying on to the pier and taking the long way home along the promenade.

He was just reaching the Harbour Tea Rooms, thinking about his afternoon there with Hetty, when he heard his mother's voice.

'Oh wonderful, you are actually coming home early tonight,' she said, catching him up. 'I was just on my way to your office to tell you the news.'

The disappointment overwhelmed him. Maybe he could tell her he wanted a walk to get some fresh air after being cooped up in the office all day.

About to open his mouth, his mother got in first with, 'We've been invited to the Beach Hotel by Lord and Lady Raynolt this evening. They're having a dinner and dance for Lord Raynolt's sixtieth birthday. I'm sure there'll be some fine and eligible young ladies there, including their daughter Isabella.'

Not this again.

'This evening? That's rather short notice.'

'Lady Raynolt telephoned me today to see why I hadn't replied to the invitation. It must have got lost in the post.'

With no prospect of seeing Hetty again, he really could not be bothered with it, but he also knew that there was no way out.

'I've already put out your suit and shirt.'

Then a thought occurred to him. Hetty was sometimes brought out of the stillroom to serve at special events. He might be able to have a word with her. His mood brightened.

'Very well, Mother. I'll have a bath first if that's all right.'

'Of course it is. You've got to look your best.'

That was his sentiment too.

–

Hetty was at early staff dinner, eating quickly as she'd been instructed by Mrs Leggett, so that she could wait at the soirée being held that evening.

'I've heard there'll be some important families attending tonight,' said Lili, who'd already finished her dinner. 'It's going to be a little bigger than Sophia Perryman's birthday party.'

'I do so love seeing all the young ladies in their gorgeous dresses,' said Hetty.

Gertie humphed. 'If you like that kinda thing.'

'You're a misery tonight,' said Fanny, comforting her toddler. 'Elsie's nearly asleep. I'd better let Vera take over.' She got up carefully and left to give her daughter back to the nursemaid.

'I'm surprised the Raynolts have booked anything 'ere again, after the disaster of their daughter Penelope's engagement party back in March,' said Gertie. 'With all the fancy food they'd been promised what never turned up.'

'Yes, but they knew that were Douglas Bygrove's fault,' said Lili. 'Lady Raynolt said as much to Mrs Bygrove. I still can't believe that we were sometimes serving food he'd bought what had been stolen!'

The conversation continued in this vein, but Hetty was only half listening, thinking about how she'd phrased the letter to Victor. She'd used the word 'cancelled' instead of 'postponed' and hadn't mentioned anything about meeting at some time in the future. Could she send another letter? But she didn't want to impose on Edie again. She could send one by post, but what if the secretary opened them all first? On the other hand, Victor could have written a reply back. Maybe he still would.

Was it possible that he'd be at the party tonight, if, as Lili had said, there would be some important families there?

Fanny returned to the dining room. 'You're looking a bit serious, Hetty.'

'Me? Well, I have an extra shift this evening, what with serving at the soirée, and I'm already a little tired.'

'We've had to use everyone we can tonight,' said the housekeeper, 'what with the dinner being served in the conservatory for the resident guests. It's lucky we're not fully booked at the moment.' She stood up. 'Well ladies – and gentlemen,' she looked towards Simon and Dennis, who'd been eating their dinner quietly at the other end, 'those of you serving this evening need to set to and get both rooms laid up. Even I'm helping this evening.'

'Very well, Mrs Leggett,' they all replied.

–

The soirée was proving to be a lot more sedate than Sophia's party, even if there were more people. The meal was a sit-down affair in the main dining room.

Hetty had served first courses at several tables before she had cause to come to a standstill by a table in the middle of the room. Sitting there, among some young ladies and a couple of gentlemen in officers' uniforms, was Victor Perryman.

Pulling herself together swiftly, she placed the plate down in front of him and the woman next to him, announcing that it was fillet of sole with anchovy sauce, avoiding making any kind of eye contact with him. She then went back to the trolley that had been wheeled in by Edie, which had more plates. On tables nearby, she spotted his father with other older men, while his sister and mother were on yet another table with a group of women. She thought this curious, until she overheard the conversation at James Perryman's table. Business, that's what they were talking about. The women, no doubt, were being excluded from this, but in a way, that was lucky for them, Hetty thought.

With all the plates distributed, it was time to start at the first table once more, to clear the plates of those who had finished.

Reaching Victor's table, she was careful once more not to look directly at him. He was engaged in conversation with the lady on his left, a pretty young thing with a low-cut and sleeveless evening gown and her hair in a bob. She would have made Hetty, in the outfits she'd worn when out with Victor, look very dull. But then, so would most of the young women here.

She walked away with his plate and that of his neighbour, placing them on the trolley that Edie was now about to wheel out of the room.

Why oh why had she been allocated his table? Luck of the draw, of course, as the room had simply been divided between her, Lili, Simon and three of the live-out waitresses. What a dilemma. She'd wanted to see him so much, and yet now she had, she couldn't talk to him.

-

Victor was so pleased to see that Hetty was serving his table. But that pleasure lasted only a few seconds. How could he talk to her here about what had happened, and about whether they could meet again? Was there some way he could follow her through the door to the staff area and talk to her? No, that might get her into trouble. And his parents had their beady eyes on him.

When Hetty reached him with the first course, he was ready with a smile, but she wouldn't even look at him, not even for a second. Had he been right then, about using her brother as an excuse to cut all contact? He felt even more bereft than he had the last few days.

'I say, this sole looks jolly tasty,' said the young woman next to him, who had chatted merrily to him since they'd sat down. 'Don't you think?'

She was attractive, and somewhat daring with her rather revealing dress, but she held little appeal for him.

'Yes, it looks delicious,' he said. And it did, but he no longer had much of an appetite for it.

He'd have to make the best of the evening and look like he was enjoying himself, otherwise he knew that both of his parents would be having words with him. He picked up his cutlery and started eating.

—

With the raspberry soufflé dishes cleared up, and some of the guests remaining seated to partake of a sherry or port digestif, others, especially the younger members, were encouraged to make their way to the ballroom. There, a string octet was playing, and Hetty knew they'd be there for the rest of the evening. No ragtime bands for this party.

'More's the pity,' she whispered to herself as she reached the scullery.

'What's that?' said Lili, catching her up, pushing another trolley of spent dishes.

'I was just thinking that it's a shame there won't be a ragtime band this evening.'

'That one we had here was rather merry. Fancied dancing myself, I did.'

So had Hetty. In fact, she'd fancied dancing with Victor. She'd even dreamt that night she was.

'Think yourself lucky that you get to hear the music and see the dancing,' said Annie, her hands elbow-deep in the large, butler sink.

Lili raised her eyes and the pair of them smiled as they turned to leave.

'Ah, ladies,' said Edie, meeting them in the stillroom. 'It's time to serve the champagne in the ballroom now.' She indicated where Tilly and Milly had already poured enough glasses for two trays.

'The Raynolts have really pushed the boat out tonight,' said Lili, picking up one of the trays. 'That was already a good deal of wine we served them at dinner.'

'They're lucky we still have a good stock of it in our cellar,' said Edie. 'With much of it coming from France, it's becoming harder to replace.'

Hetty and Lili walked through the dining room, where Simon and the others were still clearing up, and quite a few guests were still lingering with their drinks.

Entering the ballroom with the champagne took Hetty back to Sophia's party. She recalled serving a glass to Victor's cousin, Maria, who she had thought he was having some kind of illicit affair with. She wasn't here tonight, but the rather elegant woman he'd been talking to at the table was still with him, standing near the doors to the garden.

'I'll take this side of the room, you take the other,' she told Lili, wanting to avoid any contact with Victor.

As she started to offer the glasses of champagne, she noticed the elegant woman lead Victor onto the middle of the floor, where several other people were dancing to the 'Sleeping Beauty Waltz'. It was another record her father had for the gramophone.

What a forward woman she was. Hetty couldn't imagine asking a man to dance. You just didn't do that.

Oh dear, she sounded like her mother again. Perhaps women should be allowed to ask a man to dance. Why not?

All these thoughts careered around her head as she served and smiled. She looked up, about to move on, but stalled. Victor and the woman had unfortunately danced to her side of the room and were now close by. She tried not to look as she held up the tray for a young man, but she inadvertently glanced at them as they passed by. Victor looked rather happy.

With the tray empty, she headed towards the door, intent on suggesting that Simon take over, so she could clear up. It had been the right thing to do, cancelling her next meeting with Victor, even if it had been for unforeseen circumstances. She'd done him a favour, of that she was sure.

Chapter Eleven

Hetty entered the door of the flint schoolhouse in Wick around half past two, calling, 'Hello?'

'There you are, Henrietta,' said her mother, poking her head around the kitchen door. 'What took you so long? I expected you here for lunch.'

'I was on a late staff lunch today.'

'You ate before you left?'

'Just a little, as I was rather peckish,' she admitted. 'So, is Hector back? I thought you might have let me know.'

'He isn't, no. He's going to be arriving by the end of the week, so we can see him next Monday. But I do have something else for you to do this afternoon.'

'Get his bedroom sorted out. You said.'

'No, not that. We have a guest coming.'

'Who?' She noticed the pleasant aroma and took a deep breath in. 'Have you been baking?'

'Just a small fruit cake I managed to gather some ingredients for. It's made with that dreadful war flour, but it will have to do.'

'Who's coming then?' She thought it might be her sister, Iris, who she hadn't seen for a couple of months.

There was a knock at the door, causing her mother to pull off the apron she'd been wearing and toss it behind her in the kitchen. 'Go and sit down in the parlour,' she commanded on a whisper. 'Elegantly.'

Hetty was confused but did as she was asked. She took a seat on the settee nearest the empty fireplace. A few moments later her mother showed in a tall, skinny, youngish gentleman with dark, oiled hair, black clothing and a dog collar. It was the vicar of the mission church, which was just around the corner from the school.

She stood up. Was this the expected guest? 'Good afternoon, Reverend Peck.'

'Good afternoon, Henrietta. Though "good" is not how the weather is looking currently.'

'It is rather cloudy.'

'Sit down, Reverend.' Her mother pointed to the space next to Hetty, but he sat in the armchair instead. 'I'll just fetch the tea in.'

'Very good,' he said.

Hetty sat back down. Why on earth would her mother invite the vicar around, knowing she was coming home for the afternoon? Maybe, with Hector injured, she required some holy reassurance. Poor Mum. She always bustled around, taking charge and keeping busy when something upsetting happened. It wasn't in her nature to show her emotions, which is why Hetty had been surprised when she'd found her crying in Helen's office.

'So, Henrietta, I hear you're still working at the luxury hotel.' It was said in a slightly disapproving manner.

'That's right, Vicar. In the stillroom, and sometimes in the dining room.'

'Don't you think it's all rather *unnecessary* in the current times, with the war raging. The hotel could be used as a hospital.'

'People still need some distraction in the war, Vicar, to get them through. And we have put on several charity events raising money for the soldiers and for the poorer children.'

'That is something, I suppose. But all the staff there, they could be doing war work.'

'Most of the men who worked there are now fighting. What about you, Vicar? What war work do you do?'

'The reverend's war work is to look after our spiritual welfare,' said her mother, bustling in with a tray.

'I believe there are some men of the cloth who've gone out to the front, as chaplains,' said Hetty.

'They can't all go, otherwise what would *we* do for holy guidance? Now, enough of that.' Miriam placed the tray on a side table. 'Henrietta, why don't you come and pour, seeing as you have dining room experience?'

'Yes, Mother.'

'Henrietta has learned a lot of household skills, working at the hotel.'

What a strange thing to say. What was her mother up to? Then the cold truth hit her like the wet towels her brothers used to fling at her when they were children on the beach. Reverend Peck was unmarried. Oh Lord, what a thought! She sent up a brief apology to the Almighty, but also an appeal.

'I'm sure it's quite useful in teaching women wifely skills,' he said. 'But there comes a time when they must do their duty for their country and God, by becoming mothers and wives.'

She was tempted to say, *Not in that order, I assume*, but held it back.

'Indeed, Reverend Peck,' said Miriam.

'How old are you now Henrietta?' he asked.

'Twenty-five, Vicar.'

'Then it's high time you found a husband.'

'That is rather a problem at the moment, what with most of the young men away fighting.' She kept her voice civil, and even managed a smile, but inside she was boiling.

'Henrietta, don't answer back.'

'I wasn't, Mother. I was simply stating a fact.'

'They're not *all* away fighting.' Miriam glanced briefly at Reverend Peck. Hetty was glad he hadn't noticed. 'Now Reverend, do have some of my fruit cake, baked just today. I know it's not—'

'No thank you, Mrs Affleck. I'm not indulging in such things whilst there is a war on, and others would do well to follow my lead.'

'Oh, um.' Miriam placed the knife she was about to cut the cake with back on the tray and sat down. Hetty was disappointed not to be offered any.

'I wonder, Mrs Affleck, whether you've considered my suggestion of taking on one of the classes in the Sunday School.'

'Why yes, Reverend, I would be glad to. I'm sure I can fit it around my charity work.'

'Good, good.'

They started talking about the church and parish matters, allowing Hetty's mind to wander. Her thoughts came eventually to Victor. How she would like to have been with him this afternoon instead of suffering this pointless visit to get to know the vicar. A choice between a vicar and a Victor, she joked to herself. She knew which she would choose.

'What are you smiling about, girl?' said Miriam. 'Old Mrs Ball's demise is not an amusing subject.'

She had not heard a word for the last few minutes. Reverend Peck was also looking rather sternly at her.

'I'm sorry, I was thinking about how kind Mrs Ball used to be to us children at Sunday School.' It was true that she had been, even if Hetty hadn't really been thinking about it at that moment.

'A little *too* kind and indulgent at times,' said the vicar.

'I don't believe there's any such thing as being *too* kind,' said Hetty, wondering whether this man had a kind bone in his body. He'd always seemed a cold fish, the few times she'd attended a service with her parents. 'After all, aren't we called upon to love our neighbours as ourselves?'

Hetty saw her mother narrow her eyes and lips. She'd be in trouble once the vicar had left.

'Yes, we are,' he said. 'But that doesn't mean we should spoil them. You spoke of charity events you've held at the hotel. What was the last one you held?'

'It was a children's party, the funds from which went to the Arun Children's Aid Project.'

'While it's noble to raise money for the poorer children of the borough, indulging the children with lavish foodstuffs and pointless games will not enrich their souls. They need to be taught how to be frugal in such times, and to take part in activities that edify them.'

'There is certainly a place for that, Vicar, but in these troubling times, they also need a little joy to lift their spirits, as do we all.'

He ignored this last sentence, and turned back to Miriam, discussing aspects of church life, including how the rotas for flower arranging and cleaning the church were short of people. While this was taking place, she heard the bell being rung, indicating the end of the school day.

'And you, *Henrietta*,' said the vicar, pronouncing her name as if it was some kind of indulgence. 'Will you be attending Sunday service at some point? I have only seen you a couple of times since I've been the vicar here.'

'I'm usually on duty on Sunday mornings, Vicar. Mrs Leggett, our housekeeper, always says prayers at breakfast, and on occasion the vicar of St Mary's comes in to conduct a brief service.'

'That is not the same as attending church, Miss Affleck.'

'I'm sure God doesn't mind where you are when you pray to him, as long as your intentions and actions are good.'

He opened his mouth to reply but didn't get a chance to speak before the door opened and Hetty's father, Kenneth, entered the parlour, for which Hetty was thankful.

'Good afternoon, Reverend Peck. It's been such a busy day, I'm glad it's over. I suppose you've read the latest news about Russia being proclaimed a republic by the provisional government there.'

'No. I don't indulge in reading the newspapers until my day's work is done.' He rose. 'Talking of which, I must leave now, as I have to visit a parishioner.'

'Oh, oh. Well, thank you for calling around, Reverend,' said Miriam, rushing to open the door for him and accompanying him out.

Kenneth raised his eyes at Hetty and she rolled hers, making him chuckle. 'That bad, eh?' he whispered.

When Miriam re-entered the parlour, she did not look pleased. 'Did you have to be so rude to the reverend?'

'I thought I was very civil. It was him being rude, finding fault with everything I said.'

'He's not the most tolerant of men, that's true enough, but he is a single man and has a reasonable living.'

Hetty exclaimed, 'Mother!' the same time as her father's, 'Miriam!'

'He is a very *intolerant* man, who seems to have little Christian love for anyone, not even children,' said Hetty. 'He is very different to old Reverend Kent who was there before him.'

'I know he is,' she conceded, sinking onto the settee. 'And I suppose you are still writing to that Lorcan.'

'Lorcan and I are just friends. That's all we've ever been. I did tell you that.' It wasn't quite true, but she didn't have the energy to explain it all.

'I'm glad to hear it.'

'Miriam, leave the poor girl alone. I could do with a cup of tea. Is there any left in this pot?' He bent down to have a look.

'It will be cold if there is.' Her mother rose. 'I'll make a new pot. And there's a whole fruit cake left since Reverend Peck didn't want any.' She seemed a little peeved about this.

Kenneth rubbed his hands together. 'Lovely. Just what I need. Haven't you had any yet, Hetty?'

'It didn't seem right, with the vicar declaring it an "indulgence", but I will now.' She got up to serve them each a piece.

'What time can you stay til?'

'I'll leave at half past five,' she said.

She didn't have a shift this evening, but the sun was now shining, and she fancied a walk by the promenade, before sunset.

What a change this made from her afternoon, sitting on the promenade wall once again, looking out at the receding tide. It was less busy than the last time she'd sat here, when Ebony had joined her. Most of the prom-side businesses and entertainments were closed, and it wasn't as warm as on previous evenings, but she was enjoying it, nevertheless.

Her parents had assumed she had a shift this evening, and she hadn't contradicted them. She'd felt guilty at first, but as it happened, her father had a meeting to go to at six thirty, and her mother had her knitting club coming around, making gloves and scarves for the soldiers for the coming winter.

She could hear the guns, but today they were a little more distant. She opened her handbag and took out the book she'd brought to read.

'Do you mind if I join you?'

For a split second, she had a feeling of déjà vu, as if she were reliving the recent evening with Ebony she'd been thinking about. But the voice was a man's and one she recognised.

She closed the book. 'Victor! Please, do.' She felt a momentary worry about being seen with a hotel patron but decided not to let it spoil her delight at encountering him.

He sat next to her and looked out to sea. He was wearing the linen suit she'd seen him in when she'd spotted him on the beach with his cousin.

'What are you reading?' He leant over to have a look. 'Ah, *Far from the Madding Crowd*. I do like Thomas Hardy's novels.'

'Yes, they're among my favourites too.' She placed the book back in her bag.

'I'd hoped I might see you on the promenade one afternoon. I'm so sorry to hear that your brother has been injured, but will you be straight with me, Hetty, and tell me whether your letter was also to let me know that you didn't want to meet up with me again?'

She was taken aback by his forthrightness. 'No, that wasn't my intention. I really did have to go to my parents, as my mother said it was likely my brother would be back and sent to the Belgrave, and we would visit him. But he hasn't returned yet. I was hoping that you might reply in some way.'

He regarded her once more, looking happier than when he'd first sat down. 'When you didn't suggest another date, I thought that might be the end, that you were finishing it.'

'Finishing what though, Victor?' she said, wanting a clearer idea of what 'it' was.

'Whatever this is. Or might become.'

'Didn't you meet that nice young woman at the soirée?' The idea that they may have got together had troubled her, she couldn't deny.

He groaned. 'I suppose you're referring to Rosetta Stone, with whom I danced.'

'Rosetta Stone, is that her name? Like the Egyptian hiero-glyphic slab that's in the British Museum?' She giggled. 'Sorry, but I think that's funny.'

'Yes, it is. Her name's actually Rosetta Russell-Stone, but she's shortened it, I think so people talk about her. And look, we are talking about her.' He put his hands out to each side.

'I suppose it's one way to get noticed, though she was very lively and colourful, so I don't suppose she has problems with that.'

'No. I've met her before, and she's always the life and soul of the party. I, on the other hand, hate those events, especially when my mother is intent on pairing me off with some available young woman.'

'Do you prefer them to be unavailable then?' She wasn't sure why she'd said that but was looking for some clarity about what was going on here.

'I didn't mean it like that, Hetty. I had to make it look like I was enjoying myself, otherwise I would have got an earful from my mother afterwards. And my father.' He was about to take her hand, but obviously thought better of it out here, in the open.

'You seemed to enjoy your sister's party.'

'Because it was about *her* and I didn't feel I had to impress anyone.'

She noticed a guest from the hotel walking in their direction on the promenade, so lowered her head. 'Should we be here together, so close to the hotel, and where it's so busy?'

'You seem to be constantly anxious about that.'

'I don't want to lose my job.'

'Then why don't we organise another afternoon out somewhere, maybe Worthing again, or Bognor?'

'I can't do next Monday, as my brother will be back by then. Hopefully. But the following one, the first of October, should be all right.' She tried not to sound too excited.

'I'll make sure it's my afternoon off too. Can we take a walk now, as if we're just passing the time of day? There aren't that many people left, and I don't think they'll take any notice of us.'

She looked around to see what had happened to the hotel guest. They were now walking across the common towards the hotel.

'All right. But if you see anyone you know, walk away. I'll do the same. And I need to be back at the hotel before seven thirty, otherwise I'll miss my dinner.'

He nodded. 'I need to be back for dinner too. We've only about an hour until it gets dark anyway, but it's better than nothing.'

It certainly was, thought Hetty, whose mood had lifted to the sky since she'd left the hotel after lunch. She could honestly say that she was the happiest she'd been in a long time. Then she remembered her brother's injury. But he was on the mend and would be home soon. It would be good to see him after so long.

But what about Lorcan? She didn't want to think about that for now.

As they started walking, she said, 'I had a similar situation this afternoon, with regard to my mother trying to pair me off.' She told him about Reverend Peck's visit.

'Oh my, he sounds rather tedious. Sorry, I shouldn't be saying that about a man of the cloth.'

'No, you're right. Tedious, and with little empathy for anyone. The thought of spending five minutes in his company, let alone a lifetime, is quite abhorrent.'

'And your mother would be happy for you to marry such a man?'

'Sadly, I think she would. Just to stop me from being a spinster.'

He grinned. 'We should do a little matchmaking ourselves. Since Rosetta Stone and this Reverend Peck are both single, perhaps we could introduce them.'

Hetty put her hand to her mouth and giggled. 'Oh my, can you imagine it?'

'I'm trying not to, but it's too funny.'

He started laughing, which set her off again, and they found themselves chuckling helplessly for a couple of minutes, drawing curious looks.

'I'm so glad I came across you on the promenade,' Victor said when they finally stopped laughing. 'It's made my day.'

'Yes, it's made mine too.'

–

'So, ladies, I think that everything is organised for the charity concert at St Mary's on Saturday,' said Sophia, sitting in the hall behind the Congregational Church the following afternoon. 'Any questions?'

Ebony looked around her colleagues, as she thought of them. The word 'friends' didn't quite fit, not yet. She wondered if it ever would, still feeling the emptiness that was her constant companion these days.

'No questions?' said Sophia. 'Then let's get our coats and head away.'

They were all moving towards the cloakroom when Sophia halted. 'Goodness, I almost forgot. I need to tell the caretaker that we've finished.'

She headed back into the hall and the rest of them carried on. They chatted about what they were doing that evening, Ebony listening as they spoke of friends and family to visit.

'What about you, Ebony?' said Emma, as she buttoned her coat. 'Are you doing anything nice this evening?'

Not wanting to admit that she'd be dining alone once more, she said, 'This and that, you know.'

Emma grinned. 'This and that, eh? We all know what that means, don't we, ladies.'

They all giggled and another woman, named Kate, said, 'Oh yes, we certainly do. It means that you don't want to let on about a romantic tryst. A new relationship, is it?'

'Well, no, it's not—'

'Or do you just not want to share his existence with us? Eligible men are *so* thin on the ground. On leave is he? Or does he have a reserved occupation?'

'I, um, it's not really—'

Sophia stepped into the room at this point.

'Do you know about Ebony's beau?' Emma asked her.

'I didn't say—' Ebony began.

'You don't have to. We can tell the signs.' Kate turned towards Sophia, smirking. 'Very mysterious she's being, about this young man she's doing *this and that* with this evening. Or older man perhaps?'

'It's actually not what—'

'Good luck to her,' said Sophia, a little sharply. 'It's none of our business, now is it?'

'Ooh, you're such a spoilsport,' said Emma.

The other four women left, but Ebony hung back as Sophia did up her coat.

'She's got the wrong idea, I'm afraid.'

'You don't have to explain anything to me. Like I said, it's not our business. I'd walk back via the hotel with you, but I have several errands to run.'

Ebony opened the outer door. 'That's all right. I need to call in at the stationers first, anyway.'

'I'll see you at the meeting on Friday. Good afternoon, Ebony.'

'Good afternoon, Sophia.'

—

Sophia pushed open the door of the drawing room to see her mother staring out of the window at the fading light in the garden. Barbara turned, displaying a smile that didn't reach her eyes.

'Ah Sophia, you're back in time for dinner. Good. How did the meeting go?'

'Fine, fine, as they usually do.' Sophia went to her mother to kiss her cheek.

'Victor's back and getting changed for dinner. Your father's got something else on tonight.' She looked down, her lips pinched in.

'He said at breakfast that he'd see us this evening.'

'Yes, he did, but he rang to say that he's been invited out to dinner by some, well, business colleagues.' She turned back to the garden and continued to stare into the gloom.

'You seem worried about it.'

Barbara flicked her hand as if dismissing Sophia's concern. 'Oh, I'm sure it's fine. It's not like it hasn't happened before.' She paused. 'It's just...'

Sophia went to her once again, taking her arm. 'It's just *what*, Mother? You're clearly concerned about something.'

Barbara sighed and slowly looked around at her. 'I'm beginning to feel like, oh, I don't know. The housekeeper. Yes, the housekeeper, not a wife. Your father spends more and more evenings out. And the odd Sunday. It's as if he'd rather spend time with his friends and colleagues than me. And the rare occasion when he can do something, he seems to pick times when I'm already busy.'

'I suppose business is rather hectic at the moment, with more ships needed for the navy, and the hulls for the flying boats.'

'And that's another thing. Now Victor's been in the business a good few years, and runs the hull side very efficiently, why not give him more responsibility elsewhere? And promote some of his deputies, who he's always saying are so efficient and loyal. Why not take a bit more time off now he's getting older. He spoke once of us doing a spot of travelling when he got to this age. But he seems to work harder than ever.'

'I do understand your concern, Mother, but, as I said, there is a war on. You couldn't even go travelling at the moment.'

Barbara moved closer to the settee and slumped uncharacteristically onto it. 'I know. But he could still forego at least some of these social events with his peers. I suppose he prefers their company to mine.'

Sophia sat next to her, taking her hand. 'Oh Mother, I'm sure that can't be true. Why don't you arrange an evening out with him?'

'What, yet another meal at the Beach Hotel, because he's never back in time to do anything else?'

'You love the theatre. Tell him you're booking to see something at, say, the Theatre Royal in Brighton. You like it there.'

'I did ask to see *What a Catch* there, a couple of months ago, and he said he didn't have enough time at that moment. He suggested I took a friend.'

'Then ask again. He might say yes this time.'

This felt rather strange to Sophia, advising her mother on what was basically an affair of the heart.

'I suppose I could try. But, with the amount of times he's been out recently, I don't hold out much hope.'

The door opened and her brother stepped in. Sophia stood up.

'Hello Victor. I'd better go and get changed.'

'Hello. Is everything all right. You both look worried.'

'Everything is fine,' said Barbara, standing. 'Now, tell me about your day.'

Sophia left them to it, thinking back to Emma's assertion that Ebony had a 'beau' with whom she was meeting that evening. Lucky Ebony, if it was true. She wondered who it could be, with the current lack of men, and why she was being so coy about it.

Did she wish that she too had a young man? She shook her head. Men were nothing but trouble. She had surely learnt her lesson on that score. Yes, better to be single and her own woman.

Chapter Twelve

Hetty and her mother stood outside the tall edifice of Belgrave House that sat on the corner of Fitzalan Road and Irvine Road, not far from the hotel. It had been turned into a convalescent hospital at the beginning of the war. Her brother had only arrived yesterday, so it was the first chance they'd had to see him.

As they entered the grounds, Hetty said, 'This is where Lili's sweetheart Rhodri was convalescing when she met him a couple of years back. We held a do at the hotel for the men from here.'

'I remember that. It was very thoughtful of Mrs Bygrove.'

'I believe she's planning another soon. We invite other people too, and they pay for a ticket, so it raises money for the hospital.'

'It seems all the more important now your brother's here.'

Arriving in the entrance hall, they were soon directed to the correct ward. As they made their way along the corridor, they encountered several injured men, a couple with missing limbs, either heading somewhere or being pushed in wheelchairs. Hetty noticed her mother's worried frown. Was she afraid that Hector would end up losing a limb, or being confined to a wheelchair? The news hadn't suggested that, but she guessed they'd find out in a moment or two.

When they entered his ward, Hetty was about to ask a VAD nurse where Hector could be found, but her mother touched her arm and pointed to the bed right next to the door. He spotted them immediately, grinning widely and indicating for them to come over with his good arm.

'Oh Hector, how are you?' Hetty hurried to him, attempting to hug him, but not quite knowing what to do about the bandage around his arm and shoulder. His pyjama top was only half on. She kissed the top of his head instead.

'Hello, sis. I had my dressing changed about half an hour ago. They say it's healing nicely.'

Miriam glanced at her, and she wondered if her mother was thinking the same thing as her, that the smiles were all bravado, a show to make them feel better. And Hetty was sure she could see a little blood on the side of the dressing.

'How long are you likely to be here?' said Miriam.

'I'm not sure yet, Mum. I suppose that depends.'

'I thought you said it was healing nicely.'

'It is, but I'm still having difficulty using it at the moment.' He demonstrated by trying to lift his arm, which resulted in him grimacing.

'Will you come home to recuperate afterwards?'

'It depends how long it takes, I guess. One thing's for sure: I'll not be on the front again. Having a stiff arm's not conducive to defending myself or fighting the enemy.'

'But what about your army career?'

'I think we can safely say that's over, Mum.'

'I'm so sorry,' said Hetty, though she was also glad about this.

'I'm not. Fighting bits of wars and defending places is one thing. But this madness?' He shook his head vigorously, blowing out through his lips at the same time.

'Hear, hear,' said the patient in the next bed, a large man with his foot in a sling.

'What will you do?' said Hetty.

'I dunno. Office clerk? Perhaps train as an accountant, or a teacher, like Dad and Gilbert. It depends how well I heal. At least it's my left shoulder, so I can still write without difficulty.'

'Having been a lieutenant in the army should give you some opportunities. Maybe you can talk to your father about it, see what ideas he has,' said Miriam. 'He's coming in this evening.'

'And I'll try and pop in most days since I'm only up the road,' said Hetty. 'As long as visiting time coincides with the odd times between shifts.'

'That'll be something to look forward to,' said Hector. 'How's Gilbert? I haven't heard from him, being laid up in hospital the last couple of weeks. And Iris. How's she?'

'They're both fine,' said Miriam. 'Now tell us about your time in the hospital in France, and your journey back.'

'If I must,' he said, rolling his eyes at Hetty, a habit they and their other two siblings had long practised.

–

The following week, on the train to Worthing, in a carriage that contained only the two of them, Victor asked how Hetty's visit to her brother had gone.

'He was a lot better than I was expecting, given how deep the wound was. And he was very chirpy, though he always has been, even when he doesn't really feel it. I've been visiting him in between some shifts.'

It was how she'd managed to persuade her mother that she didn't need to go with her today, as she'd been four times during the week. She told Victor next about her brother's plans for a civilian life.

'We're always looking for people with good writing and arithmetic skills, which I presume he has,' said Victor.

'Oh yes. Our father wanted him to go into accountancy, but he was determined to join the army. We'll have to see how he heals.'

Victor told Hetty about his mother thinking that he and Edie were involved because of her visit to the workshop. He told it as a funny story, but she did find it a little concerning.

'I'm sure she would have been over the moon if you had been involved with her, being a baron's daughter,' said Hetty.

'Who's forsaken that life, from what I can tell.'

'But it doesn't make her any the less entitled. And I don't suppose you've told your parents who you were having a day out with today.'

'Hetty.' He took her hand. 'I haven't told them about you, not because I'm ashamed to, but because I know that *you* want to keep it quiet.'

'But how would they take it if you did tell them?'

'I'm not sure, to be honest. The fact is, I don't need to marry *up*, because, well, we are quite a wealthy family.'

'But working in a hotel, I've seen this over and over, mothers of high class or of great wealth turning up with sons and daughters, wanting them to marry into even greater status or wealth, or both. Or they only have wealth, and they want status. Someone like me couldn't offer either.'

'Me marrying someone with a title wouldn't give me a title, Hetty. It only happens the other way around. Do you know about Edie's mother, Agnes?'

'I know that her parents are Lord and Lady Moreland, obviously.'

'Well, Agnes Moreland had a very humble beginning. Her family were farmers who rented land, they didn't own it. As a young woman, I believe she was seventeen, a solicitor fell in love with her, and they married. After only a couple of months, he was killed in an accident. She inherited his house and money. Somehow, from there, she met Arnold Haydon.'

'As in the original owner of one of your shipyards?'

'That's right. She was still very young, and he was in his forties. They married, but he died of a heart attack after a couple of years.'

'Gosh. She didn't have a lot of luck, did she?'

'I wouldn't say that, exactly. Through him, she'd already met Lord Moreland. She apparently offered to sell the shipyard to him, but he married her instead, and they sold the shipyard to my grandfather.'

'Well, Edie's never told me that part of the story.'

'My point is, people and their backgrounds aren't always as simple as they seem. Now you take—' The train started to slow down and Victor looked out of the window. 'This is our stop. We'd better get ready.'

—

'You reckon there's a quintet playing there today?' said Hetty, as she and Victor started the long walk down Worthing pier, towards the pavilion at its south end.

'That's right. Just some light music, in case you're wondering whether they'll be playing serious orchestral pieces.' He smiled down at her.

She returned the smile. 'My father does like his Beethoven and Paganini, though my mother is fond of waltz music. I rather liked that ragtime band that played at Sophia's party.'

'Oh yes, so did I. I kept wishing I had you to dance with.'

'Me? I don't know any of those dances.'

'They're easy enough to learn. I'll teach you one day.'

She didn't reply as it felt like an empty promise.

'On the train, you were about to tell me something before we reached our stop.' She'd expected him to carry on once they'd got off, but they'd been distracted by the shops on the way down.

'That's right. I was talking about Edie's mother, but my family have a similar tale. My great grandparents on my father's side were also of humble stock, though no one talks much about them. My great grandfather started the first business with a small boat building workshop, and he and my grandpa built it up from there.'

'What about your mother?'

'She's a retired judge's daughter, and he has a knighthood, but even his family are descended from clerks and secretaries.'

She couldn't quite take this all in, having assumed that they were a long-standing wealthy family who had been building ships for many generations. 'Life is complicated, isn't it?'

'I suppose it makes it more interesting.'

Not when you were in their position, she thought. For all his talk of humble beginnings, she knew that families who'd gained status usually wanted to increase it by uniting with other such dynasties.

'What about your family, Hetty?'

'My father trained as a teacher, initially through the pupil-teacher scheme, and then he passed the scholarship exam to go to college. His father was a clerk to a solicitor. My mother's grandfather had three grocery stores in Chichester, and he left one each to my grandfather and two great uncles. Mum's brother now runs my grandfather's one.'

'You see, your family's story isn't so very different. It's all about people trying to do better for themselves.'

She nodded, even though she thought their two stories worlds apart.

They stopped just before they reached the pavilion, gazing out west.

'Look at that,' said Victor. 'Azure sky as far as the eye can see. You know what, I think that might be the Isle of Wight there, in the distance.' He pointed out across the water.

'You can't see that from here, can you?'

'I've heard you can on a clear day.'

They stood there for a minute or two, arm in arm. Hetty was mesmerised by the sparkles of sunlight on the gentle ripples out at sea.

'Come on, we'd better get in before the concert starts,' said Victor, leading them towards the door of the pavilion.

-

A few days later, Hetty, having an hour to spare between shifts, walked over to the Belgrave to visit her brother. She'd managed to get there at some point almost every day during one of the visiting times. On each occasion he'd seemed a little better, so she was looking forward to further improvement today.

Pushing open the door to the ward, she expected to see him sitting up, reading, as he had been almost every other time, but he was lying down. When she reached him, she saw that his eyes were closed.

'Hector? Are you awake?'

He slowly opened his eyes and looked up at her. He seemed drowsy.

'Didn't you get much sleep last night?' she asked, leaning over him.

'Not really. I was in a bit of pain. Still am.'

'Shall I call a nurse?'

'They already know about it.'

'Is everything all right?' She gave his shoulder the once over, but all she could see was a clean bandage. It perhaps looked slightly swollen, but she wasn't sure.

'Have they said why it might be hurting again?'

'It hadn't really stopped hurting, but it does feel a bit more painful. They said it could just be my body, healing.' He closed his eyes once more.

She sat in the chair by his bed. 'Do you want to talk, or would you rather rest?'

'Tell me what you've been doing since you last came. I'd like to hear, though I may not be very responsive.'

'Very well.' She started off, trying to make what had been a boring couple of days sound as interesting as she could, but soon she could hear a gentle snoring as he dropped off.

Stopping mid-sentence, she wondered what to do next. She decided to stay for the time she'd originally intended in case he awoke once more. On the bedside table was the book he'd been reading, *A Portrait of the Artist as a Young Man*, by James Joyce. She picked it up and flicked through it.

A few minutes later, a nurse passed by, so she attracted her attention.

'Excuse me, my brother told me that he's in more pain again and seems overly tired. Is he all right?'

'There doesn't seem to be anything too untoward at the moment, but we're keeping an eye on him.' The nurse smiled and moved on.

The explanation didn't reassure her as much as the woman had maybe hoped. Hetty sat back down and looked closely at her brother. His facial expression was relaxed, though he looked a little paler than normal. Maybe being tired was down to being confined to bed and not being able to move around, which might explain the pain too. She'd felt like that when she'd had influenza a few years back and had been in bed for a week.

The nurse said there was nothing *too* untoward. So, there was something? And 'at the moment', as if she expected whatever it was to develop. Hetty was probably reading too much into it. Nevertheless, she would continue to come over to see him whenever she could.

–

Hetty couldn't wait for her shift to be over, and she'd spent the morning looking up at the clock every few minutes. It has been two weeks since she'd seen Victor properly, although they had met for an hour on three evenings.

The long hand finally hit half past twelve and Hetty smiled to herself as she undid her apron.

'Hope that live-out isn't late again,' said Tilly, just as the young stillroom maid assistant came through the door.

'Phew, just in time,' she said. 'Sorry if I've held you up, Hetty.'

'Not at all,' said Hetty, glad to be a few seconds closer to seeing Victor. They'd arranged to meet at the other end of the promenade from the pier, as it was always less busy. But she'd have to beg his indulgence for half an hour later on, as she wanted to pop in to see how Hector was today.

She was just opening the door to the corridor, on the way to her room to change, when Helen appeared around the corner from her office, looking worried.

'Hetty, good, I've caught you. I'm afraid there's just been a telephone call from your father saying that your brother has taken a turn for the worse.'

Hetty, feeling a little dizzy, placed her hand on the wall to support herself. 'Oh no. I thought he didn't look well when I saw him yesterday. Poor, poor Hector. What – what should I do?' She put her hand to her mouth as she felt the tears sting her eyes.

'Your mother is at Belgrave House, sitting with him, and she wants you to come. Your father has asked that you postpone your afternoon out with Phoebe.'

'Yes, yes, of course.' That was the story she'd told her parents. 'I'll get changed and go straight away.'

'If you need time off to be with him, just say and we'll rearrange the rotas.'

'I–I'll see what they say.'

As she ran up the stairs, she thought of Victor. What would he think if she didn't turn up? But it wasn't far to that end of the promenade; she could run there quickly to explain, and then get back to the hospital.

—
.

Victor looked surprised when he noticed Hetty running towards him. Others looked at her as if she were being unlady-like, but she didn't care. When she reached him, she took several breaths.

'Whatever is wrong, Hetty?'

'I–I can't stay. My brother's taken a turn for the worse, and I need to be with him.'

He looked genuinely regretful as he said, 'Oh Hetty, I'm so sorry. Of course you must be with him.'

'I have half an hour between half-past five and six on Wednesday, if you can make it. And if I'm not with Hector.'

'I'll be here. If you don't turn up, I'll understand.'

'Thank you, Victor.'

She turned and ran back the other way, wishing so much that she could hug him, but they'd not done anything like that so she couldn't be so presumptuous.

Reaching the pavement outside the hospital five minutes later, she slowed down to get her breath, and her courage. What was she going to find? She let out a moan, propelling herself forward towards the door.

Inside, she wondered whether he would still be in the same ward, so stopped a VAD nurse to ask.

'Lieutenant Affleck, ah yes, he's been put in a side ward. Let me show you. Your mother is there, but neither of you will be able to stay for long.'

The room was small, with only one other bed, in which lay another man.

Her mother stood when she entered, her face creased with anxiety. 'Henrietta,' she whispered. 'Thank goodness.'

'How is he? What happened?' She stood by his bed, looking down at the sleeping figure. On his shoulder, arm and chest were pieces of gauze that were soaked in some kind of liquid.

'He started to get worse last night, complaining of more pain, and they noticed there was swelling around the wound and some discharge. Then he developed a fever. They think the wound has become infected.'

'Infected? What, sepsis?' When Charlie had been on leave, he'd mentioned soldiers getting this from wounds, and she knew it could be fatal. 'He wasn't so well yesterday when I visited, but the nurse didn't seem to think it was anything untoward. I don't understand. He was injured weeks ago. He was getting better.'

'These things happen sometimes, they said. At least they can treat it with this antiseptic.' She pointed to the gauze.

'Will it make him better?'

'They said time will tell.'

Hetty leant over to look more closely at her brother. 'He looks hot and is sweating.'

'That's the fever.'

Hetty went to take his hand, but her mother pulled her away. 'We're not allowed to touch him.'

The nurse who'd shown Hetty in returned. 'I'm afraid you'll have to leave now ladies, as we need to change the dressings.'

'Can we come back later, for this evening's visiting hour?' asked Miriam.

'I'm afraid not. You can come back tomorrow but will only be able to stay a short while again, to limit any further infection.'

'But, but…' Miriam seemed lost for words, which seldom happened.

'Come on, Mum. Let's get you home and let Dad know how things are.'

She nodded meekly, allowing Hetty to lead her out. She hadn't even scolded Hetty for calling her 'Mum' in public.

Chapter Thirteen

On Wednesday, Hetty did manage to meet Victor. It was gloomy and breezy as they walked in the direction of the pier, but she was glad of the fresh air, and of a chance to see him. There was hardly anybody about.

'I visited him for twenty minutes this afternoon,' Hetty said, answering Victor's query about Hector. 'He's stable, but things could still change.' She didn't even like to consider that option, but it had to be said.

Victor took her hand. Its warmth and softness was comforting. 'I'm so sorry, Hetty. I know they sound like hollow words, especially as I don't know him, but I really am. I wish there was something I could do, but I guess he's in the best place and they'll do all they can. One of my friends got to convalesce at the Belgrave, after being shot in the foot, and thought the staff very good.' He paused for a while, looking at the sky. 'I so often feel guilty about what the men abroad are going through, when I got to stay home. I might be doing war work, but I'm hardly in danger.'

'You mustn't think like that, Victor. I don't think any the less of you. There are a lot of men with reserved occupations, like the coal miners in Lili's family. Their work is to do with the ships too. We need them, we need *you* to continue doing the necessary work.'

'Goodness, *I* should be encouraging *you* to be positive, not the other way around. I'm sorry.'

'Stop apologising, Victor. Just being here with you is making me feel better.'

'There has been a good deal of progress in medicine these last few years. I think the war has at least helped in that respect, if it's done nothing else.'

'It seems a high price to pay for medical advancement.'

His hummed agreement was forlorn. 'Have you heard from your other brother, Gilbert, isn't it?'

'Yes. He sent a letter yesterday. He wants to come home to see Hector, but he can't get leave.'

'That's a shame. You told me he lived in Worthing before the war, but not what he did.'

'He was a teacher.'

She talked about her siblings until they reached the pier and walked to the end.

'It's getting windier, I think,' said Victor.

'And it'll be darker a little sooner than yesterday, being dull.'

They stopped and turned towards the sea, gazing out at it.

'After so much autumn sun, it now feels like the warm part of the year is well and truly over,' said Victor.

Hetty shivered, despite having worn her winter coat. 'It is a lot colder today.'

Victor took both her hands and kissed them. The heat of embarrassment mixed with pleasure spread across her body. Her knees felt weak, so she leant towards him. He put his arm around her and pulled her in tight, his free hand taking hers. His thumb caressed her palm. They turned their heads to gaze at each other, their faces close, remaining in this position for some while.

Eventually she looked at her wristwatch: ten to six. 'It's time for me to get back to the hotel. As much as I'd love to stay here with you.' She was going to add *forever* but wasn't sure how appropriate that was.

'When your brother gets better, and you have more time, we'll have an afternoon out again somewhere. If you want to.'

'Of course I want to.'

She pulled away from him reluctantly. 'I'd better go.'

He looked at her intently, and she wondered whether he would kiss her, but he eventually stepped back.

'I can meet briefly on Sunday for half an hour, between four thirty and five o'clock, but I'd better go with my mother to the hospital on Monday.'

'I understand. Let's meet the same place we did today.'

'All right.'

Her steps were reluctant as she walked away, but she had no choice. She looked back once when she reached the promenade. He was still on the pier, looking out to sea.

Hetty was in a world of her own as she passed the gun battery mound, until she spotted an old-fashioned brown coat and an extravagant hat. It was Lady Blackmore walking in a similar direction, towards the coastguard cottages, the only other person around. She hadn't seen her since all the fuss about the libellous letters.

Lady Blackmore looked away, saving Hetty the dilemma of whether to greet her or not. Time was getting on, so she sped up, breaking out in a run once she reached the common.

–

It had been quiet on the desk today, where Edie was coming to the end of a shift. With the gloom and cold, people seemed intent on staying in their rooms, or gathering around the fire in the guest lounge, rather than asking for advice about trips out or requesting a motor taxi. Gertie was likewise unemployed, standing by the front doors.

Edie was flicking through the reservation book, thinking about who would be arriving in the next week, when the door opened and a familiar figure stepped in, wearing a drab brown coat.

Gertie sounded rather surprised as she said, 'Good evening, Lady Blackmore.'

She ignored the portress and marched across the foyer to the desk. In her hand was an umbrella which she tapped on the ground to emphasise her words as she said, 'I wish to speak to Mrs Bygrove.'

The grandfather clock in the room struck six.

'One moment, my lady, and I will take you to her office. I'm just waiting— ah, here he is.'

Richard Watkins, smart of suit with immaculate hair as always, stepped through the door and took her place behind the desk.

'This way, my lady.'

Edie led Lady Blackmore through the door at the back of the desk area, which led directly onto the small corridor on which the manager's office was situated. She knocked, relieved when Helen's voice replied immediately.

Inside, Lady Blackmore was invited to sit down, while Edie stood next to where Helen was seated.

'I'll come straight to the point. I was out for a walk, and I saw one of your maids cavorting with James Perryman's son on the pier. It was one of your stillroom maids, I believe, as I've seen her bring trays of tea to the conservatory on occasion.'

Edie glanced at Helen, knowing it had to be Hetty.

'What exactly do you mean by "cavorting"?' Helen asked.

'Holding hands. And he had his arm around her.'

'And by James Perryman's son, you are referring to Victor?'

'Victor, yes, that's his name.'

Helen linked her hands on the desk. 'I always consider my staff's personal relationships as none of my business, Lady Blackmore, as long as it doesn't interfere with their work.'

'But, but, she's crossing a *boundary*! A guest at a prestigious hotel and a mere maid.'

Edie stepped in at this point, feeling that the older woman might give her opinion, as an 'Honourable', more credence, even if she didn't use the title anymore. 'Hetty is the daughter of the well-respected headmaster of Lyminster Council School.'

'I didn't know that, but it's hardly aristocracy.'

'And neither are the Perrymans.' *And being a mere 'lady' is hardly aristocracy, either*, thought Edie, but didn't say it.

'If you'd allow *us* to deal with the matter,' said Helen, 'we would be grateful if you said nothing to anybody else about this.'

'That is rich, coming from an establishment where rumours were rife about my relationship to Cecelia.'

'That was nothing to do with us, but was due to Miss Harvey, who caused a great deal of trouble for us too. Especially me. You must appreciate that it's not nice for people to gossip about situations they know nothing about.'

'I will of course keep this situation with the maid to myself and I, in turn, would be obliged if you did not believe anything that Cecelia might tell people when she comes in for morning coffee or afternoon tea.'

'As far as I'm aware, she has only been in once.' Helen looked up at Edie, who nodded in confirmation.

Lady Blackmore stood abruptly. 'I will be on my way, so I can get home before it gets dark.'

'I'll show you out,' said Edie.

'No need.' With that, she was gone.

'What on earth was that all about?' said Helen. 'I wonder if Hetty was really holding hands with Victor Perryman. She'd probably just come across him and was passing the time of day.'

'Well, I do happen to know...' Edie began, not knowing how to explain this. 'I do know that they're friends and meet up for an afternoon off sometimes. But I'm not aware of it going any further.'

'I thought that she and Lorcan were sweethearts.'

'Not really, not anymore. I think they were going to see how they felt after the war.'

'I see. Why do people's lives have to be so complex?'

'Like yours and mine?' Edie quipped, her head to one side.

Helen smiled. 'Well, yes.'

'How is Detective Inspector Toshack?'

'Oh, do refer to him as Sam when we're alone. And he's very well. I suppose there's gossip about us too.'

'There is some talk among the staff about whether you two are walking out.'

'I bet there is. Well, I dare say we'll come clean at some point. But it's only been six months since Douglas died. In fact, six months to the day.'

'It seems so much longer ago.'

'It does to me too, sometimes. At other times, the whole horror of those months feels like yesterday.'

'As far as Hetty and Victor Perryman are concerned,' said Edie, 'I didn't feel in a position to interfere, especially given my own situation.'

'I honestly don't think it's our business, but I suppose we should speak to her... I was wondering, whether Lady Blackmore's intention in coming here was really to make sure that we didn't believe anything Cecelia might say. She seemed to think she'd been here several times.'

'She might have been rooting for information.'

'Do you suppose it is true, that Cecelia is really her sister?' said Helen.

'Yes, I do. Cecelia said as much to Simon, which I overheard, and I see no reason why she should lie.'

'No, I agree... Now, I suppose we'd better speak to Hetty before the stillroom gets busy this evening.'

–

Hetty stood in the office, convinced she'd been invited in so they could ask about her brother's progress. Her heart sank when they told her about Lady Blackmore's visit.

'I did see her by the gun battery mound, but I hadn't realised she'd seen the two of us. I arranged to meet him today for half an hour, because we'd not been able to, well...'

'It's all right, Hetty, you're not in trouble. And I know that Edie was aware of the friendship.'

'We weren't able to meet on my afternoon off, because of my brother.'

'How is Hector? You saw him briefly this afternoon, didn't you?'

'He's the same. "Stable", they call it.'

'That's something.'

'Do you want me to stop seeing Victor?' It would break her heart, but losing her job would be bad too. Maybe she could become a Land Army girl, like Phoebe, and then her job wouldn't clash with their relationship.

'No, Hetty,' said Helen. 'I haven't asked you in here to dismiss you, or even to reprimand you, just to ask you to proceed with caution. Do either of your families know about it?'

'No. We wanted to see how it would develop. It might come to nothing.'

'Then you have to be careful about people seeing you, otherwise it might well get back to them, before you're ready to face them.'

'I thought that socialising with guests was frowned upon.'

'It's not as if he's staying here. And besides… this war, it's changed things.'

Hetty wondered if she was thinking about Edie and Charlie, and even herself and DI Toshack.

'I agree,' said Edie. 'I can't see society ever being the same again.'

'You'd better get back to the stillroom,' said Helen. 'Dinner will be starting soon, and drinks will be required.'

Hetty left the office, pondering Edie's statement about society never being the same again. She wasn't so sure. Once the war was over and the men came home, people would soon forget how brave they'd been and how the women had stepped up to the mark. The women, and the lower classes generally, would be put back in their little boxes. The 'all in it together' sentiment, would soon disappear.

Would she and Victor survive the end of the war? She was sure that it would only be a matter of time before they decided they couldn't see one another again.

In the corridor, she met Nurse Bolton.

'Don't forget there's another first aid lesson this evening, after supper, Hetty.'

She would rather have sat with her book, or daydreamed about Victor, but she'd better join in.

Chapter Fourteen

Hetty had managed to visit her brother in hospital every day, if only for five minutes. Little had changed, but at least his condition hadn't worsened.

She was sitting beside him on Friday, in between the lunch and afternoon tea shifts, when she heard a slight croaky moan. She'd been looking out of the window at the time but was soon standing and leaning over to get a better look.

'What's happening?' he said in a raspy voice, trying to open his eyes.

'Hector, you're awake.' She went to touch his hand but thought better of it.

'This isn't the room I was in? What's all this wet stuff on me?'

'You got an infection, Hector. You've been out for the count for four days.'

'Four days? What day is it?'

'Friday October the nineteenth.'

'Ooh.' He squeezed his eyelids shut for a moment, then tried to sit up, but only managed to get his head slightly off the pillow.

'No, Hector, stay still. I'll get someone.' She rushed away, soon finding the nurse who had showed her the way the first time she'd visited Hector.

'It's my brother, he's woken up,' she said in a panic.

'Calm down, Miss Affleck. Now let's have a look at him.'

Back in the ward, Hector was trying to lift his head to look around.

'Now Lieutenant Affleck, you lie back and relax. It looks like you've turned a corner. You are looking a lot better.' She turned to Hetty. 'I'd better get the doctor. He's just doing his rounds of the wards. Please stay while I'm gone but then I'm afraid you'll have to leave.'

When the nurse left, Hetty said, 'Welcome back to the land of the living. We were all so worried. I'll ask Mrs Bygrove if I can telephone Mum and Dad when I get back to the hotel, to let them know.' She heard the doctor's voice approaching. 'I'll wait outside to see what they say.'

Hetty was excited at the thought of meeting Victor by the pier on Sunday afternoon, with such good news about her brother to share.

She arrived first at their rendezvous for a change, but Victor arrived only a couple of minutes later.

'You look happy,' he said. 'There must be good news.'

'Hector woke up on Friday, when I went to see him, and now he's recovering well. I've just been to see him today, and he's sitting up.'

'That *is* good news. I'm so happy for you, Hetty. Have you got time for a walk, or do you want to get back to him?'

'Visiting time is over now, so I can't. As it is, they've been quite generous with letting me in at odd times the last couple of days, to fit in with my breaks. Let's go for that walk. I was surprised to see the sun again today, and it's quite mild, after what we said about it getting colder last time.'

'It's almost as if the weather's reflecting your emotions, and now your brother's better, you feel sunny again.'

'Oh Victor, I'm not a poem,' she laughed.

He looked at her curiously. 'Do you read poetry?'

'Sometimes. My father's a teacher, remember, and used to encourage us to read all sorts of things, not just novels.'

She'd been stalling bringing up a subject she'd rather have ignored, but she'd have to tell Victor what happened.

'After we met last time…'

'What about it?'

She told him about Lady Blackmore spotting them and going to the hotel to tell the manageress.

When he looked a little panic struck, she quickly added, 'But Mrs Bygrove has said that she isn't going to interfere, and has simply cautioned us to be careful until, until, well, we decide what to do, or tell our families.'

'That's good of her.'

'I think, with Edie's situation with Charlie...' It wasn't until she said his name, that it occurred to her that not many people outside of the hotel staff knew about their relationship.

'You mean Charlie the porter?'

'Oh dear, I shouldn't really say.'

'You can trust me, Hetty. I won't breathe a word to anyone.'

'You know Edie's situation, but what you don't know is that she is in a romantic relationship with Charlie. I don't think Edie's parents know about him.'

'Are you thinking that their situation is a bit like ours, only the other way around?'

'Yes, it has occurred to me.'

He stopped and indicated the seat, and they sat down.

'It's *not* like our situation, Hetty. I'm not a baron's son, and I'm not about to give up my life. Yes, our family moves in certain social circles, but I am going to decide for myself who I fall in love with, who I marry, not have it foisted upon me.'

Fall in love with? Marry? Did he mean...? No, he was simply illustrating that he was his own man. But was he?

'We all think that, Victor. I think it too, with my mother's efforts to introduce me to boring men who I don't want to spend five minutes with, let alone decades. But the higher up in society we are, the less choice we have, I reckon.'

'Times have changed, Hetty.'

'So people keep saying. I'm not so sure... I'm sorry, what a miserable piece I'm being today. I only wanted to tell you about Lady Blackmore and how we should be careful.'

'Shall we take a walk by the water? Or would you rather not in your shoes?'

'I have my sturdy footwear on, so yes.' She lifted her leg to show the laced boots.

They didn't have to walk far across the beach to the high tide. Once they'd reached the water's edge, they headed east once more.

'I don't have much longer before I need to go back,' she said.

'I need to get back soon anyway. My parents have invited people to dinner, and I need to bathe and change first. I think it's just people from the local businesses, so no doubt it will be a drab affair. I'd rather be having dinner with you.'

She took his arm lightly, wanting to enjoy the few minutes they had left. 'I'm afraid I will have to accompany my mother to the hospital on my afternoon off tomorrow, but now my brother's getting better, I'm going to do my best to see you next Monday.'

'I'll look forward to it.'

—

Victor considered himself in the mirror, smoothing down his thick, auburn hair, which could be a tad unruly, especially as it had a wave to it that he was always trying to get rid of. Goodness knows why his mother had insisted on him wearing his evening suit, though apparently that's what they'd all be wearing. He normally only wore that at events outside the house.

He undid the bowtie and re-tied it. That was better. There shouldn't be any cause for complaint from either of his parents about his appearance now. Hopefully the guests wouldn't stay too long into the evening, but you could never tell. If he got bored of their business talk, or the women's chatter trying to outdo each other with news of their charity work, he'd pretend he was listening and wander off into a daydream about Hetty instead.

He hadn't been downstairs five minutes, when the first of the guests started to arrive. He was surprised to see not just the wife of a local businessman, which he'd expected, but their daughter too.

Oh no, surely this wasn't another of his parents' match-making attempts? Well, it wasn't going to work, so they'd just have to be disappointed.

They entered the drawing room for sherry, and other guests started to arrive, including two other young women. He shook his head a tiny amount as he poured himself another sherry. He'd need it.

The last couple in were Mr and Mrs Russell-Stone, ahead of their daughter, Rosetta, with whom he'd danced at the Raynolts' party the month before. He would be sure to sit at the opposite side of the table to her, so that he could tell Hetty that he'd done just that.

'Victor, how lovely to see you again,' said Rosetta, planting a kiss on his cheek.

He was taken aback, not knowing how to respond. Why did she think she could be so familiar? Because they knew each other vaguely and they'd had a few dances?

Barbara came over smiling, taking Victor's arm on one side and Rosetta's on the other. 'Dinner is ready, so you two can escort me in.'

He didn't like the sound of that. Sure enough, once in the dining room, his mother made it impossible for him to do anything but sit next to Rosetta, who was chatting away about a dress fitting she'd been to earlier that day. Sophia, sitting opposite him, raised her eyebrows faintly at him, prob-ably guessing what he was thinking: it was going to be a long evening.

–

As they waited for dessert, Rosetta started talking about a theatre production she'd seen in London recently, called *Chu*

Chin Chow. This, at least, was a little more interesting to Victor than much of the conversation so far.

'You'd recommend it then?' he said.

'Oh yes, absolutely. It's a musical based on *Ali Baba and the Forty Thieves*. Do you like the theatre then, Victor?'

'He loves it, don't you?' his mother replied for him, sitting on his other side.

'As it happens, I do like it, yes. But I can reply for myself, Mother.'

Rosetta threw back her head and laughed. 'Mummy does that to me as well, don't you, Mummy?' She looked over at her mother, a highly fashionable woman in her forties, sitting at one end of the oval table.

'That's what we mothers are for,' she replied, laughing in return.

'If you both like the theatre, why not go and see something together,' Barbara suggested. 'Victor never gets out socially since his friends enlisted.'

'That's not true, Mother,' said Sophia. 'Victor and I have been to the theatre a few times in the last two or three years.'

'It's a splendid idea, nonetheless,' Mrs Russell-Stone agreed.

'Wonderful!' Rosetta declared. 'When shall we go?'

'Well, I—' Victor couldn't think of an excuse. He was sure if he mentioned work, his father, now taking an interest in the conversation, would contradict anything he had to say. This was confirmed a moment later.

'Why don't you go to the Theatre Royal in Brighton? Someone was telling me the other day that there's a very good comedy playing, called, um, what was it? *What a Catch*, that was it. If it's still on.'

'Oh yes!' said another young woman. 'It is still on, because my cousin said she saw it last week.'

'That's settled then,' said Barbara, though she was frowning slightly and he wondered why. She soon picked up. 'I will telephone tomorrow to reserve tickets. When would be convenient?'

'Tuesday evening,' Rosetta said without hesitation.

'Tuesday evening it is.' Barbara looked most pleased with herself.

'And you can borrow the motorcar, rather than take the train,' James added.

'Top notch!' Rosetta declared.

Victor felt like crawling under the table, and he wished, more than ever, that the evening was over.

–

Victor had done little but try to think of a way to get out of the theatre trip for the last two days, but it was no good; there was nothing he could come up with that wouldn't be interpreted as rudeness on his part.

They'd now arrived in Brighton, and he was finding a space to park not far from the theatre. Rosetta had done nothing but twitter on about her dresses, the latest fashion, something silly her friend had done. Finally, he tuned out and thought about Hetty instead, not least how he would explain this to her. Was it time for him to introduce her to his parents? Yet how?

'So, are we going?' said Rosetta, obviously expecting him to get out and open her door.

'Yes, yes, of course.' He got out and did his duty, under the light of a streetlamp.

On the way to the theatre, she linked her arm through his, which he wasn't at all happy about. When they had to walk around a large group of people, he took the opportunity to retrieve his arm, and made sure she didn't have the opportunity to take his again before the theatre loomed into sight. He paid for the tickets and bought a programme before they deposited their coats at the cloakroom and made their way upstairs.

His mother had reserved them good seats, in the front row of the royal circle, towards the centre.

'I've been looking forward to this since Sunday,' Rosetta said, sitting elegantly in her silk gown. 'It's meant to be *frightfully* funny.' She took his hand as he sat back.

How to retrieve it without being rude? He waited until the lights dimmed, before leaning forward as if to adjust his jacket. When he sat back, he linked his hands in front of him.

–

'That was a *terrific* evening,' Rosetta said, as he pulled up outside her house in Lyminster.

Did she always have to exaggerate everything? Whatever she did seemed to be *top notch*, *wonderful*, *terrific*, or something equally overstated. It was a huge contrast to Hetty's composure and lack of affectation.

She leant forward to kiss him on the cheek, and he let it go. But when she then aimed for his mouth, he pulled away.

'Whatever is the matter, darling?'

'Darling?'

'Oh, I call everybody darling. Ask my friends. I don't mean it like *that*. Well, not yet. But why won't you let me kiss you?'

'We've only been to the theatre, we're not courting. It's not appropriate.'

'You do surprise me.' She leant back a little, opening her unbuttoned coat and lifting her already short skirt above her knee, to reveal around a third of her thigh. 'Young men normally love me to be forward and take advantage of it.'

He wondered how far they took advantage of it, and exactly what kind of woman she was. 'It would be disrespectful.'

She grinned and looked coy. 'Your diffidence only makes me all the more interested. After all, you're a handsome man, with your lovely auburn hair.' She gave it a ruffle. 'Not to mention those big brown eyes and that rather fetching tall, slim figure of yours.'

'I think you'd better go in, before your parents realise we're just sitting here and wonder what we're up to.'

'They wouldn't bother. They think I'm big enough to look after myself. And I'm sure they'd be quite happy for me to be *up to something*, since they've despaired of me ever settling down with a young man.'

'Good night, Rosetta. I'm glad you enjoyed the play.'

'Ooh, a dismissal. Very authoritative. I will see you soon, darling.'

He got out of the motorcar and went around to her side to let her out, watching as she entered the large, double gate and walked down the pathway to her house. When she reached the door, he got back in the motorcar and set off immediately.

As he passed Lyminster School, back in Wick, he slowed down and looked up at it, even though it was mostly in darkness. The fact that Hetty had lived there was enough to give him a small tingle of joy before he carried on home.

–

His mother was excited when he got home, coming out into the hall to meet him.

'How did it go then?'

'The play was reasonably entertaining.'

'That's not what I meant. When are you seeing Rosetta again?'

'I'm not seeing her again. There was no future meeting mentioned.' Apart from her 'see you soon'. That hardly counted.

'Oh Victor, what did you do wrong?' She looked cross.

'Nothing. We went as friends, that's all. She's not even my type, Mother.'

'Then what *is* your type? You never seem interested in any girls. Are you… you're not, that is, um, you're not the *other* way inclined, are you?'

'No Mother, I'm not. Just because I'm not interested in the kind of women you're always trying to palm me off with, doesn't mean I'm— Look, it's late and I'm tired, Mother. I've got an early start tomorrow, so good night.'

Barbara tutted and went back to the drawing room, closing the door behind her. He could hear her saying something to someone, no doubt displaying her disappointment to his father or sister, or both. Let her. He climbed the stairs and looked forward to sleep, perchance to dream. Of Hetty, not Rosetta.

Chapter Fifteen

When Hetty visited the hospital five days after Hector had awoken, she was delighted to find him back in the ordinary ward, taking a little walk.

'Hector! You're looking even better than when I came yesterday.'

'I feel so much better, too. I think sitting up a couple of days ago made me feel human again.'

'I'm so glad to hear that.'

He sat on the edge of his bed, while Hetty took the chair. 'I've had enough of hospitals. They've been very good to me here, but I can't wait to get out.'

'Do you know when that might be?'

'They reckon the infection has gone, but they want to keep me here for a few more days to make sure. Then I can go home, and Mum says she'll nurse me there until I'm completely better.'

'Oh dear.' They both laughed.

'Yes, well, I haven't got a lot of choice. I suppose I should be glad I've got a home to go to and recuperate. Her fussing is only because she wants the best for us.'

'It doesn't make it any the less annoying though.'

She told him about the afternoon with the local vicar.

'Heavens above, she tried to match you up with Reverend Peck? I met him once when I was on leave. Such a disdainful person, and a cold fish.'

'Quite. Do you have any idea what will happen when you're completely well?'

'There's talk of giving me a home posting, perhaps at Shoreham camp. They have clerical positions, or I could even be involved in training.'

'Lili's sweetheart, Rhodri, went there to do clerical work, after he'd recuperated here.'

'He was the one with the leg wound, wasn't he?'

'That's right.'

'Is he still there?'

'No, he chose to go back to France and do a clerical post there.'

'I suppose that could be an option.'

'Don't be too hasty,' she said, anxious now that she'd given him the idea. 'I know having a clerical job will probably seem strange to you, after so many years in the army, but it could be a new start.' She thought about what Victor had said about them always needing clerks or people in accounts. 'You could easily get a job I'm sure, especially being ex-military and an officer.'

'Don't worry, I have a while to decide.'

–

Victor was already by the library on Fitzalan Road when Hetty arrived at one o'clock. It had been a few days since she'd seen him, and just the sight of him caused a small thrill to run through her.

His wide smile when he spotted her made her feel a little giddy as she approached him.

'I thought we might go to the picture house today, if you're agreeable,' he said. 'The Electric Picture Palace is showing *A Tale of Two Cities*, and it's meant to be very good.'

'I saw in the newspaper that they'd made it into a film. I'd love to know how they've managed it. I read it at school.'

'That's settled then.'

They started off, walking towards the town, the blue sky of earlier covered now with a few clouds.

'It'll be dark inside, but what if someone who knows one of us sees us going in?' she said.

He narrowed his lips, seeming a little perturbed by this question. 'We'll deal with that if it happens... There is something I'd like to tell you though.'

His brow creased a little more, worrying her as to what it might be.

'I, um,' he started. 'I had to take a young woman to the theatre last Tuesday.'

'Had to?'

'That dinner my parents had, they'd invited several young women, including Rosetta Stone, and made it so I had to sit next to her. When we both admitted we liked the theatre, they suggested we attend together and my mother went ahead and reserved seats. It was rather a fait accompli.'

Hetty didn't know how to feel about this. It didn't look like he'd been too enthusiastic, but she needed to know a little more.

'Where did you go?'

'The Theatre Royal, in Brighton, to see some mildly amusing comedy.'

'You didn't enjoy it then?'

'No. It was awkward, to say the least. My father insisted I take the motorcar so I could drive us, and I had her wittering on the whole time.'

'What, *wittering* because she's a woman? That's not a very nice thing to say.'

'No, not because she's a woman. Because she just talked constantly, about clothes, shopping, her friends. And she was rather... forward.'

'What do you mean?'

'She tried to kiss me when we got to her house afterwards.'

'What did you do?'

He looked at her in surprise. 'Turned away, of course.'

'Will you be going out again?'

'Of course not, Hetty. Well, not willingly. I'll have to look out for my parents trying to inveigle me into one of their matchmaking schemes again.'

'We've always got that option of introducing her to Reverend Peck.'

Even though they both laughed at this, the confession from Victor had spoiled the day a little for her.

--

When they emerged from the picture house, the clouds were covering the sky, bringing dusk a little early.

'That was most enjoyable,' Victor said, doing up his coat.

'Yes, it was.'

'It's starting to drizzle a little. There's a café just up the road here. Do you fancy a pot of tea and some cake?'

'That would be nice.'

The café was able to serve them tea but had no cakes available.

'Shall we go elsewhere?' Victor asked.

'No, just tea will be fine.' This was something she was sure they were going to have to get used to, sooner or later, even at the hotel.

After the tea arrived, he asked, 'When can you meet up next?'

'I'm not sure. I can't meet you next Monday. I really should go home, as my brother will be there by then. The Monday after, I'm meeting Phoebe.'

'You seem a little upset. Is it because of my trip out with Miss Stone?'

'No,' she said, but knew that it had made her a little anxious. 'It's not long until we have to part company again, that's all. There's a new rota for November, but I know I'm not working the afternoon tea shift this Friday. I could meet you at three o'clock, if you can get time off work.'

'I'll make sure I can. I always make it up by working in the evening, or on Sunday. Let's meet at the library again.'

'I'll have a look at the rota to see what other times there might be that we could meet, if you want to.'

'Of course I do.'

When the pot was empty, Victor said, 'I suppose I'd better get back to the workshop, see how the latest order is coming along.'

'And I don't want to be late for early dinner, as I'm working a long shift tonight.'

They left and took the route down Surrey Street, past the shops and Read's Dining Rooms, walking a little apart so it didn't look like they were together. On Pier Road, they parted, he going right to Fisherman's Quay, she carrying on down the road towards the beach. With a group of people passing them as they reached that point, they had no choice but to simply wave goodbye to each other.

Hetty tried not to think about the fashionable and pretty Rosetta Stone as she made her way back to South Terrace, but the woman's lively figure dancing with Victor kept coming into her mind all the way back to the hotel.

–

Victor could have kicked himself as he walked over the pebbles to the workshop. Perhaps he shouldn't have mentioned Rosetta, but he wanted to be absolutely honest with Hetty. If she'd found out from someone else, he would have looked like a cad.

As he approached the door to his office, he groaned inwardly. Through the window he could see his father, who at that moment looked out and frowned at him. He opened the door, indicating with his head for Victor to come in.

'Where have you been, boy?'

'Boy?' Victor muttered. 'I'm not a child, Father, and I'd appreciate it if you didn't treat me like one in front of the staff.'

He looked over to where the clerk and the secretary sat at their desks. 'Come upstairs.'

Victor led the way. Once up there, he was aware that the openness of it would mean they could hear downstairs if he talked too loudly, so he half whispered. He took his coat off and hung it on the stand.

'It was my afternoon off, so I went for a walk. You know I always make up any shortfall in my time in the evening if I need to.'

James placed his bowler hat on a nearby table that had blue-prints on it.

'But the men aren't here in the evening and need to be managed during the day.'

'Keep your voice down. We don't need everyone hearing. They know what they have to do at the moment, and I was only dealing with paperwork this afternoon. The office staff had plenty to get on with. I was only gone a couple of hours, and I am entitled to the odd afternoon off.'

'But it's not the first time you've gone missing during the day, and often when it's not your afternoon off.'

'I haven't gone "missing", as you put it. Is the work being done any the less because I've popped out for a while?'

'That's not the point. You should be *here*.' He slapped his hand on Victor's desk to illustrate his point.

'Why are you even here, Father?'

'Just seeing how things are getting on.'

'You mean, checking up on me. When have I ever let you down? When has the work here never been done?'

'Well, we want to keep it that way. Now, don't be late for dinner.'

'Mother isn't having another of her dinner parties, is she?'

'No, but you know she likes us all to be there on time.'

'You've missed a few dinners yourself recently, catching up with work.'

'Well, I have a great deal to do, running the workshops over the river, along with overseeing all the businesses. You'll understand one day. I'll see you later.'

His father picked up his hat and left. Soon Victor heard the outer door close. He breathed out a sigh of relief. If his father was going to keep checking up on him, it would make it difficult to get out the odd time to see Hetty. He'd have to work something out.

–

By Thursday, Victor was really looking forward to seeing Hetty the following afternoon. He'd thought of nothing else all week. He'd already told his secretary that he'd be popping out for a meeting with Mr Timpson, who ran the firm they sent the hulls to a few miles down the coast in Middleton. If his father called by, that's what she could tell him. He hated lying, but he still wasn't sure how to handle the situation of introducing Hetty to them, of telling them how he felt about her. Did she even feel the same way? She still seemed so worried about being seen about town with him, even after her manageress found out. Was she hedging her bets because she didn't know how it would work out with this chap called Lorcan? If she didn't feel the same way about him as he did her, there was no point in rocking the boat with his parents.

But he so hoped she did feel the same way.

He entered Surrey Cottage at the end of South Terrace, looking forward to dinner and being able to relax this evening, but as soon as he took off his coat, his mother was beside him, grinning in that way she did when she was about to tell him she'd got some activity planned. His heart sank.

'Victor, back with plenty of time, good.'

'Plenty of time for what?'

'To get spruced up for our dinner out this evening.'

'It's the first I've heard of it. I was hoping for a quiet—'

'Nonsense. You've been engaged in boring work all day, so a dinner out will be just the ticket.'

'Where are we going?'

'The Beach Hotel, just the family.'

That was something at least. Not some big affair at Sir or Lord Somebody-or-Other's house, or a party. And who knows, he might get a glimpse of Hetty, if she happened to bring something to the dining room.

'What time are we leaving?'

'The booking's for seven o'clock, so we'll leave at a quarter to seven.'

He was back down at six forty-five precisely. His parents were already there, waiting for him, making him feel that he was late, even though he wasn't.

'We're just waiting for Sophia now, are we?'

'No, she ate early because she has one of her charity meetings this evening.'

He nodded, already missing the possibility of her livelier conversation. Going out with his parents on his own took him back to when he was at boarding school and they'd come to take him out for the day.

Outside, James walked towards the Model T and opened it.

'We're not going in the motorcar, are we?' said Victor. 'The hotel's only up the road.'

'It might rain later,' said James. 'Better to be safe than sorry.'

At the hotel, they made their way to the dining room. Once there, James said, 'Table booked under the name of Perryman.'

'Yes sir,' said one of the young waiters he knew was called Simon. 'The first guest has already arrived.'

'First guest?' said Victor.

'This way, sir.'

'Off you go, son.'

'Aren't you coming?'

'Over here, Victor,' came a voice. He looked around to see Rosetta sitting at a table close by, wearing a beaded silk dress.

He looked at his parents, whispering. 'What's going on?'

'Off you go,' said Barbara.

He could hardly walk away and embarrass himself, and Rosetta come to that, as tempting as it was. But there would be words tonight when he got home.

'I'm leaving the motorcar, by the way,' said James. 'So you can drop Miss Stone home. And make sure you pay for her meal too.'

As if he'd expect her to pay; his father was treating him like a boy again. He followed the young lad, Simon, to the table, trying not to look as annoyed as he felt.

'Good evening, Victor. And how are you on this fine evening?'

'It's actually quite cold and starless.'

'You know what I mean.' Simon left and she leaned forward. 'It's a fine evening because I've got to see you again.'

'Did you know I was turning up?'

'Of course I did. Your mother telephoned me to arrange this, saying that you were too shy to do so yourself, you dear boy.'

'I said no such thing to—'

'There's no need to be bashful. Though I do find it rather fetching.' She treated him to an indulgent grin. 'Now what are you having?'

He should just get up and walk away. It would be his parents' fault if this turned into a humiliating situation. But he couldn't do that. It wasn't Rosetta's fault, after all, and it would be her who'd be humiliated. He'd make it clear at the end of the evening that this was going no further.

He only hoped Hetty didn't get wind of it before he had a chance to tell her.

—

'I am so glad my shift is over.' Hetty slumped onto the bench around the table in the staff dining room, making sure she was next to the fire. She yawned as she leant over and poured herself a cup of tea.

'It was rather busy tonight,' said Lili, sitting opposite. 'Are there any biscuits?'

'No, I've already asked,' said Gertie, seated at one end, next to Fanny. 'They've all gone, Mrs Norris said.'

'That's the third time this week there's been no biscuits at night,' said Hetty. 'Was the dining room full this evening? We were rushed off our feet in the stillroom.'

'All but one table,' said Lili. 'Unusual that is for a Thursday in November. Oh, I do have a little bit of romantic gossip though.'

'Do tell,' said Fanny, leaning forward.

'You know that nice looking Victor Perryman, him what's James Perryman's son, what owns the shipbuilding yards.'

Hetty froze at his name. Romantic gossip?

'Oh yes, him,' said Gertie, raising her eyebrows a couple of times. 'He is rather comely.'

'Comely?' Lili laughed. 'What century do you live in, Gertie? Anyway, he was having dinner this evening with that Rosetta Russell-Stone, whose parents are big landowners. She was at the party the Raynolts held, back in September. I remember her dancing with him when that ragtime band came on. Do you remember, Hetty? We were serving champagne in the ballroom at the time.'

'There were so many people there, it's hard to recall.' She tried to sound neutral, afraid her voice would shake as she was speaking. What game was Victor Perryman playing with her?

'You reckon they're walking out then?' said Gertie.

'Looked like it to me. She had that coy little face that I often see the young women put on when they're dining with young men they're courting.'

'Perhaps there'll be wedding bells soon,' said Fanny. 'And they might hold the reception here. We 'aven't 'ad many since the war started.'

'I do love a wedding reception.' Lili had a soppy look on her face, perhaps thinking of when she might marry Rhodri.

The others giggled, and Hetty joined in, but inside she felt sick.

'You know what, I'm so tired, I think I'll take my tea upstairs,' she said.

They wished her goodnight and she left promptly. In her room, she sat on the bed and put the tea on the small cabinet. They were supposed to be meeting tomorrow, her and Victor. What should she do? She'd barely had time to consider it when the tears started falling. She placed her head on her lap and sobbed.

—

Victor stopped outside the gates of Rosetta's house in Lyminster. He could see by the light of the streetlamp that she was looking at him, waiting for what exactly he wasn't sure. To arrange another meeting?

'Thank you very much, Victor. I enjoyed the meal immensely. I always do at the Beach Hotel. Even with the shortages they produce some delicious food.' She touched his arm. 'I enjoyed your company, too.'

'That's nice.' He looked ahead.

'You know, my parents are away at the moment, if you would like to come inside.'

He did look at her now. 'No, that's all right, thank you.'

'Darling Victor, why are you being so coy? I'm a modern woman.' She moved closer to him, putting her hand on his thigh and kissing his cheek. Then the hand slowly moved upwards.

He bent away and removed her hand. 'I'm sorry, Rosetta, but I'm in love with someone else.' He was? Yes, of course he was! He had simply not couched it in those words to himself before. But doing so gave him a sense of exhilaration. He was in love!

'Then why didn't you say before?'

'Because my parents don't know, and I'm not ready to tell them.'

'My my, a secret love affair. How romantic.'

'You're not upset?'

'Do you want me to be?'

'Of course I don't. I should have told you at the theatre, but I didn't think we'd meet again.'

'Tell me, what's wrong with this love of yours, that prevents you from telling your parents? Has she two heads or something?'

He frowned. 'No, of course she hasn't. It's just – complicated.'

'It's a shame you're not interested in me, but, as they say, there are plenty more fish in the sea. Or will be, when the war's over. However, if you'd like to come in, just for a – how shall I put this? For a little *mutual enjoyment*, no strings attached, you'd be welcome.'

He knew perfectly well what she was talking about but wasn't even tempted. He'd had plenty of friends who would have taken advantage, but he wasn't one of them.

'I will decline, though thank you for the offer.'

'Oh, go on. It wouldn't hurt. Men in your position cheat on their wives and sweethearts all the time. And believe me, I should know.'

'Be that as it may—'

'I am really rather good, you know, between the sheets. And you wouldn't want your parents finding out about your two-headed lover now, would you?' She laughed raucously. 'If you're nice to me, I can guarantee I'll keep it to myself.'

This was turning a lot more unpleasant than he'd bargained for. He'd thought her a little vacuous, if fun, but he had a feeling he was seeing the real Rosetta Stone.

'Are you threatening me?'

'Just trying to encourage you, dear boy. You're the handsomest man with whom I've had a chance of a dalliance for a long while. The war certainly hasn't helped on that score. And I'm definitely in the mood, if you get my meaning.'

'Oh yes, I get your meaning. And despite your threat, I'm not going to indulge you, Rosetta. I'm not like those men who cheat on their wives.'

'Oh, you will be one day, when you tire of whoever this person is.'

He got out of the motorcar and opened the door for her. She got out elegantly and touched his cheek. 'Such a shame, but never mind. Goodnight, Victor. Don't worry, I won't bother telling anyone. It was worth a try though. Have fun with your boring little secret.'

'Goodnight Miss Stone.'

–

Despite trying to open the front door quietly, Victor's mother had clearly been listening out for him and came into the hall.

'How did it go?' she chirped like a giddy girl, taking his arm and giving him no choice but to go into the drawing room with her.

James stood on his arrival. 'Victor, my boy, how was it?'

Barbara let go of him, waiting expectantly for his answer.

'I'm afraid that Miss Stone has decided that she doesn't want to see me again.' This was the best way to go.

Barbara looked horrified. 'What on *earth* did you do? She was perfectly happy to meet you for dinner this evening.'

'I didn't *do* anything, Mother. I was perfectly polite and courteous. But that is maybe the problem. I think Miss Stone likes her gentlemen a little more… gregarious. I'm just a little too quiet for her.'

'She told you that?'

'Not in so many words. It doesn't matter either way. We will not be going out together anywhere again.'

His mother sat, sighing. 'I was so hopeful too. Hers is such a respected family, and the owners of the biggest sawmills in the area. She's an only child, so would have been worth a fortune when her father died.'

'You need to be a little more spirited, boy. More attentive to a young lady.'

'Father, will you *stop* calling me "boy". You've only started this again recently after not doing it for years. I'm twenty-seven now, and it's like you're trying to put me in my place. Especially when we're in the office.'

'It's only an affectionate term.'

'Not at my age, it's a controlling one.'

'Victor, what's got into you?' said Barbara. 'Don't be rude to your father.'

'He wanted me to be more spirited. Now, if you don't mind, I'm going to bed. And please, do not try to matchmake me with anybody else. Goodnight.'

He left his parents open-mouthed and lost for words, something that didn't often happen. Now to get to his book, and dreams of seeing Hetty tomorrow.

–

It was now three twenty, and Hetty still hadn't turned up. She was probably just late, that's all. Perhaps something had come up and she'd had to stay a bit longer to sort things out. She'd come because she always did.

Victor ignored the couple of odd looks he got, waiting so long by the gate at the end of the path to the library. He wished now he'd said to meet inside. At least then he could have looked at the books.

A few minutes later, he regarded his wristwatch once more. Half past three. How long was he going to wait?

At twenty to four he decided he'd waited long enough. If she turned up now, she'd surely understand why he wasn't here. But how was he going to get any kind of message to her? Perhaps the simplest way was to send a letter.

He walked back to the workshop via South Terrace, just in case she did come out late, though it was a longer way around. He reached the hotel, but there was no sign of her. He pulled at the neck of his coat and did the top button up. It wasn't too cold today, but it was cold in his heart, with not seeing her, and not knowing when he would again. He could walk around to the staff entrance of the hotel, he supposed. He knew that he'd only have to go through the scullery to get to the stillroom, from the way she'd described it. But what if she wasn't there? And how would he explain it to the staff who were on duty?

He looked around at the hotel. No, he'd better not. And was there any point? If something had happened, she'd probably get a letter to him like she did last time, when Edie Moore had turned up at the quay. But it could be that she'd decided on Lorcan, not him. In which case there'd be no point in him sending a letter. He carried on, convinced this was the case, and the sorrow at her loss swept over him, leaving him wretched.

Chapter Sixteen

It had been nearly a week since Hetty had failed to turn up at her rendezvous with Victor. She was still wavering every few minutes over whether she'd done the right thing, but she was slowly erring on the side of yes, however much it hurt. Wouldn't he have sent a letter if he'd been concerned? Maybe he hadn't turned up at the library either.

More than likely, he'd picked Rosetta Stone over her. Why wouldn't he? She'd always known it would come to this eventually, so what was the point in putting off the inevitable any longer?

Edie put her head around the stillroom door. 'Hetty, would you mind taking a tray of water glasses to the dining room, please? They're a little short.'

'Of course.'

She picked up a tray already prepared and went to the dining room door via the corridor. It was lunchtime and the place was half full. She looked around quickly without even thinking, knowing it was Victor she was looking for on the off chance.

Placing the tray on the dresser next to where Lili was standing, she was about to speak a couple of words to her when she was thrown off her feet and landed on the floor, broken glass scattered around her.

An explosion! That's all it could have been. An almighty explosion somewhere nearby. Women were screaming and everyone was on the floor. The glass roof, which took up a third of the dining room near the garden, seemed to be covered in something.

'What the bally heck was that?' bellowed a male voice.

'Oh dear Lord, it's the Germans on an air raid! They're bombing us,' screeched a woman, causing more screaming.

'Calm down, madam,' said Major Thomas nearby. 'Panicking isn't going to help. I suggest we make our way under the tables. That would be the safest place.'

'Hetty, your hand,' said Lili, crouching nearby.

She looked down to find it bleeding. She must have cut it on the glass. How had she not realised? But now she did, the pain came quickly.

Lili pulled a napkin down from the dresser and handed it to her. 'Put that around your hand until we can find Nurse Bolton. I'd better help the major, as people are still dithering.' She stood up. 'Ladies and gentlemen, if you'd please do as Major Thomas advises, as that is the hotel policy in these circumstances.'

'Come on, I'll help you up,' Simon told Hetty, as he pushed some of the broken glass under the dresser with his foot.

People pulled chairs out and ducked beneath the tables. The major and Ebony Girard were directing some and helping others. At the same time, there was shouting and a clatter of running footsteps coming from the foyer. They came closer until a crowd entered the dining room, many in a panic, guests and staff, including Gertie and the gardeners. There was more screaming and exclamations of panic. Hetty was relieved to see Helen and the nurse with them.

'Nurse Bolton,' Lili called, pointing to Hetty as they were about to get under a nearby table.

The nurse ran over while Helen, Major Thomas and Ebony guided the newcomers under furniture.

There was another almighty explosive sound, causing the room to vibrate once more, and more mud, or whatever it was, was thrown onto the glass. People hastened to the tables, amid more shrieking and yelling.

Under the table, Nurse Bolton unwrapped the napkin and examined Hetty's hand. 'Looks like there might still be some glass in there. I'll remove it once this is over, and I might have to suture it.'

Hetty felt sick. 'What, stitches?'

'That's right. Don't worry, it'll only need a couple.'

For a while the only sound was that of whimpering and worried whispers.

'Do you think it could be the Germans?' Lili asked Major Thomas, who was under the next table.

'Didn't hear any planes, or Zeppelins.' He looked around, then leant in closer to whisper, 'But I'm not sure what else it could be.'

Several more minutes went by before there was another explosion, causing more yells and screams. It was deafening but didn't sound any louder than the last two.

A woman under another nearby table was wailing, 'We're going to die, we're going to die,' and Hetty could see her rocking back and forth.

A terrifying thought hit Hetty. If the Germans were bombing the river to get to the Admiralty ships, they might strike Victor's workshop. He would more than likely be in the office. She felt the blood drain from her face and her hands started to shake, causing more pain where she was cut.

'It's all right, Hetty, I'm sure it'll be over soon, and we'll get you fixed up,' said Nurse Bolton, misinterpreting her reaction.

There were several smaller explosions, over the next hour or so, suggesting that, if it were some kind of air raid, the Zeppelin, or aeroplanes, were moving away. Still nobody moved.

Hetty sat with her eyes closed most of the time, praying for Victor's safety. The longer it lasted, the more she was convinced that the quay would have been struck. The men there, and Victor, would not have stood a chance. She tried not to cry, but the tears started to run down her cheeks.

'There, there,' whispered Nurse Bolton. 'Not long now.'

As the reverberation faded, they heard the telephone ring in the foyer. What a time to be ringing, thought Hetty, though the caller wasn't to know what was happening if they were from outside town. There was a distant voice, as if someone had answered it, followed a few moments later by tip-tapping footsteps on the wooden floor. Several people peeped out, including Hetty, to see Richard Watkins, the head desk clerk, enter the room.

'Quickly man, under the table,' called Major Thomas.

'No need, Major,' he said. 'I've just received a call from the port commissioners' office here in Littlehampton. It seems that the Admiralty have been using explosives to widen the harbour mouth. They've finished now.'

Hetty breathed out a long sigh, and a few more tears fell with her relief.

'They've been bally well *what*?' said a tall figure in a pin checked suit, sporting a handlebar moustache and a centre parting. He emerged from under a table near the door and stood up.

'Ah, Mr Linton. They specifically rang to ask that you and your colleagues return to the office at your earliest convenience, as they are not happy with what's occurred.'

'No, and neither am I. This wasn't sanctioned by us. They didn't even ask us. The bally nerve of them.' Mr Linton's complexion became florid with annoyance. 'And why weren't we warned? Look at the distress it's caused here. I dread to think what anguish it will have caused around the town. I shall be having words with the Admiralty. Come along gentlemen.' He led the way out, and the two other men at his table followed.

Helen was standing up by this time. She looked rather pale. Hetty realised she must have been worried about her children, at school. 'Well, ladies and gentlemen, it would appear that we are not under attack. If you would like to remain for luncheon, we would be happy to close later today.'

Guests and other staff members slowly emerged from under the tables. All the diners chose to stay, maybe wary of going outside. Simon and Lili tidied the tables as they took up their places once more.

'Mrs Bygrove,' Nurse Bolton called. 'I'm going to have to take Hetty here to tend her hand.'

'Oh my gosh, you poor thing,' said Helen. Then she noticed the glass and the upset tray by the dresser. 'I'll get one of the housemaids to come and clear that up. And don't worry about getting back to work today, Hetty. You'll need to recuperate. And you won't lose any money because of it.'

'Thank you, Mrs Bygrove.' That was a blessing at least. The stress of the explosions, the cut to her hand which was still bleeding, and worrying about Victor, had made her rather lightheaded.

Helen spotted Edie and hurried towards her. 'We'd better get the gardeners to wash the windows. What a state they are. I wonder what the rest of the outside will look like.'

Hetty looked up and out. The sludge clinging to the windows contrasted with the blue sky.

'Come along, Hetty, let's deal with your hand.' Nurse Bolton led her to the door to the staff corridor.

–

'There you are, all done,' said Nurse Bolton, tying the end of the bandage around Hetty's hand. 'And now you can have a rest. It'll be light duties for you, for the next few days.'

Hetty was still tearful from the pain of the glass removal and the insertion of the two stitches. 'B–but how will I do my job? I can't do it one-handed.'

'You can get the other stillroom maids to do anything that needs two hands. You're in charge anyway.'

'But I do a lot of the manual work.'

'You can still stir, pour, open cupboards, give orders and organise people. The cut isn't too bad and I'm sure you'll soon heal. Don't forget about my first aid lessons this evening, by the way. You can watch, even if you can't practise. Now, off you go.'

Hetty stood up warily, afraid she might feel faint, but that feeling had now passed. She left the staff dining room, taking the curved staircase up to her room carefully. She was still worried about Victor, even though the workshop was a distance from the river mouth. What if he'd been outside and hit by the debris? It wasn't as if he deserved her concern, but she couldn't suddenly stop the way she felt about him. There had to be some way of making sure he was all right.

In her room, she sat on the edge of the bed and thought for a while. There was no way she was going to get any rest, worrying the way she was. The workshop wasn't far, maybe fifteen minutes' walk. It was a sunny day, not too cold. Getting out might be better for her than sitting here fretting.

She took off her apron, which wasn't too difficult with one hand. Putting on her coat was another matter. After struggling for a while, she finally managed, though doing up the buttons proved to be a challenge.

Now, how to get out of the building without being spotted? That was impossible, but if she could avoid Nurse Bolton and Mrs Bygrove, she should be all right.

She crept down the stairs, peeping through the door into the staff corridor. Good, it was empty. She hurried to the stillroom door and peeped in before entering.

'Hetty, how's your hand?' said Tilly, looking up from pouring cordials.

'Still aching, but not so badly now.' It wasn't the truth as it still hurt quite a lot.

'I thought you had to take the rest of the day off.'

She stepped in. 'I do. I feel rather panicky and confined, sitting in my room by myself, so I'm going to get some fresh air.'

'Probably not a bad idea, though Nurse Bolton gave the impression you were confined to quarters.'

'I won't tell if you don't.'

Tilly made a cross on her chest with her finger.

Getting past Annie and Alice in the scullery had been easier than she'd thought, with them readily accepting her need for some fresh air.

'Don't blame you,' said Alice. 'Hope there are no more explosions though.'

Out of the staff exit, she hurried towards the river and the quayside, holding her injured hand to somehow protect it. There was sand and shingle all over the place, increasing in quantity as she got nearer to the river. The police were on the common, talking to someone covered in mud, who was shouting and pointing. Several people passing by were complaining about the explosions and the chaos they'd caused. When the river banks towards the mouth came in site, it looked a mess with mud, and it was hard to see whether the blasts had actually done any good in clearing it.

Ten minutes later, she passed the Britannia pub at the beginning of Fisherman's Quay and slowed down. Suddenly it didn't seem like such a good idea. What would he make of her being there? Maybe if she walked across the pebbles, to look at the water, she'd spy him in a window. Then she would know he was safe and be able to go back to the hotel. Slowing down a little more, she saw that there was no damage here, not even any sign of debris. He must be all right. She glanced at the workshop, feeling foolish now. And she'd be in trouble with Nurse Bolton if she found her missing. Looking down she considered her next move. There was no point hanging around; she'd go back to the hotel and lose herself in the D. H. Lawrence novel she was reading.

About to turn, she heard her name called. She looked up to see Victor, walking towards her. He looked at her bandage, his eyes widening, then rushed over to her.

'What have you done to your hand? Have you seen a doctor? Is that why you didn't turn up last Friday?'

'No, that's not why.'

'Did you hear the explosions? I hope you weren't out.'

'I was at the hotel and dropped a tray of glasses. That's how I got the cut. Our hotel nurse saw to it.'

'My dear,' he lifted her injured hand gently, but she pulled it away.

'I didn't turn up because I assumed you are now walking out with Miss Stone, since you were at dinner with her at the hotel last week.'

'Oh, you heard.'

'It was rather insensitive, bringing her there, knowing I might find out. But I suppose that was your way of ending our friendship.'

'No, no!' He looked pained, his face crumpling. 'Hetty, I didn't even know she was going to be there. It was a set-up.'

'What do you mean?'

'My parents told me we were having a family dinner at the hotel, but when I got there, it was revealed that it had been a ruse to get me together with Rosetta. My parents left, and I had no choice but to stay. I was furious, but I couldn't take it out on her. But I told her, when I drove her home, that I was in love with someone else. Though not who.'

'In–in love?'

'Yes, in love.' He took her uninjured hand now.

'You–you love me?' She frowned, not in annoyance but confusion. Just moments ago, she'd thought he'd forsaken her for Rosetta Stone, and now he was declaring his love. Yet, didn't she love him too? Yes, yes she did, but she couldn't get herself to say the words. Instead, she said, 'Was she very annoyed? Miss Stone?'

'A little, I think. But she doesn't seem like a terribly serious person. I think she sees relationships with men as rather a… game.'

'I see. Lili was full of it, seeing you there with her in the restaurant, when we were at supper afterwards, thinking there must be a romance going on.'

'That's how you found out then. I was going to tell you about it when we met up. I promise you, there was nothing going on.

I was *so* angry with my parents. When I got home, I told them never to interfere again. For once they were speechless.'

'I–I see.'

'Do you not feel the same way?' His face creased once more. 'Did you come here to tell me it's over? Have you chosen to wait for Lorcan instead.'

'Lorcan? No, I came to make sure that you hadn't been injured in the explosions. But our situation, it's so awkward. Should you even be here, talking to me like this? What if your staff see?'

'I'll just tell them I recognised you from the hotel and was asking how you were affected by the explosions. I presume everyone else at the hotel is all right?'

'They were dreadfully frightened, but yes. There was just a lot of mud and shingle thrown everywhere. It's all over the common too.'

'My goodness, heads are going to roll if the port commissioners have anything to do with it.'

'We had some in for lunch, and that's more or less what one of them said.'

'I should think my father will have a few things to say too. Can we meet again, soon?'

'I–I suppose. But I have a lot to think about.'

He nodded. 'Send me a letter here. If you just put my name, and not the company's name, my secretary won't open it.'

'Very well.'

'You'd better get back and rest. I'm surprised they let you out.'

'They didn't. Nurse Bolton told me to rest, but I was too worried, so I sneaked out.'

'Oh Hetty, you dear, sweet thing. Would you like me to walk you back, to make sure you're all right?'

'No, I'll be fine. I'll write. You'd better go.' A fisherman came crunching across the pebbles towards some lobster pots as she was saying this, so she added, 'Good day to you, Mr Perryman.'

'Good day, Miss Affleck. Send my best wishes to those at the hotel and I hope you all get over the explosions soon.'

She walked away, her anxiety diminished. Not only was he safe, but he wasn't involved with Rosetta Stone. And he loved her! She could hardly take it in.

It didn't make deciding what to do in the future any easier.

—

'It's so nice to see you again,' Hetty said to Phoebe, when she met up with her on Monday outside the hotel. 'It's been a while.'

'I always love coming to Littlehampton. Even if it is a bit chaotic at the moment. I'm looking forward to returning to the hotel after the war.' She looked at it affectionately, her head to one side.

'I'm sure Mrs Bygrove would give you a job now, if you wanted one.'

'No, I'll remain in the Land Army until the end of the war. With any luck, it won't be too long. I fancy a walk on the promenade, before we go for tea, though I don't suppose there'll be much going on. Unless that's too much of a mess after those explosions.'

'It is in places, but we'll see how far we can go.'

'How is your hand? It was kind of Mrs Bygrove to let you telephone my farm and talk to me.'

'It's well on the mend, but Nurse Bolton wants me to keep a clean bandage on for a couple more days. After my brother's wound becoming infected, I'd rather be safe than sorry. Did he mind, the farmer, about the telephone call?'

'No, not at all. The farmer and his wife are lovely people. I've heard about Land Army girls on some other farms not being so lucky.'

They made their way down to the eastern end of South Terrace and walked up the road to the promenade, to avoid walking across the mucky common.

'My goodness,' Phoebe said as they headed towards the pier. 'It is a mess. It's amazing how far the mud got thrown. It's a good job it wasn't summer with plenty of people about.'

'Would you rather we went elsewhere?'

'No, I like walking by the sea here. And it'll be interesting to see exactly what's happened.'

Hetty gave her a rundown of the day of the explosions. She always felt comfortable in Phoebe's company, like she could tell her anything. She was in two minds about revealing her relationship with Victor though.

They came towards the end of the promenade and turned the corner to walk next to the river, passing the gun battery mound.

'Oh dear, it really *is* a mess here,' said Phoebe, pointing towards the river mouth.

'And it's been cleared up a bit in the last couple of days.'

'You said they did it to widen it for the war ships?'

'That's right. I'm not sure how much good they did. Major Thomas reckons it'll soon be silted up again because that's what the River Arun does.'

'The whole thing must have been terrifying for you, and for everyone in the town, thinking it was an air raid. It was lucky nobody was hurt.'

'There were a lot of complaints, according to the *Littlehampton Gazette*,' said Hetty. 'They reckon they should have dredged it.'

'I'm not surprised.'

They stopped outside the Casino Theatre.

'Still seems to be a few things going on here,' said Phoebe. 'Perhaps another time we could go to a performance.'

They looked at the posters there, advertising shows, including a couple of Christmas events.

'Are they doing any Christmas activities at the hotel this year?'

'Yes. We're raising money for the Christmas boxes for the men abroad, and for the local children. There's a concert and a meal for the ordinary town folk. We're doing an event for the children and Lili's leading the hotel choir again on Christmas Eve.'

'That is something I'm looking forward to when I come back, Christmas at the hotel.'

Hetty was only half listening now, for she'd noticed four men walking close to the river's shore, by the shingle edge, smartly dressed in dark suits. Two of them were Victor and his father, who was wagging his finger as if annoyed about something. Victor noticed her, staring for a moment, but quickly looked away. Luckily, neither the other men, nor Phoebe, seemed to have noticed.

'Would you like to—' Hetty began, but she wasn't able to finish her sentence.

There was a terrific boom, and the next thing she knew, she and Phoebe were cowering on the ground.

–

Victor's father had suggested a walk by the river after the meeting they'd just attended with the port commissioners and local councillors, to talk to the Admiralty engineers. Two of the councillors had decided to come along for the walk too. They were all furious with the engineers' poor excuses, and Victor couldn't blame them. He was grateful that his father had asked him to accompany him. Perhaps he'd taken note of their recent conversation on this matter.

'If they'd asked any of us who deal with the river locally, we could have told them it was a bad idea. Either way, they should have warned everyone. And even now, they're not listening,' said James.

'I suppose the only way they'll find out their mistake is when the river silts up again,' said one of the councillors.

As his father raged on, Victor noticed two young women standing by the Casino Theatre. No, it couldn't be, could it? Yes, it was definitely Hetty. And the woman with her must be Hetty's friend Phoebe.

He looked away. No point in drawing attention to them.

They sauntered along, James now wagging his finger, suggesting they complain directly to the Admiralty in London, when something happened.

He wasn't sure what, he only knew that there was a monumental explosive sound and that he was knocked over, before he passed out.

Chapter Seventeen

Hetty sat up, moaning. She'd landed on her wounded hand, and it hurt like the devil. 'Phoebe?'

Her friend roused herself. 'What happened?'

'I think it was another explo— oh my goodness.' She struggled to get up, so her friend helped her. She flung her head round to look at where Victor had been standing, her heart racing. 'Oh no! The men are all on the ground.'

Phoebe followed her as they ran across the path to the water side. There was muck everywhere, and she noticed then that she and Phoebe were also mud-spattered.

Victor and the two men she vaguely recognised were coming to, but James Perryman was still on the ground.

'Mr Perryman, are you all right?' she called to Victor.

He was sitting now, his head between his knees. 'I think I passed out there for a second. What happened?'

'I reckon there's b-been another d-damned explosion,' said the fair-haired man with him. She remembered now; he and the dark-haired man were on the council.

'Hetty?' said Victor.

'That's right, Mr Perryman. From the Beach Hotel. And you might remember Phoebe Sweeton here. Is your father all right? He's not come to.'

'What? Oh.' Victor was blinking, squeezing his eyes tight each time, as if trying to focus.

Hetty knelt down, next to his father. 'Mr Perryman. Mr Perryman? Are you awake?'

'His head's bleeding,' said Phoebe. 'I'll go to the Casino and see if they have a telephone and get the doctor here.'

As she ran over, Hetty noticed that a group of people had come out of the theatre and were running towards the Oyster Pond.

'He looks like he might have hit his head as he went down,' said the dark-haired man, who was trying to make his way over, but wobbled so much he gave up. 'Is he, I mean, is he…'

He trailed off, but she knew he was asking if he was alive.

There was a lot of blood by James Perryman's head. What should she do? The first aid lessons! She felt for a pulse on his neck first, which she found quickly.

'Yes, he's alive.'

She lifted her skirt, not caring about decorum, and tugged awkwardly at the fabric of her petticoat, her hand throbbing, until she managed to tear off a long strip.

'Could you hold his head up a little, but keep it still,' she said to Victor.

He did as she asked, and she wrapped the cloth carefully around James Perryman's head to stem the bleeding. It was tricky and painful with her bandaged hand, but she persevered. She then tore off another strip and wound it around once more.

'W-where did you learn that?' said Victor.

She had told him about the lessons, but he couldn't be thinking straight. 'The nurse at the hotel teaches us first aid.'

'Oh yes, of course.'

Phoebe returned. 'I rang Dr Ferngrove. He's going to arrange an ambulance.'

'Are the rest of you all right?' Hetty asked. 'Anything hurting that might be broken?'

They all stretched their arms and legs.

'Just a few bruises,' said the fair-haired councillor, and his colleague agreed.

'Mr Perryman?' she asked Victor.

'Just feel a bit sick...' He shuffled around next to James. 'Father?' He started to shake his arm.

Hetty stayed his hand, keeping hers there for some moments as they looked into each other's eyes. 'We'd better not move him.'

Victor nodded. 'Thank you, Hetty. I don't know what we would have done without you.'

'Hear, hear,' said the fair-haired man.

But Hetty had no idea whether what she'd done had helped, or whether anything could help. She removed her hand from his. Her injured hand was in agony. She closed her eyes and sent up a brief prayer. The last thing she wanted was for Victor to lose his father.

'If that was the Admiralty again, there'll be trouble,' said the dark-haired man. 'It's almost like it's been done on purpose because we complained.'

'That doesn't make any sense,' said his colleague. 'There aren't even any engineers here, look.'

He was right. There was no one there to set the explosives. Then what on earth had happened?

'There's the motor ambulance,' said Phoebe, as a vehicle took the corner at the end of South Terrace, followed by a motorcar. They slowed down as it neared them. When they stopped, Dr Ferngrove, who attended them on occasion at the hotel, got out of the car, coming immediately to James Perryman.

'There was an explosion. He's unconscious,' said Hetty. 'And his pulse feels a little fast.'

'Miss Affleck, did you put this around his head?'

'I did.' She was anxious that she'd done something wrong.

'You've done a good job, well done. Now, let's see.' He felt his pulse and examined him.

'Is he going to be all right?' Victor asked.

'We need to get him to hospital. You'd better go with him.' He pointed to the councillors. 'And you two had better come in the car with me. You'll all need examining.'

The two ambulance men got a stretcher out from the back and proceeded to place James Perryman on it, then carefully lifted him into the vehicle.

Before stepping into the back, Victor turned to Hetty and whispered, 'Thank you.'

She nodded. 'Let me know how he gets on,' she whispered back.

'Once again, well done, Miss Affleck,' said the doctor. 'Now let me have a look at you two while I'm here.'

'There's no need, we were further away.'

'Yes there is. What's this?' He lifted Hetty's hand with the bandage.

'I cut myself at the hotel, on some glass, during the first explosions. Nurse Bolton stitched it.'

'It'll need changing, so go back to the hotel now and ask her to see to it.' He asked them both questions and looked them over quickly.

'You both seem all right but ask Mrs Bygrove to call me if you get any pain. I'll have a word or two to say to those Admiralty officers.'

'From what I've heard, you're not the only one,' said Hetty.

—

'There you both are!' Annie declared, the moment Hetty and Phoebe walked through the door of the scullery. 'We've been so worried. Did you – oh, look at your clothes! Were you nearby when the explosion went off?'

'Very near, by the Casino Theatre,' said Hetty. 'I need to see Nurse Bolton.'

Annie clutched her cheeks with her hands. 'What's wrong?'

'Only to have my hand re-bandaged, and—'

'I'll get her and let everyone know you're all right.' Annie rushed off.

'It's nice they're so concerned,' said Phoebe.

'I didn't really expect that kind of reception though.'

But more was to come. They got a similar welcome in the stillroom from Tilly and Milly, and then, when they reached the staff corridor, there was a group of staff there waiting for news.

'Thank goodness you're safe,' said Bridget Turnbull, which was echoed by the rest of them. 'We knew you were thinkin' of goin' to the tea rooms on Pier Road, so were worried you'd be close by when we heard the explosion. Didn't sound as loud as the others, but still.'

Gertie pushed her way to the front. 'You're all muddy! Tell us what happened?'

'Let's get you sat down with a nice cup of tea, and whatever else we can summon up, and you can give us an account,' said Edie.

Mrs Turnbull was already off, calling, 'I'll see to consumables, and let the kitchen staff know you're safe.'

Edie led the way into the staff dining room, where they'd already begun the tea break by the look of the table.

With everyone gathered around, Hetty and Phoebe took it in turns to relate what had happened.

'Sorry, Mr Perryman and his son were there too?' said Fanny, bouncing Elsie on her knee.

'And two of the councillors,' said Hetty. 'It sounded like they'd been to a meeting to tell the Admiralty officers off about blowing up the river mouth.'

'And then they did it again?' said Gertie, shaking her head. 'Without any warning?'

Hetty shrugged. 'We don't know. One of the councillors mentioned that there weren't any of the Admiralty engineers around, and there surely would have been if they'd been setting up explosives.'

'Anyway, Mr Perryman was still on the ground, unconscious, and bleeding a lot,' said Phoebe, 'so I went into the Casino Theatre and they let me telephone Dr Ferngrove.'

'Oh no,' said Fanny. 'That sounds bad.'

Mrs Turnbull returned with Nurse Bolton at this point, and Phoebe gave a quick rundown of what they'd already said. 'Then, Hetty here stopped Mr Perryman's bleeding by bandaging up his head, and Dr Ferngrove said she'd done a fine job.'

Nurse Bolton, already seeing to Hetty's hand, said, 'There, you see, I told you the first aid lessons would come in handy. Now, if those of you who haven't partaken so far would like to start my lessons – not looking at anyone in particular – I'm still doing them… Goodness, this is a bit of a mess. Gertie, would you get me some hot water from the scullery please?'

She jumped off the bench. 'You'd better tell me anything I've missed when I get back.'

'Was Mr Perryman all right?' asked Mrs Leggett from her usual end seat.

Hetty shrugged once more. 'We don't know. The ambulance took him to hospital, along with Vi— his son, who did say he'd let us know how he was. And the other two gentlemen went with Dr Ferngrove.'

Gertie came back with the water, and Fanny filled her in on what she'd missed as Hetty's hand was attended to.

'There you go,' said Nurse Bolton. 'It's all done. Luckily, the wound hasn't been affected and is still healing nicely.'

Mrs Norris entered with a tray bearing scones and jam, and a fresh pot of tea. 'There you go, me ducks. It's a relief to see you. 'Ello Phoebe, it's been a while.'

'Hey, we didn't get scones,' said Gertie.

'You 'aven't been involved in an explosion. Now, tell me all about it.'

Phoebe started yet again, a lot more enthusiastically than Hetty could have managed, being too worried about Victor's father. She only hoped he managed to send some kind of message soon.

–

Phoebe had been planning to leave for the train just after five, but Helen Bygrove had insisted on driving her back home to Angmering, worried she might be suffering from delayed shock. Hetty was glad to have a free evening, feeling even more exhausted now than she had after the first explosion and her own injury.

Around six, not long after Helen had returned and was sitting in the dining room with the early staff diners, Inspector Toshack popped his head around the door.

'Um, hello… everyone,' he said with his Scottish burr.

'Sam!' said Helen, smiling broadly, causing knowing looks and grins around the table. 'Come in. I'm just having a cup of tea with the staff and catching up with what happened at the river earlier. Hetty here was involved, with Phoebe.'

'Aye, I've already heard. I understand that Miss Affleck here may have saved James Perryman's life.'

'Oh, I don't think—' Hetty started.

'Dr Ferngrove said that if the bleeding hadn't been stemmed, he would likely have died before he'd got to hospital.'

'Well done again, Hetty,' said Nurse Bolton. 'From this moment, you are my top student.'

'I think Phoebe being quick to telephone the doctor helped as well.'

'How is Mr Perryman?' Helen asked.

'Stable is all they'll say at the moment. He's in Littlehampton Hospital and still unconscious.'

Stable. Hetty had heard that one before, with her brother. He had recovered, but it didn't mean that Victor's father would.

'Do they know what happened, about the explosion I mean?' said Hetty.

'Yes, well, it seems that some explosive might have been left behind and went off by itself. It can be unstable sometimes.'

'That's going to get the Admiralty officers into even more bother than they already are,' said Hetty.

'Especially if…' Inspector Toshack didn't finish the sentence, but Hetty, and she was sure everyone else, knew what he meant. 'Let's hope for the best.'

Helen rose from the bench. 'Come along, Sam. The children are having their dinner upstairs, but afterwards, they're keen for you to read some more of *The Jungle Book* to them.'

Once they'd left the room, Hetty noticed the grins get wider, though she had no desire to join in, as worried as she was.

'She seems to be a lot more open about the relationship now,' said Mrs Turnbull.

'Well, good luck to her,' said Mrs Leggett. 'Not that it's any of our business either way, but I, for one, hope that Mrs Bygrove finds a nice man to marry, after all she went through with Douglas Bygrove, God rest his soul.' She made the sign of the cross.

Everyone around the table nodded and agreed, including herself. But romantic happy endings always seemed to be hard fought in this hotel.

–

Hetty decided after dinner to go up to her room to settle into bed and read, but once she'd got there, she had another idea. She should write to Victor to ask how his father was, and suggest they meet on Friday, if he were able, as she wasn't doing the afternoon tea shift that day. If she took a letter to the pillar box on Norfolk Road, it would only take her a few minutes, and it would probably get there by Friday morning.

What if it didn't though, or if, by the time it arrived, he'd already arranged something else? If she took it straight to the office, he'd get it tomorrow morning. And he might even be able to reply. She could be there and back within half an hour. But again, what would she tell the stillroom and scullery maids? It would be odd to be going out for fresh air this time of the evening in November.

Why not tell them that she was posting a letter, since she was. They were unlikely to ask any questions and would assume she was going to the pillar box in Norfolk Road. She got her writing paper from the top drawer and made a start at the small table that sat between her bed and what used to be Phoebe's. And hopefully would be again one day.

Half an hour later, she put on her coat and hat, and took the finished letter downstairs.

'Where are you off to this time of night?' came the inevitable question from both the stillroom and the scullery.

'Letter to post,' she said, not stopping as she held it up in a way that they couldn't see the address.

Outside, she was disappointed to see it was overcast. If they asked her why she'd been so long coming back, she had thought to say that she'd been looking at the stars. But there were none to see. In that case, she could say... oh, what did it matter, as long as she got this letter to Victor, and opened up the possibility of seeing him.

Providing something didn't happen to his father in the meantime.

Chapter Eighteen

'Oh dear,' said Sophia, pulling on a glove as she and Victor exited the hospital the next day. 'He didn't look much better than yesterday.'

'No. I was hoping he might have come around. Do you think we should leave Mother here, alone?'

'I got the impression that's what she wanted. And the staff don't want us all hanging about. We can come back this evening. If he's come around, we'll be more use then, keeping him company.'

'I suppose you're right.' They walked along the road in silence for a while, until the library came into sight, and it reminded Victor of something he needed to do.

'Sophia, I have something to tell you, and would really like your help in this matter.'

'You know I'm always here for you, Victor, as you've always been for me.'

'You see… I really need you to keep it a secret, for now.'

'Gosh, this sounds serious. You know you can trust me.' She took his arm. 'What's this all about?'

'I'm, well, I'm walking out with a young lady.'

'My goodness Victor, you are a dark horse. Can I ask who she is?'

'It, it's someone from the Beach Hotel.'

She twisted around to face him, walking backwards a few steps. 'It's not Ebony Girard, by any chance?'

'Ebony? No, why would you think that?'

'I don't know. She sent a note around this morning, to say how sorry she was to hear about our father, and she always seems interested in our family when she comes to the charity meetings. Maybe it's *you* she's interested in.'

'Well, I've nothing against her, she seems very nice, but it's not mutual. I meant, it's a member of staff from the hotel.'

'Is it Edie?'

'No.' He should just get it out to stop her speculation, but it was hard. 'It's Hetty Affleck. Henrietta.'

'The one who saved Father's life?'

'Yes.'

'Well I never. How did you two get together?'

'It was after the children's tea party that I attended with Maria and the children. I'd spoken to her a couple of times before and rather liked her, so I asked her when she had some free time. We went to the Harbour Tea Rooms and had a splendid afternoon together, so we've arranged a few others since. And I get to see her the odd hour when she's in between shifts.'

'Are you serious about her? And she about you?'

'I am about her. I hope she is too. We've had a bit of a setback with Mother and Father arranging those two evenings with Rosetta Stone. I told Hetty about the first one, but then one of the waitresses mentioned I'd been dining at the hotel with Rosetta.'

'Oh dear. I won't breathe a word, dear brother, but how exactly can I help you?'

'She posted a letter at the office, which I found this morning, and has suggested we meet on Friday for a while. I'd really like to, and I want to get a note back to her, as soon as possible. You're doing a charity event at the hotel tomorrow, aren't you?'

'That's right, an afternoon tea for the general public, to collect money for Christmas boxes for the men abroad.'

'Could you find some way of giving her a note?'

'I can try. I'm not sure how I can get it to her if she's not helping, but I'll think of something.'

'Thank you, Sophia.'

'What are big sisters for?'

–

Hetty was heading for a late lunch when Mrs Leggett caught sight of her.

'There you are. I have a letter for you. It came in the post this morning.'

Hetty felt the ripple of excitement as she took the letter from the housekeeper and placed it in her apron pocket. Victor must have replied straight away. She only hoped it was good news. They'd no doubt hear more about his father this afternoon from Sophia, when she was helping with the charity tea. As long as she came, now her father was injured.

She must remember to call her Miss Perryman if she did, which would be hard with Victor referring to her so often by her first name.

It wasn't until lunch was over, and she was on her own in the lavatory that she took the letter from her apron to open it. The smile soon slipped when she recognised the writing: it was Lorcan's, not Victor's. It was always a relief to get a letter from Lorcan, so she knew he was still safe, but it wasn't what she'd wanted today. She scanned it quickly, relieved that there was no bad news, just snippets of his current everyday life. She slipped the letter back into her pocket. There'd be time later to read it more fully.

As she entered the ballroom, three members of staff had already started making up the two long lines of trestle tables with white cloths. There was also cutlery, crockery and vases of winter greenery on several trolleys, waiting to be laid.

'Come and help over here,' Lili called from one end.

Hetty joined her and started helping.

'Mr Janus has arranged for a couple of his performers to do a few music hall numbers and a bit of comedy,' said Lili.

'Lovely.' Hetty knew she'd have felt more enthusiastic about it if she'd heard from Victor. She'd always enjoyed Mr Janus's entertainers.

'There's Miss Perryman now.' Lili pointed to where she was coming through the door.

'Ebony Girard is with her.'

'Helps with some of her charity events, she does, so she must be helping with this one. Heard she's goin' to be serving as well.'

'That'll be strange, her serving instead of being served.'

Sophia came over to them, with Ebony walking just behind her.

'Good afternoon, Miss Perryman. May I enquire how your father is today?' Hetty asked.

'He woke up this morning. Victor and I went to see him just before I came here, and he's still groggy. He's not out of the woods yet, but is making progress, so the doctor says.'

'That's wonderful news.'

'And, dear lady,' Sophia went on, 'I am told that you are one of the reasons he is making such good progress, with your first aid skills. I'm so glad of an opportunity to thank you, from the bottom of my heart, for acting so quickly and diligently. And my mother also passes on her heartfelt thanks. And my brother, of course.'

Hetty was afraid she was going to tear up but managed to keep her composure. 'I'm sure it's what any of us who've had first aid lessons from Nurse Bolton would have done. She needs to be thanked too, because if she hadn't insisted we do them, I wouldn't have known what to do.'

'Then I shall endeavour to seek her out after this event. Anyway, we're here to help, ladies. We're both capable of laying up tables.'

'That would be very useful, thank you,' said Lili.

'Perhaps Ebony could help you, Liliwen, and I'll help Henrietta here.'

'Good idea. Miss Ebony, we'll start on the other line of tables.'

Hetty felt self-conscious, being left on her own with Victor's sister, even though she didn't know about the two of them.

'Perhaps if you'd lay the cutlery, I'll follow on with the crockery,' said Hetty. 'Then we can see to the greenery.'

'Splendid. I do like being more than just an organiser at these events.'

They started on their jobs, working well together. Hetty wondered if this was the kind of thing she'd end up doing all the time, if she – dare she even think it – married Victor? How could it ever happen though, in their society, whatever people said about the war changing everything?

When they'd laid a dozen places, Sophia stopped.

'Henrietta, Hetty, before we carry on, and while everyone's attention is elsewhere, I have something for you.' She pulled out an envelope from the pocket of her skirt, and passed it to her, below the top of the table.

It was Victor's writing. She slipped it quickly into her apron pocket.

'It's about your meeting on Friday. Don't look so worried, my dear, Victor has told me all about the relationship. I'm on your side. I'm pleased he's found someone he can feel such affection for. Let's carry on.'

Hetty wasn't sure if she felt more or less awkward now. It was good that Sophia approved, but maybe a little embarrassing that she knew 'all about the relationship', as she'd put it.

'I am really very pleased that your father seems to be on the mend, not least of all for Victor's sake, of course.' She said the last bit quietly.

'Do you know, when Victor started telling me that there was someone in his life, and that it was someone here, at the hotel, I thought he was going to say Ebony. She has always seemed inordinately interested in my family when we've met up at meetings.'

'It's probably the artist in her, liking details.'

'You're probably right.'

When the room was all prepared, Hetty checked her wristwatch. 'Under fifteen minutes until people will be coming in. If you and Miss Ebony are serving, you'll need an apron each, to protect your clothing.'

'Absolutely. And a cap each too, of course.' She pointed to Hetty's head.

'Very well.'

–

The staff had now removed the empty sandwich platters from the tables at the charity tea and replaced them with trays of scones and cakes. They then stood back and watched as the guests tucked in.

'I know your head cook, Mrs Norris, is a wonder in the kitchen, but how has she managed to make so much cake for the occasion, with the shortage of flour and sugar?' Sophia asked Hetty.

'Well, and this is just between us…'

'Go on, I'm intrigued.'

'You will probably think this sounds horrible, but she found a recipe in an old cookery book, using shredded carrots.'

'Carrots!'

'It sweetens the cake, and bulks it out. It really is much nicer than it sounds, as she tried it out on some of us staff first.'

'That must be the orangey looking one. But what about the other two types?'

'She wondered whether any other vegetables could be used, so with us growing a lot of our own now, she experimented with a few, and decided, along with her tasters – the staff – that courgettes and beetroot were best.'

'How ingenious. I wonder if anyone will realise?'

'If they go down well, she might put them on the afternoon tea menu. But you mustn't breathe a word.'

'I promise.' She crossed her heart, reminding Hetty of Tilly a few days ago, when she'd left the hotel to make sure Victor was all right.

It wasn't long before a middle-aged lady, who she knew worked in the post office on Norfolk Road, called Hetty over.

'The cake is delicious.' She pointed to a piece with carrots. 'I did wonder if we'd get any with all the shortages. What sort is it? It's not orange, is it?'

'Mrs Norris calls it the Golden Beauty.'

It's what the waiting staff had been instructed to call it if any questions were asked.

'This one's lovely too,' said an old gentleman holding up a plate with the beetroot cake on. 'Proper moist, it is.'

'Looks like you *will* be putting them on the menu,' Sophia quipped when Hetty stepped back once more. Sophia was then called by a guest nearby, who wanted to tell her how much she appreciated all her charity work and how sorry she was to hear about her father.

How easily Sophia chatted to everybody, despite her troubles. Hetty had felt awkward when she'd found out that she knew about her and Victor. However, they'd got on well during the afternoon. And she still had the letter from Victor to look forward to later. It sounded like he would be able to meet on Friday, from what Sophia had said. She felt immensely cheered up, compared to before the party.

But she was forgetting about their father. Hopefully, by Friday, there would have been even more improvement.

–

Hetty was first to turn up at the rendezvous on Friday afternoon, in the cemetery of St Mary's, the parish church in town. It seemed a reasonable place to bump into somebody and chat with them, if anyone saw them.

Hetty was standing in front of a grave under a yew tree when Victor found her.

'Lady Rose Wright,' he said. 'Who is that?'

'Hello Victor. How lovely to see you again, though I wish it were under better circumstances.' She wanted to hug him but wouldn't out in the open.

'Father is recovering well. He's sitting up now, and even starting to give orders about the businesses.' He raised his eyebrows.

'Oh dear. It sounds like he should forget that for a while and rest.'

'Exactly what Mother told him. So, is this someone you knew, or who used to come to the hotel?'

'It's Helen Bygrove's mother. She lived at the hotel with her and Mr Bygrove until she died in 1912, a year after I started working there. She was a very nice lady and taken too soon.'

'So I see. Well at least now we know we won't be saying that about my father. But it might have been a different story if you hadn't been there.'

'I'm so glad I could help.'

'You did more than help, Hetty, you saved his life. And in a way, mine too.'

He looked around, she wasn't sure what for. The churchyard was empty, except for them. He placed one hand around her back, bringing her towards him, then lifted her chin, before kissing her lips. She was stunned to begin with, not having a clue what to do. Lorcan had only ever pecked her on the lips. Finally, she relaxed and let him lead. It felt good, his soft, warm lips against hers, and it brought her body alive.

He pulled away but held onto her, looking around once more. There was still no one about.

'Like I said, Father is recovering well, but he will be incapacitated for a time, so I'm having to take over the running of the other businesses until he's back on his feet. I'm not sure when I'll be free next, so it might be a little while before we can meet again. But rest assured, I love you Hetty, and nothing will stop me from seeing you. You are... you are the love of my life.'

'I—I am?' Again, she couldn't bring forth the words she wanted to say to him.

He kissed her lips briefly. 'Yes, you are.' He stared into her eyes for a few moments, his expression unreadable. 'But now, I'm sorry, I have to get back. My father's instructed me to attend a meeting at Haydon's, our shipyard over the bridge, on the west bank. Perhaps we could write to each other, either by post or via Sophia, in the meantime. And we might be able to arrange a meeting at some odd moments, maybe an evening, when you're not doing a shift.'

'All right. I imagine you'll have a lot to do.'

'I will.' He sighed. 'I'd better go.' He gave her one more kiss.

He was about to walk away when she grabbed hold of his coat sleeve, determined to say what she must. 'Victor… I—I love you too.'

He grinned broadly and kissed her hand. 'I thought you'd never say it, or that maybe you didn't love me.'

'Of course I do.' She felt one tear drop onto her cheek.

'My darling.' He took her in his arms once more and kissed her for even longer than the first time. When he finally let her go, he said, 'Until the next time,' before hastening back to the path.

She watched him, not moving until he was out of sight. She turned back to the grave. 'Keep that to yourself, Lady Rose.' She smiled, remembering how kindly the woman had been. Just like her daughter, who also knew about her friendship with Victor. But now, not the extent of it.

Chapter Nineteen

They were three days into December now, and Hetty had only managed to see Victor one evening in the last two weeks. They had met on Beach Road and taken a walk, hand in hand, around the near empty town, looking in the windows of closed shops. How she had enjoyed that simple activity. She got a whirl of sensation in her tummy, thinking about when she might see him next. His father was now home but had been ordered to do no work until after Christmas at the very earliest.

Hetty was now putting clean glasses away on the stillroom shelves. Just one more tray left, and she'd be able to get ready for her afternoon off. She was sorry not to be seeing Victor today, but also excited to be meeting Phoebe. Then she remembered: they were going to see her parents in Wick, at her mother's insistence, for lunch.

'There, all done,' she whispered to herself as she placed the last glass up. 'I'm off now,' she told Tilly and Milly, as she removed her apron.

About to open the door to the corridor, she had to step back as Lili came flying in.

'Hetty, good,' said the waitress. 'Glad I've caught you. Heard you singing in your bedroom this morning, I did. Your door was ajar.'

Hetty was confused. 'That must have been when I went back for my cap as I'd forgotten it. Why?'

'It's a good voice you've got there. I was wondering if you'd like to join our choir this Christmas Eve, you know, for our little concert.'

'Oh, well, I don't know. I was in the choir at school, I suppose.' Encouraged by her father, who'd been keen on her and her siblings getting involved with as many school activities as possible. 'Yes, go on, why not?'

She'd been looking for things to keep her mind occupied, so she wasn't spending every spare moment thinking about Victor.

'There's lovely. Thank you, Hettie.' Lili spun out of the door as quickly as she'd come in.

Hetty got ready promptly, aware that Phoebe would arrive on the train soon and be waiting for her at the bottom of Arundel Road. Outside, she was surprised to see a totally blue sky, having been stuck in the stillroom all morning and unaware of the weather. Stopping for a moment on South Terrace, she lifted her head towards the sun and closed her eyes. It was good to feel it on her face after the last few dull days. As she opened her eyes, she saw Miss Cecelia pass by, amusement on her face.

'It is rather nice to see the sun again, isn't it?'

'Um, yes, it is rather.'

Cecelia walked on and Hetty looked around, expecting Lady Blackmore to be somewhere, but she was nowhere to be seen. Just as well, as she was the last person she wanted to encounter after the woman had gone to Mrs Bygrove and *told* on her and Victor.

When Hetty finally reached the end of High Street, she saw Phoebe approaching their meeting place at the bottom of Arundel Road. She raised a hand and waved, walking a little faster.

The two women embraced when they met and Hetty was soon bringing her friend up to date on the latest news, as they walked towards Wick.

'I'm glad to hear that Mr Perryman is on the mend,' said Phoebe.

Should she tell Phoebe about her relationship with Victor? It would be good to share it with someone. 'Phoebe?'

'Yes?'

'I, um, I just wanted to say that we don't need to stay too long at my parents' house. After lunch, let's say we need to do some shopping, or need to get presents, or something. If that's all right.'

Phoebe laughed. 'Are you afraid your mother's going to try to pair you off with the vicar again? Surely she wouldn't do that with me there.'

'I wouldn't put it past her. She might try to get you paired off with the curate at the same time.'

'What's he like?'

'In his seventies with a long, grey beard and a walking stick!'

They both giggled.

'To be honest, Phoebe, I only agreed to go home for lunch to see Hector.'

'Don't worry, I'm sure we can find an excuse to leave after lunch. As it happens, I would like to visit the shops in Little-hampton. You've far more here than we have in Angmering.'

'Then that's our excuse decided.'

She wasn't sure where to start on the subject of Victor. It would have to wait for another time.

–

'Hello?' Hetty called, as she let herself and Phoebe in the front door of the schoolhouse.

'In here,' came a voice that Hetty knew was her sister Iris's. She must have come for lunch too. She wasn't sure why, but a smidgeon of trepidation slithered through her. It was as if her mother had called for backup.

Hetty led Phoebe to the sitting room, where she found her sister fussing over Hector, as he sat near the fire.

'About time,' said Iris, regarding Hetty.

'It's only twenty to one. That's five minutes earlier than I said.'

Iris didn't reply, saying instead, 'Hello Phoebe. It's been a while since we've seen you.'

'I'm back in Angmering for the rest of the war, as a Land Army girl.'

'It sounds like a much more fitting use of your time than working in the hotel.'

Iris, who had married young, had never approved of Hetty working as 'some kind of servant', as she'd put it.

'Do leave the poor girls alone,' said Hector. 'Hello Phoebe. It's very nice to see you again.'

'It's not very nice to see *me* then?' Hetty quipped, with mock indignation, giving him a peck on the cheek.

'That goes without saying, dear sister.' He took her hand. 'You're looking well, even better than last week.'

'And I'm feeling it. Which is why I wish I was allowed to do more. And go out from time to time.'

Their mother, Miriam, came into the room as he was saying this. 'You know you're not well enough yet, Hector. I'm not taking any chances. Now come along to the dining room, all of you. Lunch is served.'

Iris went to help Hector up, but he removed his arm from hers. 'Stop fussing. I can manage perfectly well.'

In the dining room, Hetty's father, Kenneth, already sitting at the table, got up to greet them.

'I'm so glad you can join us, Dad,' said Hetty.

'Only for half an hour, during the school lunch period, but it's better than nothing.'

They sat down. The sandwiches, cut into quarters, were already on the table.

'It's only three quarters of a sandwich each I'm afraid,' said Miriam. 'I can't imagine how they're managing at the hotel. I wouldn't be surprised if it had to shut down soon. In fact, it should be made law that such establishments are shut down for the duration.'

'I agree,' said Iris. 'It's dreadful that they're allowed to stay open, wasting food.'

Hetty glanced at Phoebe, who was concentrating on her plate. 'We're growing a lot of our own food, and Mrs Norris is finding ingenious ways to get around shortages.' She was thinking of the cakes bulked out with vegetables. 'And they make bread from scratch, they don't buy it from the bakers.'

'But those ingredients could be shared out and—'

'Are you suggesting that the middle and upper classes shouldn't eat at all, Mother?' said Hector. 'You consider yourself middle class, don't you, and you still go for tea in tea rooms.'

'They're not lavish and wasteful.'

'The hotel isn't wasteful,' Hetty countered. 'I bet there are ordinary people in the town who are more wasteful, and don't grow their own veg, even though the council has put by more land for allotments. Are you growing your own vegetables?'

'I'm not sure this is a subject for the dining table,' Kenneth interrupted.

'I'm not in a position to,' said Miriam.

'But you have a bit of garden.' She knew that her mother would consider it too demeaning in her position as headmaster's wife.

'Well, I agree with Mother,' said Iris. 'It's wasteful work at the hotel.'

'In which case, perhaps our mother should release the maid who comes in to clean, so she can do war work.'

'But I have important work in the community to do,' said Miriam, 'which would be reduced if I had to, to *clean*.'

'And a lot of the people who come to the hotel have important jobs, like the councillors. We also have MPs, and other dignitaries from time to time, sometimes for business lunches. We feed them and give them a break. It's about keeping people's spirits up, as it is with all the cafés, restaurants and entertainments.'

She wasn't sure why she was sticking up for the guests at the hotel, given how demanding and entitled some of them were. And others were downright troublemakers, like Lord Fernsby, who'd assaulted Gertie a couple of years before. Still, she wasn't going to let her mother get the last word in, as she normally did.

'Well *I* think—' Iris started.

'That's enough now,' Kenneth said, more forcefully. 'I don't have much time for lunch, and we have a guest. Now, pass the plate of sandwiches around, pour the tea, and let's get started. And talk about something else. I read in the newspaper this morning that there's been a suspension of hostilities between the German and Russian army.'

The conversation continued on this topic, and how they thought the allies might fare without the Russian army. Phoebe also cheered up and joined in, which Hetty was relieved about. She didn't want her friend's day off spoilt.

Talking ceased for a short while, before Miriam asked Hetty, 'I presume you're coming to the carol service at the church.'

'When is it?' She was prepared to make some kind of excuse, whenever it might be.

'Saturday the twenty-second. I'm sure Reverend Peck would be pleased to see you there.'

Hetty almost shuddered at the man's name. 'It's far too close to Christmas. Quite a lot of guests will be arriving that day, and it will mean all hands on deck.'

'Then you could come back on your day off next week, and I could invite the reverend for afternoon tea once more.'

'Mother, we didn't exactly get on.'

'Then some other nice young single man from the parish.'

'I can only make it for half an hour or so next week. I'll have to continue my Christmas shopping, which is what Phoebe and I are going to start when we've left here.'

'Aren't you staying for a few hours?'

'We can't, I'm afraid.'

'You get other breaks in between shifts though, where you have time enough to go to the shops,' Iris said with an accusing glare.

'It's the Christmas season, and we have to cover more shifts.'

'I don't think Hetty appreciates your attempts to pair her off,' said Hector. 'And I can't blame her, especially if they're all like the gloomy and condemning vicar. He certainly didn't make *me* feel uplifted when he came to visit.'

'No, he was truly awful when he came to tea that time, Victor.'

'Victor?' said Miriam. 'That's not the first time you've called him that by mistake.'

Hetty's stomach twisted and she felt sick. How could she have been so stupid? She only hoped she hadn't gone red. 'Sorry, I'm getting confused. Mr Perryman's son is called Victor, and it's what he insisted I call him when he came to thank me for saving his father's life. It's so similar to "Hector".'

'Not this again.' Iris's lips narrowed and she shook her head. 'How many times are we going to hear about your *heroics*?'

'I've only seen you once, briefly, since it happened, and you said you already knew.'

'Yes, because our father mentions it whenever I'm here.'

'No, I don't. Only a couple of times. It was a fine thing Hetty did, taking first aid lessons, and she managed to save a life. That's worth boasting about.'

'Boasting isn't—'

'Don't start again, Iris,' said Hector. 'I think you did a fine thing, Hetty. And I believe you were quick to telephone for the doctor too, Phoebe.'

'It's lucky that Mr Janus has a telephone at the Casino Theatre,' she said.

Iris made no reply but was tight lipped as she picked up her cup for a sip of tea.

'So, what does your job on the land involve, Phoebe?' Hector asked.

Phoebe smiled and gave them a rundown of a typical day as a Land Army girl.

Hetty and Phoebe had left the schoolhouse in Wick by half past two. Hetty's whole body relaxed as she shut the door behind her. She was sorry to leave her brother, but she'd pop in some other time between shifts, without warning, so that her mother couldn't arrange a 'young man' – or Iris – to be there.

'I apologise about my mother and sister,' Hetty said, as they rounded the corner onto Wick Street and passed by the church of which Reverend Peck was vicar.

'Don't worry, I'm used to it with my mother and aunt. They're just the same, always trying to organise my life. That was the biggest problem with leaving the hotel really, having to go back home. I'd got used to making my own decisions. I think Mum is angling for me to get a job closer to home after the war, but I'm determined to go back to the hotel.'

Hetty took her friend's arm. 'I'm so glad to hear you're still set on that.'

'There was one thing I was curious about, earlier.'

'What's that?'

'It was, um, you calling Hector "Victor" by mistake.'

'It's an easy thing to do.'

'When you know both people well, yes. But, when you attended Victor Perryman's father, on the riverside, I had a feeling there was more to it than you just knowing each other through the hotel. Just – something about the way you were with each other.'

'You're very perceptive, Phoebe. You always have been. You're right, there is more to it. I've wanted to tell you for a while but didn't know where to begin. It started off as a friendship. We spent some time together, enjoying each other's company. I was attracted to him the first time I spotted him in the dining room, when I was brought in to serve afternoon tea. But eventually I realised I felt much more than just friendship. He is a dear, dear soul and he, well, moves me in a way I've never felt before. And he told me recently that he loved me.'

'Oh Hetty, that is wonderful. But…'

'But he belongs to the upper classes, and the most I can boast is lower middle class?'

'I wasn't going to put it like that, only that you were different classes.'

She sighed. 'I know. Whilst my mother would be cock-a-hoop at the prospect, I don't suppose his parents would be so happy. Especially as they've already tried to pair him off with a society lady. Several probably.'

'But Hetty, what about Lorcan? You're still writing to him, aren't you?'

'Yes, but we decided on his last leave that we would see how we felt after the war.'

'Shouldn't you tell him though, that you've met someone else?'

'I don't know what to do, Phoebe. I'm afraid that if I write and tell him, he'll be upset and distracted, and that might put him in danger in the trenches.'

'It's a fair point. But you will have to tell him sometime.'

'Maybe I won't have to. Are Victor and I likely to be able to marry?' She doubted it, despite what he'd said about her being the love of his life. Though, even if they didn't, would it be right to take up with Lorcan again? She didn't feel the same way about him anymore. So, either way, perhaps she should tell him.

'It's clearly complicated,' said Phoebe. 'Does anybody else know?'

'His sister, Sophia, does. And Edie and Helen Bygrove, but not really the extent of it. Mrs Bygrove only found out because Lady Blackmore saw us talking on the pier and went to the hotel to tell her.'

'The stinking little tell-tale! Especially after what was revealed about her.'

'I know. Luckily Mrs Bygrove was understanding, probably because she's been through so much herself.'

'How is that going, her relationship with Inspector Toshack? And what's the latest on Lady Blackmore and Cecelia?'

Hetty spent the rest of their walk back into Littlehampton bringing her up to date on the two situations.

Chapter Twenty

It was the night of the concert, to be held in the ballroom, and Hetty was excited as she sat in the staff dining room, eating her dinner. Not only was she to serve refreshments again in the interval, but she knew that Victor was coming with his sister. She wouldn't be able to talk to him properly, but she'd get to be near him for a while.

She'd managed to see him for an hour on her Monday afternoon off, despite popping home for half an hour as she'd promised. Victor had arranged to meet her in Wick on the way back, outside the Dew Drop Inn, and they'd walked a slightly longer way around, past the railway station, back to the edge of the shopping streets, where he'd left her to return to work.

'You're miles away again,' said Fanny, sitting next to her. 'You seem to be like that a lot recently.'

'I'm just looking forward to serving this evening. It's always interesting to see the ladies in the latest fashions and listen to the chatter.'

'There not always fashionable young women,' said Gertie. 'Look at the likes of Lady Blackmore, her outfits are years out of date. And she's not the only one.'

'I don't suppose she'll be coming, since she hasn't graced us with her presence since she got that poison pen letter.'

'Apart from when she came to speak to Mrs Bygrove,' said Gertie. 'Goodness knows what that was all about.'

The door opened, and in walked Charlie Cobbett, in his uniform. Everyone called a greeting.

' 'Ere, Charlie, is that three chevrons on your sleeve? I thought you was a lance corporal,' said Gertie.

'Got a promotion to corporal, didn't I,' he said proudly.

'You didn't tell us, Edie.'

'I didn't know until yesterday, Gertie, when he came back on leave.'

'It only just happened, so I thought it'd be a nice surprise for my girl.'

Edie stood up and went to embrace him. It gave Hetty a warm feeling inside, even though she still saw them as rather mismatched, and yet they seemed right together.

'Are you here for the concert, Mr Cobbett?' said the housekeeper, at one end of the table.

'I certainly am, Mrs Leggett. Don't suppose I'll get a chance to attend these fancy dos once I'm back in me porter's uniform, so I might as well take the opportunity. Like a bit of a concert, me.'

Gertie laughed. 'Wouldn't 'ave thought quintets, harpists, monologists and opera pieces were your thing, Charlie.'

' 'Ere, ya cheeky so-an'-so,' he said, laughing. 'I'm very open-minded, me. And there's something for everyone at this concert.'

Mrs Leggett stood up and clapped her hands twice. 'Well ladies and gentlemen, most of you had better get yourselves ready for this evening's shifts.'

Hetty helped to stack the plates, excited that she was a little closer to seeing Victor.

–

Hetty stood in the lounge, where she was lined up with Simon, Annie and two of the part-time waiting staff, behind a long length of tables with white cloths, various jugs of cold beverages and plates of canapés. Mrs Leggett had been put in charge for the interval.

They'd heard the clapping from the ballroom so expected the audience to descend upon them at any moment. It wasn't long before they heard chatter, and people started entering the lounge. Hetty's insides fluttered with excitement as she tried not to make it too obvious that she was looking for someone. She started pouring various cordials and squashes for guests, looking out into the crowd in between.

She spotted Charlie and Edie, along with her friend, Julia, who was engaged to Detective Inspector Davis. Inspector Toshack, who'd replaced Davis when he'd been conscripted, was just behind them, accompanying Helen. Between them they'd been through some traumatic times these last few years. How nice it would be for them all to have happy endings.

Finally, she spotted Victor and Sophia, but her delight was dimmed a little a few seconds later, when their mother appeared. That would make even an innocent conversation somewhat awkward.

Mrs Leggett approached her and Annie at the end of the table. 'Miss Affleck, why don't you pour a few different drinks and take them around on a tray. It would save everyone having to queue at the table. You too, Miss Twine.'

The pair of them soon set off in different directions with their trays. Could she make it to the Perrymans before they went to help themselves at the table? They were nearby, chatting, and hadn't yet got refreshments.

As she was serving Major Thomas a lime cordial, Victor caught her eye and raised his hand to summon her. This was her opportunity.

She smiled as she joined them, holding up the tray, naming the choices.

'Just what I need,' said Mrs Perryman, helping herself to a quinine and orange cordial. 'Ah, there's Lady Raynolt. I'm just going to have a word.'

'I shall have a lime cordial,' said Sophia, picking one off the tray.

Victor chose the same. 'It's been a good concert so far,' he said, as if making conversation with the staff.

'I hear that you, Miss Perryman, were in charge of organising it.' She knew she was, but it was hard to think of anything else to say.

'That's right,' said Sophia. 'Though, of course, Mr Janus had a large part in organising the acts. I was more on the advertising and practical side.'

'And may I enquire how your father is now?'

'Well on the mend,' said Victor. 'He's at home recuperating but isn't yet well enough to venture out.'

Aware that Mrs Leggett was nearby she said, 'There are canapés on the tables, and I hope you enjoy the rest of the evening, sir, madam.'

'Thank you, Henrietta,' said Victor, as Ebony Girard joined them.

'Good evening, Sophia, Victor. I was just wondering how your father is fairing now,' she said, as Hetty walked away.

–

Victor couldn't think of anything to keep Hetty talking, and he knew that their conversation had to be brief.

As she walked away, Ebony came towards them, smiling. Victor remembered that Sophia had thought, for a brief moment, that they might be involved. She was pleasing to the eye, and he could see why men might desire her, but she held no attraction for him romantically. And the way she often attached herself to his family made her seem rather... needy. Yes, that was the word. Which was surprising, given how much confidence she seemed to otherwise exude.

'Good evening, Sophia, Victor. I was just wondering how your father is fairing now. I see he isn't here this evening with you.'

'No, despite having been home a few days, he's not well enough to venture out,' said Victor.

'But he is on the mend, I assume?' she persisted.

'Yes, definitely on the mend,' Sophia confirmed.

'It's been a splendid concert so far, hasn't it?' said Ebony. 'It's a shame we can't make a film of such things, like they do for the picture houses, and watch them again at our own leisure. Or take them home to people who haven't been able to attend.'

'That would be novel,' said Sophia. 'But you'd have to have a large camera and a room with a big screen to watch it, and probably be able to do something technical in between, so I don't suppose that's going to happen any time soon.'

'Have you been painting lately?' Victor asked her. 'I don't suppose the weather is conducive to sitting outside to work at the moment.'

'I've done a few sketches and watercolours sitting on the pier on the nicer days. I do find that the winter colours can be quite engaging.'

Victor noticed his mother making her way back towards them. Ebony smiled and said, 'Well, do excuse me,' and walked away.

When she was out of earshot, Sophia said, 'She only asked me two days ago how Father was, when we had a meeting. She does seem rather over interested in our family's business, and although I have found her good company, it is starting to irritate me.'

'I think she's just missing her own family,' said Victor, though he had thought something similar. 'Our father giving her the portrait commission did rather push her into getting to know us all, with her coming to the house every day to paint you. I don't suppose she means any harm.'

'Maybe I should help her to make friends with some of the other young women in our group. She seemed to get on well with Emma at my party, so I could encourage that. It's a shame there aren't many young men around, as maybe I could introduce her to some of them, like your friends.'

'I can think of a couple who would be most appreciative.' Victor laughed. 'But with being abroad, that's not currently an option.'

'What's not an option?' said Barbara, joining them once more.

'Introducing Ebony to some nice young men,' said Sophia. 'She seems a little... lonely?'

'I'm sure once the war has finished, she'll get company enough from young men. She's a rather beautiful young woman, don't you think, Victor?'

He and Sophia glanced at each other, both with a slight grin.

'What are you looking at each other like that for? Are you interested in her, Victor?'

'Clearly not, Mother, otherwise Sophia wouldn't be talking about introducing her to other young men.'

'Such a shame.'

Victor shook his head. 'Give up, Mother. I'll find the woman for me in my own good time.'

He glanced around the room casually but was really looking for Hetty. There she was, chatting to Major Thomas by the table. 'I'm just going to get something to eat. Does anybody else want anything?'

The other two declined, so he headed off to the part of the table where Hetty was standing.

'Ah, young Victor,' said the major. 'How is your father doing now?'

This was even better than he'd expected. Not only could he stand near Hetty, but he could bring her into the conversation too.

'Thanks to Henrietta here, he's doing a whole lot better than he might have been.'

—

'Then it was worth attending?' said James, lounging on the settee with a blanket over him in the drawing room.

Sophia had been relating the concert to him in fine detail.

'Of course – I organised it,' she said, with a slight chuckle. 'I'm joking, naturally. Mr Janus had far more input on that side of things.'

'Did it raise a good sum for the soldiers' Christmas boxes?'

'More than we'd even hoped. Aside from the ticket prices, people were very generous with throwing extra money into the buckets at the end. It seems there is no end to their generosity when it comes to our boys abroad.'

'Good, good. Who was there? Anyone of note?'

He only half listened, nodding his head, as Barbara took over the conversation to relate a list of names of several people they knew, and some they were only vaguely acquainted with.

'…and Lady Raynolt asked after you.'

'That was kind of her,' said James.

'That reminds me,' said Victor. 'Ebony also asked after you.'

'That was kind of her, too.'

'The second time in three days.' Sophia nudged his arm. 'If I didn't know better, I'd say she had a little crush on you, Papa.'

She often called him 'Papa' when joking.

He laughed. 'Yes, I should be so lucky to still be attractive to a woman in her twenties.'

'Don't put yourself down like that,' said Barbara. 'You are a handsome man, for— yes. A handsome man.'

'For my age, were you going to say?'

'Don't put words in my mouth, dear.' She walked over and kissed his head. It made him feel like a child. 'I was rather hoping that Ebony and Victor might be interested in each other.'

'I told you, Mother.'

'I know you did, Victor. You're not interested, and you'll find the woman for you in your *own good time*.'

'But don't leave it too long,' said James, yawning as he finished the sentence.

'You're tired,' said Barbara. 'I'll get Fairfax to fetch some hot chocolate, and then we'll get you to bed.'

'All right,' he said reluctantly. 'I'll be glad when I'm better and have a little more energy.'

'All in good time, dear, all in good time.'

Chapter Twenty-One

The following Saturday, Hetty, having spent the last three days thinking of her brief moments with Victor at the concert, was glad to be distracted by the children's Christmas party. She always looked forward to events that involved children. They were a lot less complicated than their grown-up guests and had a sense of joy that was often lost to the adults.

Dorothy and Arthur were in the ballroom with Helen, helping her lay up one end of the long line of tables under her instructions. Already a Christmas tree had been erected there and decorated. They normally only placed one in the foyer.

Hetty couldn't believe how much Helen's children had grown recently. They were now nine and seven. She thought back: Dorothy had been nearly three when she'd started working at the hotel, and Arthur had been about eighteen months old. Had that much time really passed since she'd first entered the stillroom? And yet, so much had happened that it often felt like a very long time ago.

Hetty and Lili eventually met Helen and the children somewhere in the middle of the tables. Although they'd grown so much, in many ways they were still the same; Dorothy with her wavy hazelnut hair, always chirpy, and her brother with his blond mop of hair, sometimes still quite shy around them. But they were both such happy children, despite what they'd been through with their father recently. Whenever she dreamt of having her own children, she often pictured them. Except recently, they'd been more auburn haired…

'Are you looking forward to the party?' Hetty asked them.

'Oh yes!' Dorothy tapped her fisted hands together. She'd grown out of jumping up and down, but her face was still bursting with excitement.

'Me too,' said Arthur, bouncing up and down on his heels.

'It looks like we're done here,' said Helen, 'and just as well, as here come Mrs Turnbull and Simon with the food.'

The storekeeper and waiter were rolling in the first of the trolleys carrying the trays. Behind them came a couple of the kitchen staff, doing the same.

'People are already queuing in the foyer, with some very excited children,' said Bridget Turnbull, coming to a stop by the tables.

'We'd better be quick then,' said Helen, indicating to Hetty and Lili to help unload the trollies.

They'd nearly finished when Helen exclaimed, 'Ah, Mister Janus!'

The entertainment manager had entered through the large door on the left of the room with an older gentleman and a young, petite woman.

'Good afternoon, Mrs Bygrove. Let me introduce you to Mr Wackett, the magician, and Miss Bonney, a children's entertainer.'

'Thank you so much for agreeing to do this for free,' said Helen. 'We're all very grateful.'

'We're just glad to be able to make some contribution to a children's charity, especially at Christmas,' said Miss Bonney.

'We'll start with the tea, with which you'll also be provided, and then we'll have the entertainment after.'

'I've often wanted to partake of the food here,' said Mr Wackett. 'Never had the chance before.'

'It's not quite up to our pre-war standard, and has been made with the children in mind, but I believe it will still prove a tasty menu.'

'And we'll do a little entertaining while the children are eating, too.'

The empty trolleys were wheeled out. Soon women and children started to enter the room. They chatted eagerly, some going to take a closer look at the tree, wide-eyed.

Hetty helped show the children to the tables, feeling their excitement. That is, until she noticed her sister, Iris, coming in with her children, Jane and Alfie.

'Auntie Hetty,' they called, as they ran over.

'Do not run!' Iris called, catching them up. 'I told you, you have to be on your best behaviour here.'

'How lovely to see you,' said Hetty, though it was aimed more at her niece and nephew than her sister.

'You mentioned the party when you came with Phoebe for lunch, so I thought we'd see if it lived up to expectation, given how much you boast about these events.'

Hetty ignored the comment. 'Come on you two, there are seats for you here at the end, next to Dorothy and Arthur, who live at the hotel.'

'I wish *I* lived in a hotel,' said Jane.

Soon, all the children were seated, still chattering with excitement. After a welcome from Helen, they were soon tucking in to the food. Mr Wackett started at the opposite end of the table, performing simple magic tricks and sleights of hand, while Miss Bonney was telling jokes to children near Hetty.

'What is heavier, a half-moon or a full moon,' she asked the children.

Some called out, 'A full moon!' while Arthur put his hand up and said, 'They're both the same, 'cos you can't see the other side of the full moon.'

'You're all wrong,' said Miss Bonney. 'It's the half-moon that's heavier, because the full moon is twice as light.'

The children giggled loudly, except one who had to ask the child next to them what she meant.

'What is it that never asks questions yet requires many answers?'

One older girl, sitting opposite Hetty's niece and nephew, held her hand up as straight as she could, straining as she said, 'Ooh, ooh, me Miss, I know.'

'Go on then,' said Miss Bonney.

'A doorbell!'

'Well done, young lady! Let's give her a round of applause.' To which Miss Bonney clapped in a circle.

The children nearby all laughed and copied.

The entertainer moved along to talk to the next lot of children. Iris, who'd gone to fetch a cup of tea, came back to where Hetty was watching the children eating and chatting.

'Mother's only trying to help, you know.'

'I'm sorry?' said Hetty.

'Her efforts to matchmake. You don't want to be left on the shelf, do you? So, the vicar is a little dull and judgemental, but he'd be better than no husband at all.'

'I beg to differ, Iris. I can think of few things worse than being stuck with him for the rest of my life. I'd rather be a spinster.'

'And work here for evermore?'

'There are worse places to spend your life. I mean, look at it?' She indicated the magnificence of the ballroom with its fancy embossed walls, the crystal chandeliers and the walnut and oak parquet flooring with its hexagons and stars.

'I presume your quarters aren't like this. Nor the scullery, where you spend most of your time. That would be a little *indulgent*.'

'Of course not. And I'm in the stillroom, not the scullery. Not that there's any shame in being in the scullery.'

'If you became a live-out and went back home, you'd be much more likely to find a young man.'

'Would you want to live with our parents at my age?'

'Of course not, but I'm married, and have been for ten years.'

'You were seventeen when you got married, and far too young, according to Mum. And I must say, I wondered then, and still do, whether you did so to escape home. You and Mum often argued back then.'

'I love my Jesse. I wanted to marry him.'

'But you could have waited a little longer.'

Iris didn't reply; it seemed that Hetty might have hit the nail on the head.

'Well, it's your life, I suppose,' said Iris. 'But if you take too long to find a husband, you'll be too old to be of interest to anyone. I believe you're meeting Mother in town on Monday.'

'That's right. We're doing a little Christmas shopping.'

Mum had been keen to meet for this purpose. It would be easier to cope with her in town, with others about. And she wouldn't be able to invite some young man to match her up with.

'Good. Make sure you turn up and don't leave after half an hour or whatever, as seems to have become your habit.'

This did make Hetty feel guilty. Had she been avoiding her family, particularly her mother, too much?

Mr Wackett was now at their end of the table with a pack of cards he was doing a few tricks with.

'Excuse me, Iris, I need to make sure everyone is provided for.' Hetty moved away, glad of a genuine excuse to take a break from her sister.

–

On Monday, Hetty met her mother outside Hussey's drapers and milliners store on High Street.

'Hello, Mother. Are you looking for a new hat for Christmas?'

'No, Henrietta, I have enough. You, on the other hand, could probably do with one.' She examined the wide-brimmed hat that Hetty was wearing, making her feel self-conscious.

'There's nothing wrong with this.' She patted it on one side. 'I only bought it a couple of years ago.'

'It's out of date. Much smaller hats are in fashion now. A young, single woman such as yourself should endeavour to keep up with fashion, especially if you are to attract a man of reasonable status.'

Like the vicar? Hetty thought.

'Let's go in and have a look. You can tell me what takes your fancy, and maybe you will get it for Christmas.' Miriam went forward and opened the shop door.

Hetty rather liked surprises at Christmas, but a new hat wouldn't hurt. And she could wear it for Victor.

She followed her mother in, enjoying the scent of new fabric. Inside was crowded with wooden shelving and drawers with glass fronts, holding all manner of accessories and items of haberdashery. On one side, there was a large display of hats. She pointed out a couple that reminded her of ones she'd seen in a *Vogue* magazine that a guest had left behind. Miriam made a note of them.

Out on the street once more, her mother said, 'Let's start at one end of High Street and keep going until half past two, when we have a booking at Read's Dining Room.'

'We're having afternoon tea? I thought such things were wasteful in wartime.'

'That's not exactly what I said. I hope you didn't have too much lunch.'

'Only a sandwich. And anyway, I'm quite happy to have afternoon tea. It'll be interesting to see what their teas are like now.'

'Not as *lavish* as at the Beach Hotel, I'll be bound.'

Hetty shook her head slightly, deciding not to reply. They walked down to the end of the street where it met Beach Road and started from there. They did mostly window shopping, popping into the odd store that might hold a gift they wanted to purchase. Despite Hetty's apprehension about this trip out, she and her mother had got on well, even having a joke or two about unsuitable gifts for certain family members. She was enjoying the afternoon, and now looked forward to the tea for more than just the treat it was.

When they'd completed around half the street, Miriam looked at her watch and said, 'Twenty-five past two. We'd better get ourselves around the corner.'

They reached the building, about halfway down Surrey Street, and took the stairs to the first floor.

'I've booked a table under the name of Affleck,' said Miriam, reaching the small desk near the top of the stairs.

'Yes, here we are,' said the waitress. 'Your other guest has already arrived.'

'Other guest?' said Hetty. She got no reply as her mother followed the young woman. She must have invited Iris too. Oh well, she'd make the best of it. But no, the children had broken up for Christmas last Friday.

When they reached the table, there was a young man there, somewhere in his late twenties she guessed.

'Henrietta, this is Archibald Olafsson. He's a teacher at your father's school. Archibald, this is my younger daughter, Henrietta.'

The young man stood and extended an arm. He smiled as they shook hands.

'How do you do?' he said, and she replied in kind.

He was a nice-looking chap, with light blond hair combed back to one side. His clothes were up to date and looked new. She smiled politely but was furious with her mother. Even on a shopping trip, she had managed to manipulate the situation to introduce her to a potential husband.

But she wasn't going to be rude to him – Archibald – as it wasn't his fault. No doubt her mother had persuaded him to come, maybe even made out that Hetty herself wished to meet someone like him.

'Let's sit down and look at the menu,' said Hetty.

'Yes, you do that,' said Miriam. 'I'll be back by four o'clock.'

'Aren't you staying?'

'No, I have things to do.' She wasted no time in walking away.

'I'm so sorry about this,' said Hetty when Miriam was out of earshot. 'Were you talked into meeting me here?'

He laughed. 'You didn't realise I'd be here?'

Something about his relaxed manner put her at ease. 'No. I thought I was having afternoon tea with my mother.'

'Oh dear. Would you rather I left?'

'No, that wouldn't be fair. Let's make the best of it. What exactly did my mother say to you?'

'She was telling me how I should be married at my age, and said she'd introduce me to you and seemed to have decided on that before I could say yay or nay. I didn't like to offend her.'

'She can be rather, um... overbearing, when she has her mind set on something. As for the "you should be married at your age" line, she says that to me all the time.'

They both chuckled.

'So, you're a teacher at Lyminster Council School, Archibald. I don't recall seeing you at any of the events.'

'Please, call me Archie. Most people do. I only started at the school in September. I moved down from Billingshurst. I fancied being by the seaside. And wanted to be more independent.'

'I don't blame you. And I'm Hetty, by the way, but Mum never calls me that in public. Sorry, *Mother*. She doesn't like being called "Mum" in public either.'

He laughed again. 'I think you and I have a lot in common in that way.'

'Olafsson sounds Scandinavian.'

'My father's parents were Swedish. They emigrated to England nearly sixty years ago.'

'Goodness. Have you ever visited your grandparents' homeland?'

'Just the once, with my father.'

'Do you mind me asking why you're not in the army?'

'Good old flat feet, I'm afraid. I did try to enlist in the first month, but there it is.'

'That's exactly like young Jack, our sous chef. I do apologise for giving you the third degree about your name and army status.'

'Don't worry. I'm used to it. My two brothers are in the war, but they wish they'd inherited flat feet too. As far as the name is concerned, I'm glad it's not German, though a couple of people have asked whether it is. And people aren't always happy about Sweden being neutral in this war.'

'I wish Britain was,' she said.

They ordered a pot of tea along with a scone and a piece of fruit cake each, then she told him about her life at the hotel.

'They sound like a nice group of people to work with,' he said.

'They're like a second family. And we've been through some troubles together and looked after each other.'

'Your father told me about the business with the poison pen letters earlier in the year, and about your boss being, you know...'

'Killed? Yes, it was a tough time for us all, especially Mrs Bygrove.'

When their order arrived, he told her something of his life.

'So, after training college, I worked in a school near home and lived with my parents. But when I had my twenty-eighth birthday last Easter, I thought it was about time I widened my horizons. And here I am.'

'Are you enjoying the change?'

'Oh my, yes. I needed a fresh start. And your father is a good headmaster to work with.'

'His staff do often say that.'

As they took a break from talking to pour more tea, Hetty noticed a group of three fashionable young women enter the room. She was surprised to see that one of them was Ebony. Now why was she here for afternoon tea, and not the hotel? Maybe to meet these friends.

'You mentioned that Mrs Bygrove has children. Are they at Lyminster School?'

'No, they go to the one on East Street, in town.'

'Of course, that would be a lot closer to the hotel.'

Hetty looked around the room once more. Ebony and the other women had been seated almost out of view, by the window. She and Archie chatted a little more, about the war and family members in it, about food restrictions.

When the large wooden wall clock said ten to four, she said, 'We'd better get the bill. I'm meeting my mother in ten minutes.'

'You don't need to worry about that. She said she'd pay the bill when she came back. I did try to persuade her otherwise, but she was insistent, and I didn't want to cause an argument. I do feel rather guilty though.'

'Please don't. It's hard to win an argument with my mother, believe me. Talk of the devil.'

Miriam appeared at the desk and was indeed paying some money to the waitress.

'Before we go, I wonder if you'd like to come to the carol service with me at the Mission Church on the twenty-second. Just as a friend. I haven't had time to make many yet, and I'd like to go with someone.'

She felt some sympathy for him, and wished for a second that she could say yes. 'I'm so sorry. Like I told Mum when she asked, it's too close to Christmas and we'll be busy. Mind you, she asked me to go because she thought she might be able to pair me up with Reverend Peck.'

Archie's eyes widened and his mouth opened in shock. 'Reverend Peck? Goodness, poor you. He's, well…'

'Yes, exactly. I put her straight, you might say. Here she comes. Don't tell her I told you.'

He put his finger to his lips. 'Not a word.'

'You two look like you're having fun,' said Miriam.

'It's been an enjoyable conversation,' said Archie.

'Good, good. Sorry we're going to have to abandon you now, Mr Olafsson, as we must get on with our festive shopping.'

'Of course. I need to get some provisions from the grocers so need to get on too. Cheerio, Hetty. I hope we'll meet again.'

'Likewise, Archie.'

Hetty and her mother left first. Outside it was even chillier than earlier and there was little light left in the sky. They'd walked past a few shops before Miriam said, 'So you're already calling each other Hetty and Archie.' She smiled. 'And he said he hoped you'd meet again. Does that mean you haven't arranged anything yet?'

'No, we haven't. He asked me to go with him to the carol service, but as you know, I can't.'

'Oh really, Henrietta! Didn't you suggest some other outing?'

'No, Mother. He is a very pleasant young man, and we enjoyed each other's company, but we both agreed that we'd like to be friends and nothing more.'

'I despair of you! He's not only a very nice young man but good looking and smart too. He has ambitions and might even make it to headmaster one day. What more could you want?'

'Love?'

'Love! So overrated. It doesn't put food on the table. And how do you know it wouldn't turn into love?'

'Let's not argue, Mother. I enjoy Christmas shopping, and I don't want to spoil it.'

'All right. Come on then. I still haven't got anything for Iris.'

–

'Good evening, Sophia,' said Ebony, as she entered the hall belonging to the Congregational Church.

'Good evening, Ebony. I trust you all had a good afternoon tea at Read's? I'm sorry I couldn't join you, but I had another meeting.'

'Yes, we had a nice time, thank you. Kate and Emma will be here shortly. I appreciate you including me in some of your social events with friends. It's not always easy to form friendships in new places.'

'I did wonder if you were lacking company. Read's isn't the top place for afternoon tea, but it's certainly adequate.'

'I'd say it was more than adequate, even if it's no Beach Hotel. Talking of which, I actually saw one of the staff members from the hotel there. Henrietta. She's served in the conservatory and at events a few times, though I believe she is a stillroom maid.'

'Oh, yes, I know who you mean.'

Ebony moved in a little closer, displaying a mischievous smirk. 'I believe she might have a sweetheart, as she was with a very nice-looking young man, smartly dressed and *very* blond, and they did seem to laugh quite a lot.'

She was surprised to see Sophia frowning a little.

'Really? And you didn't recognise the young man?'

'Not at all. Is there a problem? Are the staff not allowed romantic relationships?'

Sophia chuckled a little. 'I'm sure they are. I was just being nosy, wondering if it was anyone I knew.'

'I wouldn't have thought it would have been anyone in *your* circle of friends.'

'Who knows these days.'

'How was your father today?'

'Fine. Still improving. Anyway, take a seat, Ebony. You're the first here, but I'm sure the others will arrive soon.' She walked back to a table that had some papers on it.

Ebony chose a seat at the front of the two rows of chairs, right in the middle. Kate and Emma entered at this point, and she beckoned them over.

As Victor was coming down the stairs that evening, having changed for dinner, his sister came through the front door into the hallway.

'How was the meeting?' he called.

'Very productive.' She met him at the bottom of the stairs and took his arm. 'Can I have a word?'

She looked concerned, which in turn worried him. 'Yes, of course.'

'Where's Mother?' she whispered.

'Already in the drawing room with Father, I believe.'

'Upstairs would be best then.'

She led him around the curve of the stairs and into her bedroom, looking into the corridor before shutting the door.

'What's all this about, sis?'

'Ebony went to Read's Dining Rooms today.'

'And?'

'She told me she saw Hetty there.'

'She is allowed out on her own,' he joked.

'Apparently she was with a nice looking, smartly dressed young man, and Ebony had the impression that they were sweethearts, as they seemed to be laughing quite a lot.'

'It might have been her brother, Hector, who's at home recuperating from a shoulder injury.'

'She didn't mention any injuries.'

'It may not have been obvious. Or it could have been her other brother, Gilbert, home on leave.'

'Wouldn't she have mentioned her brother being on leave though? Are either of her brothers blond?'

'I have *no* idea. It's not something men tend to ask.'

'It's just that Ebony made a point of saying that he was *very* blond. That's quite unusual in an adult.'

'True enough. Look Sophia, are you trying to say that she might be... deceiving me?'

'I don't know what to think. It does seem a little like that. You could be right, it might be one of her brothers. I don't want to cause trouble, especially if there's none to be caused, but I thought you ought to know, just in case. I would hate to see you get hurt, little brother.'

'Thank you for your concern, though I'm sure it's nothing to worry about. You'd better get changed before Mother starts fretting about you being late for dinner.'

She nodded and he left the room. He headed down the stairs.

Nothing to worry about, that's what he'd said to his sister. And he wanted to believe that, he really did.

Lorcan. Could it be him, home on leave? If not, some other poor clod that she was taking for a ride? No, not his Hetty.

'Darn and blast it,' he mouthed, standing in the hall. He knew he'd brood about it all evening, and all night if he wasn't careful. He needed to calm down.

He took a deep breath, put on a smile and entered the drawing room.

–

As Victor had predicted, his sleep had been fitful, with him waking at least three times after vague dreams about Hetty that he couldn't quite recall. But they hadn't been good, that he did know.

He was tapping a pen on a notebook, staring into space in his office, when his secretary placed a cup and saucer in front of him.

'Are you all right, Mr Perryman?'

'Hmm? Oh, yes Miss Murrells, thank you. Just trying to work out a little engineering problem in my head.'

'I'm afraid the grocer's run out of biscuits.'

'Don't worry.'

When she'd disappeared downstairs, he put his head back and closed his eyes. He was trying to smooth out a small problem with a new design they had for the hulls, but with the mood he was in, his brain couldn't even begin to work on it.

He looked at the time. Just coming up to ten. 'Right, that's it,' he muttered, before drinking half the tea, despite it being a little too warm. Hetty had mentioned being on late morning breaks this week, and he knew that meant a quarter past ten. If he walked quickly, he could be at the hotel by then, pop in the side entrance, and ask to see her. He didn't care what the scullery maids thought, or any of the rest of the staff. He'd find his way to their dining room if he had to.

He got up and went downstairs, grabbing his coat and hat off the stand. 'I've just got to pop out, Miss Murrells. I won't be long.'

She was replying as he opened the door to leave. At least he knew his father wouldn't be checking up on him. He'd had to visit the other businesses a few times since the accident, so his staff were accustomed to him leaving from time to time. And if he didn't get this sorted out, one way or another, he'd be no good to any of their businesses.

He became ever more flustered as he dashed across the pebbles of the quay. He'd tell Hetty what he'd heard and ask for an honest answer. Was she hedging her bets because she didn't believe his statement about her being the love of his life? Maybe if he actually asked her to marry him, she'd see that—

'Mr Perryman!' a voice called out from the office. It was Miss Murrells.

He twisted around, annoyed at the delay. 'What is it?'

'There's a telephone call from Haydon's. They're asking if you can call in within the next hour, about one of the components they need. It sounds rather urgent.'

'I, that is…' His head slumped and he looked down at the pebbles. He was in charge of everything for now, and he needed to do his best. 'Yes, tell them I'm heading over now. I'll be there in five minutes.'

'Very well.'

He looked briefly at the route past the Britannia public house towards the hotel, before going in the other direction, towards the alley that led to River Road, and ultimately, the bridge over the river.

He needed to step up to the mark, to prove to his father what he was made of. And that meant forgetting his own problems for now, however hard that was.

–

Hetty was ready for a sit down when she got to the late morning break.

'My, morning coffee is busy today,' Lili said as she slumped on the bench opposite her. 'What with a full dining room for breakfast earlier, I was glad that Dennis was taking over halfway through.'

'We are busier than last year.'

'That's hardly surprising, given all the trouble we had then… You're helping with the lunch for the townsfolk tomorrow, aren't you?'

'That's right,' said Hetty. 'I'm looking forward to it. The people who come for those events are always so appreciative and it's a pleasure serving them. It's good to be able to raise money for the Littlehampton War Fund as well. And it's only a week until Christmas. I'm really looking forward to that too.'

'I'm looking forward to it being over,' said Lili.

'Why on earth are you – oh, of course. Rhodri's coming on leave on the second of January.'

'It's ages since I last saw him. I wish he'd stayed put doing clerical work in Shoreham, instead of going back to France to do it.'

'I can understand that.'

A few more staff members came in, including Gertie, Bridget Turnbull and Jack. Fanny came in a little after, holding Elsie's hand as she walked slowly beside her. At the table she picked her up and put her on her lap.

'Where bickie?' said Elsie, pointing at the table.

'Mrs Norris said there weren't enough for us to have any today,' said Jack.

'Sorry, no bickies today, sweetie,' Fanny told her toddler as she poured her a very milky cup of tea.

'Want bickie,' Elsie persisted, her mouth going down at the corners.

'I'll find somethin' for you, pet,' said Mrs Turnbull, leaving the room.

'We were just saying how busy it's been today,' said Hetty.

Fanny blew out a noisy breath through her lips. 'Don't I know it. Almost every room is booked and we've got two of the live-out chambermaids off with colds. I've had to rearrange the rota and get people to do even more extra shifts.'

'It's been non-stop in the kitchen today,' said Jack.

Mrs Turnbull was soon back with a small biscuit that had probably been a little piece of dough left after the rest of the biscuits had been cut out.

'There you are, hinny.'

Elsie didn't seem to notice its meagreness and took it eagerly. 'Tankoo.'

'Aw, you're welcome, pet.'

They all looked around as the door opened once more. Helen Bygrove entered, followed by Mrs Leggett. They stood together near the table. Neither woman looked happy.

'I'm sorry to be the bearer of some bad news,' said Helen, 'but I'm afraid I've had to cancel the Christmas lunch for the townspeople tomorrow.'

'Oh no, why?' said Lili.

'We just can't get the supplies. As much as I'd like to prioritise it, I can't leave our paying guests short. Meals have had to be pared down as it is, which the guests have been understanding about because of the war, but I can't risk rationing them anymore.'

'Come and sit yoursel' down and have a cup of tea,' said Mrs Turnbull.

'I wish I could, but I must make sure that everyone who booked is told about the cancellation and how to get their refunds. I don't want them turning up tomorrow to disappointment. I'll see you all later.'

Mrs Turnbull poured the housekeeper a cup of tea as she slumped into her chair. 'I don't wish to sound pessimistic, but I think these shortages are goin' to get worse before they get better, and we'll just have to get used to it.'

'You're right, Mrs Turnbull,' said Lili. 'At breakfast, Mr Fletcher read out that people in Pontypool are being issued with ration cards for some common foods.'

'It was sugar, tea, butter and margarine,' said Jack. 'All things we use a lot of here.'

'Even margarine's being rationed?' said Hetty.

'Yep,' said Jack. 'As for meat, we're going to have to use more pigeon and rabbit in the kitchen and create more vegetarian meals. Even fish has been harder to get hold of, despite the fishing trade here.'

'We're already having meatless days,' said Hetty. 'Just like the government suggested.'

'If there isn't enough meat to go around, then we're all going to have to get used to more meatless days, including the guests,' said Mrs Leggett.

-

The sun was sinking beyond the dunes on West Beach by the time Victor reached the pier, later that day. He leant over the end of the jetty, looking out to sea. The sky was a light orange, darkening to saffron on the horizon. The area was empty of people.

Victor was still worried about Hetty and this blond man, but he had managed to simmer down. He was now thankful for the call from Haydon's; had he rushed over to the Beach Hotel in that state of mind, he'd have made a complete idiot of himself.

He still needed to sort it out, but he would do it sensibly, calmly, however much his heart was hurting.

He caught sight of Hetty as she approached the pier. She was the only person he could see in the immediate vicinity, wearing her navy wool coat.

He looked back at the sea, not turning around until she had nearly reached him.

She stood next to him, taking his arm and kissing his cheek. 'Have you been waiting long?'

He didn't kiss her in return but kept looking out at the water. 'Only five minutes. The sky's beautiful this evening.'

'It is, but I'd trade it for summer sun any day. I've never been fond of long winter nights. You sound rather melancholy. How have you been? And how is your father?'

'He's getting better all the time, but he's still confined to home by my mother. I can't help thinking he'd be better off going out for short walks. Maybe if it wasn't winter she'd let him.'

'And you? How are you?'

'Busy. Sophia's even spent a bit of time in the office to help out. She's been very useful. It's a shame Father denied her a part in the firm when she asked to be involved a few years back.'

'What's wrong? You seem very down, and not particularly pleased to see me.'

He turned to look at her. 'I'm sorry. It's just…'

'What?'

'Are either of your brothers blond? Or Lorcan?'

'Blond? No. My brothers both have brown hair, and Lorcan's is black. Why do you ask?'

'Hetty, are you seeing someone else as well?'

She stepped back, letting go of his arm. 'What do you mean, seeing someone else?'

'I mean, another man, another – sweetheart.'

'Of course not! Why would you think that?'

'Ebony Girard told Sophia that she saw you in Read's Dining Rooms with a young man who had blond hair.'

'Oh my. I didn't think Ebony had noticed me.'

'Then you *were* with another man?'

'No, Victor, I wasn't. Well, I was, but it wasn't… oh how can I explain?'

'Just tell me.' He looked down at his hands, gripping the pier wall, anticipating the worst.

'I'd never met him before and didn't even know he was going to be there. His name is Archibald Olafsson – Archie – and he's a teacher at my father's school. I was out for the afternoon with my mother, and she said we were going for tea at Read's, but when we got there Archie was at the table and she left us two alone.'

'She was trying to matchmake the two of you?'

'Yes, like she tried with the vicar, and how your parents tried with you and Rosetta Stone.'

'Ebony thought you were getting on rather well.'

'Goodness, she *was* taking notice. He was a nice chap and we did get along, but only in the same way as I would with, I don't know, Edie, or Annie in the kitchen. We had a laugh about my mother trying to match the two of us up. We agreed that friendship was the only thing on the cards. I felt sorry for him, to be honest. I don't think he's made many friends since he arrived here in September. I'm sorry, I should have told you that when I first arrived. I was going to tell you later.'

Victor blew out a long breath that showed up in the cold air. Then he smiled. 'Hetty, I'm so relieved.'

'Did you really think I would do that to you? And it should have occurred to you, especially after what we've both been through lately with our mothers trying to matchmake us.'

'You're absolutely right. I didn't want to think it, but I suppose I was afraid. Stupid really. I'm so sorry.'

'I suppose it's nice to know you care so much.'

She pushed her fingers through his thick, auburn hair and kissed his cheek. He turned his head and brushed her lips with his. Soon they were in each other's arms, kissing deeply.

It was a minute or two before their faces moved apart slightly, but they remained in an embrace.

'Oh Hetty, I'm not going to leave it too long before I tell my parents about us. I can't. Being parted from you most of the time is unbearable.'

He thought about his earlier plan to ask him to marry her. That really would not have been the time, and neither was this, not an actual, down on one knee proposal. Not yet. He wanted to do it somewhere different, somewhere special.

'Are you sure it's wise to tell your parents?'

'What else are we going to do? We can't just exist like this for the rest of our lives. I need you with me, properly in my life. I'll have to leave it until after Christmas though. Father will be better by then. But it has to be done. How do you think your parents will take it?'

'How do you think? My mother in particular would be thrilled. You would be all of her dreams come true.'

'Am I all of *your* dreams come true?'

'Definitely, but not for the same reasons as my mother's. I don't care about your money or status, or whether you dress smartly or have a fashionable hair style. I only care about you. I love *you* for *you*.' She pressed her palm against his chest twice as she said the word 'you'. 'I love you more than anything else in this whole world.'

'And nothing matters more to me than you. You are everything to me.'

Somewhere in the sky, a seagull keened several long notes.

'You see, my feathered friend agrees with me,' he said.

'I've always thought of the seagulls' cries as mournful,' said Hetty, 'but from now on, whenever I hear it, I will remember this moment.'

They kissed once more, then turned to look at the western sky as the orange became a deep ruddy bronze, like a pool of blood across the sky. It felt to Victor like they were the only two people in this darkening world, and at that brief moment in time, he was content with that.

Chapter Twenty-Two

Barbara had left James to dress himself that morning, and for that he was grateful. He felt like a toddler, her helping him on with his trousers, shirt and jacket, doing up his buttons. Perhaps, seeing that he'd managed today, she'd allow him to dress himself from now on.

He was currently sat by the fire in the drawing room, watching the flames. He looked up at the carriage clock on the mantelpiece. Half past nine. Not long now.

The reason Barbara hadn't helped him this morning was that he'd got up late and she'd had a meeting to attend for some Christmas charity event. She'd asked Perkins the valet to help him dress before she'd left, but James had dismissed him when he'd come to assist. He'd never needed a valet to help him dress, and he wasn't about to start now.

She wasn't due back today until lunchtime, by which time he'd be long gone. He'd give the butler, Harries, a message to pass on. Barbara had said that it didn't matter about him giving them all Christmas presents this year, that the fact he was getting better was all the present they needed, but he just had to get out and buy them all something. They deserved it after all they'd done for him in his time of need.

The butler appeared in the hall just at the right moment. 'Harries, when my wife returns, would you tell her not to worry and that I've just walked into town. And would you get Perkins to fetch my coat, hat and scarf, please?'

'Would you like somebody to walk there with you, sir?' Harries sounded a little concerned.

'No, no. I'll be fine.'

'But Mrs Perryman said—'

'My wife over fusses, Harries. It's only because she cares, but I will be all right.'

'Very well, sir.'

Harries left, and soon Perkins was in the hall with the required items.

He put on his coat and placed the bowler hat on his head and left, not looking back as he walked away from Surrey Cottage. What he hadn't told Harries was that he was actually taking the train to Worthing. No need to worry anyone unduly.

–

Ebony smiled as she left the last shop she needed to visit in Worthing. It had been a successful day and she'd managed to get all the presents she needed for her family. She'd parked on Marine Parade, close to the pier, so she headed back along the main thoroughfare of Montague Street in that direction.

She was just passing Perilli's Refreshment House, when she saw a familiar figure come out of the door, carrying several brown paper bags and looking rather the worse for wear.

'Mr Perryman! Oh my goodness, are you all right?' She hurried towards him. 'Is someone with you?'

'Uh, no. I came to Worthing by myself.'

'Why on earth did they let you? You're clearly not well enough.' She used her free hand to help him along a little. 'I'm sure I could fit your packages in my basket. I made sure I brought my large one.' She stopped and took the bags from him.

'That's most kind of you. And nobody let me. I'm afraid I escaped.' His expression was half smile, half grimace.

'Did you drive here?'

'No, I took the train.'

'In that case, I will drive you home. Your wife must be worried sick.'

'I really don't need help. I need to do things for myself. And I haven't quite finished yet.'

'You've clearly already done too much for one day. You are looking decidedly pale. Now come along.' She took his arm and matched his pace, which was slower than usual. 'Honestly, men! Always thinking they have to be able to cope with everything. My motorcar is right near the pier, so we don't have too far to walk.'

–

Ebony pulled up outside Surrey Cottage a little after two thirty. James dreaded what might be coming next, the telling off for not only going out, but for doing it in secret. Still, it was his own fault.

'Thank you for giving me a lift, Ebony. I'd better get inside and face the music. You get off back to the hotel. It looks like it might rain.' And he didn't want her to be a witness to whatever was coming.

'I'll carry your parcels to the door,' she insisted.

As he got out, the front door opened and Barbara came running down the front path. 'Where on *earth* have you been?' She frowned at Ebony as she carried the parcels from the car. 'What is the meaning of this?'

'I was shopping in Worthing, and came across your husband looking decidedly fatigued,' said Ebony. 'He said he was going to take the train home, but I couldn't let him in that state.'

'Thank you, Miss Girard, that was most kind of you.' She took the parcels from her. 'What a stroke of luck you came across him. Now for pity's sake, James, get inside and sit down.'

'Yes, dear.' He took one last look at Ebony before limping inside. Despite being agitated about his lack of independence, he had enjoyed the trip back with her. Her liveliness reminded him of his youth once more, of the lovely Irene. But that was all a very long time ago. And at this moment in time, he felt the very opposite of young.

As he sat in the armchair in the drawing room, Barbara entered, her expression a mixture of anxiety and irritation.

'Where have you been, James?'

'You know where I've been.'

'But you told Harries you were going into town, not to Worthing.'

'I didn't want to worry you.'

'I was already worried by you just leaving the house by yourself.'

'I'm sorry. I just wanted to get away to do some Christmas shopping.'

'Oh James, why did you have to lie? I could have driven you to Worthing.'

'I wanted to be by myself, so that I could buy you a present.'

'You could have got Victor or Sophia to go with you. Or Perkins.'

'It wouldn't have been the same though, as going on my own, especially to get something for you.'

'Oh James! I'll get Perkins to store your gifts.'

'I can do that myself.'

'Very well. They're on the hall table. But come straight back and you're not moving again today, except to walk to the dining room and then later to bed.'

'Yes, dear.'

Chapter Twenty-Three

'All right, everyone, this is the last chance we're going to get to practise before tomorrow's performance,' said Lili, as the makeshift choir gathered in the ballroom late Sunday evening. 'It's our dress rehearsal, if you like.'

Hetty was already nervous, and this wasn't even the real thing. It was the first time they'd all managed to sing together, as in the other rehearsals there'd always been different people missing, including herself. She only hoped it worked out as well as Lili seemed to think it would. The choir consisted of Annie and Alice, Mrs Turnbull, three of the young men, four other live-out members of staff, and Lili and Hetty: twelve in all. Edie was at the piano, which had already been sent over by Mr Janus. Her skill was adequate for the rehearsal, but elementary, so she wouldn't be playing on the night.

'We'll start with "The Twelve Days of Christmas", the second song in our programme, which begins with – oh.' Lili scanned the group in front of her. 'Simon isn't here.'

The nearest door opened, and Simon came rushing in. 'Sorry I'm late. Hope I haven't missed too much.'

'No, we're just about to start,' said Lili. 'But you are the first voice in "The Twelve Days".'

He took his place, and they began, each of them representing a different day, every verse ending with Simon's enthusiastic, 'And a partridge in a pear tree.'

Hetty was the ninth day of Christmas; she was grateful only to have to sing her solo part four times.

They practised ten other carols, having to restart a couple. Hetty was impressed with Annie and Alice's duet, harmonising beautifully together on the melancholic 'Coventry Carol'.

'Right, now let's finish with the carol we're going to start with,' said Lili. 'Since this is your county's carol, let's give a rousing performance.'

During the first verse, Hetty noticed the door open slowly, before Ebony Girard stepped in. She remained against the closed door and smiled as they sang.

When the song came to an end, Ebony clapped eagerly. 'Bravo!'

Lili swung round in surprise, clearly not realising she'd come in. 'Oh, yes. Thank you, Miss Girard.'

'I'm really looking forward to the concert tomorrow. Good luck, everyone.'

There was a round of thank yous, before Ebony left the room.

'How long was she standing there?' Lili asked them. 'I wish she wouldn't creep up on a body like that.'

'She only arrived during the first verse,' Hetty said, laughing. 'She was hardly creeping up on you.'

'Anyway, off you all go now. Don't shout or strain your voices between now and tomorrow, look you.' Her pointed forefinger panned across to include them all.

'You're starting to sound like Mrs Leggett,' said Annie.

'Didn't know she had a Welsh accent,' Lili quipped.

'No, I mean the—'

'I know what you mean. Now get along with you all.' She grinned. 'I can appreciate, being in charge of this, why she's so bossy sometimes.'

There was a chorus of 'goodnight' and 'see ya tomorrow!' as the choir dispersed.

Soon only Lili and Edie were left, gathering up song sheets. Hetty went over to them.

'Are you sure my voice is good enough for my solo in "The Twelve Days of Christmas"?'

'Of course it is,' said Lili. 'Believe me, I wouldn't let you spoil it if it weren't.'

'You have a good voice,' Edie confirmed.

'Thank you.' She was encouraged by their words. 'I'd better get to bed as I have an early shift tomorrow. Night night.'

–

Ebony heard the familiar voices before she saw the figures enter the foyer on Christmas Eve, late morning. First in was her mother, fussing over her father, then behind came Marigold and Hazel, with their mothers behind them. Bringing up the rear were two of the family's chauffeurs, overladen with cases.

'Mama, Papa,' called Ebony, rushing over to them, kissing each of them on both cheeks. She repeated the ritual with her aunts and cousins, then greeted the staff. 'You've arrived almost exactly the time you said you would.'

'You know I always work these things out as closely as I can,' said her mother, resplendent in a violet swagger coat.

'It's so lovely to see you all. Especially you two.' She took hold of Marigold and Hazel's hands. 'I've missed you so. You must tell me all about your exploits in the hospital and in France.'

They smiled at her, but both looked tired.

'Let's get checked in first,' said her mother, 'and settled in our rooms. It will be luncheon soon, and we can catch up with all our news then.'

'I'll get us all checked in, Irene,' said her father. 'You organise the staff to bring in the rest of the luggage.'

'Very well, Humphrey.'

Ebony chatted with her aunts and cousins about the journey as her mother gave instructions to the chauffeurs.

'And there's a short carol concert this evening, with the hotel staff choir. They were splendid last year, led by the head waitress,

Liliwen, who has the most divine voice. And it does put one in the Christmas spirit.'

'Oh yes, it was very good,' Marigold confirmed, and Hazel agreed.

When all the luggage had been brought in and stacked neatly, ready for the porters to transport to the rooms, Irene took a moment to do a circle, taking in the foyer.

'My, it's been a good many years since I came in here, and then it wasn't to stay of course, only for afternoon tea, since we lived nearby.'

'Yes, we all came together a couple of times,' said her sister Rachael, who was Marigold's mother. She grinned. 'And there was that ball, held by the family that Father knew.'

Irene's brow creased. 'I can't say I remember it much now. Ah, here are the porters, oh, and a portress. How novel.'

'I did tell you that a lot of the female staff have taken over the male roles now, Mama.'

'So you did. I must say, I don't remember it being as splendid as this. Come along now, let's get to our rooms and get changed for luncheon.'

'Do you need any help?' Ebony asked, not wanting to be on her own.

'You can come and help us unpack,' said Hazel. 'Marigold and I are sharing a room.'

This information made Ebony feel left out, but she smiled and replied, 'Of course,' being keen to be in their company once more.

–

As Hetty stood in the staff dining room, with the rest of the staff who were in the choir, she felt her nerves grow. Victor had said he would try to get to the concert, and she so hoped he did. But at the same time, she was afraid that she'd make a fool of herself, and that her voice would be less than adequate and obvious to all, despite what Lili and Edie had said the night before.

Lili led them in a few exercises to warm up their voices. Hetty looked around at the others as they sang. They were all smiling, looking confident, but maybe they felt the same as her inside.

At five past five, Lili said, 'All right, it's time for us to go. We need to do our very best, as we'll be collecting money for the kiddies after.'

Of course, they were collecting for the children's charity that Sophia ran. This just added to her nerves, as she wanted to do the very best she could for Victor's sister.

They slowly filed out in a pre-decided order, so that they could easily take up their positions on the makeshift stage that Mr Janus had again arranged for them.

Entering the room, Hetty could tell that the audience was at least as large as last year's, as there were now people standing at the back. And last year's had been considerably larger than the year before, the first time they'd put on the concert in the foyer.

She hadn't been standing in her position long before she spotted Sophia and Victor at the front with their parents. Her heart thumped in her chest as the piano, played by Mr Janus himself this year, began the introduction to 'The Sussex Carol'.

On Christmas night all Christians sing
To hear the news the angels bring...

–

Victor, sitting between his mother and sister, waited eagerly for the choir to appear. As its members started to fill the stage, he sat forward slightly, looking to see who was coming on next. When Hetty appeared, he wanted to announce, 'There she is!' but could only do so in his head. Sophia touched his arm lightly, not looking at him, and he knew she was acknowledging Hetty's presence.

The choir started up with a carol he liked, and he managed to stop himself singing along, as he often did when he was happy. And he *was* happy. Ecstatic. He'd had crushes on girls before, but had never felt this overwhelming feeling of joy, which contrasted with the despair when he couldn't see her for a few days. If only he could jump up and shout, *This is her, this is the woman I love!* But he couldn't. Not yet.

Hetty was his world, his future; the thought of life without her was absurd. Whatever it meant, he would have to find some way of revealing his feelings to the world at some stage.

But then, it wasn't the world he was worried about, it was his parents.

—

The concert had finished with Sophia thanking everyone concerned, then asking them to be generous for the charity. Following that, there had been a long period of clapping and cheering before the audience was finally invited to go to the dining room for refreshments.

'That was rather a triumph,' said Barbara. 'What an excellent choir they are; a good match for any other I've seen.'

James was only half listening, wondering how long it would be until he could return to work.

'Are you listening, dear?'

'Hmm? What was that, Barbara?'

'I said the concert was a triumph. Come on, Sophia and Victor have gone ahead.'

When they entered the dining room, where refreshments were being served, James looked around the room.

'Who are you looking for?' said Barbara.

'No one in particular. Just wondering who's here this evening.'

Sophia and Victor joined them with two glasses of wine each, having brought over some for their parents.

'There are mince tarts if anybody wants them,' said Victor.

He'd barely finished when James noticed Ebony heading over to them, with what he presumed was her family in tow.

'Good evening, Sophia,' she said. 'And Mr Perryman, it's nice to see you out and about after your accident. I was just telling my family here.'

'I hope you told them about the splendid portrait you did of me, too,' said Sophia.

'Oh, I hadn't got around to that.' Ebony gave a modest smile. 'Let me introduce you to my family. My cousins I'm sure you already recognise. These two ladies are their mothers and my aunts, and this is my father.' She turned to her family to introduce the Perrymans, and they all politely greeted each other.

'Is your mother not with you?' said Sophia, and James had wondered the same.

'No, unfortunately she came down with a headache, so is resting in her room. She wants to feel fit for tomorrow.'

'Of course,' said Barbara. 'She wants to be well for Christmas.'

'Do I know you from somewhere?' said Aunt Rachael. 'We used to live in Littlehampton as youngsters, and you look a little familiar.'

'I don't think so,' said James, not sure if he recognised her. It could just be a line to start a conversation, as people sometimes did. 'I spent much of my youth away at school.'

'You always think you recognise people,' her sister joked.

'Well, I hope you all have a splendid Christmas, Miss Girard,' said James.

'Yes, happy Christmas,' said Barbara.

'A happy Christmas to you all.' Ebony turned to her family. 'Some of you haven't been introduced to Major Thomas yet, so do come and meet him. You will like him in particular, Aunt Amelia.'

When they'd walked away, Sophia said, 'It's nice to see her with her family. I always felt she was rather lonely here on her own. We both did, didn't we, Victor?'

'I felt she was quite needy and must be lacking company.'

James laughed. 'She always strikes me as very self-sufficient, don't you think, Barbara?'

'No, I agree with the children. She seems more self-assured with her family here. Maybe it's time she went home to Surrey, so she could have them nearby.'

'Well, I suppose she'll do what she wants,' he said. 'Her avant-garde type always do.'

'Drink up your wine, James,' said Barbara. 'I still have some presents to wrap. And you've been out long enough.'

'Very well, I'm sure I have a few things to do too.'

–

Ebony was listening to Major Thomas talking to her aunts about living in a hotel, when she noticed the Perryman family leave. They were so lucky to be a close-knit family, and she'd envied that, being here alone for so long. But she had Marigold and Hazel here, along with her dear aunts and her caring parents. At least for now.

What to do about the future though? How much longer was she going to stay here, brooding?

Her father and aunts laughed at something the major had said, and she joined in, even though she'd been miles away and hadn't heard what it was.

Ebony noticed Marigold and Hazel beckon her over from where they were standing near the drinks table. She left the other members of her family, who were clearly enjoying the major's company.

'Did you manage to get a mince tart?' she said when she reached them.

'Yes,' said Marigold, 'though they were very small. Tasty, nonetheless. My goodness, I've been looking forward to coming here for some decent food after the substandard fare we've been served at Netley.'

'I don't suppose it will get any better when you leave there,' Hazel said flatly. 'You have to tell Ebony.'

'Tell me what?'

'I'm going to France, in the new year.'

'You're joining Hazel in the WAAC?'

'No, I'm going as a VAD nurse, to one of the hospitals on the front.'

'Oh, Marigold, you too?'

'I want to feel I've done something useful by the time this war is finished.'

'Isn't it useful, treating soldiers at Netley?'

'It is, but they're short of nurses on the front, and that's often where the soldiers need the most critical care. By the time they get to Netley, they're often through the worst.'

'I see. In that case, I'm even more pleased that you were able to come here for a few days off before you go to France.'

'Have you thought of doing something towards the war effort?' said Hazel.

'I've been helping with Sophia Perryman's charity events around the area. Much of it raises money for the soldiers and the hospitals.'

'It's a start,' Hazel said, dismissively.

Marigold put her arms around both Hazel and Ebony. 'We all have to do what is best for us. There's no need to argue.'

Ebony wasn't aware it had been an argument, though maybe her cousins had already discussed it. Did they think less of her for not volunteering for something?

'Let's just forget it for Christmas,' said Hazel. 'I'm too tired to quarrel anyway.'

'Look, people are being escorted out. They must want to get the room ready for dinner. Why don't we go to the lounge and relax,' suggested Marigold.

'Let's do that,' said Ebony, though a small piece of her wasn't looking forward to Christmas as much as she had been before this conversation.

Chapter Twenty-Four

Victor and his family were in the living room, sitting with a pot of tea after breakfast on Christmas Day, ready to open their presents, as was their tradition. He pictured Hetty sitting next to him, wondering what it would be like to be married to her, to be able to share these special moments.

'Victor, are you with us?' said Sophia, placing herself next to him.

'What's that?'

'Youngest goes first.' She handed him a present.

'Still?'

'When you start producing the next generation, there'll be others who'll be the youngest,' Barbara said light-heartedly, but he knew that beneath the smile was a deep-rooted desperation.

He took the small present and read the label. 'From Mother and Father.' He opened it to reveal a watch. 'That's very nice, thank you so much,' he said. 'I have had my other wristwatch a few years now.' He put it on.

Sophia opened a present from her parents next, another watch.

'When your father showed me the wristwatch he'd bought for Victor, I thought you ought to have a new one too,' said Barbara, 'as you've had yours even longer than Victor has.'

'You next, Mother,' said Sophia, handing her another small present.

When Barbara unwrapped the box, which was clearly from a jeweller, she smiled. But when she opened it, the smile slipped.

'Oh, emeralds,' she said, lifting the necklace out of the box. 'Green doesn't really suit me, it never has.'

Now Victor thought about it, this was something he'd heard her say a few times. He was surprised his father hadn't remembered.

James's smile was now strained. 'You won't know until you've tried it on. I thought you liked emeralds.'

'It's sapphires that I like, dear. You should remember, as you used to say that they matched my eyes.'

He slapped his head as if it were obvious. 'Of course, how could I have got them mixed up?'

Victor wasn't sure whether he was more cross with his father for forgetting such a thing, or his mother for acting so ungraciously. She'd always told him and Sophia to accept gifts with a smile, whether you liked them or not.

Sophia, as was often the case, came to the rescue. 'Maybe Father could take you to the jeweller and get it exchanged for something that does suit you, Mother.'

'What a splendid idea,' said James. 'Let's open the rest of the presents. I'm sure there'll be plenty of things among them you'll enjoy.'

As his sister went to find the next present, as had been her role since they were children, Victor glanced at his parents. His mother had a slightly worried frown, while his father looked a little remorseful. He'd likely bought it the day he'd gone off to Worthing by himself. And that might be why his father had bought something unsuitable, being too tired to concentrate. He had been exhausted that evening.

Never mind, he'd work with Sophia to improve the festive mood again, even though he was missing Hetty. He wondered what she was doing at this moment. Probably making pots of beverages for morning coffee. He looked forward to rescuing her from that, and all her other chores.

–

Hetty had been working all morning, and was now at early staff lunch, one of the first to arrive.

'There was a lovely festive atmosphere at breakfast, especially with Ebony's family,' said Lili, bringing in a plate of sandwiches from the kitchen. 'My, it's lively they are. Christmas lunch should be interesting.'

'Let's hope they and the other guests don't mind the mixture of meats,' said Bridget Turnbull. 'Mrs Norris has had a devil of a job gettin' hold of partridge and turkey. They've had to add lark and good old pigeon to the mix.'

'I don't suppose the guests would have done any better had they stayed at home,' said Hetty.

Lili sat next to her. 'Are you going to see your folks this afternoon?'

'For an hour or so, after lunch. I'll be back to help lay out the buffet supper for the guests.'

Hetty's mother had not been pleased about the short amount of time she'd be spending there, but it had been the same every year. At least she was visiting for a long afternoon on Thursday. She'd rather have spent it with Victor, but he had work and family commitments too.

'It's so glad I am there's no proper dinner to serve on Christmas Day,' said Lili. 'For it gives us a chance to have a seasonal feast all together.'

'I agree,' said Mrs Turnbull. 'But I'm not sure how much of a "feast" it'll be this year, though I'm sure Mrs Norris and the cooks'll do their very best.'

Fanny entered with her toddler. She sat down, placing Elsie, clutching a rag doll, next to her.

'Was that a present from Father Christmas, pet?' Mrs Turnbull asked the little girl.

'Fada Cwismas?' she replied, looking a little confused.

'Gertie gave it to her,' Fanny added. 'She's still a bit young for Father Christmas.'

Staff trickled in and soon the table was full. People chatted about the presents they'd received.

'I saw Inspector Toshack arrive earlier,' said Fanny with a cheeky grin. 'Looks like he's spending Christmas Day here.'

'Well, I for one am glad of that. That poor lass deserves some happiness. And, my, he is handsome.'

'Mrs Turnbull!' said Hetty, giggling.

'Well, got to get my pleasure somewhere, and looking at him certainly is a delight.'

'Perhaps we should find you your own beau,' said Fanny. 'How about Major Thomas?'

Everyone laughed as the storekeeper said, 'He's a fine figure for his age. I'm surprised he hasn't got a lady wife.'

'He once told me that he'd been married to the army, so had never got around to it,' said Lili.

The door opened, and Helen entered with Dorothy and Arthur.

'Happy Christmas, everyone,' the children called. The staff echoed their greeting.

'And what did you get for Christmas?' Hetty asked.

'I got a steam train that puffs out real steam and a railway to push it along,' said Arthur, beaming.

'I got a doll's house,' said Dorothy. 'And I got this from Sam.' She produced a book from under her arm. 'It's *The Lost Princess of Oz*.' She turned to Fanny. 'Would you like to borrow it when I've finished. I know you like the Oz books.'

So, the children were calling Inspector Toshack Sam now, thought Hetty. That did suggest the relationship between him and Helen had come on a pace.

'That would be lovely,' said Fanny, looking inordinately pleased. Dorothy had loaned her the previous books as well. 'You're right, I have enjoyed them. Imagine having an ordinary life on a farm and being whisked off to a fantasy land.'

Yes, thought Hetty, fancy having an ordinary life, in a hotel in her case, and being whisked off to… Could a life with Victor be considered a fantasy land? It seemed almost as implausible.

'Pass the teapot, pet,' said Mrs Turnbull.

Hetty obliged, determined not to think so negatively, especially on Christmas Day. She and Victor would be together eventually. If it were meant to be.

–

'The end of another year,' said Hetty, as she placed a pot of tea on the table and sat down next to Gertie for afternoon break on New Year's Eve.

'And still the darned war ain't over,' replied the portress.

'I have a feelin' in my bones that it might be over by next Christmas though,' said Mrs Turnbull.

Mrs Norris came in with a plate of plain biscuits which she put in the middle of the table. 'There you go, a little treat. They're all a bit misshapen, but I'm sure they'll taste as good. Only one each now, else there won't be enough for everyone.'

'I don't care what shape they are,' said Gertie, leaning over to pick one up.

'I'd make the most of it,' the cook went on. 'Will Fletcher told me he read in his newspaper that the government is gonna be rationing sugar for everyone. Eight ounces per week. We're gonna have to start getting creative again with fruit.'

'I had a bumper crop to preserve this year,' said Hetty, 'so that's something. And the cakes you've made with vegetables have gone down well.'

'That's the spirit,' said Mrs Turnbull. 'We'll get through this. And if that feelin' in my bones is right, this time next year we'll be celebratin' a new year without war, and who knows, some of our boys might be back too.'

'I do hope you're right,' said Gertie. 'I'd like to see me brothers back 'ome.'

The storekeeper's optimism lifted Hetty's spirits. The war being over would mean that her brother Gilbert would be back. And maybe, just maybe, it would make the situation easier for her and Victor.

Then it occurred to her: Lorcan would be back too. What was she going to do about him? Whatever they'd said about their relationship, it still didn't seem right to keep him in the dark about her new situation.

Alice entered the room. 'Ah, there you are, Hetty. I'm so sorry, but I've had this for you since this morning and forgot all about it.' She pulled an envelope out of her apron pocket and handed it to her.

There was only 'Hetty Affleck' written on the front, and no address. It looked like Victor's handwriting.

'Some messenger boy brought it to the back door,' said Alice.

Had her positivity been a little presumptive? What if Victor had changed his mind, and this was a letter saying he wanted to end it.

'Aren't you goin' to open it, pet?' said Mrs Turnbull. 'Ooh, or is it a billet-doux from a secret sweetheart?'

'Of course not,' she said. 'I think it's from my mother.'

'Only one way to find out, pet.'

Hetty opened it and rapidly scanned the contents. Far from breaking up with her, Victor had written that his father was starting work again in the new year, albeit slowly, which would mean they could meet more regularly once more. He went on to say how desperate he was to see her.

Why did she always think the worst? She felt like she'd been lifted to the heavens on the wings of an angel. But she couldn't tell the others what it said. Another fib, but what else could she do for now?

'It's just my mum wishing me a happy new year, as I haven't been able to get home the last few days. And, um, she says "Happy New Year" to all the staff here too.' As she knew she would have done had she sent a letter.

'That's nice of her,' said Gertie. 'Now, have we decided what games we're playing after supper this evening, to see the new year in?'

Soon ideas were being shouted out, and Hetty joined in with the fun.

It was only two days into a year that Hetty had started having hope in, when a letter came for her from Lorcan. She was sitting on her bed, looking at the contents once more, knowing that she had to make a decision. But the more she thought about it, the more tangled her attempts at a solution became.

There was a knock on her slightly ajar door, and she could just spy Lili's black hair.

'Come in.'

Lily poked her head around the door. 'Am I disturbing you? It's just, it were a little out of sorts you seemed when you were reading your letter earlier.'

About to say she was all right and that she needed to be alone, she had a change of heart. Maybe talking to somebody about it would help her decide what to do. And come to think of it, Lili was probably the best person for this.

'Come and sit down,' Hetty said. 'I could do with someone else's advice.'

Lili sat next to her on the bed. 'What's up?'

'What I'm about to tell you, only Phoebe and Edie know so far. And Mrs Bygrove knows a little bit. You see… you might actually have a better idea of what I'm facing, since you sort of went through something similar.'

'In what way?'

'You and Norman, with you thinking he'd been killed, and so walking out with Rhodri, and then discovering he was still alive, and not knowing what to do.'

Lili still looked confused. 'Lorcan hasn't died, has he?'

'No, I did say it was *sort of* similar. Look, the truth is, Lorcan and I had agreed that our relationship hadn't really got going when he left, and to see how it went when he returned. But, but… I've found someone else, Lili. With Lorcan not coming back on leave until last August, and it being nearly three years since I'd seen him, I suppose… Oh, I don't know. I liked him a lot, but I didn't realise that what I felt wasn't enough until I met somebody and was immediately swept away with an emotion I'd never felt before.'

'Oh dear. Yes, I know how that feels. You think you're in love with someone, and then you meet someone else and realise you had no idea what love was until that moment.'

'That's it exactly.'

'Can I ask who it is?'

Hetty hesitated only for a second. She knew Lili was trustworthy. 'It's Victor Perryman. So that, you know…'

'Causes a whole other set of problems?'

Hetty nodded. 'His parents don't know yet. Neither do mine, but they wouldn't be the problem.'

'Oh Hetty, you poor thing.' Lili put an arm through hers. 'Is the letter from Lorcan then?'

'Yes, and, despite him saying he'd probably go to Ireland on his next leave, he's coming here first, on Monday. So, I have what, five days to decide what to do.'

'I'm not sure how much help I'll be. I was silly enough to break off with Rhodri to be with Norman because I thought it were the right thing to do. And then look what happened. So, maybe what I'd say is, you'll have to tell Lorcan, if it's Victor you really want to be with. But then, what if that doesn't work out? Are you sure he feels the same?'

'Yes, I am. And if his parents interfere, and it can't happen, I couldn't in all conscience keep Lorcan hanging on, just in case, as a second best. And besides, no other man would be good enough now.'

'I think you've answered your own question then. And you're right. You need to follow your heart. I know I wouldn't want to be someone's second best, and I'm sure Lorcan wouldn't really want that either.'

'You're right. Neither would I. I owe it to him to tell him. Thank you, Lili.'

'Ooh, I don't think I've done much, but I'm glad you've come to a decision.'

'Yes, I have.'

—

Hetty had been glad of Lorcan's early arrival, during breakfast, with a full staff dining room, so that he'd made no attempt to kiss her.

They were walking now along a near empty promenade, on a cold, cloudy day.

'I'm sorry I have to push off again this afternoon, like,' he said. 'I did say I'd have to visit my family. Things are no better really, over there, so they're not.'

'I quite understand, Lorcan, and to be honest, maybe it's for the best.'

'How do you mean?' He tried to take her hand, but she pushed it into her coat pocket.

'What we said, about restarting the relationship when you returned after the war, and to see how it went… I don't want to do that anymore. I'm sorry.'

He didn't say anything for a while but stared at the ground as they walked. 'You don't want us to be sweethearts anymore?'

'We haven't really been since you left, Lorcan. You admitted that yourself back in August.'

'So I did. Did that… make you not want to start again? Did I offend you?'

'No, it wasn't that. When we said about seeing how it went when you returned, I thought that was what I wanted. But it wasn't long after that I realised, I suppose. I do like you, Lorcan, you're a great person, but you're just not the one for me.'

'I see. Is there someone else?'

She could take the easy way out and say no, but when he did return, after the war, he'd find out she'd lied, and she hated the idea of that. He would probably feel deceived.

'Yes, there is someone. I didn't go looking for another love, but it found me all the same.'

'I see. Don't suppose you want to tell me who it is?'

270

'Not at the moment. Hardly anyone knows yet.'

'I see.'

He was hunched over now as he walked, his hands clasped together in front of his military coat. 'You could have told me this in a letter, saved me the extra journey.'

'That's just what I didn't want to do, Lorcan. It seemed too… cold.'

'I see.'

How she wished he'd stop repeating that phrase. If he'd got a bit angry about it, she would have understood. It might have even made her feel better, that she was getting a telling off, as she deserved, not these monotone responses.

'I–I can still write to you, if you like, as a friend.'

'That's what you've already been doing really. No, it's all right. I'll ask Simon to write to me. He seemed quite keen to keep in touch after I had a talk with him when I was here last.'

'If you're sure.'

He came to an abrupt halt. 'Is there any point in us walking along here anymore? I'd rather be by the fire in the staff dining room, so I would. I can have morning coffee. Then I'll head off for the train. No point in delaying. I'll get to Fishguard earlier and won't have to wait until tomorrow morning for a ferry.'

She nodded, not knowing what else to say.

They headed back to the hotel in silence. It wasn't as if she'd broken off an actual romantic relationship, just changed the future possibilities of one, yet it was almost as sad as if she had.

Chapter Twenty-Five

Ebony drew up by the pavement on Brighton's promenade road, thankful that it was mild today, even if it was gloomy. Should she find somewhere for morning coffee first? No, she wanted to get straight on with her shopping.

She set off, passing grand Regency buildings and negotiating the narrow shopping streets, until she reached the long, wide Western Road. Here, she headed for a leather goods shop she knew. Marigold had bought a handbag there on the last trip she'd been on here with her cousins. The memory made her melancholic.

In the shop, she quickly picked out a large black handbag with a seal grain finish and two handles. The assistant handed it to her and she examined it. 'Yes, just the ticket,' she announced.

After she'd paid and was presented with a paper bag bearing her purchase, she stepped onto the street once more.

A young man, maybe around her own age, but in a suit that had seen better days, lifted his fedora as he passed, and wished her, 'Good Morning.' He had a pronounced limp.

She smiled, only half answering back, wondering if she was supposed to know him from somewhere. Perhaps he had mistaken her for somebody else. She took a long walk past the shops, stopping to look into windows that were not as full as they had once been.

She crossed over, to peruse the shops on the other side, wondering where to go for luncheon, when the same young man passed by once more, lifting his hat in greeting. A few shops down, she stopped to look at the window display of a fancy depository. She was wondering whether to buy some small tokens for her new friends at the charity, when she found the same young man by her side.

'They've got some nice pieces in here, haven't they?' he said, in a surprisingly middle-class accent. She hadn't expected that.

'Um, yes, they have.'

'A bit wasteful in war time, of course.'

'Well, maybe.'

He was quiet after that, and she took the opportunity to carry on. But she soon realised he had caught her up and was limping beside her.

'I'm Michael, by the way. How do you do? What's your name?'

She didn't want to divulge her name, so she said, 'I'm Miss Smith.'

'You live in Brighton, do you?' he asked.

'No, I'm just here on a trip out.'

He chuckled. 'All right for some. Wish I could have a trip out. Brighton born and bred, I am.'

She felt it would be rude not to reply, although she would rather have not. 'Are you on leave then?'

'You think I'm in the forces with this limp? No, my injuries led to me being discharged.'

'I'm sorry to hear that.'

'I'm not. Nor would you if you could see it out there.'

'So... it's your day off work then?' She wasn't sure how else to reply.

'Work?' He laughed. 'I wish. The paralysed arm put paid to that.' He lifted his right arm up a little with his left, then let it drop back down. 'Can't even use my writing arm anymore, and a woman was taken on to do my job when I enlisted.'

'I'm sure you'd be able to do some kind of work. Postman, or something like that maybe?' She wanted to be encouraging.

'What kind of work do you do?'

'I'm an artist.'

'Artist? That's just a hobby, a pastime. What good is that in a war? Why don't *you* be a postwoman?' His voice was starting to sound irritated.

Ebony stopped outside a grocery store, hoping he might move on if she went inside. 'I'm sorry, I didn't mean to offend you. Now I must—'

His voice became louder as he said, 'Perhaps you should think about your own contribution before you criticise other people.'

Stumped for a moment, she wondered what to do next. Then she heard a voice say, 'Is this man bothering you, madam?'

She turned to see a police constable approaching. He was frowning at Michael.

Not wanting to get him into trouble, given the problems he already had, she said, 'It's fine, thank you, Constable.'

The young man limped away, his face puckered with anger.

'Very well, madam.' He lifted his helmet slightly and carried on in the opposite direction.

Ebony watched as Michael disappeared into the crowd. Rather than feeling annoyed with him for harassing her, she felt guilty. He shouldn't have been bothering her, but…

She looked at her watch. There was a tea room she liked, where she could get some lunch. She'd go there and try to forget the incident. But as she headed there, she couldn't help but think of Marigold in a hospital near the front, and Hazel doing her dangerous signalling job. She knew it had given her much to ponder.

–

This was Hetty's first long afternoon out with Victor in over two months, and so far all they'd managed to do was sit in a Tudor style refreshment room in Arundel and look out at the pouring rain as it bounced off the road and splattered against the windows.

'I'm sorry about the weather, Hetty. I think we might be stuck here for a while. I was hoping we could go for a stroll in the park.'

Hetty stroked his hand, which she was already holding. 'The most important thing for me is that I'm here with you.'

'And for me too, my love.' They gazed at each other for a while before he turned to look out of the window. 'How I hate this time of year. It's always so gloomy. And we do seem to have had an inordinate amount of rain in the last few days, even for January.'

'When the days get lighter, it'll make it easier for us to meet on my odd hours off.'

'I'm hoping that by the time we get there, all this subterfuge will be unnecessary. In fact, I was thinking about telling my parents in the next couple of weeks. Now my father's much better again and back to work, it's the right time. Especially now you've spoken to Lorcan.'

As if she needed reminding. She wondered, as she had several times in the last ten days, how he was. She'd likely not find out until Simon received a letter from him. The young waiter had been thrilled at the idea of writing to someone in the war, and being able to pass on the hotel gossip, as he'd put it.

'Are you sure about telling them, Victor?'

His eyebrows drew together as he regarded her. 'That's what you said before Christmas when I mentioned it. It makes me wonder whether *you're* sure, whether *you're* ready.'

'I don't think there'll ever be a time when I can say I'm sure or ready, but not because of any lack of feeling for you, Victor, but because of what's going to happen when you tell your parents. I'm, well I'm *scared* that it won't turn out well, and that they'll split us up.'

'I wouldn't let them do that. If we want to be together, how can they stop us?'

'I'm sure they could think of a few ways. Your father might threaten to throw you out of the business.' She shrugged.

'No, he wouldn't do that. My grandmother told me that he was relieved when I was born, because he wanted a son to pass the business on to. He's proud of what his family has achieved over the generations, and I don't think he'd want to jeopardise that, or sell the business to someone else.'

Despite his words, he didn't sound totally confident.

'I'm just advising caution, that's all,' she said. 'And we should be prepared for a, well, a fight, for want of a better word.'

'I'm sure Father wouldn't want to do anything to risk our relationship, his and mine that is, particularly in the business. And he and Mother would want me to be happy.' He sounded more sure of himself now. 'Besides, Sophia will support me.'

None of these statements gave Hetty any more confidence than she'd had. Was she being too pessimistic, or was he being overly optimistic? After all, he knew his parents better than she did. But if he really thought it was going to be that easy, why hadn't he told them about her before?

The waitress approached the table. 'More tea, sir, madam?'

'I think we'd better.' Victor pointed out of the window. 'We're not going anywhere in this.'

'Hopefully it'll rain itself out,' said the waitress, removing the empty teapot.

'I do hope so,' said Victor, when she'd left. 'Then maybe next time we meet, we can actually do something other than sit around in a refreshment room.'

'And I'll look forward to you not having the weather to moan about.'

She placed her hands around his arm and they both laughed.

–

Four evenings later, Hetty was in the staff dining room, darning a hole in one of her wool stockings, wondering exactly when Victor was planning to tell his parents about them. He hadn't mentioned a specific day, and it sounded like it would happen when he'd built up the courage to do it.

276

'I hope none of the guests have gone out this evening,' said Mrs Leggett, standing to look out of the window at the pouring rain. 'Not that there are many to go out at the moment.'

'I was supposed to be popping up to Wick to see my parents this evening, but I asked Mrs Bygrove if I could use the telephone to cancel the trip,' said Hetty.

She put the darning down and walked across the room to stand next to the housekeeper. 'What a noise it's making. I think it might be windy as well.'

The dining room door opened and Jack came in, his hair and face wet, along with his apron. 'Blimey, it's blowin' a hooley out there,' he said, confirming Hetty's assumption. 'Only went out to the dustbins and got soaked.'

There was a sudden, explosive clap of thunder, and both Mrs Leggett and Hetty stepped back from the window.

'Did you hear that?' said Fanny charging into the room. 'I 'ope it don't wake Elsie up. She's a good little sleeper, but this is bloomin' loud.'

'I'm sure Vera will keep an eye on her,' said Mrs Leggett. 'To think we had a bit of blue sky this morning.'

'I had hoped that the rainy weather had finally come to an end,' said Hetty. 'But it wasn't to be.'

Jack scoffed. 'It's British weather. What d'ya expect?'

'It's not going to help trade,' said the housekeeper. 'And we're already having to take fewer bookings because of the increasing rationing.'

'Anyway,' said Jack, 'Mrs Norris says can people come and collect the dishes from the kitchen for supper.'

Hetty helped bring the dishes with the vegetables in, whilst Mrs Leggett and Fanny brought in the plates, each with a piece of fish already served on it. Lili and Gertie joined them. There was only a small gathering for late supper tonight.

'I 'ope this storm don't last long,' said Fanny. 'They never used to bother me, but since the one last April...'

'And that was only wind,' said Jack.

'I remember going with Hetty and Edie, to a guest room upstairs,' said Lili, 'to watch the wind before it got dark. It were fascinating, if terrifying.'

'Wasn't it?' said Hetty. 'The waves were crashing onto the beach.'

'Caused a bit of damage it did, what with blowing the chairs and tents on the beach all over the place.'

'Not to mention Bygrove's demise,' said Jack.

'That wasn't the wind as much as that councillor bloke, whatsisname, strangling him,' said Gertie.

'Adrian Bloomfield,' said Fanny.

'True, but there's meant to be a high tide tonight,' Jack said. 'So who knows—'

'I think that's enough of that talk,' said Mrs Leggett, putting her hand up to bring the conversation to an end. 'I'm sure it will all blow over soon and we'll wonder what all the fuss was about.'

Hetty hoped so too. And she didn't want it lasting until the day after tomorrow, when she was due to see Victor again. They had a trip to Bognor planned. She hadn't been there for a while.

Not that it mattered where she went, as long as she was with him.

–

Despite Mrs Leggett's words of hope, the storm was still raging at two o'clock in the morning.

Hetty, unable to sleep, had gone downstairs in her dressing gown to the staff dining room, to find Bridget Turnbull, Gertie and Edie there.

'You can't sleep either?' said Mrs Turnbull. 'Come and pour yoursel' a cuppa tea, pet.'

Hetty sat down. 'I think it's got worse. And the thunder and lightning is constant now. It's been flashing through my curtains every few seconds.'

'The storm's right above us and has been for a while,' said Gertie. 'I looked outta me window at it, 'cos thunder and lightning's always fascinated me. We've 'ad a few corkers here, but I've never seen nothin' like this.'

'It gives me the shivers,' said Edie, demonstrating the emotion. 'It's because it reminds me of, you know, Bygrove.'

Gertie leant over to pour herself another cup of tea. 'We was saying that earlier. Mrs Leggett didn't like us talkin' about it though.'

'I can understand that.' Mrs Turnbull pushed the milk jug towards her. She almost knocked it over, jumping at the next ear-splitting crack of thunder which roared at the same time as a flash appeared at the window.

Edie held her arm. 'Are you all right?'

'Yes pet, well, I will be. I wonder if any of the guests are worried.'

'Perhaps we should get dressed in case they come down and need reassurance,' said Edie. 'We could make tea for them as well, in the guest lounge. Being gathered together might make them feel better too.'

'Like us,' said Hetty.

She thought about Victor and his family, only up the road in Surrey Cottage, and wondered if they were all up, gathered in what Victor referred to as the drawing room. What she would have given to have been held in his reassuring arms at this moment in time.

'Come on then,' said Mrs Turnbull. 'Edie's right, we should get dressed and make sure the guests are fine. It's just as well that we're in a slack period. I dunno about you, but I'm not goin' to sleep a wink while this cacophony's goin' on.'

–

When Hetty arrived at the lounge with Edie, Mrs Turnbull and Gertie, it was clear that some of the guests had indeed found solace in gathering together. There were two young couples, a trio of middle-aged male friends and two older ladies who were widows.

'Thank goodness you're here,' said one of the widows. 'Do you think this is likely to last long? Do you often have these storms?'

'We have them every now and again,' Edie confirmed, 'but I believe this is the worst one for a while, isn't that what you said, Gertrude?'

'That's right. And there's no way of knowing how long it'll go on for, I'm afraid.'

Edie nodded dolefully. 'We thought, in the meantime, you might appreciate some tea.'

'Oh, yes please,' said one of the young women.

'Henrietta and I will fetch it. Mrs Turnbull, would you and Gertrude build up the fire, please?'

Helen Bygrove entered with Mrs Leggett as Edie was speaking. 'Good, I see you've had the same idea as us,' said the manageress. 'This is probably the cosiest room to gather in.'

In the stillroom, Edie helped Hetty prepare several pots of tea. As they were doing so, Mrs Norris popped her head around the door. 'I'm not the only one up then?'

'No,' said Hetty. 'About half the guests were already in the lounge when we went there. And some of us staff have been up a while. We're just making tea for everyone.'

'I wish I had some spare biscuits to offer, but I don't wanta be short for morning coffee and afternoon tea.'

'I'm not sure how many people will be in for those, Mrs Norris, or any meals if this weather keeps up. It will only be our staying guests I should think.'

'You could be right, but I'd better hang on to what I've got all the same.'

When Hetty and Edie returned to the lounge, people seemed a little more settled. The fire had been built up and it was feeling a little warmer in there now.

Hetty was pouring tea for the three gentlemen who'd arrived together, as one of them was saying, 'It's rather like being back in London, with the Germans bombing us. I hope this storm doesn't wreak that kind of havoc. Gosh, who needs the Hun when you've got British weather, eh?'

One of the young men said, 'To me, it's like being on the front, with the constant ear-splitting booming of the cannons.' He sighed heavily.

One of the older men got up to pull the curtain to one side, just as there was a flash of lightning. The ensuing thunder came a second later.

'Oh, do put the curtain back,' said one of the older ladies. 'We can hear the noise well enough without having to look at it too. And that wind! Will it ever subside?'

Her friend said, 'That nice Major Thomas was telling us at dinner that there was a gale here back in April.'

Hetty noticed Helen and Mrs Leggett glance at each other. They'd probably be wondering, as she was, how much the major had told them.

'But even at dinner he reckoned this one sounded more serious.'

'I don't suppose we'll know for sure until it starts getting light,' said Mrs Leggett. 'And that won't be until at least half past seven. Maybe later if it's still cloudy.'

'I won't be going back to bed until it dies down,' said one of the young women. Her husband sat and put his arm around her, pulling her to him.

All of a sudden, there was a crash against the window. A couple of the women screamed and one of the young men clattered his teacup onto the table.

'What on earth?' said one of the older men.

Helen and Hetty both went to see what had happened, pulling back a curtain each. By the light of the room, they could see bits of white wood and glass outside. There was now a crack in one of the lounge windows.

'Oh no,' Helen said under her breath. 'That looks like part of the greenhouse. Mr Hargreaves is not going to be pleased.'

Hetty could only agree. The head gardener had been upset for days after the last storm had made a mess of the garden. She only hoped a similar fate didn't befall the large windows and outside glass doors of the ballroom, or even worse, the conservatory.

'It doesn't feel very safe in here,' said one of the young wives.

'Let us adjourn to the foyer,' said Helen. 'There's less glass there and it's away from the direction of the wind. We'll carry out some of the chairs and settees, and the coffee tables for you.'

She organised the staff to do that and helped them too. The furniture was put close to the desk, away from the front doors and windows, Mrs Turnbull brought through the tea trays. While she was doing this, a few more guests were coming down the long curve of the stairs, including Major Thomas and Ebony. At the same time, Jack Sinden appeared from the staff area with Mrs Norris.

'It's less blowy down here than on the upper floors,' the major announced as he approached them. 'And there was some almighty rumbling not long ago. Not the thunder, something else.'

'I don't like the sound of that,' Gertie whispered to Hetty.

'Why?'

But she didn't get a reply before the major carried on with, 'Looks like everyone's gathered here.'

'Just about,' said Helen. 'I wonder if we should get Fanny, Vera and the children down.'

'If they're sleeping through this lot, I'd let them,' said the major. 'No point worrying the youngsters in particular. Your quarters are on the other side from where the wind's blowing, so less likely to sustain any damage.'

'Then I think we'd better make more tea and sit it out until the morning. I don't think the rest of us will get back to sleep now.'

'I'll see to that,' said Hetty, making her way to the staff door.

By half past seven, as a vague light started to appear with dawn, the storm had finally abated, and people had gone back to their rooms with instructions to report any damage immediately. Edie and Hetty had been sent on a mission around the ground floor to assess the damage, while Helen went to help with the children.

In the conservatory, a branch had broken through one of the top windows, while one of the dining room windows had a crack in it, similar to the one in the lounge. They couldn't see what had caused it. The ballroom, much to their surprise, had escaped unscathed.

'I wonder if any of the windows upstairs are broken,' said Edie. 'My goodness, the glaziers are going to have their work cut out if a lot of other buildings have sustained damage.'

Hetty shook her head. 'That's a good point. It might take ages to get one to replace the broken panes if a lot of people need new windows.'

No other windows downstairs had been broken, but even in the dim dawn, the garden from the dining room looked a mess of branches, and it was evident that bits of wood from at least one greenhouse had blown all over the place.

'Where are the guests going to eat breakfast?' said Hetty.

'I think, if we close the curtains where the cracked pane is, they'll be all right in here. With the broken roof in the conservatory, I suspect we'll have to serve morning coffee and afternoon tea in here as well, though it will make it rather hectic, clearing up after one meal while preparing the room for the next.'

'The lack of custom we're likely to have today will be a help there.'

'You'd better get to the stillroom and get ready. Breakfast is going to be late as it is. I'll go and report to Helen.'

Hetty did as she was told, glad that she didn't have to break the news of the broken glass to Mrs Bygrove.

Fifteen minutes had gone past in the stillroom, and still Milly hadn't turned up for her shift, and neither had Annie and Alice arrived in the scullery. Maybe their houses had been damaged and they'd had to stay and help.

Hetty was just checking her watch again when Gertie, now in her porter's uniform, barged through the door.

'Oh my gawd, Hetty, have you seen outside?'

'No, I've been busy as no one else is here in the scullery or stillroom and I've had to—'

'For gawd's sake, come upstairs and 'ave a look.'

Gertie led the way to an empty guest room that looked over the common and towards the river. It was light enough now to see outside.

Hetty gasped. 'Oh – my – giddy – aunt!'

Chapter Twenty-Six

'Jack wasn't joking when he said it was meant to be a high tide,' said Hetty, as she and Gertie looked out. 'I do hope that nobody's been hurt.'

'That's more than an 'igh tide,' said Gertie. 'Look, there's water as far as the eye can see. It even comes up to our walls but I'm not sure if it's got in the garden. The road out the front is flooded too, and there's water between our gates and the door. It's what I feared when Major Thomas mentioned the rumbling. The river's been breached, I'm sure of it. It's not the first time, but it ain't 'appened in a while.'

Hetty couldn't quite take it in. She'd seen the river flood before, but not this much. She wondered what it was like at Victor's house. Being right at the other end of the long promenade road, it might not be so bad, but she wanted to know.

'What's it like on the other side of the hotel?' she asked.

'The flood seems to go up to at least Norfolk Road, maybe beyond.'

'No wonder Annie, Alice and Milly haven't turned up. I hope they're safe. Who knows what it's like in the town.'

Or by the actual river, she thought. Humphrey Wilmot's and Haydon's were both on the riverbank, Wilmot's this side, and Haydon's on the west bank. There was no way that they hadn't been affected. Her heart sank. More trouble and responsibility for Victor, and his father who'd only recently recovered from the explosion.

Hetty looked along the part of South Terrace that could be seen from the window. 'I dread to think what's happened to all those basement rooms in the houses here.'

'They'll be flooded for sure. A lot of people have their kitchens down there, and those what are landladies or landlords sometimes live in them rooms, as they let out the apartments above to tenants. Let's hope they all managed to get out in time.'

'I remember Edie saying that her old landlady there lived in the basement. Look, there are men over there, wading through the water. They seem to be helping someone out of one of the houses. Poor things... I wonder what our guests will do.'

'January's not much of a month to have time away at the seaside as it is, but they're not even gonna be able to walk by the beach or river. Blimey, I 'ope the motorcars at the 'otel garage are all right, otherwise some of the guests are gonna have trouble driving 'ome.'

Hetty hoped they were all right too, though it was a slightly selfish wish since the garage was just around the corner from Victor's house.

'I'd better get back to preparing for breakfast,' she said. 'If we can't do anything else, we can at least provide some food for our guests.'

–

With mostly only the live-in staff able to do shifts, it was all hands on deck as they cooked the food and served it to the guests in the dining room.

The staff didn't sit down for their own breakfasts until nine thirty, much later than normal, by which time Hetty was starving. Fanny was almost last in with her toddler.

'Elsie's very chirpy,' said Hetty. 'How was she in the night?'

'Slept like a log, unlike me. Vera told me that Dorothy and Arthur didn't stir neither.'

'That's a blessing. I don't suppose they've gone to school today?'

Fanny laughed. 'Nah. Don't think no one's going nowhere for the foreseeable.'

Mrs Leggett came in and stood by her chair. 'It's been decided that morning coffee will be served in the lounge, but not until ten thirty, to give us time to eat our breakfast.'

'What about the cracked window?' Gertie asked.

'Mr Hargreaves and a couple of the other gardeners have made it in and have boarded it up.'

Jack looked up from his bacon and toast. 'I suppose they've seen the state of the garden and one of the greenhouses.'

'They'd have found it hard not to, Mr Sinden, though there are people no doubt worse off in the town. Anyway, they're making a start on clearing up as well as salvaging any of the winter vegetables they can, but it'll be hard with the garden being rather wet.'

Edie, the last of the staff due for breakfast, came in and sat next to Lili.

'How's Mrs Bygrove copin'?' Mrs Turnbull asked.

'She's on the desk, ringing various people to try to find out what's going on. She rang the glazier she normally uses, and he says he'll be able to come round and have a look today. Whether he'll be able to change the glass straight away we don't know. Maybe it's just as well that most of the guests have expressed a wish to check out, though how they expect to get anywhere with the flood, I've no idea.'

'What about their motorcars?' Hetty asked.

'Mr Burgess at the garage telephoned to say that although there's water on the road, it's only slightly wet in the garage, so the vehicles are fine.'

The door opened and Hetty was surprised to see Inspector Toshack standing there, in his mackintosh and a long pair of gumboots, his fedora in his hand.

'Good morning, all,' he said, 'if "good" is the right word. I've come over to make sure you're all right here in the hotel.'

'Mrs Bygrove's on the desk,' said Fanny.

Toshack went a little red as he said, 'Um, yes, I know. I came in that way and saw her.'

'How on earth did you get here, Inspector?' said Mrs Leggett.

'I walked around the town and down St Augustine's Road, opposite.' He pointed as if they wouldn't know where he meant. 'There's still several inches of water there, but not nearly as much as the area closest to the river.'

'What exactly has happened, Inspector?' Edie asked.

'Along with the gale force winds and exceptionally heavy rain, there was a high tide, but that's not what caused most of the damage.'

'I bet the Arun broke through again, didn't it?' said Gertie.

'Aye, it did. The harbour master reckons there was a breach to the west bank around two in the morning, down by the bridge and Railway Wharf.'

Hetty felt sick. That's where Haydon's was.

'A large area of farmland over that way has also been flooded.'

'Just what we don't need with the food shortages,' said Mrs Turnbull.

Mrs Norris crossed her arms under her bosom. 'It's a good job we've got a plentiful store of our own veggies then.'

'Around the same time, the river breached the east bank and flowed over in this direction,' he went on. 'The water's now all over the common from the river to the hotel and beyond, and the basements on South Terrace are damaged. The fishermen's cottages on Pier Road and the Harbour Tea Rooms have been half submerged, and they reckon the water was five feet deep on South Terrace at one point. Some of the roads coming off it got flooded too, and the shops on Norfolk Road haven't fared well. People reckon they've seen groceries, furniture and all sorts floating around.'

'Has anyone been hurt?' asked Hetty.

'Nothing of note's been reported so far, amazingly. A few bumps and bruises at the most, it seems. I've got my officers out getting around to as many areas as possible, knocking on doors, checking up on people, and the ambulance crew is on standby.'

'I do hope everyone's all right,' said Mrs Turnbull. 'They must have been terribly frightened at the very least. And so much of their possessions will have been ruined.' She placed her head in her hand, tutting several times.

'I wonder whether the Admiralty blowing up the river mouth had anything to do with it being weakened,' said Edie.

'I'm sure questions will be asked about that,' said the inspector.

Helen came through the door. 'You've brought them up to date, have you?'

'Aye. With as much as I know anyway. My officers are out trying to assess the situation more fully.'

'Mr Watkins has managed to get in, so he's taken over from me at the desk. The guests with motorcars are checking out and are going to get to the main road via Rustington. I do hope the rest of my staff are all right. Some of them live close by.'

The door opened once again, and Annie and Alice almost fell in.

'Here you all are,' said Alice, standing in the doorway with her sister. 'Sorry we're so late.'

'Are you flooded up in Wick as well?' Mrs Leggett asked.

'No, but we was on our way here earlier and started to hear from people what had happened, so we went to see our mum's cousin what has a room on Bayford Road to make sure she was all right. But they've had some water in the house so we helped her take a few bags up to ours.'

'Sorry that we've missed some of our shift, Mrs Bygrove,' said Annie.

'I quite understand,' said Helen. 'A number of the live-outs haven't even made it in yet.'

'Excuse me, ladies,' said Mr Watkins, waiting for the scullery maids to move into the room. 'Mrs Bygrove, I wonder if I could trouble you. You said we wouldn't be taking any more bookings for the next week.'

'That's right, Mr Watkins.'

'It's just that, er, Lady Blackmore is at the desk with Miss Cecelia, and they're asking if they can have a room, as the kitchen is flooded in their home on South Terrace.'

'Lady Blackmore? Goodness, she must be desperate. Oh, well, I suppose we should be accommodating to people who are without facilities for the next few days. Though I'm not at all sure how reliable the food supplies are going to be.'

'It might be the right thing to do, though,' said Inspector Toshack, 'with people in need.'

'Yes, yes, you're right Sam.' She smiled warmly at him. 'Mr Watkins, tell her ladyship and Miss Cecelia that we would be happy to accommodate them.'

'Very well, madam.'

When he'd left Helen added, 'In fact, what am I thinking? We should make ourselves a centre for people to come to today, until they can sort out alternative accommodation.'

'We're rather short staffed at the moment, madam,' said Mrs Leggett. 'And we're not going to be able to feed them.'

'But we don't have many guests to see to, so I think we can extend some generosity and do whatever we can. They could gather in the ballroom, where we could provide tables and chairs.'

'We could move the ones in the conservatory and some from the dining room that won't be needed,' said Edie.

'Exactly! And we might not have much food to offer, but we can provide tea and keep people warm for the day.'

'I'll go and spread the word then,' said Toshack.

As he was about to leave, Hetty got his attention. 'Inspector, what's happened to the businesses down on Fisherman's Quay and along the river there up to the bridge?'

'I dread to think, but I shall find out,' he replied, placing his hat back on. 'At the moment, we need to make sure people are safe, and worry about the businesses later. Good day to you all.'

He and Helen left the room together. Her heart ached for Victor and his family. She wanted to cry, but now was not the time.

'Let's finish breakfast quickly,' Mrs Leggett called. 'Then we'll start organising the rooms and get morning coffee for whatever guests we have left.'

Hetty had lost her appetite, but she finished off the toast as it would have been wasteful not to. She only wished she had some way of finding out more about the situation for Victor's family.

–

Tables and chairs were quickly set up in the ballroom, and it wasn't long before the news had been spread that the hotel was somewhere to go while people sorted themselves out. Hetty was soon making pots of tea and helping to serve them in the makeshift reception room.

'It's very kind of the manageress here to give us a place to sit until we can find somewhere else to stay,' said one old gentleman to Hetty, with several sacks of belongings around him. 'I've got a first-floor room on South Terrace, but my landlord wants it for his family until he can sort out their living quarters in the basement. I'm sure my daughter'll accommodate me, but she's working in Angmering, so won't be back til later.'

There was a middle-aged couple Hetty served tea to next, the landlords of another property along the road. The wife was crying.

'It's all ruined,' she wailed. 'Our kitchen and our living area. The water's even seeped into the guests' dining room. I don't know how long it will take to dry, and we'll have to buy new furniture and the water could be there for days.'

Everyone had a story to tell. Hetty's heart went out to them, but she really wanted to know about Victor and his family.

Could she go there, to his home, in a break? At this rate, she wouldn't be getting one, and what would she say when she got to Surrey Cottage? And it was likely he wouldn't be there but trying to sort out the devastation of the flood. Oh Victor, what new catastrophe had befallen him now?

'Has your home been affected by the flood, lovey?' said an old lady as Hetty poured her a cup of tea.

'I live-in at the hotel. I think we were lucky to have the wall to protect us from much of the water. And my parents live up in Wick, so they should be all right.'

'You're a lucky girl, and a lovely girl for looking after us in our troubles. I'm a tenant in Bayford Road and nearly all the houses down there have been flooded.'

At the end of the room, Hetty recognised the Italian owner of the Harbour Tea Rooms.

'Mr Crolla, how are you?'

'Ees terrible, my poor business, and all my lovely decoration and the tables and the cloffs and everyfing.' He gave a deep sigh.

'I'm so sorry.'

'I've no idea when we'll be able to open again. Ees a tragedy, for me and my family and all these poor people 'ere.'

'There, there, Mr Crolla,' said a man who was the owner of a shop on Norfolk Road, patting him on the shoulder. 'Someone'll have to take responsibility for this, mark my words, and I'm thinking it'll have to be the port commissioners or the Admiralty. And once we've sorted out accommodation, I'll be getting together a group who'll be asking a few pertinent questions.'

'Count me in,' said Mr Crolla.

People were upset, but they were also very angry. Hetty wouldn't have wanted to have been the port commissioners or the Admiralty facing their fury, but they were right: someone had to take responsibility.

Back in the stillroom, she was glad of some moments alone, until Milly came flying through the door from the scullery.

'I'm so sorry, Hetty, but me Auntie Betty, what 'as a room on Granville Road, has had to come and stay with us and we 'ad to 'elp her. The place she rents is a right mess with water. I'm still wet from 'elping.' She pointed to the bottom of her coat and dress. 'There seemed to be a lot of people coming into the hotel when I walked past.'

Hetty gave her a rundown of the morning.

'Crikey, how are we gonna cope?'

She didn't have time to reply before Mrs Norris was flinging open the opposite door. 'You got some of them pickled beet-roots left, Hetty?'

'We've got loads Mrs Norris. We had a bumper crop last year.'

'Good, 'cos I'm making one very large stew, mostly veg, as we're feeding them what's taking refuge 'ere for the day. The paying guests will have to put up with the same, even if it is presented in a fancier way with some decorative bits on the side.'

'All right, Mrs Norris, I'll go and locate the beetroot in the store for you.'

Victor walked with his father onto the top of Norfolk Road. Both were silent, crestfallen. Victor was trying to think of Hetty, of their last meeting, to take his mind from the sight they'd witnessed, but the devastation kept flashing into his mind, obscuring thoughts of the afternoon they'd had together. Even then it had been pouring with rain. It was no good, he was going to have to face what had happened, and the quicker they got on with doing… what? Doing something. It all rather depended on what happened next.

'It's still mayhem down here too,' said James, as they waded through the water in their gumboots, the end of their coats soaked, along with the knees of their trousers.

There were crates, food items, knickknacks, chairs, bedding, envelopes, milk bottles, boots and all manner of things around them, the smaller items still bobbing along in the water, while the larger ones had come to rest.

'Look at it,' said Victor, feeling as sorry for the residents on the street as he did for himself. 'The shops here will have lost so much.'

'They're not the only ones,' James said forlornly.

As they passed the post office, the postmistress was in the doorway, attempting to push the water away with a broom.

'Good day to you, Mr Perryman, Mr Victor. Rum do this.'

'It certainly is, Mrs Riddles,' said James.

'People are pointing the finger at the Admiralty after them blowing up the river. Your businesses must be badly affected.'

'All the businesses in Beach Town and by the river are.'

'What about the town, do you know?'

'Only the shops on the bottom of Surrey Street and River Road.'

She tutted several times and carried on sweeping at the water, a thankless and ultimately pointless task, as far as Victor could see.

When they were out of earshot, James said, 'She has a point, about the Admiralty.'

'The Arun has breached its banks in the past, long before the Admiralty arrived here.'

'But I've never seen it flood this much. And if this breach is partly down to them blowing up the river mouth, that will be twice they've nearly ruined my life.' He said this stiffly, looking ahead.

Nearly ruined. It implied some kind of optimism about the current situation, even if it looked hopeless.

Victor placed his hand on his father's shoulder. 'Once the water's subsided, we'll be able to assess the damage properly.'

'And we'll work day and night to put it right. My great grandfather started the business with nothing and built it up, and I'm not going to let him down, God rest his soul.'

'We'd better go down here.' Victor pointed towards one side of Western Road, which was another way to get to their small street. 'It looks a little less wet.'

His father nodded, and they were silent again until they reached Surrey Cottage.

Inside the scullery, Perkins was already waiting to take away their boots and coats and provide clean footwear.

'I shouldn't tell your mother too much,' said James, as they were both doing up their laces.

'Tell me too much about what?' said Barbara, entering the room with Sophia. 'I'm not a child, James, and I don't appreciate being treated like one. I want to know *exactly* what the situation is. And if you don't tell me, I'll go down to the riverside myself.'

Victor and his father glanced at each other, before James said, 'All right. Although you wouldn't get near the riverside at the moment. Fisherman's Quay and the area around the bridge are completely flooded, as is the whole river area.'

Barbara let out a long moan. 'And the businesses?'

'Under at least five feet of water,' said Victor. 'Maybe more. We couldn't get anywhere near the quay, but Wilmot's will be quite well submerged, I am sure of that.'

'Haydon's has been badly flooded as well from what we can see,' said James. 'It seems that the river breached the western bank on that side first of all.'

'So, what is the plan of action?' said Sophia, ever the practical one.

'We'll have to wait until the water subsides,' said James. 'Then we'll call the men in and clear it all up. I dare say it will take a fair amount of time, not to mention a good deal of money. We'll have to be at the workshops and warehouse seven days a week until everything is back to normal, and so will the men, even if we have to pay them for the extra hours. There'll be no time off for anyone for the foreseeable future.'

'If you need someone to oversee the other businesses in the meantime, I'm at your disposal,' said Sophia. 'I'm sure my committee can manage the charity events in my absence.'

'And I'm happy to help in that way too,' said his mother.

His father's, 'But—' was interrupted by Barbara's, 'Don't underestimate me, or Sophia, James. We may not understand the ins and outs of the business, but we can certainly ensure that the people who do get the job done. Now, come and have some tea and we'll set about making plans.'

They followed her out of the scullery, Victor being the last to leave. No time off for the foreseeable future, his father had said. It was only right, but a wave of despair washed over him. He was due to see Hetty in two days' time. It would maybe be possible if work hadn't already started on repairing the damage, since they'd agreed to meet at St Mary's which was away from the flooded area. He'd have to wait and see what happened.

–

Thursday arrived, and Hetty found herself daydreaming during the early morning break, as others chatted about the current situation. She was seeing Victor this afternoon and could hardly bear the wait. Not only was she desperate to see him, but she wanted to know what had happened to his business.

'The water has subsided quite a lot today,' said Hetty, 'and it's sunny, so I wouldn't mind betting there'll be a few outside guests in for morning coffee, lunch and afternoon tea too, wanting to cheer themselves up.'

'I think you could be right, Miss Affleck,' said the house-keeper.

'What happened about them two families what Mrs Bygrove put up in the empty guest rooms?' said Jack.

'They found accommodation this morning,' said the house-keeper.

Annie entered the staff dining room and handed Hetty a letter. 'Here, Alice found this shoved under the door with your name on when we came in this morning. She stuck it in her apron and forgot about it. Sorry, that's the second time she's done that. She is inclined to wool-gathering. Someone must have come round early to put it there.' She went around the other side of the table, closer to the fire, making a point of rubbing her hands together in front of it before sitting down.

Hetty knew immediately that it was Victor's writing. She opened it and read the short missive within. It was clear that the businesses in Littlehampton had suffered greatly, and that his attention would be turned to that for a long while to come. He was also preparing for a public meeting with the Admiralty and Port Commission next Thursday.

She was swamped with so much disappointment that she could have wept there and then. And yet, she should have expected it.

'You got a secret sweetheart?' Annie joked.

'It's from an old friend I was due to meet today, but they can't make it.'

'Is that Phoebe?'

'No, I'd say if it was.'

'What you gonna do with your afternoon off then?'

'I'll probably go and see my family. They'll be wondering what's been happening down here and would probably appreciate an update.'

Helen had allowed her to telephone them the day of the flood, so that they would know she was all right. Her mother had asked then about her visiting on her day off, and she'd told her she was seeing Phoebe. Now she'd have to tell her that Phoebe was unable to make it. Fibs, fibs, fibs: how she hated them. If she and Victor had been able to be open, she could have been more of a support for him in this time of trouble, as well as when his father had been injured. And at the back of her mind was that recurring fear that *this* would be the event that finally put an end to their relationship.

Victor hadn't been looking forward to this meeting with the Port Commission and the Admiralty, but as he entered the hall where it was taking place, he was astonished to see just how many people had turned up. Already the voices were loud with concern, as people spoke to each other, awaiting the start.

'Everyone seems quite angry,' said his father, beside him.

'Can you blame them? Are you sure you're up to this, Father?'

James regarded him, his eyes narrowed with annoyance. 'I am perfectly well. Please, do stop fussing. I get enough of it from your mother.'

'I'm sorry, it's just... All right.' He'd probably have felt the same if his parents had been constantly fussing over him in this way. 'It looks like it's going to be a lively meeting.'

'Yes. Let's hope they're all here to give the Admiralty what for.'

'Whether they'll take any notice is another matter.' Victor found two seats near the front and invited his father to sit first.

'There's Paul Flower, the council chairman.' James indicated a young middle-aged man, climbing the steps to the stage. 'He's apparently chairing this meeting.'

'Good luck to him!'

Several other men climbed the stage, who Victor recognised from the Admiralty, the Port Commission and the council. They sat down on a line of chairs, facing the audience.

'Order, order!' Mr Flower bellowed, in a voice that carried and got everyone's attention. 'We're here today to discuss the matter of the flood that occurred on the twenty-second of January—'

'We know when it happened!' called a voice from the audience. 'Get on with it!'

'We *will* have order in this meeting, and everyone who needs to will get a chance to speak.'

298

'We'll be here all day if just *anyone* can speak,' said Commander Truss, the Admiralty representative.

'We've got a right to,' said someone near Victor, who he knew to be Mr Caffyn, the butcher on Norfolk Road. 'You and your explosives caused that flood, and you've cost me and my business a good deal of money, cleaning up all that filth!'

'We did not cause the flood. The explosives were used last year, and they were successful in widening the river only. You've had floods here before, so it's nothing we've done.'

'The hell it isn't!' said a large, tall man, all in black. 'Yes, we've had floods, but not ones as bad as that in a long time. You made the river unstable.'

'If the river is in need of attention, that is down to the port commissioners and their wilful neglect of the riverbanks, a long time before we came here. It was noted that—'

One of the port commissioners stood abruptly. 'I can assure you, Commander Truss, that our river was well maintained until *you* turned up in 1916 and took over. We have dredged the riverbed in the past, to keep the banks wide enough for shipping, but when they needed further maintenance, you did not consult us, the experts, on the best way, but went ahead like a bull in a china shop with your damned explosives!'

'*We* have experts in this field, and we were of the correct opinion that explosives were the way.'

Victor had heard enough. He stood up and shouted, 'Then it's a pity your so-called experts were stupid enough to leave explosives behind which went off later and nearly killed my father!'

James pulled at his sleeve. 'Sit down.'

'No.'

'Well, that, that's not—' the commander blustered.

'It's a good job the riverside wasn't busy that day,' called Mr Janus, who Victor hadn't noticed until now. 'Otherwise there could have been a lot of casualties.'

'If the port commissioners and council had maintained the riverbanks adequately,' the commander persisted.

'The *council*?' roared Mr Flower. 'We're not responsible for the river, we're responsible for the town!'

'The river is part of the town,' said the port commissioner.

'There you go,' said the commander. 'The council is liable.'

'We bally well are not! The Admiralty took over the riverside in 1916. You are responsible for maintenance.'

'And for compensation!' yelled a small woman. 'Our house on South Terrace has been *ruined*. We live in the basement and let out the rooms upstairs, and we can't live in our area anymore with the water damage, because it's going to cost so much to repair it and replace our furniture. We lost nearly everything,' she said, sobbing.

The man sitting next to her stood and put his arm around her. 'She's right, we did. And we demand compensation.'

Commander Truss shrugged as if it didn't matter. 'We are not responsible, and I urge the Port Commission to do their duty and repair the breaches in the banks as quickly as possible.'

'That is strange that you should make that claim,' said one of the councillors who had been on the riverside with Victor and his father the day of the explosion. He'd just arrived and was climbing the stage. 'When the Admiralty took over the river in 1916, you impressed upon the Port Commission that you not only assumed responsibility for the financing and mainten-ance of the entire harbour, but you insisted that you would compensate them for loss of harbour revenues during the time you were in control. Now you're saying it's nothing to do with you.'

'Yes, that's right,' said the port commissioner. 'If you're now claiming that you're not responsible, then you lied to us. You've taken advantage of the good people of Littlehampton, and our goodwill in allowing you to use our harbour.'

'You had no choice but to hand it over,' said Commander Truss.

'So, you thought you could bully us, and then say we were responsible for the cost?'

'We said, we gave, um, we made no such agreement.'

'Yes, you did,' said James, standing up now. 'The councillor is absolutely right about what the Admiralty claimed in 1916.'

'Oh, do sit down, man. I'm not listening to any more of the proletariat. I don't know why you lot are even part of this meeting.'

There were a number of indignant remarks and a fair amount of booing.

'I am the owner of several shipbuilding companies along the coast, which are now all engaged in building vessels for military use, as you well know, including Haydon's and Humphrey Wilmot's here in Littlehampton.'

'Oh, it's you, Mr Perryman.'

'Yes, it's me. But it shouldn't matter if it were a shop owner on Norfolk Road, a landlord on South Terrace, a fisherman in Pier Road or a tenant on Bayford Road. We all have a right to express our concern after what's happened to us. Now, as far as the businesses by the river and on the quay engaged in making ships and naval parts are concerned, water is still coming into our workshops intermittently. If those breaches aren't sorted out, our work for the Admiralty will come to a standstill.'

'Oh, I agree it needs sorting out,' said the commander. 'But it's the council and Port Commission who are responsible, as far as I'm concerned.'

'That is *utter* nonsense, as we've already ascertained,' said Councillor Flower.

'Balderdash!' announced the port commissioner.

The room descended into uproar, with people shaking their fists and shouting their opinions.

'This could be a long evening,' said James.

'And I've got a feeling we're going to get nowhere,' said Victor.

—

'Another note from your friend?' said Annie, joining some of the staff for the late afternoon break.

Hetty looked up from the letter which she'd just begun reading. 'That's right. It's from – Victoria. We've started writing to each other since it's difficult to meet at the moment.'

That last part was at least true, as she and Victor had exchanged several letters in the past fortnight, although hers had been sent to Sophia to pass on to him. He rarely received private correspondence, but his sister did all the time, so it wouldn't look odd, he'd said. She'd been so relieved to receive that first letter from him. Every time he sent one now, she put it under her pillow and touched it with her fingers as she settled down, thinking of him.

'Would you fetch us a fresh pot of tea, Miss Affleck,' said the housekeeper. 'This one is nearly empty.'

Hetty resisted sighing at the interruption. She placed the letter in her apron pocket and headed off to fulfil the request. When she returned, the conversation had moved on to the aftermath of the flood.

'At least the water's finally gone from most of the area,' said Gertie, before slurping at her teacup.

'For now,' said Hetty as she placed the pot on the table and sat back down.

'What do you mean?' asked the housekeeper.

'When I had a walk down by the river yesterday, I got chatting to someone who told me there was still intermittent flooding by the bridge. It's affecting the wharves where the shipbuilding takes place, and the farmers' fields beyond.'

In truth, Victor had told her this in his last letter.

Mrs Leggett shook her head. 'That's not good.'

'And it's still a right mess on the common and along the river,' Jack added. 'I had a walk there a coupla days back. And we thought it was bad when they blew the river up. That meeting they had a few days ago, with the Admiralty and the port commissioners, I 'eared there was a right to-do.'

'Yes, nobody's taking responsibility apparently,' said Mrs Leggett.

Victor had written of the meeting in one of his letters. He had sounded upset and angry, and she couldn't blame him. It seemed that the man from the Admiralty had not only denied any responsibility for the damage, but didn't even care that so many lives, and livelihoods had been ruined. She was dying to get the current letter out to read once more but thought it might look rude while they were having this conversation. Eventually, people broke into smaller groups to chat, and Hetty had a chance to get the letter out once more.

She'd only read three sentences when the urge to shout with joy almost got the better of her. No one seemed any the wiser even though her smile was wide. She took a moment to calm down and continued reading. Victor was asking to meet on Thursday, if that was still her afternoon off. It was, and she wanted to reply as soon as possible. She finished her tea quickly and rose.

'You off already?' said Annie. 'Tea break's not over yet.'

'My friend wants to meet on Thursday, so I want to get a letter sent as soon as possible since it's only three days away.'

'Shame it's a friend and not a sweetheart,' said Annie wistfully. 'What with it being Saint Valentine's Day. It would have been nice to spend it with someone special.'

Saint Valentine's Day? She counted the dates in her head. Of course it was. Then she'd have to get him a card from somewhere. In the town, in a shop where she wasn't known by anyone. Or she could make one. Had he realised what date it was? She felt even more excited about seeing him now, and once out of the dining room, rushed up the stairs.

–

James hadn't been out of Littlehampton since his trip to Worthing before Christmas. Even after he'd started work again, Victor had deputised for him at a couple of the meetings out of town. Mostly, they'd been organising clearing up the mess caused by the flood, but today, he'd been glad of the opportunity to drive to Bognor for a meeting with one of their suppliers.

The meeting had gone well, and since it was over by lunchtime, he'd gone for something to eat at the Royal Hotel, where he'd eaten a few times. Far from feeling lonely, he was happy for the opportunity to be on his own for once, without people fussing about how he was doing. Having emerged from the hotel just after two, he hadn't wanted to travel back just at that moment, so had gone for a walk on the pier instead.

He was standing about halfway down the pier, the only person there. The sun was trying to break through the clouds, causing a bright patch and a hazy effect.

'Why, Mr Perryman, fancy seeing you here.'

'Oh, Miss Girard. Good afternoon. I'm here on business. I had a meeting. But I'll be leaving soon.' He felt slightly uncomfortable but wasn't sure why. 'And what brings you here today?'

'I like coming to Bognor from time to time, to visit different shops.'

She stood with her hands on the rail, a slight breeze blowing the large bow on her small, narrow brimmed hat. It felt like he'd gone back thirty years; it could almost have been Irene standing there. It wasn't the first time he'd thought that, and it still made him feel... odd.

'In many ways, I prefer the seaside in winter,' she said. 'There's something more mysterious, about it. The fact that it's mostly empty, alone, gives it some kind of... ghostly air, like it's the spirit of the coast, waiting for the warmer days to awaken it.'

That was the kind of thing Irene would have said too. 'How very poetical, Miss Girard. Do you write at all?' He stood next to her now.

'Me? Gosh no. I'm not a poet, I'm an artist, but I suppose because of that I do see things in rather a symbolic way.'

She leant away from the railing and was in the process of swapping her handbag from her right wrist to her left, when she dropped it. She was about to bend to retrieve it, when James beat her to it.

'Don't worry, I've got it,' he said. 'There.' He was placing it back in her hand, when he heard a voice.

'What on earth do you think you're doing?'

James was confused at first, thinking Ebony had said it, yet the voice was wrong and her mouth hadn't moved. Then he realised the words had come from behind him.

There, standing next to them now, was his daughter, Sophia.

'I *said*, what on earth do you think you're doing?'

Chapter Twenty-Seven

With a little time to spare before she met Victor, Hetty made her way down to the riverside to see what it was like today. There was still debris everywhere, including silt and stones from the river, while the area still hadn't dried out. It looked like it had been pouring down for hours, but although it had been continually dull, there'd been no rain for several days.

Down Pier Road, she saw fishermen, still fixing broken boats and mending nets. The Harbour Tea Rooms was still closed, with a notice in the window saying that they hoped to be opening soon. Cleaning the windows on the inside, she saw Mr Crolla. He spotted her and waved, so she waved back.

She headed straight on towards the pier, where she was due to meet Victor. On the way she saw Mr Janus talking to someone in the door of his Casino Theatre. He looked exasperated as he spoke with manic hand gestures. As far as she knew, the theatre hadn't reopened either, even though it normally put on a few shows in the winter.

Victor was already on the pier when she arrived. As they'd both anticipated, there were even fewer people than normal, given the recent turn of events. When she reached him, she placed her arm through his. They kissed briefly, then did so again for longer.

'If there is one benefit of all this mess, it's that it's put people off coming for a walk,' he said.

'I don't suppose your father would appreciate that sentiment,' she said.

'No, he definitely wouldn't. But luckily he's gone to a meeting in Bognor, so he can't hear me.' He chuckled. 'I am so glad to see you again, Hetty.' He kissed her once more.

'And I you, Victor,' she said, when he finally let her lips go.

'Let's walk along the empty promenade and find a seat at the other end.'

They dawdled, speaking of how things were going at the hotel and with his business.

'You should have heard the people shouting at the various authorities,' he said, telling her again about the meeting a few days ago. 'The local residents and businessmen were all furious, wanting answers about who was ultimately responsible for the floods and ensuing damage. Talk about the show that will run and run. Meanwhile, nothing has been done to fix the problems we now have and to ensure it doesn't happen again.'

'It sounds like they're all trying to pass on the blame,' she said. 'We're more or less back to normal at the hotel and starting to get bookings again after the initial run of cancellations. However, there are so many people still trying to fix the damage and get back to normal. I tell you who is still at the hotel though, apart from the major, of course.'

'Do you mean Ebony Girard?'

'No, though she seems to have set up home there, too,' she laughed. 'It's Lady Blackmore and her sister, Cecelia.'

'I think it's taking a while to dry, clean and refurbish some of the basements in South Terrace. Didn't you say Lady Black-more's kitchen was down there?'

'That's right.'

They'd reached the part of the promenade where the main road swung up and carried on to Rustington, next to the promenade. They sat on the first seat they came to, snuggling up together. He struggled to pull a small envelope out of one pocket, and a present out of the next.

'Happy Saint Valentine's Day, Hetty.' He handed them to her.

'Oh Victor, I only bought you a card, because I didn't know what else to get.' She unclipped her handbag and handed it to him.

'Hetty, all I really need is you on this special day. On any day, because every moment with you is special.'

'I feel the same way, Victor.' She undid the card, with its hearts and roses, feeling warm inside, despite the weather. 'That is lovely, thank you.' She kissed his cheek, then unwrapped the present, revealing a small box. Inside was an oval, silver brooch. She read the writing etched onto it. '*May the Lord watch between me and thee when we are apart one from another.* Oh Victor, it's a Mizpah brooch. How lovely.' She kissed him again, placing her arms around his shoulders as she did so.

When Lili had received one from Rhodri last year, Hetty had thought it terribly romantic, so was thrilled to have her own. It wasn't as if the pair of them were separated in the same way as Lili and Rhodri, but in some ways, they were more apart.

Victor opened his card and admired the embroidery work. 'That's beautiful. Whoever made it is wonderfully skilled.'

'*I* made it,' she said, chuckling.

'You did?' He looked delighted. 'It must have taken you ages.'

'I'm quite quick really. I did an hour or two every night before I went to sleep.'

'Oh Hetty.' They kissed once more and she sighed, enjoying the thrilling sensation that ran through her.

When they parted once more, Hetty placed the brooch back in its box and put it and the card in her handbag. 'I will only be able to wear this when I'm alone at the moment, but I will look at it every day and kiss it.'

Victor slid the embroidered card back in its envelope and carefully placed it in his pocket. 'That's it. I've come to a decision. It's been delayed long enough because of the flood. I'm going to give it another couple of weeks, so that we can get the businesses up and running properly, and then I *will* tell my parents about us. Absolutely definitely.'

'Are you sure it's the right time? It might take a while before things get back properly to normal.'

'When will the right time be? We've been through a lot in the last few months, and life might yet have a few more things to throw at us. I want us to be together. Life won't be worth anything to me until we are.'

They placed their arms around each other and hugged tightly. She was thrilled about his decision, but also scared. He was right though, when was there a right time? Eventually they'd either have to come clean or split up, and she knew what she'd prefer, whatever the trouble it caused along the way.

–

Ebony was confused about Sophia's question. Was it aimed at James, who maybe shouldn't be here for some reason?

'I *said*, what on earth do you think you're doing?'

James looked equally confused. 'I'm in Bognor for a meeting, Sophia.'

'But what are you doing here, with Ebony, holding her hand?'

'I'm not here with Miss Girard. I was on the pier, and she happened to walk on. And I wasn't holding her hand. She had just dropped her handbag and I was handing it back to her.'

'That's right,' said Ebony. 'And I came to Bognor to shop, not to meet your father.'

'Oh yes, that's a likely story. How could you, Father? I thought you were better than that.'

'I can assure you—'

'And I never want to see you at any of my meetings again, Ebony. I thought you were a friend. Now I see that you wheedled your way into our family by offering to paint my portrait. No wonder you were always so interested in my family, and always asking after my—'

'I commissioned her to do the painting,' James interrupted.

'In order to pretend that your acquaintance was all above board? You make me sick! Mother is always wanting to go out and do things, and you say you don't have time because of work, but here you are, carrying on with another woman. And one who is the same age as your daughter!'

'I am most certainly not—'

'You can keep your excuses! I will make sure, *Miss Girard*, that everyone knows what a deceitful little she-devil you are.'

'Oh, but there really is nothing going on!'

'That isn't nice, Sophia. What are you even doing in Bognor?'

'I've just had a meeting with a children's charity here, and I was having a walk on the pier before I left. Fate obviously wanted me to catch you in the act.'

'You haven't caught us in anything. And I suggest that you say nothing to your mother about this and I will talk to her, otherwise you'll give her the wrong—'

'Oh, shut up, Father!' Sophia stormed back the way she'd come and was soon out of sight, past the theatre and picture house.

'I'm so sorry about that, Ebony. I haven't seen her have a tantrum like that since she was fifteen.'

'Oh dear, what are we going to do? She seemed very quick to jump to the wrong conclusion.' She tried to keep her voice steady, but a cold dread invaded her being and she felt slightly nauseous.

'Yes, that is a little strange.' He pushed himself away from the railing. 'I need to get home as soon as possible.'

'Yes, I must too. If I could just speak to Sophia alone.'

'I wouldn't. You might make it worse. She can be very stubborn. Did you come by motorcar?'

'No, by train.'

'Then I might as well take you home.'

'No, Mr Perryman. I can easily catch a train to Little-hampton from here.'

'Please, at least let me do that for you, after the upset Sophia has caused.'

She was on the cusp of refusing, but realised she was weary and wanted to get back to the Beach Hotel as soon as possible.

'All right. But let us hope that this misunderstanding is cleared up quickly. I will come and speak to your wife, if necessary.'

'I don't suppose you'll need to. I will talk to her.'

Chapter Twenty-Eight

'You'd better not drop me off right outside the hotel,' Ebony said, as they drove down South Terrace. 'In case people see us.'

The anxiety she'd felt after the encounter with Sophia had grown during the journey home and she longed to be alone now.

'There's barely anyone about. And me dropping you off can be easily explained.'

As he came to a halt, Ebony noticed a woman walking towards the hotel. She couldn't tell who it was from here as she was looking down and her hat obscured her face. James jumped out and came around to open the door.

'Thank you for the lift. Good day to you, Mr—'

'Ebony, is that you?' a voice called.

She looked up. 'Mama? What are you doing here?'

'Thank goodness you're back.' Her mother hurried towards her. 'I arrived late morning, and they said you'd gone out for the day. I decided to go for a walk. I know you told us in your letters about the flood, but what a terrible mess it still is.'

Aware that her mother was looking curiously at James, she said, 'Let me introduce you to Mr Perryman. He's the father of Sophia, who runs the charities I help with. He was just giving me a lift from—'

'James?'

'Irene Belfiore?' he said, his eyes wide with bewilderment.

'Do you two know each other?'

'We knew each other a long time ago, when we were young,' said James, seeming to dismiss the connection.

'It was a little more than that, now wasn't it, James? And I'm Irene Girard now, by the way. We were walking out together, although our parents weren't really aware of it. Then we moved away to Kensington – Amelia, Rachael and I. You've hardly changed at all, James. A little older and greyer, but essentially the same face.'

James looked rather awkward. 'It never occurred to me that you were related, but now, I can see the resemblance.'

Ebony was too bewildered to know what to make of this news. She wondered how close they'd been.

'How interesting to see you again, after all these years.' Irene smiled, looking a little puzzled at the same time. 'Anyway, I'm not here for my health or a break, but have news. Marigold has been injured in France in an air raid that bombed her hospital.'

Ebony's gloved hands flew to her mouth. 'How dreadful. Is she all right?'

'She'll survive, but her leg is badly wounded.'

Tears stung her eyes and one spilled over onto her cheek. 'Oh, poor Marigold. And she does so love dancing.'

'I think that's the least of her worries, darling. Anyway, I've decided to come and stay here with you for a week or so, as I think you need a family member with you.'

'Maybe I–I should check out and come home now.'

'No need to do anything rash. To be honest, I could do with some time away from London, and Amelia is on hand to comfort Rachael.'

'I'm so sorry to hear about Marigold,' James said. 'I hope she recovers soon. Good day to you, Miss Girard, Irene.'

'Good day, James. It was interesting seeing you again after all these years.'

He nodded his head once and got back in the motorcar. They watched as he drove up South Terrace, towards his house. Ebony wondered what kind of reception he would get at home. Hopefully he'd be able to sort out the misunderstanding.

'Now tell me all about Marigold, Mama.'

'Let us go inside. They'll be serving afternoon tea and I could do with a sit down and some sustenance.'

—

James drove away in the direction of Surrey Cottage, but was not in the mood to go home yet. Nor could he face the shipyard. On reaching the corner, at the end of South Terrace, he turned right and carried on to the part of the road that ran next to the promenade. He'd go for a walk, try to sort out in his head what to do.

But how strange that Ebony should be Irene's daughter. If Barbara found that out, it might add fuel to the assumption that there was something going on. No wonder he'd had flashbacks to that time when they'd been together. She did have a look of her mother. And her voice was very similar. It should have occurred to him before. Hadn't Ebony said that they'd come to Littlehampton as children? But that hadn't been enough to make the connection.

He needed a walk to clear his head. He veered to the side of the road and brought the motorcar to a halt. After stepping out, he looked down both lengths of the promenade, the one that led ultimately to Rustington, and the other that led to the pier. The weather was even gloomier than it had been in Bognor.

He decided on the route towards the pier and headed off. The area was almost deserted; there were just two lone figures sitting together on a bench part-way down. They looked like a couple. His head was a muddle with the scenarios that might play out between him and Barbara. If only Sophia hadn't turned up, or hadn't jumped to the wrong conclusion.

If only, if only. There'd been a few of those in his life, including if only Irene hadn't moved away. But he had to face facts after all these years: he hadn't really been the one for her. He'd always suspected that she'd been biding her time with him, until she found something better, but, as in love as he'd been with her, he had never examined the thought too closely. Barbara had been quite a different story. He had known from very early on in their relationship that she considered him to be the only man for her. She'd said as much on many occasions.

He was in a world of his own, taking no notice of the waves lapping onto the beach, or the terns pecking at the wet sand as he would normally have done, looking straight ahead. It was only when he was approaching the bench with the couple on, that he chose to glance briefly at them. But the glance became a horrified glare.

'Victor? What on *earth* are you doing here? You should be at the quay. And who is this? Good grief, it's the maid from the hotel.'

Victor stood up, rigid. 'This *maid* from the hotel is the one who saved your life, and she's called Henrietta Affleck. Hetty. So please have some respect.'

'And very grateful I was to her for that, but that doesn't mean she can inveigle my son into a romantic liaison because of it.'

'She hasn't *inveigled* me into anything. I was the one who pursued *her* and did so before your accident. And I love her more than life itself.'

'Don't be such a fool! How could she ever be a suitable wife for you? Can you imagine what your mother would say?'

That's all he needed, for Barbara to have two things to dismay her.

'I couldn't care less about class! She's my equal in every other way.'

'You're being ridiculous. That's just your lust speaking. I hope to goodness you haven't got her with child.'

'Don't be disgusting, Father. She's not that kind of woman. And I'm not the type to take advantage. Don't you know me at all?'

James grabbed hold of Victor's coat collar and dragged him a few steps away from Hetty.

'You will come home now, otherwise I will go to the hotel and complain that the maid has been bothering you, and maybe worse.'

'That would be a barefaced lie!' Victor yelled. 'And I would tell them otherwise.'

'You wait until I tell your mother. She'll have a few choice words to say to you.'

Victor shoved James's hand away. 'I will come home, but it'll be by my own volition.' He turned to Hetty. 'Don't worry, my love, I'll sort this out. I won't let him complain about you. You go now and I will see you soon.'

'No, you will not see her soon,' said James, grabbing Victor's arm and pulling him along. 'And I will make damned sure you don't, believe me. The motorcar's parked up here.'

'I can walk home.'

Hetty turned and started running across the common.

'That's it, run away!' James called after her, then said to Victor, 'How do I know you'll go home and won't go after *her*.'

'Because I have said I will come, and I will.' Victor started running in the direction of home, and James left him to get on with it. His son had been a competitive runner at school, and he couldn't match his speed, especially at his age.

An explosion had almost seen him off, a flood had nearly ruined two of his businesses, and now he had a misunderstanding to explain and an ill-advised relationship to extinguish. The sooner it was all over, the better.

–

By the time Victor had reached Surrey Cottage, his father was parking on the road outside. He made sure he was ahead of him, charging into the drawing room, where his mother was sitting, warming herself by the fire.

'Mother, I have something to tell you—'

James interrupted with, 'I have just found this idiot on a bench, snuggled up with a maid from the Beach Hotel. A maid, would you believe? He—'

'There is nothing wrong with being a maid or working in a hotel. Look at Edie Moore, with her titled father.'

'Do not interrupt me.'

'Why? You interrupted me. Mother, Hetty and I have been seeing each other for a few months, and we are in love. She is not some silly girl, but is the daughter of the headmaster of Lyminster School, very intelligent and well read. She would make a perfect wife for me, whatever *he* thinks.' He pointed an accusing thumb at his father.

'You don't know what you're saying, boy.'

'Do *not* call me "boy". I will be twenty-eight at the end of this month. I am *sick* of being treated like a child. Mother, you should meet Hetty, not just as a maid giving out drinks at a function. I know that you would like her.'

Barbara was looking straight ahead, stony-faced. She must be really angry with him for being with someone to whom she had not given her approval.

'Mother?'

At that moment, Sophia walked in with a tray of tea.

'Why couldn't a servant have done that?' said James.

Sophia didn't reply, but instead started pouring. 'Would you like one, Victor?'

'No.'

His father persevered. 'I'm right about Victor and this maid, don't you think so, Barbara?'

'What I think, James, is that you have a nerve berating a young bachelor like Victor about seeing a single woman, when you, a married man, have been seeing Ebony Girard. What a hypocrite you are.'

'Ebony?' said Victor. 'Father?'

'I have absolutely *not* been seeing Ebony Girard. I came across her on the pier at Bognor, where I went for a walk after the lunch I bought myself.'

'Or the lunch your bought yourself and Miss Girard,' Barbara went on. 'It all makes sense now, with the large number of occasions in the last few months that you've told me you have "things to do and people to see", as you put it. No wonder you wanted her in the house, painting Sophia's portrait. Then you insisted that you had to take her out for that lunch to thank her for the portrait, even though I couldn't make it and you knew I was unhappy about it. And at Christmas, when she brought you back from Worthing. I suppose *that* was a coincidence, too.'

'Yes, it—'

'And that emerald necklace you bought me. I suppose she had something to do with that. Emeralds would suit her, with her green eyes. Green, like Irene Belfiore's. I've been trying to think who she reminded me of, and it only occurred to me the other day. But I didn't think for a moment you'd be stupid enough to—to—'

'I've done nothing!' he said, fearing now she'd find out that Irene was Ebony's mother. This made the whole situation worse. Barbara would never believe that he hadn't known.

'And to think she befriended our daughter, and all the while...' She turned her head away. 'I can't even bear to think of it.'

'But there is nothing going on. It was a pure coincidence that she was on Bognor pier. Sophia had no right to tell you otherwise. She got the wrong idea and I told her—'

Barbara stood abruptly and faced him. 'There is no such thing as a *pure coincidence* when it involves a grown man and woman, especially when there have been a few of them. What do you take me for?'

She marched out, knocking James's arm, albeit accidently, as she fled, but Victor could see her face pucker as the tears fell. Sophia quickly followed her.

'And you have the cheek to tell me who I should be in a relationship with?' said Victor. 'How long has this been going on?'

James squeezed his lips together for a few seconds. 'There is nothing "going on". Nothing whatsoever. It is just as I said, I promise you. And it is neither here nor there with regards to you and that girl. You must give her up.'

'You can go to hell!'

Sophia returned at this point, with the portrait that Ebony had painted of her. She tossed it on the floor. 'I certainly don't want *this* anymore. Now, I'm helping Mother move bedrooms.' She was about to leave when she twisted back. 'And by the way, I already knew about Henrietta, and I approve. She is a very nice young woman and would make a splendid wife for Victor.' On which note, she left.

'Sophia knew, and she didn't tell me?'

'Why should she? Mother's right, you *are* a hypocrite.'

'How many more times? There is *nothing* going on. You, on the other hand, have been having a dalliance with someone who is not in our class and—'

'Our class? Three generations ago, your great grandfather was working class. Have you forgotten that? And times are changing, particularly since the war. Look at Edie Moore.'

'You've already mentioned her.'

'But I didn't say that she's now in a relationship with one of the porters from the hotel. You remember Charlie, don't you?'

'She's chosen to give up her privileged position. Is that what you're proposing to do? Would you like me to find someone else to manage Wilmot's? Because that's the only thing keeping you from being conscripted. Healthy young man like you, out of work, they'd soon have you in the army.'

Victor stepped towards his father. 'Is that a threat? What are you going to do, bring Sophia in to manage? Not that I'm saying that's a bad thing, for I'm sure if you brought her into the business she'd do very well. She certainly proved herself while you were unwell.'

'Don't be ludicrous! She has no engineering qualifications. And why would she? She's a woman.'

'I won't even dignify that chauvinistic opinion with a reply. And you know, maybe fighting for my country wouldn't be so bad.'

'If that's what you want, it can be arranged. But if you do, don't expect to be welcomed back into the company when the war is over. And don't expect me to hand it over to you when I retire. There's a few around here would be glad of the chance to buy it. And do you know what else I'll do? I'll report Henrietta to the hotel, then tell them you enlisted because she'd been pestering you. And I'll tell the police she's been harassing you. I swear I will.'

'She has not been harassing me. She's not that sort.'

'Not that sort? She's after you for what you can give her.'

'You're right. Because I can give her love. That's what she's after.'

'Nonsense. She wants a rich husband. Or she wants the opportunity to steal from you. Yes, I could tell the hotel that too. And the police. What's it to be then? A spell in the trenches with no future to look forward to while your so-called sweetheart is disgraced and out of a job? Or are you going to be sensible?'

Would his father really do that to his beautiful Hetty? And did he really want to be uprooted from here, to join the war so late in the game, not see the flying boat project through? Fighting for his country would be a noble thing, but what he was doing at the quay, producing the hulls for these invaluable aircraft, was important too. How could he stay and, more importantly, keep Hetty safe too?

'Father, you're a scoundrel.'

'No, I'm not. I'm a concerned father. Now, you have an opportunity to do the right thing. Your mother wouldn't be very pleased if you brought someone like Hetty into the family either. She wants someone refined for you, who can carry out the wifely duties she needs to, just like your mother has always done for me. And she'd be devasted if you had to go off to war.'

Victor said nothing for some moments, staring at the fire instead. What should he do? He could feel his heart thumping in his throat. Was his father calling his bluff, or would he honestly report Hetty for something that could get her dismissed, or even locked up?

Eventually, he looked up at his father. 'If I agree, will you give up Ebony Girard?'

'I've already told you, there is nothing to give up, but I guarantee there is nothing and will never be anything between us.'

'All right, it's a deal.'

'And you're not to tell Sophia about this, otherwise the deal will be null and void. I'm having to put up with enough trouble from her and her wrong assumptions.'

'All right.' He still wasn't sure if he believed his father when it came to Ebony, but he'd have to trust him on that one.

'We'll shake on it, then.'

Victor eyed the outstretched hand offered by his father, stalling for a few seconds before shaking it.

'Good. Then we will say no more about it.'

James walked out of the room and closed the door, leaving Victor alone. He slumped onto the settee and placed his head in his hands. What on earth had he done? There was no way back from this. He'd always considered himself a man of honour, and he wouldn't renege on an agreement.

He felt a tightness in this throat. Soon after, his chin wobbled and he was dismayed to find himself trying to sniff back tears. The effort of doing this was making it hard to breathe, and eventually he had to let it go. He pulled a handkerchief from his pocket and sobbed into it for some minutes.

Finally, pulling himself together, he blew his nose and stood up. He'd better go to his room and write a letter to Hetty. It would be the last he would ever write to her, but it had to be done to keep her safe.

James took the stairs two at a time, like he would have done in his youth. He needed to change and be alone, just for a while, before he spoke to Barbara again. His skull was thumping with the stress of it all and he feared he'd end up with a severe headache.

'Mother and I have put your things in Victor's old bedroom,' said Sophia, standing at the top of the stairs. 'You'll have to sort them out yourself.'

'This is ridiculous!'

Sophia ignored him. James went to the bedroom and shut the door. His clothes on hangers were draped over the bed. The items from the drawers were piled on top of the chair, while his toiletries had been discarded haphazardly on the dressing table.

What a mess, not just his personal items, but the whole situation. He perched on a small space at the edge of the bed. His hands were shaking and his breathing was rapid. What had happened to him? It was as if he'd turned into a different person, someone he didn't even like. And he wasn't even guilty, but it felt like he was.

What he'd done for Victor was for his own good. What would it look like if he married a maid from a hotel? He'd lose any respect he had from those they did business with, or those of status in the town.

He got up and walked over to the dressing table, sitting on the stool and regarding himself in the mirror. He looked tired, which made him look older than his years. How would he ever persuade Barbara that he was telling the truth? He'd had several moments of misgiving over the years, about losing Irene, but, seeing her today had convinced him that Barbara had been the right woman for him. He considered now how fortunate he'd been that Irene had left.

Sophia had been right about one thing though: he always had things to do and people to see, and they'd not really involved his wife for a long time. Then, he'd convinced himself it was her fault. But she had tried, he knew that. And now, *he'd* have to make the effort. But he'd have to convince her of his innocence first.

Chapter Twenty-Nine

Hetty had slept little last night, her dreams filled with variations of the scene that had played out on the promenade the day before. She was worried for Victor, what his father might have put him through in front of his family. If only she could have stood and helped fight his corner. But what good would she have been?

Annie joined her at the table in the staff dining room for morning break. 'Are you feeling all right? You look a bit pale.'

She yawned. 'I didn't sleep well.'

'Have you, um, heard from Lorcan recently? You normally say if you've had a letter.'

'Not for a month or so. Why?'

'Just wondering how he's getting on – the same as I do with all the others. We don't seem to have heard much from any of them recently.'

'It sounds like they're all a bit busy. We'd hear if anything had happened to any of them though, I'm sure.'

Annie nodded but didn't look consoled. Hetty wondered if she'd been fond of one of the men who'd worked here, maybe Jasper, who'd been a porter, or one of the waiters.

'Annie, to be honest, Lorcan and I aren't writing to each other anymore. I believe he's writing to Simon though, to keep up with the news, so you could ask him.'

'Have you split up?'

'I don't think it ever really got going.'

Annie didn't seem to know how to take it. Maybe she was worried about saying the wrong thing and upsetting her.

Her sister Alice came in next, holding a letter. 'Hetty, this has just come for you. It was delivered by hand by someone. No idea who it was.'

'That's funny, we was just talking about letters,' said Annie.

Edie entered, bringing in a tray with a coffee pot and cups. 'Letters? Has there been another postal delivery already?'

'No, just a hand delivered one,' said Alice.

It was Victor's handwriting, so probably news of how it had gone when he'd returned home. She needed to know he was all right, so opened it in eager anticipation. She hadn't got far when she felt like she could hardly breathe. She got up, exiting the room immediately, the letter still in her hand.

In her bedroom, she sat on her bed and read it again, hardly believing that it could be from the man who'd just declared that he loved her more than life itself. Could his father have written it, pretending it was from him? No, it was Victor's writing, she was sure of it. She scanned it once more, certain she must have misread the contents.

> My dearest Hetty,
>
> I am truly sorry about what happened on the promenade yesterday, when my father found us.
>
> I have been thinking deeply about this situation, and I have come to the conclusion that our relationship could never ultimately work, given our circumstances. I would only end up making you unhappy, and that I never want to do. I want you to have a happy life, with someone who will not cause you undue stress or trouble.
>
> Forgive me, my love,
> Yours,
> Victor

No, how could it be, after the way he argued with his father about it, about them? What could have happened to make him change his mind so quickly?

She leaned forward, dropping the letter as her head reached her knees. She emitted a low keening sound as her chin trembled and the tears began to fall.

'Hetty? Hetty, what's wrong?'

Edie sat on the bed next to her, leaning over so their heads were level. 'I'm sorry, the door was ajar, and you sounded in distress.'

'The—the letter.' She pointed to the floor.

Edie picked it up and read it. 'Oh. So things had moved on with you and Victor. If you don't mind me asking, what happened with his father?'

Hetty slowly pulled herself up. Her face was drenched, but she had no urge to wipe the tears away. She explained briefly how the relationship had developed, then went into more detail about what had happened the day before.

'I'm so sorry, Hetty. Victor has always seemed such a nice young man.'

'He *is* a n-nice young man. This will be down to some threat or other, after what his father said about reporting me to the hotel.'

'Do you think he'd honestly do that? Mr Perryman has always seemed a decent enough sort.'

'I s-suppose they all do until they think their family, or lifestyle, might be threatened. He'll be afraid that I'll bring the family down in status.'

'What nonsense! I've always thought that you weren't achieving what you were capable of, Hetty. You're clearly intelligent and knowledgeable. You could do anything. Why are you even a stillroom maid?'

'That's strange, coming from the Honourable Edith Moorland, daughter of a baron and rich industrialist.'

'You're right. I'm being a little hypocritical, but I've started again to climb in a different world, under my own terms. I was a chambermaid when I came here, and now I'm under-manageress. Maybe, in a few years and with some experience,

I could be a manageress somewhere. To me, that is infinitely more desirable than being married off to someone I have no love for, as would surely have happened.'

Hetty thought back to her younger days. 'I wanted to be a teacher, you know, go to one of the training colleges, but my mother said no.'

'I'd have thought it would have been just what your father wanted.'

'It was, but my mother overruled him, saying I needed to look for a good husband instead. If I had been a boy, like Gilbert, it would have been a different matter.'

'Things are changing, Hetty. And if you really can't be with Victor, maybe it's time to, I don't know, achieve something else you'd like to do. I'm sorry, I'm not being much help. I know how I'd feel if someone said I couldn't be with Charlie.'

'It's actually good to have someone to talk to about it.'

Edie took her hands. 'Don't worry, I won't tell anyone else.'

'I don't mind Lili knowing, as she's already aware of the relationship. She's been through hard times too, where love is concerned.'

'I'll tell the others that you're feeling unwell and that it had nothing to do with the letter. We'll find someone else to do your shift.'

'No, it's all right. By all means, tell them it wasn't the letter, but I'll say I've made a quick recovery.'

'Very well. I'll leave you to wipe your tears and tidy yourself.'

When Edie had gone, Hetty looked in the mirror. What a state she looked. For now, she'd have to pull herself together and make it through the day. The time for tears would be later, during another sleepless night.

'Victor? Victor?'

There was a rapid knocking on his bedroom door as he was about to knot his tie. He knew it was his sister's voice. He sauntered to the door and opened it a little.

'What is it, Sophia?'

She looked around. 'Can I speak with you?'

'I need to get down to breakfast. We've a shipment of parts coming in later this morning, and I don't want to be late.'

'Just five minutes, please.'

He opened the door wider and she marched in. He had the feeling he was in trouble – again – but for what he didn't know this time.

'I've just heard from Father that you have given Hetty up. Why?'

'What did Father say exactly?'

'That he managed to talk some sense into you.'

If he let her believe that, he knew she would argue against him, and tell him he should follow his heart. And if she ever found out about the bargain they'd made, she'd be incandescent, especially as it might confirm their father's guilt concerning Ebony in her eyes. What should he say?

'Yes, and I'll let him keep on believing it. I had no intention of giving her up but, well… Last night I received a note from her, saying that she didn't want any trouble, so she didn't want to see me again.'

'What? That doesn't sound plausible. Honestly, Victor, are you sure our father didn't get a maid to write it? And how did it get here?'

More fibs to weave. He was so fed up with it, but he'd have to continue now or cause another row.

'It was her writing, I'd know it anywhere. And I was coming down the stairs when someone knocked at the door and, um, Fairfax answered it.'

The maid had been a good choice, since she'd gone to visit her family for a few days that morning.

'But are you sure she means it? She might just be trying to make it easier for you, thinking it's for the best?' She stepped forward to take his hands. 'Oh Victor, you should never abandon love when you've found it. It's not as if either of you is married.'

She was thinking of her affair a few years back, he was sure. He'd often wondered whether it had made her reluctant to pursue any other relationship.

'But there are other barriers. Maybe we could have overcome them, but she doesn't want me, Sophia, and that's the biggest obstacle now. Perhaps Father finding us put things in perspective for her, and she realised she didn't love me enough for all the trouble it would cause.'

The very idea that this might be true was enough to knock the wind out of him. He had to keep it together. He didn't want Sophia to see just how distraught he was.

'If that is the case, then I'm truly sorry, Victor.'

'And now, I want the family to be restored to harmony. Don't tell Mother, or particularly Father. Let him believe I did the right thing and he'll be happy.'

'What about Ebony Girard?'

'I'm pretty sure that there was nothing between them, and that it was a coincidence that she was in Bognor. What exactly did you see on the pier? Were they arm in arm, or anything?'

'No, he had hold of her hand, I thought, but claims she'd dropped her handbag and he was simply giving it back to her. But it seems strange, after her apparently coming across him in Worthing before Christmas. And what about all that interest she took in him?'

'I don't know, Sophia. I just feel that Father was telling the truth. Maybe you jumped the gun a bit. Do you think that, you know, your, um, affair may have coloured your judgement?'

She looked down, frowning. 'I… I suppose, it might have done.'

'Do you know who this Irene Belfiore Mother mentioned was?'

'Apparently, she was Father's sweetheart before he started walking out with our mother. She left the area and went to London with her sisters.' She emitted a long sigh and let go of his hands. 'Oh dear, maybe I have jumped the gun a bit. I need to find out more, though I'm not sure how. I shall leave you to finish dressing and see you at breakfast.'

When she left, he leant against the door and put his head back. If breakfast was anything like dinner last night, it would be a cold affair. Maybe they'd eventually get over what had happened, and things would be back to normal, whatever that meant anymore. At this moment in time, he had severe doubts about that.

—

If there was one thing Ebony had feared with her mother being here, it was that she would find out about the trouble with Sophia and the misunderstanding, once she started telling everyone what a 'deceitful little she-devil' she was. It had been two days since the incident, but still no one was even looking askance at her.

She was in the dining room currently, sitting under the glass-roofed portion, next to the window. Her mother had gone to visit an old friend in Arundel, so she was lunching alone. Those sitting on the next table were talking of the end of the hostilities between Russia and the Central Powers, made up of Germany and her allies, and debating whether this could be the beginning of the end of the war.

She thought about Marigold, still in a hospital near the front, and soon to be returned to one in this country. Hopefully it would be one nearby, where she could visit her regularly. Maybe, while she was convalescing, post hospital, Marigold could stay at the hotel. Or was that her being selfish, longing for her cousin's company? She was sure Aunt Rachael would want her home to recuperate. So maybe that would also be her cue to return to… what? She'd stayed here so long it had started to feel like home. She felt she had more of a purpose here, painting seaside pictures to mount an exhibition at some point, and helping with Sophia's charity events, of which there'd been many. The latter was no longer open to her, and both of these activities she could do back home, but she did so love the seaside.

Despite her efforts to distract her mind, it returned to the situation with James Perryman. Could it be that any gossip spread by Sophia just hadn't reached the hotel yet? Was it only a matter of time?

All this worry and supposition wasn't doing much for her appetite. She perused the menu, not tempted by the reduced choices, then placed it down. She gazed out at the blue sky, wondering whether to take a walk instead, and return for afternoon tea, should she fancy it.

She didn't know what to do, not right now, not in the future. She picked up the menu once more.

—

Hetty watched Ebony as she placed the menu down and wondered if she was ready to order, but then she picked it up again. She'd been brought into the dining room to serve luncheon, but she was struggling to keep the smile on her face that the customers always commented on.

'You all right, Hetty?' said Lili, coming to stand next to her.

She and Edie had been keeping an eye on her for the last couple of days, she was aware of that.

'No, Lili, I'm not, but you keep carrying on, don't you?'

'You do, that. Thought my life were over, I did, when it seemed like Norman had perished. Then I found Rhodri, but of course, Norman still actually being alive complicated things, so I sort of know what you're going through. But I found happiness in the end, and I'm sure you will too.'

Hetty had nothing to say to this. People were often full of these well-meaning encouragements when others were in·

trouble, claiming that everything would be all right, but it wasn't always the case.

'Oh look, there's Miss Perryman. I wonder if she has news for you.'

Perhaps Lili *had* been right about finding happiness. Could Sophia be coming to tell her that Victor had changed his mind, and wanted to see her?

'Good afternoon,' said Sophia. 'I wonder if it would be all right to join Miss Girard at her table.'

'Of course,' said Lili. 'I'll show you—'

'It's fine, I can take myself over.'

Sophia wandered over to the window, leaving Hetty bitterly disappointed. That would teach her to build her hopes in any way.

Lili patted her arm. 'I'll serve that table now. You can do my table seven instead.'

Hetty nodded, praying that the day would go quickly, so she could enjoy the oblivion of sleep. Or at least, try to.

—

Ebony looked up to find Sophia looming over her, or so it seemed.

'Do you mind if I join you?'

There might be a fuss whether she said yes or no, so she'd go for the more polite choice.

'Take a seat.' As if she didn't have enough worries, without James's daughter coming to, what? Tell her to leave this town, like some dramatic Western at the picture house?

'It's good to see the sun today,' said Sophia.

She was resorting to a conversation about the weather?

'It might be better if you said what you've come to say.'

Sophia sat with her hands linked on the table, her lips pinched. Her mouth opened, but before she had a chance to say anything, Lili had arrived with another menu.

'I'll be back in a while to take your orders.'

When the waitress was out of earshot, Sophia said in a soft voice, 'I'm sorry I jumped to conclusions.'

'There really wasn't anything going on. I would *never* have an affair with someone's husband. What a terrible thing to do to another woman. The meeting in Bognor, and before Christmas in Worthing, really were coincidences.'

'It's all right. I am willing to give you the benefit of the doubt. I went to Bognor yesterday, to the Royal Hotel, asking if my father had left an umbrella behind. When the head waitress inevitably said that he hadn't, I said that I wondered if he'd lunched with a colleague and whether he'd taken it by mistake, and she confirmed that he'd lunched alone. Of course, that doesn't mean that there wasn't something going on, but my brother is satisfied that there wasn't. And I think I am, too. My mother, however, is still not convinced.'

'Oh dear, that's a shame. I wish you'd found out a little more before you presented your accusations to your mother.' Ebony was cross now, and could have said a whole lot more, but she would rather fix the situation, if she could.

'Yes, you're right. I've caused trouble where there needn't have been anyway. I am sorry.' They were silent for some moments, before Sophia said, 'How are your cousins, by the way?'

'My mother arrived Thursday afternoon, to tell me that Marigold has been injured in France. She is to return to a hospital in England soon.'

'I'm sorry to hear that.'

'When she goes home to finish her recuperation, I will also go home, to help nurse her.'

Ebony had only that second come to the decision, but with it came a kind of peace.

'It would be the right thing to do,' said Sophia. 'What will you do when Marigold has recovered?'

'I thought I might become a VAD nurse too. I have much to think about. This unfortunate incident with your father has, if nothing else, made things clearer to me.'

The waitress came back to the table, her notebook and pen ready to take their order.

'Have you come to a decision, ladies?' said Lili.

'Indeed we have,' said Ebony.

Chapter Thirty

It had been six weeks since that fateful Saint Valentine's Day, and Hetty was feeling no less broken-hearted about Victor. She'd gone home for all her Thursday afternoons off except one, when she'd met Phoebe and poured out her sad tale.

According to Lili and Edie, apart from Sophia having lunch with Ebony a couple of days after the event, the Perrymans had not visited the hotel. And with Marigold now at a hospital in Surrey, Ebony had finally returned to Richmond.

'Are you going home again for your afternoon off?' Lili said as she walked through the staff corridor, on her way to early lunch.

'Not until later. I need a few things in town and want to buy my niece and nephew an Easter egg each.'

'Can't believe it's Easter this weekend already. The year's going so fast.'

Not for me it isn't, thought Hetty. 'Wish the weather was a bit more spring-like.'

'April it'll be on Easter Monday. Maybe the weather will improve then. I 'ope so, for the guests' sakes. About two thirds of the rooms are booked.'

'Huh! More likely the April showers will start.'

'True. It'll be like being back in Wales! I'll see you later.'

Hetty turned back to the mirror to pin her hat on. Lili had tried hard to cheer her up, and she was grateful for the effort, but nothing was working. She still felt like her heart was filled with pebbles, weighing her down with sorrow.

She'd already decided to take a walk by the sea before heading to the shops, despite the cold, overcast day, so headed for the promenade. There were a few people on it, considering the weather, and she guessed that it would be fairly busy over the weekend, whether it was sunny or not. The tide was quite low, exposing the large island of sand that always appeared during these times. There were small pools of water on the wet sand where there were dips and ripples. She tried to clear her mind, to simply enjoy the walk. Inevitably the thoughts broke through, the never-ending ones with no answers that she could figure out.

One that had come to her mind more and more recently was what Edie had said that fateful day, about how she could achieve anything she wanted. It wasn't true, of course, with her being a woman. There were still so many things she couldn't do, including voting, though, from what she'd heard there might soon be some progress made on that front. Perhaps she should concentrate on what she *could* do.

She could go somewhere else to work, Worthing, or Bognor maybe. But she wouldn't only be leaving her own family, she'd be leaving the one at the hotel too. Yet could she bear to continue living just up the road from the only man she'd ever loved? She might hear of him getting married, and her heart would break all over again.

These constant, battling thoughts wearied her. She sat on the next bench, looking out to sea, wondering what Lorcan might be doing right now over the other side of the water. Was it possible she could develop an affection for him again, when he returned, one that could grow to love? No. That ship had sailed.

She was aware of someone approaching and was put out when they sat next to her. Normally she would politely greet someone who had done this, but she continued to stare ahead, not wanting to get into a conversation with a stranger.

'Hello Henrietta.'

Hetty swung around, surprised. 'Oh, Miss Perryman. I'm sorry, I was miles away.'

'I saw you here and wanted to take the opportunity to tell you how sorry I was, about the way things came to an end. But I have to ask, are you sure you wanted to give Victor up? The two of you seemed very... close.'

Hetty thought at first she'd misheard. 'Give Victor up? Is that what you said?'

'He told me about the note you sent.'

She shook her head vigorously. 'I didn't send any note. It was Victor who sent a note to me, ending it.'

'I'm sorry, I'm confused. He sent *you* a note?'

'Yes. I have it in my handbag.' She wasn't sure why she'd squirreled it away in there. A reminder of her foolishness in getting involved with him, maybe. She opened the clasp and found the letter tucked in next to her purse, then gave it to Sophia.

As she read it, she started shaking her head.

'I have to confess, I couldn't understand it, after him defending me so vehemently when your father found us. Though... I don't know.'

'Go on.'

'I did wonder if it had something to do with your father threatening to report me to the hotel for bothering Victor, which I wasn't of course. I suppose I wanted to believe he still loved me and was trying to protect me... Please, don't tell Victor. He'll think me foolish. It's quite clear now, with all the time that's passed with no word, that I was wrong about that. I was wrong about it all.' She felt the tears threatening but was determined not to cry.

'I think you should talk to Victor.' Sophia handed the letter back.

'What's the point?' She replaced the letter and regarded her watch. 'I have to get to town now, as I'm seeing my parents later. Good day to you, Miss Perryman.'

Sophia leant forward and opened her mouth as if to object, but her face relaxed as she said, 'Good day, Henrietta.'

–

Sophia's pace was quick as she walked back to Surrey Cottage, matching her racing thoughts. Why had Victor told her that Hetty had given *him* up? Was it so she wouldn't have another go at their father? And this was the first time she'd heard that he'd threatened to complain to the hotel. There was something else going on here, and she was going to get to the bottom of it.

At home, she found her mother arranging dark pink camellias in a vase in the dining room.

'Sophia, there you are. Perhaps you'd like to help me organise a few things for Easter.'

'Mother, I want to have a word with you about Victor.'

'I do, too. I've been thinking about this business with Henrietta lately. I know your father didn't want this to be discussed any further, and I've kept my mouth shut even though I'm not sure he has any right to expect anything from me. I did it for Victor's sake, and for peace in the family. But, now...'

'Go on. I'd be interested to hear what you have to say, as I have a few thoughts of my own.'

'The poor boy has been miserable since he gave Henrietta up, and I do wonder if he did the right thing. Yet it seemed to be his choice.'

'This is what I don't understand. Victor told *me* that *she'd* written to *him*, breaking it off, but I've just seen her on the promenade, and she even showed me the letter he sent her.'

'Why would Victor tell you that? And you never mentioned it.'

'Because he told me not to, that he wanted Father to believe that *he'd* done the right thing, and that he'd really had no intention of giving her up until the letter came.'

'That is strange. To be honest, Sophia, I'm not sure what all the fuss has been about. Yes, it's a little unconventional, but it's not like she's some wanton piece he's picked up off the street.'

'No, I agree. I didn't think Father was that much of a snob. Could it be that he wasn't thinking straight because of the to-do involving Ebony? You know, I'm convinced now that it was just a coincidence, them being on the pier together. I really should have thought twice before jumping in the way I did. I feel I've caused so much trouble.'

Barbara looked thoughtful for a while. 'I've been asking around about Henrietta and gather she's a headmaster's daughter and very bright.'

'So, you don't mind that Victor was seeing her?'

'I've had a long, hard think about it, and no, I don't.'

'But you were always the one trying to pair him up with women from high status families.'

'Only because they're the ones we socialise with, and I didn't want him to grow old alone. The same as with you. Of course, it is often more important that women marry up—'

'Mother!'

'I know, I know. I wish it were not so, and maybe in the future it won't be, but women's position in society still gives them little power or money.'

'I can't argue with that. And after the war, make no mistake, I will be banding together with my suffragist sisters again to fight for a more equal world for women. But right now, it's Victor and *his* situation that I'm worried about. I think there's more to it, and I intend to find out what. The way he felt about her, the way he argued against Father, I don't understand why he'd give her up so easily.'

'It does seem rather strange. I agree, we need to get to the bottom of it.'

'You tell me everything you know, and I'll tell you all I know, and we'll work from there. And maybe I'll go and talk to Henrietta again, to find out exactly what happened when

Father found them. All I know is that he threatened to report her to the hotel for bothering Victor.'

'James did? It doesn't seem like him at all, not the man I thought I knew, anyway. I do feel that he's overreacted.'

'I'm thinking the same. So, this is what Victor told me...'

—

On Saturday evening Victor was in his bedroom, changing into the evening suit his mother had insisted on for dinner. He was already tired of the long Easter weekend; he yearned for Tuesday and the return to work. It was bad enough, spending time without Hetty, but having to endure the still strained atmosphere at home, despite his father's falsely upbeat manner and Sophia's attempt to make out everything was normal. His mother barely said a word these days, and neither did he.

Perhaps he could go out tomorrow or Monday, especially now the weather had improved. But where to, on his own? The picture house? That wouldn't be open until Monday, but it was a possibility.

There was a knock at his door, causing him to look heavenward. Why couldn't they just leave him alone. The knock came again.

'Come in,' he called impatiently.

He turned to see his mother enter. At least it wasn't his father.

'Victor, I'd like to speak to you.'

This sounded more serious than he could be bothered with. 'What about?'

She took a couple of steps in, dressed for dinner as if she were dining at the hotel.

'I don't appreciate that tone. I am trying to help you.'

'I don't need your help, Mother. I'm fine.'

'You do, and you're not.'

'If this is about Hetty, it's over. That should be enough.'

'But how did it end?'

'I'm sure Father told you.' He lowered his voice in case Sophia was nearby. 'I sent her a note, ending it.'

She looked at the ground, her mouth pinched. 'That's strange, because you told Sophia that it was Henrietta who sent *you* a note.'

'Um, well, she must have got mixed up.'

'She did no such thing,' said his sister's voice as she pushed the door further open. 'You definitely told me that she'd sent you a note, one that Fairfax took delivery of. I've asked her whether anything came for you that night, and she says she has no recollection of anything. But then, I already knew she'd say that.'

'What do you mean?' Victor felt like he was in the witness box, giving evidence, like in a trial he'd gone to watch once.

'I came across Henrietta a couple of days ago, and she showed me the letter you sent her.'

'You've been investigating me like some criminal?'

'It was quite by accident. I saw her on the promenade and told her how sorry I was that she'd felt the need to break up with you. She said that wasn't the case and showed me the letter.'

He rubbed at his eyebrow as he bit his bottom lip.

'I've been to speak to her again since, to find out what happened when Father found you on the promenade, and it was quite enlightening. He accused her of "inveigling" you into a romantic liaison as a kind of payment for saving his life after the explosion. Then he threatened to report her to the hotel for bothering you. He said something about Mother having a few *choice* words when she found out. And finally, he would make *damned* sure that you wouldn't be able to sort this out.'

'It sounds much more aggressive, and even threatening, than the way your father described it to me,' said Barbara.

Sophia came closer to him. 'What you said in Hetty's presence made it sound like you were determined *not* to give her up, under any circumstances. Yet, within an hour or so, you had.'

340

'What's going on, Victor? I demand to know. Did your father threaten you with something so you'd give her up?'

He couldn't keep this up any longer. The lies, upon more lies, and all because of something that should have been wonderful: love.

'Look, we made a gentleman's agreement, that's all.'

'Involving what?' Sophia narrowed her eyes.

'I did it to bring peace to the family, and to protect Hetty.'

'What did you agree, son?'

'I'm not even sure how we ended up there,' he said. 'It started with me pointing out that Edie Moore had a sweetheart who was a different class, and he said she'd given up her position, and if I wanted to do that, I'd be out of the firm and would have to enlist, and then he'd...'

'Go on,' said Barbara.

'He'd tell the hotel, and maybe even the police, that Hetty had been bothering me, or trying to steal from me.'

'He *what*?' Sophia put her head back and closed her eyes, while throwing her hands out in frustration. 'You do know he was almost certainly bluffing, don't you? Don't you remember how incensed he was when Helen Bygrove was falsely accused of sending those poison pen letters? He said that anyone who gave fake evidence should be locked up for a very long time.'

'Yes, that's right he did,' Barbara agreed.

Victor had forgotten about that. 'I'm not sure that proves anything. People often have different standards when it comes to their own concerns.'

'While that is true,' said Barbara, 'I really don't believe he would have carried out that threat. Nor would he have thrown you out of the firm. He told me, while he was still incapacitated, that he didn't know what he would have done without you in charge, and that you had the makings to run the place when he finally retired.'

'He said that?' Victor had always had the impression that his father thought him rather useless.

'Yes, he did. I think Sophia is right; it was a huge bluff on his part to get you to toe the line.'

What a fool he was. He'd been so worried about ruining Hetty's life, that he hadn't stopped to examine the situation. He held his forehead with his hand and rubbed his temples.

'You really shouldn't have been so hasty,' said Barbara.

'What do you care? You wouldn't want Hetty in the family either.'

'Have you ever asked me what I thought? I've had a few weeks to consider it all, thinking about Great Grandad Perryman's position in life, about Edie Moore, and particularly her mother Agnes Moorland, or Agnes Haydon as she was when we knew her. As I said to your sister, I wouldn't object to the relationship. From what I've heard, Henrietta is a bright girl, from a respectable family who are well known in Wick.'

'How do you know that, Mother?'

She patted his arm. 'Never mind that now.'

'You know that Father will never accept her, and I couldn't allow Hetty to live with that.'

'You leave him to me. I've come to a point where I feel I can deal with him now, after the recent debacle. Don't say anything to him about this conversation though.'

'That's not a problem. We're barely even speaking, and when we do, it's business.'

'We're going to have to change that. Come along now, dinner will be served soon.'

Victor picked up his jacket and put it on. He wasn't sure what his mother had up her sleeve, but if there was any way she could mend the situation, he'd be happy for her to have a go. He didn't hold out much hope though.

—

'Where have Victor and Sophia gone?' James asked, as they sat down for their lunch, at opposite ends of the table.

'It was such a lovely sunny day after so much gloom, they decided to drive to Brighton,' said Barbara. 'I dare say there'll be a few more entertainments going on there than here.'

'But it's Easter Sunday, and that should be a family occasion.'

'Don't be such a misery, James. It's good that they can go out and enjoy themselves. And let's face it: sitting around an almost silent table with us wouldn't exactly put them in the holiday mood. They deserve a rest from that.'

'I have tried to explain to you, on numerous occasions, that it was all a mistake. Even Sophia and Victor believe me now. How much longer can we go on like this, with you treating me like I'm merely a visitor.'

'It's the way *you've* acted the last few years.'

'Well it's—'

She suspected an outburst from him, but it was stayed by Harries, the butler, entering with two plates containing chicken, while Fairfax came in behind with a large tray containing three tureens of vegetables.

They were dismissed, and a few seconds later James carried on. 'It's ridiculous, this impasse between us, when there was absolutely nothing going on.'

'There still seem to have been rather too many coincidences, given that you employed her to paint Sophia.'

'Purely a business transaction.'

'And she was always overly interested in our family.'

He slumped a little. 'That's hardly my fault. Maybe she was lonely.'

'I know how she feels. I've had my children, they've grown up, and now what is there for me? A husband who's always working or has some other excuse not to be with me. When was the last time we took a holiday?'

'It is wartime.'

'I know that, but people come to the Beach Hotel for a holiday. Even the working classes turn up in trainloads in the summer for days out. We don't do anything like that anymore.

The only thing we do is eat out at the Beach Hotel. How do you think that makes me feel? I might be fifty-four, but I still feel like I have a lot of life left in me.'

'I'm sorry.' He looked down, closing his eyes.

'You always being absent only added to my suspicion about you and Ebony. And another thing: Why were you so horrible to Hetty the day you found them? It's almost as if you were taking it out on her because your affair had been discovered.'

'No, no, it wasn't... No. I—I was, um, just trying to make sure that Victor—'

'Toed the line?'

He nodded.

'You made some serious threats, about reporting Henrietta to the police, about expelling Victor from the company, about him being conscripted. What have you become, James?'

'I only did it to save him from himself. I didn't want him ending up in a relationship he'd regret in years to come.'

'Why, is that how you feel about me? Are you still hankering after the wonderful Irene Belfiore, after all these years? Like I said, Ebony does have a look of her.'

Barbara and Irene had belonged to the same large circle of friends but hadn't themselves been close. He'd told her about their past relationship in their early days of courting. Should he tell her what he'd now discovered? Yes. It was the time for truth.

'It is, um, strange that you should bring her up. It's just, and I swear to you I did not know this until that day it all came out. Really, I didn't.'

'Know what? What are you talking about?'

'I drove Ebony back to the Beach Hotel, from Bognor, because it seemed the right thing to do, after my daughter had been so awful to her. When we got there, there was a woman outside, who turned out to be her mother. It was Irene Belfiore, or Girard, as she now is.'

'No! Surely not. How could you not know that Irene was her mother?'

344

'Why would I know that?'

He got up and walked around the table, kneeling next to Barbara before taking her hand. 'I know it seems like another impossible coincidence, but it really is, Barbara, my love.'

'*My love?* You haven't called me that in a few years.'

'I'm sorry about that too. Please, can we mend this situation?'

'I don't know. Even before any of this, I was feeling that I'd become just a housekeeper, one who's been mostly in the way of your life. A poor replacement for Irene.'

He could see the tears starting to form at the corner of her eyes and felt regret and guilt.

'I thought you liked being the lady of the house, doing your local charity work and going to events with other wives.'

'I do, but I'm *bored*, James. And I want my husband back, the one who used to make me feel special, like there was no one in the world like me. Perhaps that was never true.' She sniffed and a tear fell down her cheek.

'Yes, yes it was. It is! And I'll tell you something, Barbara. And I swear this is true too. That day I saw Irene, outside the hotel, I was so grateful that she did run away to London all those years ago, as I might have ended up with her. And really, she's not a patch on you.'

'Oh James, do you mean that?' she said, her voice croaky.

'Yes, yes, I do. What if I were to organise a holiday, just the two of us, an opportunity to be alone and get to know each other again? You liked Cornwall when we visited as a young couple.'

'I'd like that.' She pulled a handkerchief from her pocket and dabbed her eyes. 'Go and sit down. First of all, we have something else to sort out. Or rather, you do. You've put a terrible weight of responsibility on Victor, who feels he is obliged to keep to this ridiculous agreement. Victor is clearly miserable without Henrietta, or Hetty, as he calls her.'

'But she's a maid—'

'With a headmaster for a father and a mother who helps with Sophia's charity endeavours in Wick, so I have found out. But that doesn't matter. Have you forgotten about Edie Moore's mother, Agnes?'

'She worked her way up slowly.'

Barbara let out a huffed laugh. 'Not that slowly. Goodness, she went from farmer's daughter to solicitor's wife to shipyard owner's wife to baron's wife within a mere five years. Admittedly with much tragedy and loss in between.'

'Yes, but—'

'Yes, but *nothing*, James. Your own great grandfather was a labourer in a shipyard in Littlehampton, while your great grandmother took in washing.'

'But he was the one who started the first small boat building business that's become what it is today, and enabled my father and I to buy up other businesses.'

'Exactly. But it started with a humble beginning. When Henrietta served us, she seemed like a very nice and tidy young woman. As a headmaster's daughter, she didn't have to do any job, she could have simply waited for a husband, but she decided to fend for herself and become a stillroom maid, learning how to make preserves and pickles. Then she became the head stillroom maid. It may not seem like much of an achievement to some, but she's clearly a hard worker.'

'How do you know all this?'

'I've talked to a few people, including Edie. She didn't have a bad word to say about her. Quite the opposite. Now James, if you are genuinely repentant and want to make things better for us all, you will allow Victor to follow his heart. As Arnold Haydon did, and as Baron Moreland did, all those years ago. And for him to do this, you will have to free him from the agreement.'

She was right, he knew she was. The happiness of his family was dependent on him doing the right thing. 'Yes, all right. I will do that.'

'Thank you, James… Now, I think our meal might be rather cold. It's such a nice day, maybe we should follow our children's example and go out for the afternoon. We can ask for the food to be stored and reheated this evening. I'm sure we'll find somewhere out to eat.'

After weeks of misery, he suddenly felt more… He couldn't think of a word to describe it initially. *Relieved*. Yes. A simple word, but with such power.

He stood up. 'You call the staff to clear up, and I will get the motorcar out of the garage.'

Chapter Thirty-One

'Don't you have an hour break now?' said Milly, as Hetty polished one of the silver teapots in the stillroom.

'I'll wait for Tilly to arrive, just in case.'

'In case of what? We've just finished the lunch shift and the tea shift's not for another hour. The only orders we might get are room service, and I can deal with that.'

'I'll just finish polishing this then.'

The truth was, she didn't know what to do with her break. A walk by the river had occurred to her, but that reminded her now always of the day of the explosion. How ironic it was that she should have saved James Perryman's life, only for him to ruin hers. Not that she regretted saving him.

As for having a stroll on the promenade, that still brought back bitter memories of that terrible afternoon...

Perhaps she'd be better off sitting in her room, reading. But no, it was sunny, and that would be a waste of a nice day. She couldn't avoid it forever.

Tilly rushed in, out of breath, as Hetty decided this. 'Sorry I'm a coupla minutes late. I saw me Auntie Beryl on the way, and she don't 'alf talk.'

'Gawd, yes, she's a right gossiper,' Milly confirmed. 'Now, off you go, Hetty. We can manage 'ere.'

'I'll get myself organised, then.'

She was undoing her apron and taking off the cap when she heard a male voice in the scullery, though she couldn't quite make out the words. The other two took no notice, but it soon became apparent to Hetty that she recognised it. Or thought she did. Wishful thinking on her part. She was leaving the room to collect her jacket from the corridor when the slightly ajar door from the scullery was pushed open by Annie.

'Go in, they won't bite.'

She took a huge intake of breath. Victor was in the doorway.

'Hetty, I've got to speak to you. Can you spare me five minutes?'

'What about?' she said, wary of what might be coming, fearing something that would crush her spirit even more.

'I don't want to say here, please. It's private.' His eyes puckered in a beseeching manner, and she knew she'd have to hear him out.

'Very well. Let me fetch my jacket and hat, and I'll meet you by the gate.'

She could hear Milly and Tilly giggling from the corridor. She supposed she would have, too, at their age.

When she returned to leave via the scullery, Annie said, 'Will you be all right, going to talk to him on your own? He seemed a bit troubled.'

'I'll be fine, Annie, don't worry.'

She clearly had no inkling of the relationship that had been between them, and that was just as well.

Victor was by the gate when she arrived, pacing up and down.

'What has happened?' she said.

'How long have you got to spare?'

'I have a gap in my shifts now, so have an hour off.'

'Then, can we walk by the beach?'

'Your father might see us. I don't want either of us to go through *that* again.'

The worry melted from his face and a smile appeared. He took hold of her hands. 'It doesn't matter if he does, my love.'

'I–I don't understand.'

'Oh, gosh, where to start? Are you willing to walk with me? It will take a while to explain.'

'Yes, all right.'

'But there are things I will have to tell you that you'll need to keep to yourself.'

'Don't worry, I've become very good at keeping secrets.'

The dread she'd felt initially eased and she allowed herself a tiny morsel of hope.

As Hetty listened to what had gone on in his family, his father's assumed affair with Ebony which had not been as it seemed, the unfair agreement, the involvement of his sister and mother in sorting out the mess, she became ever more amazed.

'The only reason I agreed to father's terms was to protect you, Hetty. I was so afraid he would do or say something that would ruin your life, and I couldn't have endured it if he'd done that. If he had gone to the police, and they'd got the idea that you were some kind of loose woman, I dread to think what might have happened.'

'Would he really have done that?'

'No, I don't think so now. It was all a bluff. But I was so wound up at the time, and afraid for you, I couldn't risk it.'

'Oh Victor.' She felt her love for him grow even more, and she hadn't thought that possible.

They'd reached the promenade by this time. Normally she'd have been fascinated by the various people there, the women in their fashionable clothes, the children enjoying the sand, the various entertainments, but she was so taken by the story he was weaving, and his obvious devotion to her, that he was all she could concentrate on.

'After Mother had a word yesterday – or many from what I can make out – my father seemed to realise that he'd made a terrible error in trying to split us up. Whatever it was she said, and I only know a little of it, she persuaded him that I should be with the person I love. And, there seems to have been some healing in their own relationship, for which Sophia and I are immensely grateful.'

Hetty's brain was reeling. 'There's so much to take in. It sounds like I have a great deal to thank your sister and mother for. What I don't understand is, after trying to pair you off with women of status like Rosetta Stone, why your mother thinks *me* suitable.'

'She said that it wasn't the class she was worried about so much as finding me a companion, so I wasn't alone. She mentioned Edie's mother, as an example from a lower class who climbed the social ladder via marriages. I told you that story.'

'Yes, you did.'

'I think I've relayed all the important things now. So...'

She waited for him to continue. Although it seemed that this conversation had a predictable ending, she couldn't be absolutely sure until she heard him say it.

They carried on but still he said nothing. They arrived at the pier and kept walking until they reached the middle.

'Oh dear,' he said. 'I'm afraid I've inadvertently brought you to the wrong place for this conversation.'

'In what way?'

He pointed at the crowds. 'Let's keep walking to the end. There are fewer people there.'

At the pointed tip of the pier, Hetty scanned the whole area, taking in the mouth of the River Arun and West Beach beyond, then the wide expanse of sea, and finally the crowds on the beach and promenade. In the distance she could spy the Beach Hotel, sitting magisterially on the common.

'Hetty, now the objections have gone, would you do me the honour of being my sweetheart for good, and for all to see? I know you've been put through a lot, and I fear it has placed a barrier between us, but my father says he is truly sorry for what he said about you. This is no excuse for his behaviour, but I do believe that he was under a lot of pressure and was not himself. Both he and my mother want to meet you, or rather, meet you as yourself, not a waitress or stillroom maid. And the sooner the better.'

This had all been said almost as one sentence, causing him to take a deep breath when he'd finished.

'That's a nerve-racking prospect, but I suppose I will have to, if I'm going to be your sweetheart for good.'

'Then, you will?'

'Yes, of course I will. And you will have to meet my parents.'

Her mother would be beyond herself with delight, she knew for sure, while her father would be happy that *she* was happy.

He frowned. 'I hope they like me.'

'Oh Victor, they'll think you're wonderful!'

He looked a little embarrassed as he took her hands in his and they gazed at one another.

After a while, he put his hands on her shoulders and leant forward, before hesitating part way. He shook his head. 'Oh, what the heck!'

His mouth touched hers and they kissed as the seagulls above sang what seemed to Hetty a celebratory chorus.

'Aw, young love,' said an old lady nearby. 'That used to be me and you, Cyril!'

'What d'ya mean, ducks, it still is!'

As Hetty and Victor parted, they saw the old gent put his arm around his wife and the elderly pair giggled.

'That'll be us one day,' he whispered.

'Yes, I believe it will be,' she said, and they kissed once more.

A Letter from Francesca

Dear Reader,

Hetty the stillroom maid's story takes place in a time of turmoil in Littlehampton. Although what happens to Hetty and her fellow staff at the Beach Hotel involving the River Arun is fictional, the events involving the river itself really happened.

The first event, the Admiralty blowing up the river to widen it for ships, certainly took place in 1917. When in that year it happened remains a mystery to me, despite extensive research. Littlehampton Museum even got on the case for me but had no more luck. Consequently, I decided to place it in November of that year. If anybody reading this knows the precise date, I would really love to know!

The second river related event, the flood, did actually take place on 22nd January 1918, as it does in the novel. The Arun was always prone to flooding long before this, and for many decades afterwards. In the 1960s, '70s and '80s, I remember my father having sandbags in the cellar of his restaurant on Pier Road, and a small concrete barrier built in front of the outside door which you had to step over to enter. This was to prevent the waters of the Arun entering and ruining the food stored there.

A few years ago, they built up the bank next to the river on Arun Parade and Pier Road as a flood defence. While I can understand why they did it, it's sad to think that the customers and staff of the cafés on Pier Road will no longer have that lovely view of the river and West Beach opposite, as we did when I was young, and as Hetty and her friends would have had in the 1910s.

The public meeting on 30th January 1918, involving the port commissioners, the Admiralty and the council, also occurred in real life. I could only find an outline of what was said, but it's clear that the public was angry and that nobody would take responsibility. So, the conversation at the meeting in the novel is fictional, but I think it conveys the essence of what took place.

Thank you to all the readers who've sent messages and have supported me on social media. I'm always happy to chat. If you'd like to contact me to discuss the novels, or discover more about them, you can find me here:

Website and blog: www.francesca-capaldi.com/
Facebook: www.facebook.com/FrancescaCapaldiAuthor
Twitter: @FCapaldiBurgess
Instagram: francesca.capaldi.burgess
TikTok: @francesca.capaldi.author

Acknowledgements

A big thank you to Keshini Naidoo and Jennie Ayres, at Hera Books.

Thank you to the Littlehampton Museum for the research they did for me, and also to the Bygone Littlehampton Facebook page for all their wonderful and informative old photos, which really bring the period to life. Thank you to Lucy and Mike at Pier Road Coffee and Art in Littlehampton for their support.

Thank you to the writing groups and organisations who've been a great help over the years in my writing journey, particularly to the Romantic Novelists' Association and the Society of Women Writers and Journalists.

And last but not least, thank you to my children Carmela, Peter, Giovanna and Jack, and my grandchildren, Luca, Seren and Phynn, for all their encouragement.